ANDRONE

ANDRONE

DWAIN WORRELL

Published by 47North, Seattle

www.apub.com

Amazon, the Amazon logo, and 47North are trademarks of Amazon.com, Inc., or its affiliates.

ISBN-13: 9781662511974 (paperback)
ISBN-13: 9781662511967 (digital)

Cover design by Faceout Studio, Paul Nielsen
Cover illustration by Danny Schlitz

Printed in the United States of America

I dedicate this to you, Mom, my light.
And to my own old man, Dad.

PROLOGUE

They wouldn't tell her anything. They dropped her at the bottom of a hole with Sinatra and Crosby knotted into a pair of off-brand earbuds, and they told her to listen; listen to the oldies, they said, not the prisoner you'll be guarding. The descent was fast. Down the elevator shaft, past checkpoints—flashing IDs, then deeper, around a spiral stairwell, barbed in rust and reeking of tarnish. And at the deepest bend of this winding walk was madness—prayers shrieked in Arabic, cusses in Somali patois, fingernail stretch marks clawed across naked bodies. This was solitary. This was their Guantanamo-inspired abyss. But for her, only this single square cell was of any significance, and its single unnamed occupant. Rumors had swirled around the ranks that every officer who had monitored the prisoner had disappeared, ripped clean off the face of the earth. And now she sat there, across from this bogeyman, armed with only Sinatra and Crosby and that knot.

But she was different. She had made corporal in six months, Medal of Honor in three. Purple Heart. Silver Star. Top of her class. This corporal believed in the cause and would die for it—was dying for it: no feeling in her left thumb, toes lost to frostbite, and half-deaf in her right ear. The US Army was killing her, softly, gently, nibble by nipple.

It was a cell within a cell, a separate room partitioned off by thick steel walls, and soundproof, the entire nightmare beyond barely a muffle now, just white noise scratching against the walls. There was a bench for her outside the cell, positioned under an AC duct that showered her with a cold draft from above. The cell's steel beams played a sort of xylophone with the mechanical breeze; that quiet, hollow lullaby between each bar seemed to keep the prisoner asleep.

The man rolled away from the air, from the light—away from her. The blanket slipped off the knoll of his bare shoulder. His mucus-filled snout half snorted on his pillow. But then he went still; a moment after that, he went quiet. And that relieved her. She exhaled and realized she had been holding her breath. The corporal unhooked the top button on her shirt but still felt noosed in her collar, noosed in the cold air, noosed in that room, so she unbuttoned one more and breathed even deeper.

Complicated scents gusted from food trays adjacent to the bench and journeyed through her nostrils, through her thoughts and taste buds. Three square meals for the bogeyman, while she dined on the leftover half-pack of gum in her back pocket and chewed it into submission.

One earbud hung from her left ear, and the other earbud couldn't quite reach her right because of the knot. The corporal couldn't hear much in her right ear anyway, but it was about symmetry; she had never let on about her disabilities before, so why start now?

As the corporal dug her fingernails into the knot, she noticed tiny surveillance lenses and microphones dotting the interior of the cell. More obvious cameras hung over the doors and along the corridor, many aimed at him, just one aimed at her. If anyone was watching, they must have been having a chuckle at her fighting with the knot for minutes on end and only just now feeling something beginning to slip.

"Good morning," the prisoner said, rising up from his back to his tailbone. He sat and stared at her with such alertness that the corporal wondered if he had been awake the entire time. "Is it?" he continued, without a hint of grogginess. "Morning?"

It wasn't. It was probably about 5:40 in the evening, an early light most likely cutting across the San Diego skyline. Soft drinks and sunshine, but here she was, at the bottom of a sunless pit with a traitor—a bogeyman.

"What's that you're listening to?" He gestured to his ear as he aimed an eye at hers. "I heard they like to dole out the oldies: Johnny Cash. Muddy Waters."

She kept her head down. Her fingernails kept gnawing into the knot in the wire.

"They told you not to talk to me." He nodded as if imagining her response. "But I'll talk to you." He stood then and dragged his feet toward the front of the cell. He pressed his face between two bars, and fifty years of wrinkles squeezed back. "Your life, that little drumming behind your kindergarten cleavage there, that's in my hands." He reached out of the cell. His fingers coiled in, pre-fist, and squeezed an invisible heart: *boom—boom, boom—boom.*

She buttoned the top of her shirt and regretted the moment she did; she could hear him chuckling. She could see him in her peripherals, choking the bars of the cell, and she could feel the five-fingered noose tightening around her.

"Show respect," the prisoner said as he backpedaled toward the bed. "That's all. Show respect and you make it through the night. You should fare better than the others."

The knot loosened. It nearly cost her a fingernail, but it began to open up, the hard trappings giving way to a sort of sponginess between the wires. He kept quiet for a minute, and she could hear the music again. Treble whispered. Lyrics hissed. She wouldn't consider what he had said until much later, until the knot loosened further and she could slip a fingernail in between. Those rumors, *which were just rumors*, of soldiers disappearing—that was only gossip among the recruits. From his prison cell, he couldn't know what they were saying about soldiers dying on his watch.

"Unless it were true."

Talking to herself again—bad habits, and the corporal had a million of them: short tempered, confrontational, and antisocial, the latter of which made talking to herself all the more necessary. At the same time, her antisocial behavior made solo assignments like this manageable—the stakeouts in non-English territories, burying herself in ice with a sniper rifle like a snow woman. And now, sitting in a cell with a madman, her self-induced alienation made it all the easier.

"What's for breakfast?" he said, eyeing the cart beside her.

The cart had three shelves: breakfast on the first, lunch on the second, and supper on the lowest rung. Breakfast was toast, bacon, a bowl of fruit (sliced apples, grapes, oranges), and the redundancy of fruit juice. A single-dose medicine bottle, small enough for four or five pills, lay on its cylindrical side and swayed as she touched the cart; the label read "take two every six hours."

"Let's go," he said, his hand stretched out between the bars.

"Hold on." *Goddamn it*, the words had slipped out of her mouth— thinking out loud. *Don't talk to him.* She winced in regret and he saw. He smirked. He leered.

"Oh, I'm holding on," he said, and with two hands wrapped around the prison bars rocked to and fro. "What do we got?"

The corporal carried the tray of fruits and juices toward the cell but stopped in front of it. "Back toward the wall," she ordered. *Too late for any silent treatment now.* "Back of the cell."

He withdrew, hands in the air, as if she were holding a gun. She laid the tray at the foot of his cell. He picked at the fruits. He gulped down the juice. Everything was in foam containers. No glass, not even plastic forks—only finger foods.

"Shit," he said as the medicine bottle cracked against the cell floor and pills rolled out. "I need another one."

She reached for another medicine bottle but had a sudden thought. The absence of glass or even sharp plastic may not have been to protect her but to protect him from himself. Another medicine bottle with two doses might just cause the onset of a seizure.

"No," she said. "I can't do that."

"Excuse me?" He gestured to the scattering of pills on the floor. "Why the fuck not?"

"Because I said so."

"You remember what I said about being respectful?" he asked. "I said, I need another packet of pills."

"Then pick up the ones on the floor first. Throw them out, and I'll give you another bottle."

"More," he demanded, without even glancing at the pills on the floor. "Now."

"You're not killing yourself on my watch," she said. "Not going to happen."

"Then how about I kill you?" He paused to fold half his fingers into a fist and aim the barrel of his remaining two fingers at her. "You're killing yourself. Because not giving me those pills would be suicide."

"Just give me your pills," she said, reaching and wiggling her fingers in anticipation. "I'll give you another one."

"Do you want to know why I'm here?" he said, and didn't wait for a response. "The answer to that question is no. You don't want to know. The reason I'm here is classified. The reason I'm here has gotten me a death sentence, and like many terminal diagnoses, it's infectious. If I tell you why I'm here, they will kill you too."

She faked a half scoff, a half smile. But then she revealed herself as she reached for the earbuds, plugging one end into her right ear, but the other earbud wouldn't reach. That *fucking* knot!

"Last chance," he said. "More pills."

"No," the corporal said, so quietly it could have been a whisper.

"No?"

"No," she said, even quieter, as she considered the surveillance cameras glaring down at her. "No." Quieter yet as she pondered on how every noncommissioned officer monitoring him had caught themselves in the coincidence of KIAs. "No." Now she said it to herself.

"Fine," he said, and smiled and kicked his food across the cell. "Why am I here, then?"

The corporal squirmed away from him, her hips and heels twisting out of sync. She could feel him breathing on her back, cold on her spine—*or were those his eyes?*—stripping her uniform down to her skin and scars.

"I'm here because I figured something out."

The corporal scratched at the knot like a mad itch. It loosened, but still the spaghetti-sprawl of wiring was dizzying. She dragged the earbud out of her ear and looped it through and around the wires as "Fly Me to the Moon" drifted in and out of audibility.

"The war upstairs," he said, and chuckled. "The drones and tanks, that whole thing, it's not what it seems."

Footsteps pounded in the stairwell. They were coming, and fast, so *fucking* fast, stampedes of boots on metal, heavy soldiers with heavy weapons galloping down the spiral steps. But they wouldn't be fast enough.

"They started a war they couldn't win." He paused. "A war with *them*."

And the knot loosened.

"Fly me to the moon," Sinatra interrupted. *"And let me play among the stars. Let me see what spring is like on Jupiter and Mars."* But the prisoner kept talking and explaining, his lips mouthing as she raised the volume: *"In other words, please be true. In other words, I love you!"*

The door to the stairwell swung on ancient hinges and shrieked into the space. A huddle of men marched in familiar three-by-one formation, riflemen on the flanks, shooter at the hub. Weapons hung from slings on their shoulders, and their fists throttled the grips. The one at the center didn't have a rifle; he had authority.

The corporal lowered herself to her knees, raised her arms, and opened her palms, their shadows black against her face. "I didn't hear anything," she said, but then noticed the buds in all their ears. "I didn't hear." Louder. "I didn't hear!"

But he reached for the handgun on his hip anyway—a SIG M17.

"He didn't say anything!" She screamed it, as if shouting wasn't loud enough.

But he flipped the safety and cocked the SIG all the same.

"I didn't hear anything," she pleaded, hands up, head shaking, bilingually in English and sign language—*don't shoot.* "Please!"

But still, he aimed his SIG at her. "Don't move," he said.

But she did. She kept moving. Kept shaking. She couldn't stay still. And it wasn't the gun—she didn't care about the gun. It wasn't the soldiers, nor an end to her career, nor even the prospect of death. Something else shook the corporal at her core and wouldn't stop shaking.

"I didn't hear," she said, and pointed to the broken eardrum she had hid her entire antisocial career. But now she flaunted it, paraded it around to the highest of military ranks—she had to. "I promise to God I can't hear. I didn't. I didn't hear a thing."

But she had. The corporal had heard what the bogeyman had said, and it shook inside of her, like an echo growing louder, heavier. Tremors in her palms. Quivers on her lips. What he had said was of such impossible terror, and yet she knew it was true. It had to be. And now she knew—and she knew she would die.

PART I

1

"Sergeant Paxton Victor Arés." He whispered his own name as if it were a secret to him now, reading through enlistment papers, through his rank, race, religion, reminding himself of who he was. It all dribbled off his lips in incoherent mumbles: "Staff sergeant, single, twenty-nine years old." But as the vocabulary swelled beyond twelve years of public education with "proprietaries," "NDAs," and "confidentiality agreements," he went quiet. He surrendered to the pen, ending up right back where he had started—his name, now on a dotted line: *Paxton V. Arés*.

It was 5:39 a.m. First light twinkled through window grime. A dirty dew melted out of the windowpane, squiggling down the glass as if the night itself were melting away. He saw himself vaguely reflected there, ghostly against the glass, and fading into the Oakland suburbs outside as sunlight glossed the window. There was a metaphor there, he thought, something about him leaving Oakland to return to active duty or the drones he piloted and their images on glass screens. Somewhere in there was a metaphor but one that he wasn't smart enough to parse.

Now it was 5:40, and Paxton eyed the clock with contempt; he'd leave for deployment in just over an hour. He laid his documents onto the glass bed of a scanner and listened as the purr of his enlistment papers dissolved into digital. His fingers tap-danced across the touch screen display, delivering the email to its virtual post.

DRONE PILOT, it read on-screen, but that wasn't completely accurate.

"Landrone," Paxton corrected, amending the nondescript category of drone. Not the aerial drones, with their glossy, streamlined designs and billion-dollar budgets, but the grunts—the remote-controlled cavalry, crawling across Iraqi and Afghan dirt. "Fucking landrones."

He flipped his laptop shut and eased back onto the squealing spring mattress where Callie was still asleep. As he tiptoed into his socks and slippers, he felt her breathing ebb and flow on the blanket beneath him. He heard her, a soft sniffle crackling at her nostrils. Her scent was ever present; the taste of her lips still hung on the tip of his tongue, but of all his senses, Paxton's eyes spurned her. Callie hung in his peripherals, his lover, eclipsed by the crescent of her six-month-pregnant belly.

He tried not to wake her and kept his toes tipped as he eased down the stairway's wooden planks. The curtains drawn over the window squeezed out any hints of sunrise, and he left it that way. He sat in the dark and eyed the bowl of oatmeal stewing in his lap. When he did open a window, the sunlight shrapneled off the old man's military plaques on the wall, like lighthouses bringing back memories of base camp, back to made beds and the *sirs* and *ma'ams* suffixing every sentence.

The old man never discussed his decade in the Marines but provoked hearsay with the medals and ribbons, the framed pistols, the pressed uniforms, and the nickname WULF tattooed along his wrinkled arm. And because he never discussed them, hearsay became rumor, became myth, then legend. But maybe that was the old man's tactic—let them do the talking, let them pass down the legend.

Paxton stirred the thick, swelling oats; it reminded him of Nevada's desert air, the drills, the mechanical food, and that eight-hour bus trek across the Mojave. He didn't touch the oatmeal, feeling the beginnings of stomachaches or gastritis, or was that homesickness already kicking at his chest?

It changes after a child, the old man would preach, but by now Paxton had seen it enough himself to know. Paulo, Scotty, Larry—most of his old squad had blended into the suburban sprawl, the strollers and diapers, the picket fences and family sedans. Yet the truth of what the old man had said never truly clicked until that dinner last summer. A former staff sergeant homecoming, returning from a stint in the Pacific with a Korean wife and two-year-old in tow.

The child had screamed and flailed in his father's arms the entire night. He squirmed around the man's body, his shrimpy fingers snatching at everything, and it seemed to Paxton that as his friend had thinned, that baby fat now swelled on the infant's body—the man's bouquet of blond hair had receded, and those same curls had begun to sprout from the child's scalp. Amid the diaper changes and bottle feeds, something sinister had occurred, a sapping of one generation by the other, and Paxton felt it too now, that slight snag at the seam of his youth.

Paxton heard movement upstairs, wood wheezing under the labor of heavy footsteps. He listened for the direction of the steps. Callie's first destination would be the bathroom, but these feet treaded along the corridor. It was the old man. He took a cigarette to his lungs every morning, nicotine in place of caffeine, as he hung out of the window and watched the day begin.

The oatmeal had gotten cold. Paxton dumped the mush into Hudson's feeding bowl; they fed that old dog anything and he ate as much. The rottweiler–German shepherd mix buried its graying snout into the meal and wagged his ancient tail in approval. The elderly dog peered up, wet- and doe-eyed, staring at his best friend. Paxton knew that this might be the last time he'd see Hudson, and he caressed the dog's grizzled fur as if it were.

His shower water was the usual seesaw of ice and scalding hot, Paxton spending the better part of his shower trying to balance out the temperatures. He changed into his uniform and pedaled up the stairs, nudging the bedroom door open, but didn't find his bags. Instead he noticed Callie's hair tossing like tentacles underneath the fan. He pulled plug after plug from the noodle knot on the extension cord. The entire room died—alarm clock, lamps, phone charger—before the four tongues of the fan finally stopped their movement.

He stared at her, the Chinook girl he had met at that bar just outside the base. Callie was uniquely pretty, with her wide jaw, undefined eyebrows, and that sour-eyed look she always carried. She was pretty like abstract art but in the end not his type, and he suspected that he wasn't hers. Callie enjoyed reality television—the worst kinds. He preferred ESPN and football highlights with a lager and something meaty. He fixed engines and changed tires and drove fast, with quick reflexes behind the steering; her—carsick or morning sick, and she had a favorite seat on the bus. No mutual friends, friends of friends. He was an atheist, and she had many gods. They were opposites, nothing in common, except the strange proclivity to not talk about it. Paxton and Callie's intersection of common interests met and ended with that bump on her belly.

Their pregnancy had been unexpected but shouldn't have been; they were reckless lovers, impulsive—remiss, so quickly tangled into each other that there was only time for the taking off of things and none for the putting on. Opposites attract in that way, coarse, blunt, without a thought to compatibility. But if Paxton was anything, he was reliable, raised with that military devotion. He would be there for the baby—there for her, whether she needed him or not.

Callie's feet poked out from underneath the blanket with uneven toenails polished in a verdant turf green. The bottoms of her feet were rough, all the walking up the rock-riddled back hills in her sandals, even with a belly in full bloom, just to reach those sunflowers she craved.

Something moved him to touch her then, to press his palm against her thigh. Love maybe, or was that pity? Was that him thinking of the blisters on her legs and the swelling on her toes? Love and pity—it was funny how those two very different emotions mingled their sensations. But if Paxton did love Callie, he had never said it. It was not that he didn't feel something between them. He did, he felt it now; he'd just never been able to put it into words.

"Did you eat something?" Callie said, awake now, *or had she been the entire time?*

"What?" he said, responding before the question sank in—then it did. "Oh, no, I wasn't really hungry."

"You should eat."

"I made a sandwich," he lied. "I'll eat on the bus. Go back to sleep."

Callie stared at him with her hooded eyes and shook her head. She climbed out from under the blanket and sat back against the headboard. She did her best to groom herself in the morning light, finger-combing her hair and knuckling the corners of her eyes.

"I'll be back in no time," he said, trying to fill the quiet spaces between them.

"Until when?" she asked. "April?"

"Yeah, 'round about," he said, retreating back to the door. "You take care of yourself. I'll miss you."

Callie stared down the barrel of his eyes without a word—without even a flinch in reaction. The duo had never exchanged sweet talk, none of the honey-cottoned vocable of young lovers and never, ever a reference to that L-word. So she was illiterate to this dialect, untutored and failing on the spot. But she did nod; a single nod and a faint smile.

"I'll miss the bus," Paxton said, and withdrew into the doorway.

On his way down the stairs, though, Paxton considered turning back—a kiss or tight embrace might ease the blunt goodbye. But by the time he reached the bottom he figured it was better like this, with none of the awkward entanglement of bodies or verbs.

Paxton couldn't remember bringing his duffel bags downstairs in the morning—he hadn't. So where were they? He glanced behind the couch, in the closet. He even took a desperate peek into the half bath and found nothing.

"You lost something?"

The old man sat in the back corner of the kitchen, cigarette tip lit, two duffel bags and a backpack lying at his feet, accompanied by a single plastic bag with contents unknown.

"You packed light," the old man said, nudging the bag with a toes-fist; the arthritis appeared to be particularly bad this morning. "Just the basics, huh?"

Paxton responded with a nod. He lifted the bags over either shoulder and smirked, attempting to conceal their heaviness.

"You're one of the good ones, Paxy," the old man said, and Paxton knew right then that he was rearing for a speech. "But your genera-tion . . ." He paused and shook his head slow. "Spoiled little things. Attention span of squirrels." He laughed. He sucked on his nicotine straw, and the laughter vapored into white swirls from his nostrils and lips. "And why they have to take pictures of every goddamn thing? And all their protesting—rebels without causes, all of them. But you're one of the good ones. You remember it."

"I will," Paxton said as quickly as he could, jumping in before the old man went on.

"My shoes," the old man said, holding out the plastic bag. It trem-bled, dangling from his frail fingers. "They match your uniform. I'd be pleased if you wore them."

Paxton kicked off his boots without hesitation. He shoved his feet into his grandfather's glossy oxfords. He felt air pockets behind the heel of each shoe and at the front, where his toes wormed against the empty space.

"They fit," Paxton said, not to seem ungrateful. It meant something to the old man, so he would try to make it meaningful. "Think they match the suit better too."

The old man hummed agreement, examining Paxton's look, up and down, and finally nodding his full approval. He gestured a salute, and Paxton smiled and returned the same. Sometimes the old man was cute.

"Callie's got a doctor's thing this Thursday," Paxton said.

"You don't worry about old girl," he said and gestured upstairs to Callie's bedroom. "I got my eye out. You take care of business out there. Since the Ninety-Nine everything's been tech, satellite system this, drone pilots that. You never been too sharp, no disrespect, boy, but you know that. But it's brain over brawn nowadays, you remember that."

"I will," he said, but Paxton knew he wasn't smart and didn't need any more reminders. Multiple failed aptitude tests, OAR exams, even as early as high school, repeating the ninth grade twice. He didn't have it, whatever *it* was, and wasn't even sure that he wanted it. But they had all pitied the orphan raised by the old wolf, and that was enough to get him through.

"Nellis Base is your godfather's range," the old man said. "Top brass now. A colonel. He rose up fast."

"He was stationed on the East Coast when it happened?" Paxton asked.

"Front and center at the gates of hell." The old man stepped forward, bringing his lips close to Paxton's ear. "I put in words," he said at a whisper, as if anyone cared to listen. "You don't let on, but I put in words. Your godfather has sway, and he'll shove you as far up that ladder as he can. Fixin' jeeps ain't gonna cut it no more. Commissioned officers get their pay, and you got enough responsibilities to pay for now."

They embraced, and it was as uncomfortable as he had imagined. They held on too long and compensated with man-size pats on the back. The old man's jagged beard felt like pine needles against Paxton's neck, and his nicotine breath exhaled from every pore. The old man whispered promises to watch out for Callie and take his cigarette passions into the backyard where the breeze picked up the smoke and Hudson licked the cigarette butts dry.

"Pax," the old man said as Paxton dangled out the doorway, midstep, midbreath, whiplashing back to his grandfather. "Your momma wanted to call you that, Paxton. They'd fight sometimes like mad. Months 'fore you came popping out. All that over what, a name? But she always did find her ways to win, you know?"

He did, but Paxton wouldn't hang around again to listen about how he had bled out his own mother at birth: "It all changes after the baby." That old lecture would have to wait. Taxi horns beckoned outside, and Paxton retreated to marijuana-fumed polyester and oldies stuttering on a scratched disc. Callie waved into the taxi's midnight-black tinted windows; she wouldn't see him, but still he waved back.

The driver kept conversation to a minimum—"Service roads or highway?" and "Is the music too loud?" They took the highway, and it was loud, but he didn't say so. When the driver did aim his eyes into the rearview to hold actual conversation, he discussed only the Ninety-Nine; it was all anyone ever wanted to talk about, especially in the company of military men and women. Rumors and conspiracy theories filled the hour-long trek, and even after Paxton stepped out of the taxi, the bus driver picked up where the taxi driver had left off.

"It's almost the anniversary," the bus driver said, ice-breaking as they waited for the bus to fill. Paxton realized he should have sat in the back. "You know, the anniversary of the Ninety-Nine."

It was. September 9, the day every major American and foreign military installation had been wiped out: Russian tanks mangled like aluminum foil, American aircraft carriers dragged to ocean floors, hundred-acre Chinese bases scorched to ash, and the most inconceivable part of it, the complete mindfuck of it all, was that there was no enemy. Nowhere to send the drones. No targets at which to aim all their fancy new cruise missiles. Thirty-six percent of the world's military infrastructure had been obliterated in minutes, and no one knew how. No one knew *who*. Global military intelligences had stated publicly that no foreign nation was responsible—everyone had been hit. It wasn't Russia, it wasn't China, it was neither terrestrial nor extraterrestrial, neither AI nor organic in nature. Military intelligence had scratched every possible villain off their list, and they were left with nothing but the same unanswerable question now spray-painted across the columns of the Golden Gate Bridge: *WHO?*

"Who are we fighting?" the bus driver inevitably asked.

Paxton didn't know; no one knew, but the media had invented their names for it: Invisible Warfare. The Enigma Campaign. World War Who. And there he was, rolling willfully toward invisible front lines, their ace drone pilot, their joystick jarhead, their war machine.

2

The road was long.

Round mustardy hills and yellow dried shrubs colored the I-45 vista. Sand-whipped road signs had the neon peeled back and served as graffiti canvases: FUK DA GOVERMENT . . . DRONE ZONE . . . ENEMIES UNKNOWN. It all appeared abandoned—ancient—an unending road with crippling cracks and weeds bleeding through. That highway was like a spinal column running along the bone-dry vestige of America: dead roadside lights, billboards like scarecrows, hollowed-out gas stations rotting on every side of the road, and then the human tumbleweeds with cardboard signs begging in poetry, like civilized oases amid all the illiterate infrastructure.

The sixty-seat charter bus housed only seventeen; Paxton had counted. He had strolled the aisle, pretending to touch seat backs for balance, but in fact he was counting: fourteen . . . fifteen . . . all the way to the lavatory in the back. It was the monotony; it highlighted every detail of the nine-hour drive, from gum stains on seat cushions to the names carved into the toilet-bowl seat.

A hundred engraved signatures scarred the lavatory walls, names carved over names, like one generation burying the other. And they had. Tens of thousands had died in the Ninety-Nine, and that was such a strange thought now—dying in war. Casualties over the past few years had dwindled to nothing. As the world's militaries rebuilt, drones had risen in fashion—en vogue. No more fathers lost to gunfire, no more daughters returned limbless. This would be the era of lifeless combatants, as their puppeteers fiddled far away and at safe distance.

Paxton walked back down the aisle at an angle to conceal his limp. Years of hiding the pins and metal plates in his heel and knee had made it instinctual. He barely felt the half-degree slope in his step, and it had even, at times, seemed like a sort of sashay—a swagger, common in the bravado of injured vets. Still, the old battle scars from a tour in Sri Lanka challenged him in the off-balanced rattle of the bus. Inertia tugged on his left, then in front of him; the floor lifted and fell, and then it slipped; Paxton limped. He caught himself on a seat back. He re-angled himself and glanced around the charter bus. No one was watching. No one cared.

The flash of diffidence took his eyes off the aisle, and Paxton bumped into number eight of the seventeen passengers. She was younger than him, or appeared to be, short and flimsy with a hunched posture. Her features were hard, sharp angles in her jaw and around her brow, yet she had wiry carrot hair and full lips. Her look was unique, a collage of disconnected features, and that trapped him in her face for a few seconds too long.

She broke the silence, but barely, so soft spoken, coy even, that the engine's rattling, heavy against the body of the old bus, drowned out her voice nearly completely.

"I'm sorry, what?" Paxton responded.

"Eighteen," she said again, and smiled.

That was actually what he thought she had said, but it didn't make sense the first time and surely wasn't any clearer now.

Eighteen what? He gestured the question with a bend of his neck and lift of his brow, but he also smiled, and she must have misread it as understanding. She never spoke on it again.

But conversation sparked soon after—small talk, names and places. Hers was Bella, hers was Sunnyvale, California. She was a corporal and formerly a drone pilot in DC before the Ninety-Nine—*before*, and therein she broadcasted her age. Bella listened more than she spoke and kept her answers succinct. Yet she seemed eager for conversation. Her body language explained it, a posture that bent toward him, eye contact fixed on his, and she nodded her enthusiasm, whispering "really" and "that's interesting."

Bella relocated to the seat across from Paxton's and leaned over the aisle to chat. He talked about fixing Jeeps and SUVs and the once-in-a-lifetime Lamborghini. But Paxton kept the conversation mostly impersonal; Hudson burying bones in the backyard was the closest he came to talking about home. She had majored in military history at Cornell University and nerded out on the Greek phalanx, the blitzkrieg, and *The Art of War*.

Suddenly the brake hydraulics squealed and gravel crackled under the tires; the bus hissed to a stop. Outside the window, a wooden-faced man with whittled-out cheekbones and chin escorted a military-trained German shepherd along the side of the bus. Another couple of wooden soldiers stood at the door—nutcrackers with uniforms, hats, and long, grizzly beards.

"Let's go!" the drill sergeant hollered as he slammed his fist against the side of the bus. "Hit the concrete and keep moving—let's go!"

Paxton and Bella were the first off the bus. The drill sergeants lined them up, from fresh-faced recruits to more seasoned veterans. The line stretched seventeen long . . . *no, eighteen*, as he counted again and noticed a short buzz cut at the head of the line that he had overlooked.

That's what she had meant—eighteen.

Bella had noticed him counting on the bus. *Perceptive*, he thought, and leaned over to tell her, but the drill sergeant howled commands to cadets and corporals alike.

"Knees high, back straight, and march!"

The sergeant directed them across a field of solar arrays. It spanned nearly two miles, maybe more. Paxton had never seen so many: football fields upon football fields, with tens of thousands of sun-sucking silicon sponges. They wrapped around the main facility like rings around Saturn, a solar-powered halo that shone blue in the moonlight, brightening their path through the dark.

He lined them up outside a pair of stairways that led down to underground barracks. Scents wafted out. Sour and saltine flavors lifted

Paxton's nostrils to breathe deep. He slavered and swallowed and imagined the tastes. There were noises too, rhythmic reggaeton beats and laughter rising up from the barracks at their feet.

"The party's started without you," the drill sergeant said. "And if you don't form a proper fucking line, it will end without you."

It took them a few minutes to find their footing in the dark, but eventually the line straightened up enough for the drill sergeant to holler approval. He chased them down into the barracks, and even his promise to let them sleep late the following day somehow sounded like a threat.

Paxton's room was badly lit. Two pairs of aging fluorescent lights hung and hummed, luring wanton flies to dry-hump the phosphorous bulbs. The walls were unpainted gray with fine fissures sprawling like stretch marks across the concrete. Then there was the bunk bed, standing at a bowlegged hunch with lazy mattresses that drooped in the middle.

Paxton tossed his bags into a rusted locker squeezed into the corner and stepped right back out, coming up for air from the claustrophobic space. He found Bella roomed a few corridors down, with the other women of war, and their conditions weren't any better. She shared her room with a staff sergeant. A pipe ran along the ceiling, and it leaked water into a puddle at the foot of the sergeant's bed.

Staff Sergeant Olive Oya slept in the bunk above Bella. Oya was a mother and had the proof of it tattooed over her exposed cleavage. Her braless bust dangled at the neck of her shirt with a pair of names: Eliyah, Elijah. And the tattoos kept going. Oya had ink stitched into her shoulders, arms, and legs. She was a tapestry of her own identity, from a thunderbolt on her right wrist to a map of Nigeria tattooed into the flex of her left biceps.

Now in her second year at Nellis, Oya fielded questions about the infinite stretch of solar panels, the cafeteria food, and Colonel Marson, Paxton's godfather. Yet to Paxton's surprise, there was no mention of the landrones they would soon pilot, the quadrupedals, the bipedals, and the rumored new War Machines. It was all middle-school queries, playtime and days off and how to kill time in between.

The youngest of them, Privates Inga Qamaits and Solomon "Solo" Oro, both still recovering from pubescent acne, hung in the doorway, wide-eyed youngsters asking one unnecessary question after the other.

"Are the conspiracies true?" Private Qamaits said.

"Where's the secret bunker?" Solo asked.

The gravity of their laughter pulled the party to Bella's bunk. And even as midnight approached, socializing continued to reach a crescendo. Paxton listened to privates and sergeants trade names and things in common. Basketball came up often, and Japanese anime seemed to color many a childhood, but eventually that inevitable topic came up, that one inescapable depth of modern conversation.

The Ninety-Nine.

Solo squinted into the haze of childhood memory and recalled dodgeball, recess, and school lunches smuggled onto the playground. He remembered how the math teacher and principal had dragged the entire sixth grade off the monkey bars and hopscotch trails and huddled grades three through six in the gym. He and his classmates had watched the spectacle of flames and smoke on a projector used for sex ed. He said he hadn't understood the magnitude of it and was just glad to get out of a history exam.

Private Qamaits, nine on the day of the Ninety-Nine, said that she just remembered her mother crying but didn't know why. Bella was even less forthcoming with anecdotes. Even as a legal adult, seventeen at the time, and active-duty ROTC, Bella had lost consciousness in the attack on Fort McNair and couldn't remember anything besides waking up in the infirmary days later. Paxton shrugged his experience off in a single sentence, saying that he had seen the aftermath of things on TV, but that was just a blatant lie.

All eyes then turned to Sergeant Oya. She had experienced the Ninety-Nine from a base in South Korea. The enemy hadn't hit Kunsan Air Base, but intelligence from Washington indicated a Chinese aggressor. So they had loaded up every gunship, stealth jet, and submarine with enough artillery to put a hole in the world. They had galloped toward China, full head of steam, pistons burning, but Beijing wasn't there. Oya said she had stood on the deck of the USS *Washington*, a hundred miles from the coast of China, and she could see the smoke and hear the impossible being said—

"Beijing is gone," Sergeant Oya said as she stared out into the memory on the tip of her thoughts. "Beijing is gone."

And Washington was gone, or at least a part of it—Fort McNair, Dupont Circle, Georgetown, and most of the surrounding counties. Moscow was gone. London. North Carolina. New Delhi. Rome. Tokyo. Rio. *Sri Lanka*. Twenty-seven separate attacks worldwide, and the only ones who had seen the attackers were dead.

"Who are we fighting?" Solo said, eyeing Sergeant Oya as he did.

"You think I know?" Oya said, and frowned.

"There's rumors," Solo said at a conspiratorial whisper, and the room turned to him at once, like a hydra, a half-dozen heads pivoting in sync.

"I don't listen to rumors," Oya said.

But that didn't satisfy Private Qamaits. "There're rumors?" she asked. "What rumors?"

"Okay, good night," Oya said, pointing to the door. "I'm going to bed. Talk your rumors outside."

The night ended on that note. Conversation didn't continue in the corridor. Mandatory brownouts beginning at 12:15 forced the crowd of enlistees to bottleneck the shower doors with only enough time to either brush teeth or wash faces; Paxton chose the latter.

He retreated to the claustrophobia of his room and kept the old man's shoes on as he lay down. A bunkmate never came, and the quiet let in all the chirping thoughts in his head. He thought of Callie and her morning sickness, then wondered if the old man would keep his promise not to smoke inside, and if Hudson still barked like a canine rooster at sunrise. Paxton wandered far too deep into his homesick mind and couldn't sleep. And then he had to wake up.

3

Dreams fade faster in the daylight. Sunshine dissolves the subconscious in the same way it does the pupils in dilation. But those underground barracks' fluorescent dawn kept Paxton's dreams stuck to the corners of his mind, lingering long after the cold shower, the shots of mouthwash, and the artwork of making a military bed. It was that same dream again: Callie swaddling her stillborn babe in the thick of the old man's cigarette smoke. Paxton sighed, full of melancholy, but abandoned her there in that nightmare, climbing out of his subconscious, the taste of cigarette smoldering on his breath.

Breakfast was the usual mess hall assembly line: eggs, sausage, toast, and lukewarm oatmeal in a foam bowl. He didn't have much of a taste for any of it, sleep still bending his posture, his vision still a blur like mucusy static, but he wrangled what they handed and ended up with oatmeal, eggs, and some brownish juice. He liked the smells, the warmth rising up to meet his nose. He hung his tired head over the bowl, staring into the grainy slush, almost exfoliating in the steam of swelling oats.

Paxton spotted the back of Sergeant Oya's head at the off-ramp to the breakfast line and followed a trail of familiar voices to her table. Oya sat between Private Qamaits and Solo on one side and another sergeant, Calum Woden, on the other. Paxton took a seat opposite the foursome and quickly found himself privy to Sergeant Woden's theories about the Asian Bloc, India's rise to dominance in world affairs, and its perceived immunity to enemy attacks. The sergeant's spiel sounded more like first-world envy than any classified intel, so Paxton followed Sergeant Oya's lead and kept his head down.

"Colonel Marson's speech this afternoon is mandatory," Sergeant Woden reminded them. Paxton squirmed at the idea of standing in the Nevada sun for the better part of the afternoon, and Woden noticed. "Sitting in drone cockpits for so long make you soft, Arés?"

Paxton shrugged. Maybe it had. But Paxton had already seen the leaflets taped to the corridor walls: ANNIVERSARY SPEECH @ 12:50 FOXTROT. RUNWAY 9, with a black-and-white photo of the general absorbing half the page—his godfather, the four-star general, with all the prestige of a professional athlete. Colonel Marson had been there on the Ninety-Nine, leading drone strikes against unidentifiable enemies—little more than a staticky haze on the screen. Marson was part of a coalition of a hundred nations and over a hundred million troops, making him one of the most powerful military leaders alive. If anyone knew anything about who they were fighting, it was him.

"You sleep good?" Oya asked all of a sudden, as if he was giving away something in his lazy look.

"Not bad," Paxton said, quickly tightening his expression—locked lips, focused eyes.

"Don't look like it," Woden said. "You got stuff in your eye."

Do I? Because as Paxton dug into the corners of his eyes, he found nothing but soft, sleep-sore flesh. His vision blurred in the efforts, and squinting into that haze he saw Bella roaming lost with a tray of breakfast in hand.

"Bells," he half shouted, but she didn't hear him.

"Corporal Columbia!" Woden shouted, and smirked.

Bella heard her name and swiveled, neck and waist, spinning her in circles.

"Hey, B!" Oya shouted even louder and waved at her bunkmate. "Here!"

Bella approached and planted herself between Sergeants Woden and Oya. A thick book weighed down her lap, something about military tactics. Bella smiled a nonverbal hello to Paxton, but he couldn't reply. Instead he gaped at a smearing of marker graffiti swirled across Bella's face: vulgar words on her forehead, inappropriate drawings on her cheeks. Paxton stared at it all, and again, stared just a second too long.

"What's up?" Bella asked.

But as Paxton poised to speak, Woden interrupted. "You know what I hate," he said, voice aimed at Solo but eyes on Paxton. "Snitches."

"Fuck snitches," Solo chimed in.

Oya ignored both Woden and the artwork on Bella's cheeks, seemingly not amused by the juvenile larks. Paxton attempted to do the same, quickly stuffing a spoonful of oatmeal into his mouth without the hunger for it. But it was too late. Bella appeared to realize that something was off, brushing her hair, rubbing her nose, as Solo and Woden flashed their obvious teeth.

"Hey, Bella," Woden said as he nudged her shoulder. "You clean up nice."

"Thanks," she said, and lowered her gaze to the coffee of her breakfast tray. She ran her tongue along the front of her teeth, seemingly searching for some fragment of breakfast lodged therein.

"You're gonna be turning a lot of heads around here," Woden continued.

Woden's face remained inexpressive, but Solo's lips rippled with smirks and dimples. And Bella kept running her tongue along the face of her teeth and sucking at the spaces between them. *She knows*—not what the joke was exactly, but she seemed to be aware that it was on her face. Paxton tried to signal to her, a subtle rub of his knuckles against his cheeks, but too subtle, and she glanced past it.

"Your girlfriend's here," Woden whispered to Oya as someone else captured his attention. "Fresh cut and all. Blow her a kiss."

"Fuck off, Woden," Oya said, never raising an eye toward an approaching woman.

She stood nearly six feet tall, a first lieutenant, her rank stitched into the grayed green of her uniform. She rounded the aisle and approached the opposite side of the table. Sergeant Oya kept her eyes down and lifted the coffee cup to her face as if she could hide behind it.

"Sergeants," the woman said, greeting them.

"Crown Vic," Woden addressed her as he stood and saluted. "Victoria the Great."

"Sit down, jackass," Victoria said, then turned to Bella. "What's your name, recruit?"

"Corporal Bella Columbia," Bella said, and saluted before she could even climb to her feet, which she eventually did. "I'm a—"

"At ease," Lieutenant Victoria said, cutting Bella off with a lazy hum of disinterest. "Go wash off your face, Corporal Columbia."

Sergeant Woden managed to keep his reaction tied down to a simple smirk. Solo, on the other hand, fell face-first into the palms of his hands and muffled a laugh that attracted three tables full of glances.

Bella's fingers spidered across the collage of vulgarity on her face. She understood. Her eyelids peeled back. Her irises stood on end. Bella backpedaled from the table, aiming one glance of disappointment at Paxton before charging away from the crowd.

He had tried to warn her, but that was just it—he had *only* tried. Now Paxton felt this older brother's irresponsibility ringing at his chest, an alarm he couldn't turn off. Bella wasn't built for this habitat, he thought: the anti-effeminate lingo, the slang, the boyish minds and bodies of men, the protein bars and creatine, the Gatorade and urinals reeking of testosterone. She wasn't built for it, and neither was he.

"Permanent marker!" Sergeant Woden shouted and chuckled between the words. "Gonna need a facial, baby girl!"

"Facial!" a few of them clamored. "Facial!" More joined in. "Facial, facial, facial!" The entire mess hall rioted. Fists pumped into the air, feet thudding against greasy tiles, every voice swept up in the holy ghost and repeating the same as Bella swerved toward the exit and disappeared into the corridor.

"Enough!" Lieutenant Victoria's voice exploded over the crowd, snuffing out laughter, grins, all of them, but she fixed her eyes on Paxton as if he had started the whole thing, or maybe because he should have stopped it. There was disappointment in her look, like she expected better of him. Paxton considered saluting or nodding, but the longer she stared at him, the more he thought he shouldn't. In the end, he figured he should at least introduce himself, starting with his name.

"Sergeant Paxton Arés," Victoria said, cutting him off before he even mustered the breath to speak. "I'd like to speak to you."

"Yes, Lieutenant?" Paxton said.

"In private, Sergeant," she said, as if it should have been obvious, then motioned toward the exit, her gesture like a leash lifting Paxton off his seat. "Follow me."

4

Her office had a library: four shelves against the four walls in a rectangular room. The shelves bulged with books, everything from military history to quantum theory to the scrawny fantasy novellas in between. On her desk—nothing. Bare-naked mahogany gleamed in the early-morning light beaming down from a skylight above.

Yet even with the desk, matching mahogany shelves, and reclining swivel chairs, her office sprawled to spacious lengths; vased ferns breathed green into the office flanks, and oriental lamps shone down on framed Hebrew calligraphy. The decor all seemed to have a symmetry about it, balanced around the four corners of the room. The floor and windowpanes gleamed as if freshly polished, and the entire room seemed to sparkle.

"Nice office," Paxton said, and waited for a response.

And she kept him waiting, never coming forth with a response. She may have actually nodded, *maybe*, but it was so slight that he couldn't tell. She had been sending and receiving texts since they got to her office and hadn't spoken a word. But after Paxton voiced his compliment, she seemed to remember that he was there. She multitasked, a cell phone in one hand and the other reaching deep into the drawer by her feet. She lifted a single sheet of paper from inside. Paxton's information—those same lines of legal dialect from the morning before.

"Have you ever piloted Furies?" she asked with that accent that he couldn't place. "The aerial drones?"

"No, ma'am," he said.

"So, landrones only?"

"Yes, ma'am," Paxton said. "Rovers mostly."

"K9s," she said.

"K9s?"

"We called them K9s in Israel," she said, *and that explained a lot.* First, why she would use the term K9 and second, it explained that accent. "But you've never piloted a bipedal—an Androne?"

Androne. That word again—was it a thing now? A year ago in San Diego and Fort Irwin the term didn't exist. Even as the use of the bipedal drones had become the new standard, pilots called them bipedals or landrones. At first Paxton had thought maybe the term Androne originated by subtracting the *l* from landrone, but now he realized the words *android* plus *drone* would equal out to *Androne.* He debated with himself for half a second longer than he should have and nearly lost sight of what he was talking about in the first place.

"I've piloted an Androne in simulation."

"Sim." She sounded disappointed.

Lieutenant Victoria reached back to the bookshelf and pulled a thick white book from between two other fat thousand-page binders. Paxton felt the weight of it as she handed it to him. *Bipedals: The Androne Series.* Paxton quickly flipped it open to a random page to feign interest. He saw two separate blueprints on either page, one of a Shogun Series Androne and the other an Apache Series.

He had to squint at the fine print naming all the individual parts. There were so many pieces. The Androns were created in the human image—like gods with human proportions, optical lenses, synthetic spinal fluids, and metallic fibrous muscle.

The Shogun Series stood six feet plus and were armor heavy, with a tungsten carbide body and shifting tungsten alloys surrounding the joints—and faceless, except for a single cyclopic eye. The Apache Series appeared to be built for speed, a sprinter's aerodynamic design, less armor, lighter guns, and a nearly empty face, except for its triceratops-fashioned optical lenses.

Paxton turned the page and found blueprints for two more Andrones, a fifth and sixth on the pages after. Each with a distinct look and function: combat, recon, extraction.

"How many?" Paxton asked.

"Eight series, or nine, depending on who you ask."

"If I'm asking you?"

"I count nine." She flashed nine fingers. "The Cooks name them after the greatest and most respected military war machines throughout history. The Spartan Series, the SPQR Series 1 and 2, the Mongol Series, Shogun, Apache, Z Series or Zulu Series, and the Kingsman Series."

"What's the ninth?" Paxton asked.

"The Americana," she said. "But it's not a series. They're only making one."

"Why one?"

"Because there's only one God," she said, and half smiled for the first time. "That's what the Cooks tell us, at least. And they are right about one thing: it's godlike in nature."

Paxton thumbed through the subsequent pages. Detailed diagrams on antennae, satellite signals, and infinitely complex optical lenses filled the pages. Though what Paxton was searching for was a blueprint for the Americana.

"It's not in there," she said.

"What's not?"

"You're looking for the Americana?"

She had read his mind.

"They're just in the conceptual phase right now—brainstorming: hurricanes and twisters. They won't start any actual construction for another ten, fifteen years at least."

"Gotcha," Paxton said, and closed the book thereafter.

"You want to see them?"

Not right now. But she would show him anyway. Her body language alluded to it—the slope of her wrist, the tilt of her elbows. The lieutenant leaned forward and eyed the door before even finishing her sentence.

"There are prototypes here on base," she said as she stood and moved toward the door. "This way."

Paxton followed Victoria into the Mojave oven, lagging a few steps behind her enlivened haste. They cut through the field of solar arrays; the mile and a half of gleaming metals appeared like stalks of diamonds in the daylight. Barbed vegetation knotted the trail and somehow smuggled their thorns into his footwear. Paxton limped, as either pebbles or thorns or both rattled around his socks, making them into cotton maracas. At the top of the winding trail, they reached a deep-fried warehouse, rusted and corroded to perfection, crowning the ridge.

"Why me?" he said to himself. "Why just me?"

And he kept on wondering why the lieutenant would reveal every bell and whistle within the Androne Program a full day before orientation. He had expected Victoria to reveal this in her office, but no. Why wasn't Bella here? Neither Solo nor Private Qamaits had any Androne training—why weren't they on this grand tour? Or any of the 117 fresh recruits, now resting in the air-conditioned bunks—why weren't they cresting this hill in the cutting late-morning sunshine?

Two pairs of patrol officers slouched on either side of the extra-crispy warehouse rust; cigarette fumes huffed from their nostrils, chewing tobacco sprayed from their gums. America's finest guards hadn't even noticed Paxton's and the lieutenant's bright uniforms moving against a palette of infinite desert grays; and they wouldn't notice, not until Victoria whistled and threw up her hand to wave. The young men straightened their postures, dusting their sleeves and snuffing cigarette butts under their heels.

She flashed her badge, but they had already taken the locks off the barn doors and begun sliding them back. Complicated smells poured out: tarnish, motor fuels, battery acids, all singeing his nose hairs and seeping into his taste buds the deeper he journeyed inside.

The interior was black, and Lieutenant Victoria's dark navy uniform dissolved in the void ahead. Paxton entered more cautiously, feeling in front of him and catching fistfuls of cobwebs.

"Watch your eyes." Her voice echoed somewhere in the distance.

"What?" he said, and as he said it floodlights exploded into the darkness. He squinted into a fifty-some-odd high-wattage nova burning down from the ceiling. A massive space yawned out in front of him. A space large enough to host a 747. The words HANGAR 18 were painted over large twin doors at the opposite end.

"Sergeant," Victoria said and gestured. The wide, empty space splintered her voice into echoes, ricocheting from every direction. "The Andrones are over here."

Their naked tungsten bodies glistened under the incandescent shine. Stainless steel joints twisted the luster into whirlpools of dazzle, the glare dizzying his eyes. The Andrones appeared godlike and at the same time ungodly, monstrous behemoths, with an unlimited capacity for destruction. *Built in our image* came to mind again, but not born from women—these were the children of Men.

"Shogun, SPQR Series 1, Apache, and Spartan," Victoria said, pressing her palm against the Spartan's reinforced-steel chest as if feeling for a heartbeat.

The Spartan in no way resembled its Greco-Mycenaean counterparts in fashion or design; it was modern, mechanical muscle, at least six feet, nine inches vertically and four feet broad, with built-in titanium body armor giving it a reflective grayish-brownish hue and wielding a Gatling gun–size assault rifle.

"Are they functional?" Paxton asked.

"All four. The Spartan was the first model. SPQR Series was the second version—"

"Chronologically," he cut her off, thinking he understood. "Spartans are Greeks. SPQR is the Roman Empire, and the . . ."

She started shaking her head before he could finish.

"You would think so, but then they made the Apache before the Mongol, the Shogun before SPQR Series 2. Great engineers. Bad historians."

"Where are the rest?" Paxton said, glancing around the room searching for the Mongol, Kingsman, and Z Series depicted in the book.

"They're . . ." She hesitated with the answer. "Not too far out."

Paxton rapped his knuckles against the chest of the armor-heavy Shogun. He ran his palms along the Spartan's monstrous assault rifle. He prodded the hundred individual parts along the back: pistons in the arms and legs, a titanium-reinforced spine and the synthetic fluid therein; Paxton disassembled it all in his head, examining the individual parts and their functions, like he had the used cars at Larry's mechanic shop back in Novato. But all of his poking and prodding was just a hesitation move—a buying of time, as Paxton waited for the lieutenant to address that one question swelling malignantly in his brain—*Why me?*

But a buzz from her cell phone dragged Victoria outside. Her voice faded, then disappeared, and Paxton could only stand and wait among the company of the Androns. But a five-minute wait turned into ten, turned into twenty, and eventually a cigarette-wielding private came in her stead, relaying a message from the lieutenant.

"'Tenant said you should get back to camp."

She left? he thought, then it echoed out of his lips: "She's gone?"

"No, she's 'round back, but—"

Paxton nodded as if the private were finished and treaded toward the doors just a skip short of jogging. Trails of kicked-up sand followed the soles of his shoes, and he found her curled up under a spot of shade, ending her phone call just as Paxton stepped within earshot of her voice.

"You should get back," she said, standing under the barbed-wire shade of a cactus. "The colonel's speech is about to start."

"You do this for all one hundred seventeen of us?" Paxton asked. "The whole grand tour?"

"No," she said with her eyes fixed on him as if bracing for the next question.

"Then why do it for me?"

"For you." Lieutenant Victoria glanced back at the warehouse entrance dangling ajar in the breeze. "You feel special?"

"No," he said.

"No, what?"

It took Paxton a second to remember his rank. "No, ma'am!" he said, straightening up and looking her in the eye. Maybe he *was* starting to think that he was special.

"Maybe you are," she said, and shrugged. "Maybe you could make a difference." And then as she stepped away, moving back the way they came, Victoria said, "Maybe you could end the war."

5

The way down stretched on for many minutes and miles. The oases of shade that had sheltered him on the way up now angled away from his path, and Paxton bore the full brunt of the sun. Yet Victoria's words ran dizzying loops around his head, distracting him from the sweat puddles under his arms and the twigs stabbing at his heel. There was something she wasn't saying, something hiding in her vagueness.

He had considered the possibility that it was *him*—his godfather, Colonel Marson. The old man had mentioned that he had *put in words* and that Marson would *keep an eye out*. That was the logical answer, wasn't it? Marson had commissioned Lieutenant Victoria to give Paxton a leg up. It explained almost every random act of favoritism therein. Although, there was the part of the brain that longed for ego, that hankered for the spark of individual worth; and somewhere therein Paxton wanted to believe her—he could end the war.

It was around noon when he arrived back at camp. The cattle pen of troops stampeded out of the barracks and filed into rows and columns, advancing toward Runway 9. And Paxton followed, without question or answer, marching in sequence: *left, right, left,* dancing to their choreography, concrete drums beating under his size-twelve drumsticks. End what war? He was no different from the rest of them: *left, right, left, right, left.*

They sat Paxton opposite the tide of afternoon shade as if to reemphasize that he wasn't special at all. The sun burned him down. He melted to puddles. He evaporated to body odor—like a vapor, like an out-of-body drift that carried Paxton floating out over the buzz cuts and applauding hands.

Regiment banners and state flags soured the stage a lemony gold, and the old men stood in their shade. A hundred colonels and sergeants stood in full military dress as statesmen and congresswomen took the stage. Colonel Marson gave the penultimate address. He paralleled the anniversary of the Ninety-Nine and the emergence of the Androne Program, calling it "fitting" and dubbing it as a tactical turning point in the Enigma War.

Yet Paxton managed to ignore the stripes, the banners, the elderly men standing on their dais, and instead he watched *them*—the nicotine-faced youth, flaunting black gums and copper-stained teeth and skin sponged up beneath their dreary eyes. They applauded Marson, standing center stage with the podium dwarfed under his height. And Marson had the voice for it, a deep valley of resonance from tobacco-scratched lungs.

"Nine years ago it happened—the sky fell."

He was a storyteller. His words painted color onto the whites of their eyes, and it animated them. Cadets and corporals nodded their respect. Lieutenants and colonels applauded their reverence. They stood for ovations; they whistled and cried and screamed. And they even dangled on the edge of sentences as the storyteller colonel strategically lulled and paused.

"Who are we fighting? Who has the technological know-how to cripple the entire world?"

Paxton felt something then, and it wasn't the fugue of dehydration or the preludes to heatstroke—or maybe it was. But right there, Paxton felt a need *to be*—to be something, anything. He felt inspired. Rather than drift through the rest of the tour, he could be part of something bigger: the military evangelical. He could climb the rungs to lieutenant, first lieutenant, and beyond. So he listened. He found the sound of it comforting. Paxton listened to them, the recruits—the believers. He listened to them listening to him.

"Conspiracy theorists indicate the United State of Korea, or even India. Science fictionists point to extraterrestrials—aliens or AI. No! We've analyzed every ounce of data, from attack patterns to the targeted installations. It wasn't artificial intelligence. It wasn't E.T. or interdimensional fictional, fantasy forces. So who? Who is it that we're waging an invisible war against? Doesn't matter who we're fighting. What matters is who we're fighting with. We fight with our allies abroad, a hundred nations, a hundred million soldiers. We fight with each other, every soldier to the left and right of you. And we fight with the fury of the most advanced weapons ever introduced into the War Machine Program— the Androne Series. From the Spartan to the Americana—you now fight with Andrones!"

Applause rioted across the expanse, shrill cheers and whistling from giddy cadets, and even more seasoned officers, and Marson himself applauded his own speech, or maybe he was applauding them. Tomorrow they would all climb into the Androne cockpits and steer their mechanical bodies, take their first baby steps in hundred-pound feet. *Tomorrow*: Paxton pondered the word now deeper than he ever had before, with purpose. All his potential, all those goals, it would all begin tomorrow in that cockpit.

6

The night was short and his breakfast rushed, all so he could be the first to Hangar 36, the first to his cockpit. He wasn't; Paxton stood somewhere in the middle of a line a hundred pilots long. All of them groaning, griping, huddled so close behind one another they nipped at each other's heels. They had been assigned the cockpits in the days and weeks before deployment and yet still, there was this bottleneck of confusion. After forty-five minutes, Paxton eventually stood in front of it—the cockpit, labeled 9027, his window into the war, standing just a few inches taller than him.

From the outside it appeared like a mechanical eggshell—rounded, ovular, with cables like veins sprawling across its metallic hull. Dozens of these spherical pods stood in an old plane hangar with a towering gate large enough to swallow the largest jetliners. It was as if to remind onlookers of the bygone era of true piloting, the person literally within the machine.

Inside the cockpits were wombs of claustrophobia so tight only limbs were allowed freedom of movement—pedals for the legs, gloves suctioned onto palms to reach and swing. And every surface was rounded, every valve and node constructed to spiral and loop around the ovular design.

These cockpits were smaller than the ones Paxton had operated in Fort Irwin. The tilt of their seating hunched his posture, brought the foot pedals higher and glove controls tighter in on his six-foot frame.

The pedals and control shifts seemed thicker, denser, more robust—more expensive.

Still, any differences between the quadrupedal cockpits at Fort Irwin and these bipedals at Nellis Base were cosmetic at best. The only stark difference was in movement—quads had gas pedals, much like any motor vehicle, but the motion pedals on bipedals simulated walking, resembling elliptical machines and all the sweat that came with them.

Another difference was the gloves—carbon-steel gloved controls that suctioned around Paxton's palms, enabling finger and thumb movement to be remotely mimicked by the bipedal. But even more amazing, signals from the field would be sent back to the cockpit's gloves. If the Androne picked up a stone, for instance, that signal would return to the cockpit and prevent the pilot from closing their fist completely.

The last major difference was the Optical Output, or OO, an overused acronym because of the resemblance between the letters OO and a pair of eyes. The original OOs from the Fort Irwin cockpits had a slightly curved LCD screen, the same as any high-end television, displaying high-definition Afghan landscapes or Syrian ruins. The Nellis Base OOs were light-years more advanced. Screens curved across nearly half of the cockpit space—above, below, side to side, all of it covered in smooth synthetic glass. But this was only half of the visual display. A second glass display was a helmetlike visor that was placed directly over the eyes. These dual screens worked in tandem to create the optical illusion of depth of field. There was no visible discrepancy in watching from the cockpit and actually being in the field.

But after mere glances at the ins and outs of their cockpits, pairs of bony cadets, elbows and knees like edges on their uniforms, set up geriatric folding chairs, many of them bowlegged and rusted at their hinges. Other senior staff set up an array of projectors, spray-painting light across the massive hangar walls. But the video too was ancient, shot maybe twenty years ago. So old in fact that liver-spotted VHS static dotted the screen. An older man, likely of South Asian descent based on the flags behind him, appeared in the image, explaining an unnecessary tutorial of cockpit and satellite sciences.

Paxton took his seat amid familiar faces. Bella nodded her hello, mindful of not outshouting the presentational audio. Then Woden, his neighbor for the afternoon, drowned out the speakers with his boisterous greetings.

"Sarge Arés," Woden shouted, and Paxton offered him a tepid salute.

"The signals from your cockpits will be sent to our AN satellites in orbit," the man on-screen said in the thickest accent. "Once your signals hit the satellite, they will then be ricocheted down into an Androne in the field."

"India," Woden whispered. "The centennial bourgeois?" Woden aimed his first-world envy at India with the now in-vogue verbiage— *centennial*; the generation that came of age during the Ninety-Nine would fittingly be dubbed one hundred. "National debt and Hindi debt collectors, and we're still borrowing those rupees." Woden pointed up to the lights above. "But they keep the lights on, right?" He leaned in, lowering his voice. "You know how much power this place runs on? Like raw electric power?"

Out of the corner of Paxton's eyes, he noticed someone's head aimed in his direction, or was it Woden's direction, or both? As he glanced toward this person, she glanced away—Bella glanced away. Paxton caught her in a visual getaway, spinning her head to avoid his gaze.

"Heard the Cooks are gonna start more brownouts in the afternoon," Woden said. "And they're installing another couple thousand solar panels, like, how much power do you need?"

Woden must have noticed Paxton's lack of interest. He scowled lightly and sighed heavier and moved on to other crowds and conversations. And that was fine. Paxton didn't care much for Woden, and Woden likely cared even less for him. He thought of approaching Bella, but that would entail navigating rows and aisles of foldout chairs and the pairs of outstretched feet hurdled in between. Instead he continued his conversation with the video, quipping at its outdated references, questioning its basic terminology—quadrupedals, hexapods, and buggers. Even the term *sandbox* (the perimeter that individual Andro">nes were confined to) had been basic-training vocab since the first Gulf War, and still they explained it to death.

"Do not travel beyond the perimeter of your sandbox," the man on-screen said. "Your sandbox is home. Going beyond the border of your sandbox is trespassing and may result in a court-martial."

Now that was new. "A court-martial?" Paxton asked the man on the old video as the screen abruptly went black. "A fucking court-martial."

There were stakes here. Back at Fort Irwin, Paxton's quadrupedal consistently ran off course, in and out of the sandbox perimeter. His supervisor had barely docked a single point, *but here*... What were they hiding beyond the confines of those sandboxes, beyond the curtain of Sri Lankan smog or Afghan sandstorms? To be honest, Paxton didn't care. His thoughts had already drifted by the time he climbed into that claustrophobic cockpit. Notions on rising up the military ladder crawled back into his head, climbing above and beyond the Sergeant Wodens of the world. Higher, he thought, so high no one would ever be able to look down on him again.

7

Afternoon orientation began with an exploration of the Androne's motor functions, treading on the pedals, clenching the gloves. And remotely the Androne, somewhere out in that desert, responded, racing across rocky surfaces and gripping stones as it climbed mounds of granite and sand. The pedals at Paxton's feet reacted to the different terrains, feeling the drag of muddy soil or the sink of grainy dunes. His gloves reacted too, easily squeezing in on glass and plastics but unable to fully close the fist when squeezing the polymer of an assault rifle.

Pilots were required to operate the entire gamut of Androne Series: the Spartan Series, Shoguns, Apaches, and so on. By day three, Paxton had found his soulmate—the Kingsman; its speed and agility didn't sacrifice armor or artillery. Three layers of metal alloys, the densest among any Androne, and yet it felt feathery on every terrain. The Kingsman was a gymnast, so strong, yet light—*impossibly light*.

And then there was the Kingsman's rifle, a hundred-round monstrosity designed to resemble the British redcoat's rifle of old, including a four-foot-long bayonet attached to its barrel. It was icing on its metaled cake.

The Kingsman felt tailored to Paxton's reflexes and sensibilities, and over the subsequent days, he pushed the Androne to its limits. This machine's foot speed could top off at sixty miles per hour while towing nearly half a ton in body armor and another thousand pounds in artillery and ammunition. And each time Paxton saw it perform, he knew he was watching the impossible. No quadrupedal he had ever operated at any previous base could move that fast, *none*, even without body armor. *Not even close.* But he wasn't bothered by the scientific surrealism. He simply hung on for the ride.

They got an hour and change for lunch and "recess," which was mostly outshouting every nearby conversation as sports events played like silent films in the background. Paxton had considered getting a short lunch and heading back to the cockpit early—*show initiative*. But then he saw Bella sitting solo in front of the lavatory doors. She seemed to be multitasking between her soup and taking notes on something in front of her, so he approached, mouth first.

"Hey, Bells," Paxton shouted over the buzz of cafeteria noise. "How you been?"

"Paxton," she said casually before even turning to him, as if she already knew he was there. "I'm okay."

"How's orientation going?" He sat next to her and leaned into her notes. "Mine's a fucking drag."

"Good," she said and folded her notebook shut as politely as was possible. "It's fine."

"Sorry. Classified?" Paxton said, leaning away from her notebook with a smile. "Hey, has that lieutenant, what's her name, Victoria? Has she taken you out on the town? Seeing the sights?"

"Sorry," Bella interrupted, uncoiling her hunched-up posture from her seat. "I have to get these notes to my supervising officer. Maybe I can meet you after orientation?"

"Sounds good," he said.

"Great. Talk to you soon."

But she didn't. Paxton wouldn't find Bella in her bunk nor in the mess hall later that afternoon, and not for lack of trying. He roamed those corridors for at least an hour before surrendering to the idea that she was holding a grudge because of Woden's abhorrent display yesterday.

In the evening, Paxton called home, but no one picked up. "Just checking in," he said in the briefest of messages, but waited by the phone for thirty minutes for a callback. He skipped dinner and caught up with Sergeant Oya and Solo and hovered on the outer edges of their conversation. Solo was recounting the monotony of accompanying Oya and two other recruits that morning, escorting a convoy of diesel fuel back to camp. Paxton drifted in the dull drone of Solo's voice and saw Callie's pregnant anatomy in different shapes and outlines: hips in the hump of a tree trunk, breasts in the heads of cactus. But then a joke somewhere in Solo's monologue and a pop of laughter brought Paxton back to a conversation that seemed to have just hit its high note.

"You know they power this base with nuclear reactors?" Solo said. "We drove right past one today. Few hours' drive north. It could power all of Manhattan with power to spare, and Captain Laran let it slip that it was 'one of the nuclear reactors.'" Solo hooked those last few words in quotations. "Subtle, but I caught it. *One* of the nuclear reactors."

"And?" Sergeant Oya said.

"We got what, one hundred seventeen servicemen, about a hundred in the civvy population, plus higher-ups and the guard. That's like—"

"Four thirty-two," she interrupted. "Total population of four thirty-two. What's your point?"

"The captain said 'one of the,' one of the power plants, which means there's more than one nuclear plant out there sending electricity solely to us. Manhattan, bright lights, millions of people, and they only got one. How many nuclear plants are we using?"

"Don't know," Oya said. "Don't care."

It was there that the ember of curiosity kindled—a glint, warm, inviting—and it was there that Paxton leaned in. A nuclear reactor *was* excessive, but two? Though it was less Solo's stirred-up conspiracies that intrigued him and more Oya's cagey dismissals. What was she afraid of?

"The kicker," Solo said, now eyeing Paxton and pointing at nothing in particular. "I think there's at least two more."

Oya scoffed and turned away, but not playfully. She twisted in the opposite direction and glanced around, as if looking, searching, afraid that someone was listening.

"It's the way Captain Laran said it," Solo continued. "The way he gestured to two other locations. Like there was more than just one more. Could you imagine? Three total nuclear reactors powering this tiny base?"

"Captain Laran's an overmedicated mess," Oya said.

"No," Solo said. "Even if there's just two nuclear plants, that's over-kill like a motherfucker!"

"Not to mention all those solar arrays," Paxton said. "I've never seen this many."

"That's *right*," Solo said, as if just remembering this detail as well. "I bet that many solar panels could power this place on its own."

"Probably," Paxton said.

Sergeant Oya's eyes rolled to Paxton, appearing annoyed at him for encouraging the younger private. Solo rocked back and forth as he spoke, muscles in his face clenched, as if the onion layers of a great mystery were falling away.

"Where's all that power going?" Solo said.

"You should be careful—" Oya paused on the cusp of that last word, not long, but long enough. Her eyes darted, eyelashes flitted, glancing at something in the window ahead of her.

On the other side of that window was an office, but it was empty and unlit, nothing to see inside. But the window's glass was full of reflections: streetlamps, red blinks on distant taillights, a stream of passersby, even Paxton's own empty expression slurred across the bevel glass. And in the corner of the window was another reflection—a man, his horn-rimmed glasses twisting the streetlight above him. His eyes, lit like incandescent suns, were aimed directly at the trio.

Paxton whipped around to get a better look at the man. He wore modest blue jeans and sneakers stained in cooking oil and food dyes. A smock corseted the bump on his waist, and a hairnet swallowed greased hair like a black cobweb. He was a civvy, likely working the lunchrooms on base. It was nothing—he was nobody, and yet all around Sergeant Oya, false alarms seemed to detonate, footsteps on gravel like land mines, laughter bursting like verbal fireworks. Oya's clenched shoulders, her swiveling neck, the crook in her backbone, it all cried wolf. These false alarms were maybe more revealing than the real thing. Truth was, there was a sense of paranoia to this place; there was something to what Solo had said about the amount of power usage at the base—*but what?*

"You should be careful about the questions you ask," Sergeant Oya said, her eyes burning through Solo. "There're spies. Their spies. Everywhere. People get locked up just for hearing shit."

Solo seemed to comply with a reluctant shrug, and that ended it. And his conspiracies never came up again.

8

The old man had sent Paxton pictures via text: Hudson, the dog, chewing on plastic cups; Paxton's Toyota with its guts still hanging out over the hood; and one of Callie wearing one of Paxton's faded green T-shirts with her belly poking out from underneath. She stood by the window with deflated arms hanging off her shoulders and a dead expression on her face. Paxton smiled at that. That was how she always looked at him, with her lifeless love. Maybe he missed her. Maybe that meant he loved her—*maybe*, he thought.

Thanks, Paxton texted back, then in a separate message, How's Callie?

His cell phone lit up moments after with a text message from Callie's phone. A colon-and-half-parenthesis smile. He guessed that meant she was okay but couldn't think up an appropriate emoji reply.

It was the last day of training, or orientation, or whatever it was they were calling it, before their Androne's deployment into the field. Senior officers marched between the forest of techno-egg chambers— the cockpits. They strutted down their militant runway, all military vogue, pinned sleeves and striped collars, heels high as they saluted. Their physiques and postures hinted at former muscle-framed glory, but now it had all melted away; bulging guts and rubbery waists dripped off their uniforms. *Nothing against Time's scythe can make defense*, the old man would often quote; that Shakespeare sonnet was the scholarly excuse for his own withering frame.

They had set up an improvised stage in the hangar—very improvised, wood planks for elevation, sandbag holding the thing in place, and a coffee-brown carpet, though that likely wasn't its original color. All the named names stood in attendance and at attention: Lieutenant Victoria, her posture upright but her expression slouched on her face, heavy with an apparent boredom. Paxton's godfather colonel stood at the microphone introducing speakers and shaking hands. And then there was Captain Laran, the one Solo had mentioned, the overmedicated mess of a man, as Oya had described him.

Colonel Marson introduced Laran as a specialist in the cockpits, clocking more hours than any other drone pilot alive. But Laran didn't approach the stage and microphone with the swagger of a five-star pilot and instead hobbled between the cockpits with a limp. He had more pins and stripes than the others but was hunched over the microphone with his gaze sifting through the crowd of onlooking pilots, as if searching for someone.

"Thank you," Captain Laran said eventually, but paused again as if possessed by stage fright. "Tomorrow, most of you will be piloting on the front lines. Lives will be in your hands. Death will be on your trigger finger." He stopped there and glanced down at the next note card trembling between his fingers. "These pressures and fears are the gifts of war and, for better or worse, will follow you for the rest of your lives." Another pause, another note card. "So today there will be no pressure. There will be no fear. Today, you will be competing in Androne versus Androne combat." The crowd began to rumble, and he had to raise his voice. "These one-versus-one simulations will implement what you've learned over the past two days: defensive strategy, adaptive camouflage, artillery accuracy. Let's find out who's the best among you."

Applause, hooting, hollering, it all exploded together in the hollow hangar. Thirty-some-odd drone pilots applauded from the footsteps of their cockpits. But Captain Laran didn't move. He didn't untie his gaze from the crowd; he kept sifting, each blink and squint shoving bodies aside, digging deeper into the throng, searching for something, for someone.

"Thank you, Captain," Colonel Marson said, shuffling to him. "Now, let's get this thing started."

Thirty-six pressurized doors hissed open as the cockpits exhaled their oxygen. Paxton climbed into the narrow gap. It was hotter in there than he expected, his palms clammy, his scalp running wet. But not just hot—Paxton noticed his breathing echoing in that tight cockpit space, his heartbeat racing. It wasn't hot in there at all; it was him, his nerves twisting into knots.

Paxton had never been particularly high-strung, aside from expecting a son. He was mostly aloof about the ways of the world, but this new thing, this stir in the soup of his gut, this was the burden of ambition, wasn't it? He couldn't tell at the moment and wouldn't get the time to dwell on it either. The simulation started midthought, midbreath. The headset over his eyes lit up. The audio buzzed in. The setup was simple: two simulated Androns, a simulated location, and a fight to the simulated death. Paxton faced an unknown opponent, identified only by a series of numbers on-screen. His opponent chose a Shogun Series. Paxton decided on a Kingsman.

The simulated rain forest environment wasn't well rendered. Paxton noticed pixels in the leaves and the casting of shadows, but the sound design was pristine. He heard the Shogun's heavy footsteps on approach but couldn't see it. The Shogun's dark crocodile-chrome shade melted into the shadowy rain forest green. But Paxton's Kingsman Series flashy blue-and-red color scheme clashed with the rain forest environment. And the Shogun lit him up—a flash-bang grenade and consecutive point-blank Gatling shots; the Kingsman lost its right arm in the opening seconds of the contest. The arm didn't tear off clean and dangled by warped metal and wires, weighing down the Androne's right side. From there, the battle turned into a hand-to-hand contest, where the Shogun Series excelled. Even if Paxton's Kingsman had both its hands, he would have been outmatched. The ensuing fight lasted just under a minute. Paxton was the first to lose, his simulated Androne torn apart in minutes, and he ranked in the bottom 10 percent of the pilots.

So much for climbing the ladder.

Paxton crawled out of the cockpit, wiping his sweaty palms on the lap of his pants. His fingers felt sore and still clenched up as he replayed the dodges and countered strikes he should have used against the Shogun's attacks.

"Sergeant Arés." An unfamiliar voice hollered up from behind him. "Jesus H. Christ. It's like looking at a ghost."

Colonel Marson stood behind Paxton, appearing to have recognized him though the two had never met. The man's bushy brow opened up, his eyes bounding wide open, full of visual embrace. He had a wiry mustache and a coarse sprawl of facial hair across his cheeks.

"You don't know me," Marson said. "But it's an honor to meet you."

"Colonel Marson?" Paxton asked, but he knew who this man was.

"Colonel Marson," he agreed, and reached for a handshake. Marson had a firm grip and held firm as he continued, "The godfather you never met. Your grandfather mention me?"

"Many times." But that was a lie; the old man had spoken highly of Marson, but only on the one occasion had he mentioned him by name. "He speaks very highly of you, sir."

"I owe my life to that man," Marson said, and then as if remembering someone else raised two fingers. "I owe my *life* to your father; my livelihood, my career, I owe to the old man."

"You knew my father too?" Paxton said.

"I served under your grandfather in the last years before he retired. Later I requested to be assigned with your father. He was a couple years my junior." Then Marson nodded as if confirming something to himself. "You look more like him . . . your grandfather, I mean."

"I've been told."

"He ever tell you how he got that nickname? Wulf?"

"No, sir."

"Ah, well don't let me ruin the ending." Marson turned then with a gesture to the personnel trafficking around them. "This generation. They lack a certain . . . unity, you know?" He didn't, but Paxton nodded nonetheless, eyes rapt in faux captivation. "They've lost our ideals, lost our traditions—a lost generation, the way I see it. But you're different, according to the old man." The colonel stepped closer. "He said you're devoted—disciplined. And I want you to know, Arés, you got eyes looking out for you."

"Thank you, sir."

"You're a sergeant, right?"

"Yes, sir."

"You could go from enlisted to officer overnight. You come see me when you're ready. We'll make that happen."

That was what he wanted, and it was divulged in his smile, in the way he dipped his head and offered him a firm salute.

"You'd like that?" Marson asked, seeing through Paxton's ponderous poker face.

"I would, sir."

"Why?" Marson asked.

"Why . . ."

"Why do you want to rise in the ranks? Why do you want to give orders instead of taking them?"

He didn't know. Paxton stood dumbfounded in front of the one man who could change his future. He knew that he wanted to ascend the ranks, he knew it for a fact. Feeling it now in every fiber of his being. He just didn't have a word for it yet. No notion nor explanation came to him then.

But Marson would rescue him again. A soft smile and a softer pat on Paxton's shoulder. "I hear you have a little one on the way," he said. "Little boy?"

"I do," Paxton said. "Yes."

"There's your reason. There's all your reasons."

Was it? Paxton pondered on this for as long as was acceptable mid-conversation, but still he wasn't sure. Though it sounded better than greed or power-hungry motives. Status and trendiness, it all sounded so gross to him, but for family, *yes*, he liked that. This was the vocabulary he was searching for. He *was* doing this for them, wasn't he? For Callie. For the next generation. And he made himself believe, starting with a nod, a purse of the lips, and finally a word.

"Yes," Paxton said. "I'm doing it for my family."

"Good," Marson said. "You need that. A man needs to know what he's fighting for."

"Thank you, sir. And I've spoken to Lieutenant Victoria already. She's been very generous with her time and support."

"Lieutenant . . ."

"Victoria?" Paxton said, wondering now if Marson even knew her.

"Right, Victoria," he said, nodding, but slow, and his eyes wandering as if trying to recall the face that went with that name. "Top brass is always so in and out that . . . Anyway." He stepped back, elusive now, retreating with a wave of his hand. "I'll check in from time to time, and you give me a progress report, all right?"

"Yes, sir," Paxton said with only half a salute, as Marson had already disappeared into the frenzied oblivion before Paxton could even finish raising his arm. And a thought struck him just then, as the crowd closed in like curtains on the colonel's back: If Marson hadn't sent Victoria to talk to him, then who had?

9

Paxton found Bella curled up under a solar panel's shade, a book on her lap, a straw between her teeth, and her eyes fixed on the fiery sunset ahead. The solar grid had become the sunset hangout for off-duty pilots, a retreat from the million-eyed surveillance with romantic views of the desert-topped peaks. But today, as far as Paxton had seen, it was only her and him.

"Hey, Bells," Paxton said. "Where you been?"

Bella sat barefoot, propped up on two hands in the dirt. She pivoted but didn't turn all the way, eyeing him from her peripherals. "Same as you, I guess."

"Cockpits?"

"Cockpits," she agreed, melancholy deepening in her voice.

"Didn't do too well?" he asked.

"No."

Paxton couldn't tell whether Bella was just tired or tired of him. He stepped closer, around the curb of her peripheral vision, and caught her eye to eye.

"You wanna talk?" he asked cautiously, like approaching a feral animal. "Anything . . ." He considered how to say it. "Bugging you?"

"No." Bella looked at Paxton and squeezed out a smile, and that would've been it, but the smile died so quickly after that it nearly resembled sarcasm. Paxton kept wondering, was Bella mad at the world or mad at him? He'd never been one to pry, *never*, but he would now.

"Okay," Paxton said, clearing the dirt beneath him of twigs and stones before taking a seat. "You mind if I—" Then he stopped mid-sentence, noticing Bella's toes curl up, dirt under the nails, and her legs recoil into her chest. Her arms, once propping her recline, now folded in on her chest and ended in fists. She imploded in on herself—even her expression had a gravity pulling down her brow and tightening her lips. And then she exploded on him.

"Don't do that," she said without even a glance, keeping her eyes on the dirt. "Don't!"

"Sorry, I don't know what you're—"

"Pity," Bella said. "Don't pity me."

"What?" Paxton said. "I don't pity you." But he did, didn't he? The girl without a friend, the girl who couldn't fake bravado and camaraderie. He pitied her and she saw it. "Why would you say that?"

"Can you just leave?" Bella said.

"Bella—"

"Please!"

"Okay," he said, and stood, but figured he'd give it one last try. "And you are right. I feel bad about what happened yesterday, and if that's pity, then . . . I should have said something."

"You should have. I only ask one thing of people and that's to be true. Loyalty. And I know you lied about where you were during the Ninety-Nine."

"You're right," he said, no hesitation, figuring there was nothing else to do standing in front of a human lie detector. How did she read that from him on that first night? "I lied about the Ninety-Nine. But I'll tell you the truth now. If you want to listen."

She stared at him, seconds on end, reading deeper into his eyes. And finding something, *maybe*, that she appeared to trust.

"Yes," she said. "Tell me."

"I was in the Marine Corps. A grunt. Boots on the ground in Sri Lanka. No drones. I sort of looked down on drone pilots back then . . . still do."

"Active combat?" she asked.

"No. The old man 'knew people,'" Paxton said and threw up quotations.

"Your old man?"

"Grandfather. He pulled strings. Got me a safe gig. Removing mines."

"Mines. Safe?"

"We had landrones—quadrupedals. And they did most of the dirty work. I just stuck a few safety flags in the dirt. It was a nice gig. Good people. And the beaches out there, the food . . . Sri Lanka was beautiful, until the Ninety-Nine. The attack hit Galle Base Port so hard that entire aircraft carriers were like shrapnel. It started raining down ships and planes and bodies. All of a sudden, the minefield was covered in debris and smoke, and everything caught fire. I tried not to run through the smoke, but it was so hot, and I barely got twenty feet before I stepped on a mine. It knocked me back. Tore holes in me. My leg. Arm. Chest." Paxton pointed. "I was just lucky it was old."

"The mine?"

"Right. The medic said it wasn't even a quarter of its full strength—monsoon flooding, heat, the explosives had degraded—and still they replaced bone in my foot, my heel is mostly metal, and so is the front half of my knee."

"That's why you limp?"

She'd noticed. Larry, Paulo, Scotty, none of the guys at the mechanic shop knew. He concealed it well. Even Callie needed four months of intimacy before she eventually registered it.

"Don't worry," she said quickly. "It's not noticeable at all. Really."

"Funny thing," Paxton continued. "Those land mines were set by the US military forty-five years earlier. They had planted them there when they were fighting with the rebels—my grandfather's generation. Now we're fighting against the rebels and our own mines."

"Taliban too," Bella said, and seemed to see immediately that Paxton didn't understand. "We fought with the Taliban in our grandfathers'

generation, armed them, created them. Now we fight against them."
She paused then, a bigger question on her mind. "Why'd you lie? You
were on the ground, not sitting behind a drone. That's brave. Why
didn't you tell us?"

Good question. Why had he lied? The answer didn't come at once,
but she was patient as Paxton rolled into himself, like a snail drain-
ing down the whorls of its shell. He approached the question backward: What if he had told the truth? Would they have eyed his leg and
cringed? Maybe even noticed his limp? And would every single one of
them have pitied him? And that was it, wasn't it?

"Pity," Paxton said, recalling the RNs and field medics saying *poor
thing*. From the wheelchair, to the casted leg, the screws in his ankle,
and pins in his knees—*poor thing*. And they'd been saying it since the
very day he was born. The poor boy who bled his mother to death at
birth. The poor orphan whose dad shot himself in the head. That poor
thing.

"Pity." He said the word again, confident of the truth of it. "I didn't
want you to pity me."

"I wouldn't have," she said.

"I know."

"If we're gonna be friends, you can't lie. We shouldn't keep secrets."

"No lies," he said, smiling back at her. "And no secrets. So I showed
you mine. You? You never said where you were during the Ninety-Nine."

Bella's eyes rolled away from his and seemed to see a memory
manifesting in front of her. "I saw," she said. "I was an aerial drone
pilot then, so I saw it from my screen—the fires, the smoke, and all
those bodies." She turned away from the manifestation, unable to look
anymore, turning back to him. "I watched the entire world burn, Pax,
and I did nothing."

"What'd you see?"

"Betrayal." She paused as her mind appeared to drift back.
"Someone gave intel. Someone let the enemy in."

"Do you know something?" Paxton whispered. "About the Ninety-Nine."

"No, but I know there was a betrayal," she said. "I'm from a military family, uncles, grandparents, and you hear things." She paused then, as if there was more—as if she didn't want to say, but then she did. "And my brothers died that day. Splattered across concrete."

"I'm sorry."

Bella stared through Paxton. Her face went white—a hollow eggshell, like there was just empty space on the inside. But her eyes seemed to hold relics of emotion, shadows under her eyes, wrinkles tracing her young skin, as if sadness had once been there, centuries ago.

"Bella," Paxton said, and nudged her, two fingers against the edge of her shoulders.

The pit of her eyes lit up, and she let out a quiet gasp as if she'd been holding her breath. Bella woke up and stared at Paxton with an awkward smile that would open up all the way. Then she said something, but whatever it was, it was muted by the sound of gunfire.

10

The shooter was in full uniform, pins on his collars, clovers and stars on his chest, and an M4 carbine cradled in his arms. He looked frail, fragile, and maybe even familiar; his facial features slowly slipped into focus the closer he came—Captain Laran. He shot with either inept aim or aimed at nothing, stumbling at every snap of the trigger, and seeming to follow a path through the solar panel forest directly toward Paxton and Bella.

"Go, Bella!" Paxton said, shoving her into a stumble, forgetting how small she was.

"Does he see us?" Bella asked, bouncing back to her feet. "If we move, he'll see us."

"Doesn't matter. We can outrun him. You head down that way."

"Split up?"

"Just go."

Bella bolted downfield, deeper into the solar panel forest, glancing back at Paxton before disappearing into the metal thicket. She moved slow, like a pilot, and Paxton had figured as much. He could outrun Laran. He could outrun most of these noncombat pilots, especially an already-winded shooter carrying an eight-pound weapon.

"No," Laran shouted under a barely discernible gargling for air, and he seemed to be shouting at Paxton. He lifted the weapon above his head with one hand and waved with the other. "I won't shoot. I won't."

Paxton backpedaled but didn't run. He was actually listening to him—why was he listening? Laran had lowered the rifle completely, dragging the muzzle through the dirt. Paxton's backpedal slowed as Captain Laran staggered toward him with a wild wobble of his feet. Paxton wasn't even sure if Laran had energy enough to lift the rifle again.

"What do you want?" Paxton shouted back, the men now twenty feet apart.

"Wait," Laran said, tripping, then lifting himself back to his drunken gait.

"I said, what do you want?"

"You," he said, the duo now mere feet apart and Laran drawing even closer. "You're in? I've seen you two. You're in, right?"

"What?" Paxton asked with his eye on the rifle that had now become the man's crutch.

"They're gonna kill me," he said, trying to squeeze his fist into Paxton's hand, as if trying to shake his hand. "They're gonna kill me." Then something slipped out of his palms and was now in Paxton's fist. "And if they find you with it, they'll kill you."

And that was it. Laran dropped his rifle in the sand and scrambled onward, his pace slower, his balance swaying, the dips and stones in his path bringing him to palms and knees. He was a tumbleweed, dropping and rolling across the dead terrain.

Humvees shrieked across the solar maze; jets of black soil sprayed from their rear tires. They bounced on the pitted dirt, clipping solar panels in their pursuit of Captain Laran. The vehicles caught up quick. A handful of young men in camo-spotted uniforms leaped from the doors—cheetahs toward their gazelle. They ripped him off his feet and slammed him against the dirt, sand cratered up and clouded around them, and then all that was visible was the frenzy of limbs.

Paxton watched and caught his breath. His fist clenched around something he'd yet to even glance at. He hadn't noticed the crowd gathering behind him. He hadn't even noticed Bella's hand on his shoulder until she spoke to him.

"Pax?" she said as he glanced back. "You okay?"

"Yes," he said, but he wasn't sure.

"He said something." She wasn't asking.

"Something," he said, knowing that she must have seen the exchange.

"What?"

"Mostly gibberish."

And there it was. His very first words since promising honesty were a lie. But he had to. No one had seemed to notice the seconds-long inter-action between him and the gunman, and Paxton needed it to stay that way. Something was in his hand that, according to the now-handcuffed captain, could get him killed. Paxton hadn't even had a chance to look at it. Not even a glance. But the object was small, no larger than a ball of bubble gum.

"Did he shoot anybody?" Bella asked.

"I think so," someone answered.

Paxton glanced back to find a small crowd beginning to gather, curious faces squinting and pointing ahead.

"Who'd he shoot?" a second voice uttered.

"Tech scout," a third replied. "But he's still breathing."

"You got lucky," Bella said.

Paxton nodded his reply.

Armed troops dragged the gunman toward the Humvees as security personnel approached the crowd. Paxton backpedaled, trying to dissolve into the mob, but the crowd had thickened. He had to push his way through, clipping shoulders and stepping on the toes of a faceless few.

"Sergeant Arés," she said—a voice of feminine familiarity. "What happened?"

Victoria—Paxton realized it even before he turned to her, standing at his left flank, all too calm and patiently waiting for Paxton to reply. But he jostled past her. That unseen thing in his hand felt unbearably heavy now, weighing down on his arm and putting a crook in his shoul-ders. He could drop it right now and no one would know the better, but curiosity and all of its cats scratched at Paxton's mind. He had to see.

"Paxton!" Bella shouted over the crowd and into his ear. She grabbed him by the wrist and pulled him through a tunnel of bodies, and they emerged at the back of the crowd. "You shook up?" she asked, her eyes inside of his.

"He said they were gonna kill him," Paxton said. "You know, I feel there's something else going on at this camp. Something they're not telling us."

"Fighting a war against an enemy no one's ever seen. Probably a lot we don't know about." He started toward the bunks, and she followed. "And with active combat starting tomorrow."

"Active combat," Paxton said as if he had forgotten, as if taking on the enemy was the least of his worries. "Right. I should get back to the bunk and—"

"What's in your hand?" Bella said, barely allowing the last syllable to leave Paxton's lips. Goddamn it she was perceptive; a fucking mind reader. Paxton couldn't flinch now, no way—any hesitation or mutter of words, she would see through. He was see-through at this very moment, so he did the only thing he could.

"Just this thing," Paxton said as he unwrapped his fingers, one by one, having no idea what was inside. Right at the center of his palm was a round metal sphere, just bigger than a marble, but heavier, so much heavier. He could swear it weighed as much as ten pounds.

"Oh," Bella said, surprised and almost disappointed. "You play with those things too?"

"Not really," he said, having no idea what she was talking about, and it wasn't until he returned to his bunk and got a better look at the marble that he realized it resembled one of those remote-control balls that the kids played with, some adults too. But what was it, this ball that they would kill him for?

Paxton lost an entire night of sleep thinking about Captain Laran and the ball, and by the time it rolled to the back of his mind it was morning. It was time for war.

11

They gave him a Spartan—some Series 1 titanium-armored bullshit. Spartans were the first models in the Androne Series, the basic building blocks in the War Machine Program. Speed: average. Durability: average. Body armor: average. Endurance and artillery: below average. In fact, the only attribute that ranked above its counterparts was battery expenditure, and that was because it didn't pack as much power per punch.

But these were the least of Paxton's problems—his real problems (insomnia-bruised eyes, headache, a caffeine-heavy heartbeat) all stemmed from a single marble. He had left it in the bunk. He had wrapped it in a T-shirt and shoved it to the back of his locker, and now he needed to shove it to the back of his mind—he had to. The cockpit's switches and displays lit up, and the entire thing hummed. This was wartime. Butterflies danced around his gut, or was it the thrum of electricity flowing through the cockpit? Wintry steel gloves suctioned around his hands and wrists. Somewhere in heaven, a satellite synced in, racketing signals from his cockpit to advanced Androne technology somewhere in the middle of nowhere. The glass visor covered his eyes, and the monitor lit up with true-to-life pixels and colors and light.

And just like that, Paxton's problems were literally a thousand miles away.

The Spartan's eye opened to a desert ocean, sand in every direction. There was a miles-long barbed-wire fence, bending and folding in the breeze, and a half-buried concrete highway dead-ending into a dirt road. This used to be a border crossing for some forgotten country, abandoned and decades old, now just separating sand from sand.

The location was undisclosed—"classified" was the terminology offered during the morning briefings. But the familiar monochrome landscape betrayed itself. The static black and white, the discolored gray skyline propped up against sawtooth mountain ranges—this was Afghanistan. Paxton had navigated similar Afghan vistas in his quadrupedal years before.

His sandbox stretched the four-and-a-half-mile track that ran alongside the fencing. It was an unpopulated relic. No one and nothing had traveled there in years, not a single insect or weed, nothing but spoiled dirt that puffed under the Spartan's feet.

Paxton marched the Spartan Series back and forth along the dead dirt for nine hours. Bathroom breaks required a voice-activated request; a temp pilot, usually a cadet, sat in his seat while Paxton stood in front of the urinal and took his time. He flushed and listened, flushed again, and watched the clear water swirl. He washed his hands twice or three times too many, then dragged his feet back to the egg carton aisles and rows of cockpits. Lunches came the same way, from the same cadet, a young woman with braided hair and glasses who never gave a name even after he offered his. He strapped back in for another four hours of this shit. The front lines were empty. The war was over. Whoever they were fighting had come, conquered, and gone.

That last hour dragged. Knots squeezed into his knuckles, his right leg fell unconscious, and his eyes were a watery blur. Eventually a knock rapped on the cockpit door. He undressed himself of the metal gloves, visor, and seat straps as fast as humanly possible and nearly fell out of the cockpit. Solo stood outside, ready to relieve him for the night shift.

"Good luck," Paxton said, sarcasm hot on his breath.

Conversation concurred through their mess hall dinner. They had all seen the same thing: unending desert, hills, and grassless plains. It was then that Paxton felt halfway fortunate to at least have had a fence to look at. Bella had a diminutive 126-square-foot sandbox and a small hill where she stood watch for hours; others whined about the miles of dunes or rocky paths, dry bluffs or abandoned mines. They were all the same place—*nowhere.*

"But where is nowhere?" Private Inga Qamaits asked, running her hand across a recent buzz cut. "I mean, where do you think we are?"

A few regions were offered up, but the overwhelming consensus was Afghanistan, and that was even without Paxton's vote.

"Afghanistan is the only non-UN nation with that landscape," Sergeant Woden said. "And they won't let lower ranks patrol populated regions. We don't get to mix with the population. That's upper brass only, 'tenants and caps, but you didn't hear that from me."

Paxton hadn't seen any upper brass in the cockpit hangar besides a lieutenant standing in the wings, overseeing and organizing but never approaching the filthy blue-collar trenches of a cockpit.

"I saw one," Bella said. "Lieutenant Powers was in the Rooster's Nest. And only top brass gave him lunch and piss breaks, 'tenant or captain, couldn't count all the stars on his chest."

"They don't trust us around the civvies?" another corporal said. "Or they don't want us talking to the civvies?"

Conspiracy again, but Paxton wouldn't play a part this time. Yawns kept cracking into his dying expression, and he slipped away from the conversation. Bella watched and waved as he smuggled dinner out of the mess hall in a backpack; foil-wrapped sandwiches jockeyed against his back.

He took the scenic route, past the hangars and solar arrays and through the food truck parking lot. It gave Paxton a few more minutes to think. And he thought. But after rounding the entire base twice he realized he was avoiding going back to the barracks because of the marble hidden at the back of his locker.

Eventually, the cracks and croons of a half-filled gut interrupted Paxton's train of thought. He imagined the sandwiches were still warm and tasted like the spicy mutton Callie had cooked on Labor Day. He imagined her, the belly bulged, the fingernails bitten, the hair long and frayed, plain Jane—plain Callie. And for a second Paxton forgot that marble. It drifted, like dreams in daylight.

Paxton moved toward the bunks. He'd call her when he got back. He stepped down the stairwell, dodging bodies, and still he bumped into someone, but as that someone grabbed him and dragged him aside, he realized *she* had bumped into him.

"Paxton," Bella whispered, dragging him into the corner.

"Bells?" he said, but she pressed her finger against her lips, gesturing for him to shut the fuck up.

"Brass," Bella whispered. "In your bunk."

A chill wrapped tight around Paxton's spine. His heartbeat quickened. His breathing lost its rhythm.

"Brass?" he asked, but he'd heard her. He knew what this was about.

"Yes," Bella shrugged. "Just a heads-up."

"Thanks." He nodded.

Paxton dawdled onward, his feet heavy and that appetite from a moment earlier dead. He rounded the doorway into his bunk. The lights were off, and a figure sat on the edge of his bed with her cell phone ablaze in the shadowy room.

"How was the first day?" It was Lieutenant Victoria. She lifted her head from the phone screen and squinted at him.

"Quiet," he said, eyeing the room—eyeing his locker.

"Quiet's good."

"I thought we were fighting a war?"

"Don't be too eager." She put away her phone. "You haven't been reading?" Lieutenant Victoria fingered the leaves of a book next to her. The pages flapped and came to a rest on the cover—the Androne manual she had lent him days earlier.

"I read a couple chapters," he said.

"Liar."

But he wasn't, not entirely. Paxton had glanced over a chapter on the design of Androne, focusing on joint function and mobility.

Following his loss in the competition, he had assumed them to be weak points in the Androne's structure.

"Not lying," Paxton said. "And I've been busy."

"Busy?" she said. "Doing what?"

"Girlfriend, back home."

"How many?"

"One."

"So unambitious?" she said, smirking.

"With all due respect, ma'am." Paxton gestured to her, then himself. "What is it you want?"

"I'm trying to figure out if you are who I think you are, Sergeant."

"Who do you *think* I am?" he asked, but Victoria only stared at him as if she could figure it out by just watching him long enough. "Colonel Marson didn't tell you to give me the grand tour the other day . . . did he?"

"No," she said. "Why would a colonel tell me to do you a favor?"

"Because he's . . ." Paxton paused, waiting, surprised she didn't know. "He's my godfather."

Her lips broke in genuine surprise. "Marson," she said. "Didn't know that."

"Is there something *I* need to know?" Paxton said. "You know things about the Ninety-Nine, right?" He glanced back at the doorway—no one there and still he whispered. "What's the secret people are hiding out here?"

"If your question is, Did I catch a glimpse, a glance, at who was on the other side of the battlefield? The answer is no. All I saw was fire. As if it were all the fire in all the world. But what I do know . . ." Victoria stopped there and eyed that same space in the doorway behind Paxton. "What I know"—she lowered her voice—"without a doubt, is that they, *them*"—she pointed beyond the doorway—"out there, with all their stars and stripes, they do."

"They do what?" Paxton said, and found that he had begun to whisper along with her.

"They say that it isn't another foreign country that we're fighting. It isn't extraterrestrials. It isn't artificial intelligence or any other sort of sci-fi, apocryphal fantasy. And they're right. And they know they're right. But have you ever considered how they know that for sure? How we could possibly eliminate every other alternative?"

Paxton shook his head.

"Because they *do* know. The United States and her allies have crossed off every other possible enemy because they know who we're fighting. Not ETs, not AI, not any fantasy media could conjure up. It's something else."

"What?" he said, without breathing. His heartbeat held still, nothing pulsed, he listened with every thread of his eardrum. "What are we fighting?"

Victoria shook her head and buckled her lips as if forcefully holding back. "I'm not sure myself."

"You don't trust me," Paxton said.

"No," she said, and paused to stare at him as if confirming something in her head. "Like I said, I'm not sure if you are who I think you are . . ."

"Who do you think—" he tried to ask, but she freight-trained through his babble.

". . . but even if you were that person, you'd figure it out eventually anyway."

"You came all the way down to the bunks to say that? Say . . . nothing."

"No," she said. "I came for this." She opened her hand, and it rolled to the center of her palm—the marble. "Where'd you get it?"

Paxton stopped breathing. He was the deer in her headlights, with every muscle fiber knotted into one another. He thought about Callie and his baby boy, and as much as he loathed the idea of fatherhood, he at least wanted to see the little thing.

"Don't worry," she said. "You're not in trouble. Not yet. Where'd you get it?"

"He gave it to me," Paxton said, gasping between each blurt of words. "Captain Laran. That fucking guy that got arrested. He said that if they catch me with it, they'll kill me."

"We will."

"But I'm still breathing." *Barely.* His nostrils flared, trying to catch his racing breath.

"He wasn't arrested for this. Captain Laran. This was just one small string in a web he made for himself."

Victoria's eyes drifted around the room. She saw something on those peeling white walls as a projector from her mind cast images against them. And she strayed from the conversation as the candles in her eyes went out.

"You know him," Paxton said, not a question but a discovery. Her thoughts seemed to be on him.

"I know who?"

"Captain Laran."

The name seemed to sour in her ear as if it were an insult. And still she nodded.

"He was an amazing pilot but started dabbling in cockpit manipulation. That's why he was arrested. That and linguistics training."

"Linguistics?"

"He was trying to learn a language that he shouldn't have. Among other things."

"Language? What language carries a federal offense?"

"Here," she said, avoiding the question completely, then holding out her hand and the marble.

"No," Paxton said, but she dropped the marble in his palm nonetheless. "What are you doing?"

"He gave it to you."

"Why?"

"You should ask him."

"He said . . ." Paxton had to think about it; he had almost forgotten. "Something like: 'You're in, right?'"

"Shhh." She hushed him with a finger against her lips.

"Was he talking about you? Are you in on this?"

Victoria turned to the door and gestured to the marble lying in Paxton's palm. "Ball's in your court, Sergeant Arés."

"What does it do?" Paxton asked, following her to the doorway.

"Nothing," she said. "Hiding in that locker, it does nothing." Victoria approached the door, then closed it. "In your cockpit, though," she said at a softer whisper, "it opens up the sandbox."

"What do you mean?"

"If you take the Androne beyond the boundary you're assigned, alarms will be signaled. Security personnel pull you out of your cockpit, and best case you get a slap on the wrist. Worst case, you get court-martialed. That marble there has a jamming mechanism. It blocks those signals. You can cross that boundary. You can take your Androne beyond the map they made for you. Think of it like a passport."

"What's there to see but desert?"

"That's up to you to find out."

Lieutenant Victoria stepped into the corridor, and Paxton kept following. He had more questions but found a small crowd huddled outside, Bella and Oya among them. They saluted as the lieutenant marched by with a regal sashay. Then the stargazers turned to him, squinting, lifting eyebrows, questioning with a hundred looks and gestures.

Paxton answered the same way, with a smile, a shake of the head, and a shrug, like it was nothing. The crowd thinned without any answers, but Sergeant Oya loitered, cuddling against the women's-room doorway, half in, half out, and watched Victoria every step of the way. Then her eyes met Paxton's. Their eye contact lingered under the canopy of the crowd, him trying to figure her out, and her—he wasn't sure what she was thinking. But there were snitches everywhere, he remembered, snitches employed by top brass. And Paxton flinched on that thought—he blinked first, stepped back, and retreated to his bunk, their staring match done. Oya had won that round.

12

By Thursday, Paxton had adapted himself to the cockpit, or rather the cockpit had adapted to him. The stiffness in the cushions and armrests had thawed to fit his form; the compression in the pedals had loosened after days of active use; even internal temperatures had adjusted to a Goldilocks balm. Most of the day he found himself—the Spartan—shadowboxing beside the border fencing, dodging assaults from invisible enemies and countering them with the same. Friday was identical. Nothing changed, inside the cockpit or out. Saturday the cockpits were down for maintenance, and on Sunday Paxton dozed off inside the cockpit for the first time. On Monday he found himself inching closer to the boundary of his sandbox, and just under ten yards away his display winked with warnings, red lights—*thou shall not pass!* And so he settled back in, back to the fence, back to his side of the border.

The very next day in the cockpit, Paxton dozed off completely—full-blown sleep—and still he dreamed of piloting the Androne through the empty desert. He dreamed that he brought his sophisticated marble into the cockpit and stepped beyond the sandbox and into the unknown. Wednesday was the same, and so was Thursday, and after a full week Paxton lost track of the days—he couldn't distinguish weeknights from weekdays from daydreams, until someone woke him up.

"It couldn't be Afghanistan," Sergeant Woden said, and Paxton snapped out of it, *daydreaming again*, and finding himself in the high-calorie banquet of the mess hall.

"What's that?" Paxton asked, half listening, half-asleep. He loosened his knuckles, his fingers so accustomed to being wrapped under the steel gloves that they clenched in physical withdrawal. "You said Afghanistan?" His toes uncoiled. "Afghanistan couldn't be what?" And his eyes unglazed as he blinked back to life.

"I'm saying," Woden reiterated, "the time zones don't match. The sunlight isn't right. They're in early morning during our afternoon—that would put us somewhere between eastern Russia, Indonesia, or Central Australia."

Oh.

But Woden wasn't the first to realize this. Afghanistan was about nine hours ahead of eastern standard time. Paxton had noticed that by the second day in the cockpit, *or was it the third?* And still, Woden kept on flaunting his deductive reasoning, a gesture that proved him to be more witless than clever. Even so, this was the first Paxton had considered Australia as an alternative. The time zone didn't quite work, *but maybe*, that time of year, that side of the hemisphere.

"Yeah, maybe the Aussies," Paxton said, and ran his spoon over a bowl of dry oatmeal. "The deserts match up."

Callie had an uncle in Australia, a lieutenant stationed off Perth. He spoke to her about it that afternoon, though she couldn't offer any real insight. Callie's pregnancy had reached a full bloom; her belly was busting now, and for the first time, she whined. For the first time, she said she couldn't wait for it to be over.

"Just nine more weeks," Paxton said.

"Twelve weeks," she corrected him. "Twelve and change."

Paxton's side of the line went quiet. The cockpit was tangling up the time line in his head. And what was Callie thinking right now? Probably that Paxton didn't care. That there were more important things on his mind.

"Callie—" Paxton started, but she cut him off.

"I have an appointment tomorrow," she said, saving him from whatever convoluted apology he'd yet to conceive. "I should get some rest."

It was only late afternoon, and Paxton decided to walk through his thoughts. Callie's visage walked beside him, hand in hand, her imagined belly in his mind's eye. She was his oasis of thought in that desert, even if he didn't want her to be.

The humidity had hollowed out the roads outside. Air-conditioning hummed heavy from rooftops as he walked along grainy, unswept concrete. Tumbleweeds meteored across the yellow lines, and skeletal oaks offered spotted shade. It seemed like the desert just kept trying to take the land back.

And nearly on cue, a street sweeper passed. Spinning yellow brushes skimmed the grit off the road, and gravel sprayed into particles that pinched at Paxton's eyes. The driver, a wide, gray-haired woman, apologized with a wave of her hand as Paxton wandered off the road and along the dusty path between two office buildings, still squinting, still rubbing his eyes. That led to an even narrower path between two other buildings, which led to a back alley, which led to fences with barbed wire, and a werewolf.

A howl, half-human, half-canine, exploded from deep in his peripherals. Paxton spasmed, watts of synaptic current surging down his spine. And he stumbled back as his limp popped completely. He picked himself back up only to stumble again. A German shepherd of doubtful pedigree tugged forward on its leash. The guard's thick, veiny arms barely held it back.

"What the hell are you doing back here?" the guard barked as if translating the dog's mad furor.

"I . . . I was . . ." Paxton fumbled the words, nerves still shot and shorted out as that hellhound kept on bellowing from the other side of the fence.

"You're telling me you didn't see these?"

See what?

There was nothing on the empty plot of land, not even a latrine. But Paxton followed the sharp point of the guard's finger nonetheless— Restricted Area. It was printed red and bold on pairs of signs against either building, and on the fence, and in the alley. He must have missed the signs because of his eyes, still dust red and pinching in the corners.

"Sorry," Paxton said. "Really, I didn't see it."

"You a private?" the man asked.

"Sergeant, sir."

"Well, you should know better."

Paxton knew he'd seen something he shouldn't have, *but what?* The way the sentry angled himself in front of Paxton blocked the view beyond the fence. But there was nothing there: dirt, weeds, the tiny yellow triangle of a marker flag in the ground with a Y-like symbol and the number nine printed on it. The broad sentry stepped into Paxton's line of sight, with one hand on his hip, a trigger finger away from the pistol therein.

"Head back to your barracks, Sergeant."

"Yes, sir," Paxton said, though he believed his rank was probably on par with the sentry's.

Paxton pivoted fast and strode back in the direction he came from. The mongrel carried on woofing taunts at his hasty retreat. As he rounded the corner to the main road, he glanced back just in time to catch the sentry plucking the Y marker flag out of the ground.

Bingo! That was what he was trying to hide.

Paxton paced back to the barracks, eyes hanging over his shoulder the entire way. He changed his shoes, washed his face, checked for the marble in his locker—still there. He called Callie, listened to an infinite ringtone, then texted her: Call back. Waiting for a reply, Paxton doodled the Y symbol in a notebook and its number: nine. He doodled them on top of each other, around each other, until he filled the page, until it overflowed into the margins.

Callie didn't text back, and he hadn't thought she would. Paxton roamed the corridors for familiar faces and eventually found himself in the mess hall. He found Bella, Solo, and Oya there too and hoped Bella's military degree might shed some light on the symbols.

"Hey, Bells," Paxton said. "Let me show you something real quick."

"What's up?" she said with a mouthful of waffles, syrup on her lower lip.

He didn't want to show her here, in front of everyone—in front of Oya. He hesitated, gripping the notebook tighter in his fist and digging it deeper under his arm. And they all must have seen the obviousness of it.

"What's in the notebook, Arés?" Sergeant Oya said and grinned. "Secret diary?"

"List of the nosiest people on base," Paxton responded.

"Dear diary," Oya squealed, squeezing her vocal cords and pitching them to pubertal highs. "Today, Bella and I held hands. It was magical. I felt a twinkle in my pants."

Solo laughed. Paxton aimed a middle finger at Oya and returned the smile. She raised two fuck-fingers and smiled wider, gums and all.

The jig was up. He opened the notebook to the fourth page—the fourth draft of doodling, and incidentally the cleanest drawings of all. He angled the pages away from Oya, and still she leaned in.

"You seen this before?" he said. "The symbol?"

"No." Bella shook her head. "Why?"

"It's a receptor," Solo said with confidence. "Yeah, receptor."

"Receptor?" Paxton asked.

"A receptor receives power from a nuclear plant and spreads energy through the base. I saw it when we went off base the other day. It had a one on it, but you know my theory: there should be at least two."

"You're saying the number on the symbol correlates to the number of nuclear reactors?" Paxton asked.

"Right," Solo said. "There's only one receptor per nuclear plant. So like I said, I think there might be a second receptor somewhere on base with a two on it. Meaning there would be two nuclear plants powering the base. Could you imagine?"

"You're saying . . ." But Paxton did the math of it in his head. *Nine.* The number terrified him. Nine power stations: nuclear, geothermal, dams, who knows, but enough power plants for half of the East Coast were pumping energy into the tiny base. Add to that brownouts after midnight. Add to that a rain forest of solar arrays outside. Where *the fuck* was all that power going?

"Paxton?" Oya asked, squinting at the look on his face. The shock bouncing around in his head must have been showing. "Why do you ask?"

"Nothing," Paxton said. "Just curious."

13

The web of conspiracy tightened around him, and it showed. It showed in the reddish bags under his eyes. It showed in an off-kilter hunch in his posture. It showed, but no one saw it, no one besides him. He knew too much. Too many power plants, one too many illegal marbles, and a lieutenant, Victoria, who seemed to be actively recruiting Paxton for mutiny—*They know who we're fighting*, she had said. And even though Paxton knew too much, he still wanted to know just that little bit more.

But Paxton wouldn't find out anything in that sandbox. For eighteen consecutive days he had stared at nothing but dirt and desert and that rotting fence. The Spartan moved back and forth along that border, and he knew in his heart that something lurked out beyond the confines of his sandbox. The enemy was out there. And whether it was curiosity, career ambition, or a newfound paternal instinct, Paxton felt a burning need to find them, stop them, save the world.

He kept one eye on the screen and one eye on the clock, counting down the minutes to the end of his shift like counting sheep. He drifted off, came back with drool on his cheek, then drifted again. For the first couple of weeks, Paxton had made games of dodging and dipping between spools of kicked-up sand, shadowboxing and testing the Spartan's speed limits, preparing himself for war. But that motivation had died. Now his Spartan dragged its titanium-plated feet back and forth along the fence as Paxton daydreamed and doted on the horizon.

Ten minutes left, and at that moment Paxton considered something he never had. He walked the Spartan toward the border. Slow, contemplative steps carried him to an invisible red line, and he stood closer than he ever had. He felt like he was dangling over the edge. He felt something pulling at him from the other side. But in the peripherals of his visor, red alarm signals flashed: THREATENING, warning Paxton not to take a step farther. And yet his foot hovered over the pedal, just one more step.

What would happen if he broke protocol? Would they send him home? That would be welcomed punishment. Callie would still be pregnant. It would be good to see the old man and feed Hudson and share a beer with Larry. But then Paxton stutter-stepped as he considered that stepping out of the sandbox might bring unwanted attention to him, attention to the marble, to his conversations with Victoria, and everything he knew.

The knocking from the cockpit door was a relief. Solo was early today, and Paxton would pretend he didn't notice. He backed the Spartan away from the border as he stripped off his gloves and removed his visor. But it wasn't Solo—Sergeant Olive Oya stood on the other side, and she must have noticed the look of bewilderment on his expression.

"Nice to see you too," Oya said as Paxton paused, considering where he'd left the Spartan, how far from the border, the direction it was facing. "Come on," Oya said and gestured for him to climb out.

"Since when do you cover me?" Paxton said.

"Since today," Oya said. "And from now on. We're on that long-term shit." She held up her ring finger. "Put a ring on it."

Paxton smiled and left the hangar and headed back to the barracks. An NCAA exhibition football game outside had emptied the corridors and barracks of all noise. Paxton was apathetic to the whole college football revelry, but he did look forward to the draft beers and Chicago-style hot dogs. But he'd check the marble first.

Paxton leaned against the locker and held it between his index finger and thumb, wheeling it around like candy on a fingertip tongue. It was like a drug for touch, infinitely smooth, a high for his shot nerves. His muscles unwound, and even though there was a voice telling him to throw it out, there was another voice, a louder voice, telling him not to.

"Pax," Bella called from the doorway. "You're not going?"

Paxton twisted around, startled, as he stuffed the marble into the side pocket of his jeans—*his* marble now. "Hey, Bells," he said. "I'm going. Right behind you."

The afternoon was particularly hot. The bleacher's long, ascending steel rows burned under Paxton like skewers. He simmered; they all simmered, Bella next to him, Woden a couple of rows below, Solo and others scattered about, all of them roasting under the Mojave sun. Paxton kept one hand in his pocket and twirled the marble between his sweaty fingers, still his drug, still calming his nerves. That worried him—why would this illegal device, this string on his web of conspiracy, calm him?

The athletes bathed in the sunlight, helmets shining, cleats glistening under their feet. They lined up, tied score, two minutes left in the third. Two lines of colossal men, green on one side, yellow on the other, crashed into each other. The quarterback aimed and launched a Hail Mary into the opposition's end zone. Touchdown!

Football was war. The tactics, the opposing front lines, the fortification, attacks, and stratagem—no other sport resembled warfare more than American football. Helmets, padding, war paint. "Hut-hut-hut," the quarterback barked, short form for, "Atten-hut!" And of course the blitz—blitzkrieg—as the opposing team attempted to invade and pillage the enemy's advancing forces. The game was war, through and through, stopping just short of death.

The crowd exploded with cheers. Their bodies lifted up off seats, blocking Paxton's view. The semilocal Californians scored on the very foreign Bostonians.

"Who's winning?" Bella asked as fireworks blazed the sky in color.

"Nobody," Paxton shouted over the fireworks. "They just tied."

They watched the fireworks detonate in the sky, like a rainbow boiling, bubbling, popping away in the distance. Bella waited for the fireworks to settle and the crowd to calm before speaking again.

"You know . . ." But Bella's voice stopped right there. Her arms folded, she crossed her legs, recoiling in on herself. "Never mind."

"What?" Paxton asked.

"It's nothing, just the fireworks . . ."

"Fireworks, what?"

It took her a second to think it through, the thought rippling across her expression. Lips bit and nostrils flared, then she coughed it up. "I saw lights during my shift a few days back."

"In your cockpit?"

Bella nodded. "Right around the evening. Sunset. Way, way out in the distance. These spotlights, like the ones in lighthouses, you know? Two of them. Big and wide, but moving together . . ."

"There's something out there," Paxton said.

"I know," Bella said. "But . . . we got our orders, right?"

They did. And for today those orders were to endure the sunlight and overtime finale of the game. It ended with a field goal from fifty yards out. The kick was good, and a hundred thirsty voices rejoiced. Paxton used the distraction to escape the inevitable bottleneck that would flow into one of two exits. He got out of the makeshift stadium, back to his bunk, and flopped onto his bed without a shower. He called home and talked with Callie for an hour before falling asleep.

He dreamed of breakfast: bananas and cold oatmeal. He dreamed that he dragged his sleepy feet back to the hangar, exchanging seats with Oya. But then, as Paxton woke up, he found visors over his eyes and gloves on his palms and discovered he was staring out of the eye of a Spartan. He had dreamed through the entire morning, barely remembering that cranny of consciousness between his bed and the cockpit.

It took minutes for his pupils to dilate and the haze to lift from his brain, but when it did he found his Spartan a few feet from the edge of the sandbox, looking out at the horizon beyond. It felt like the universe was daring him to do this, and it might have been the intoxication of drowsiness, but if he had brought that marble with him, he would take that step beyond the barrier, right there and then. And then he felt it, *like the princess and the pea*, the tiniest bump in his pocket, the marble.

Somewhere between sleep and his morning fugue, Paxton must have forgotten the marble in his pocket. He dug into the lint-filled corner of the pocket, and there it rested. And right then, Paxton took a few steps toward the sandbox's border, yet none of yesterday's alarms flashed. He stepped closer, still nothing—still moving, closer to the edge. Nine steps away . . . seven . . . five . . . and he closed his eyes for the last few steps beyond the boundaries of his sandbox.

When Paxton opened his eyes, the Spartan stood with one foot outside its sandbox, and not a single alarm rang, not a single message or beep sounded off—*nothing*. He dawdled forward so slow, so cautious, on two-hundred-horsepower legs. The Spartan climbed over the mound that for the past three weeks had blocked out any visibility on the horizon. And standing there, on the Spartan's colossal shoulders, Paxton could see on to forever. There was no turning back now.

14

Cracked, yellowed dirt sprawled out into an endless haze. The ground snapped like eggshells under the Spartan's colossal feet. The landscape was flat and rolled out to an empty horizon. Nothing but dust and fading sunlight. No life whatsoever.

But Paxton kept moving the Spartan forward. He'd barely walked half a mile out and knew he could easily get back to the sandbox before his shift was up. But direction was the decision of the hour, and Paxton decided it best to go against the push of the wind, westerly. The gusts were strong and cool against the Spartan's temperature gauge; the breeze might be coming off a body of water, however unlikely that may have been in the middle of a desert. And wherever there was water, there was usually civilization. But after eight hours in the wilds, Paxton didn't find his oasis, not even so much as a puddle, just more desert and stronger winds.

On the verge of turning back, Paxton stutter-stepped on the pedals—a yellow blur fizzed on the horizon ahead. He squinted. He tiptoed on the pedal like it was thin ice. The Spartan took a few timid steps forward toward the blur. And the closer the Spartan approached, the more that blur slipped into focus, the more it grew on the screen, and the more Paxton realized that he wasn't moving toward it—it was moving toward him.

"Sandstorm." He said it before he saw the thing.

An entire wall of migrating sand whipped on the horizon ahead, approaching fast. Even as Paxton veered back toward the sandbox, particles of debris clattered against the Spartan's body. The wind caught up with the Androne and rocked its metal frame from side to side. It was like a dry monsoon as the light dimmed and shards of sand deluged down. He pushed hard on the pedals, but the Spartan's feet sunk in shifting dunes. The end of Paxton's shift was quickly approaching, and for all his effort, he didn't even know if he was headed in the right direction.

The light got clogged in the knots of sand, and the cockpit went black. The full breath of the sandstorm hampered the Spartan's movement. He was in the eye of it now, all dark, with the only light gleaming from the displays: battery, external temperatures, and the twenty-seven minutes left before Oya came banging on the cockpit door.

Paxton's body leaked sweat as he panted heavily through his throat, as if he himself was running fifty miles an hour through the dark. He was lost and off-grid with an illegal gadget cloaking his location. They'd bury him under that jail, dishonorable discharge, interrogation, torture, with a minimum of a quarter century in some offshore military prison.

He watched minutes go to seconds, until nothing but zeros lit the top right corner of the screen. And immediately—prompt as *fuck*, Sergeant Oya pounded on the cockpit door.

Goddamn it! Paxton couldn't open the door now—*not now!* Not with all this: sand meteoring down on top of him and the rug of dirt shifting and lifting underneath the Spartan's unsteady feet. There was one more hill ahead of him, a round lump on the ground that appeared familiarly high, familiarly sloped. It might be right over that ridge; the fence and sandbox would be just on the other side.

"Arés?" He could hear her voice through inches of thick steel.

The pounding on the door went beat for beat with the Spartan's dense steps. Paxton couldn't distinguish between the two as the Spartan pedaled against a cascade of loose stones and splitting dirt. The Spartan mounted the top of the hill—and it wasn't there. No fence. No sandbox. Nothing. The Spartan's eye zoomed and panned and lit its night-vision candle in the dark, but nothing was there.

Sweating, panting, Paxton was as exhausted as the Spartan's beating quad-piston heart. Steam fizzed out from the gills on the side of its neck. He had never pushed the Spartan that hard, and all for nothing.

"Sergeant Paxton Arés?" Oya said. "If you are incapacitated or unconscious, I'll have to get security staff to remove the door."

Paxton held his breath and kept listening, but Oya's voice had gone quiet—gone to find security and unhinge the door. And take him away.

He was done, and he knew it. Paxton pulled his hands from the gloves and sat back, staring out at the sand-strewn landscape one last time and right then, something dove down from above. It was too dark to tell what exactly, but it moved snakelike down into the sand. It was long and thin and hurtling toward him. Paxton grabbed blindly for his gloves, lifted the Spartan's assault rifle, and aimed.

He straddled the two worlds, peering through the rifle's scope and cocking his ear to the clinks of metal on metal at the cockpit door. They were coming in. But it didn't matter now; he had something in his crosshairs slithering in and out of focus. And then he saw it—the snake, the dragon, *the fence*—half of it writhing in the winds, the other half still tethered to the dirt. Paxton was right there. Right where he needed to be. He punched the pedal. The Spartan dashed down the path ahead, following the fence like a trail back to the sandbox. And the instant he parked the Spartan, he ungloved his hands, took off his visor, and opened the door.

"Arés?" Sergeant Oya stood outside, staring at Paxton's sweaty, wild-eyed countenance.

"Hey," he said, staring at the monuments of security personnel standing behind her, tall, bulging men with faces built of stone. "Sorry, I . . ." *Dozed off? Didn't hear you? Lost track of the time?* "I was caught in this sandstorm here and . . . wind was really pushing me and I . . . didn't want to go off sandbox."

Not bad, he considered but watched closely to see if his cohorts agreed. Security barely waited for Paxton to finish the sentence, shaking their heads in disgust and moving on. They had better things to do. And

Oya seemed more concerned with the sweat pasted to the back of his shirt. She narrowed her eyes and nostrils as if she could smell something that wasn't right.

"Well, come on." Oya gestured for Paxton to step out.

He crawled out. Every muscle tense, legs and arms like tentacles—boneless limbs lazy and uneven, and a limp noticeable in his step. But Oya seemed far more occupied with the moisture on the seat. She tucked her arm into her sleeve and wiped the polyester dry. He had dodged the bullet, he thought. He had backpedaled, almost away, almost out of earshot, when Oya turned and shouted to him.

"By the way," she said, holding on to the seat inside the cockpit and letting her body dangle out the doorway. "Your girlfriend's in lockdown."

Paxton paused. *What girlfriend?* Then he realized—"Bella?"

"There was active combat today. Warfare," Oya said, like it excited her. "Bella came across the enemy and it tore her Androne in half."

"Seriously?" he asked, but her expression was as deadpan and serious as ever. "Who? Bella fought one of *them*?"

"I don't know shit else. Classified, right? But she'll probably need a little snuggle-up after her debrief, so ask her yourself."

For a half second, Paxton felt the tug of that distraction. For a half second, his mind's eye lost sight of the paranoia and trepidation that still had the hairs on his arms standing on end. Bella had fought one of *them*, and for that half second, the grand question—*Who are we fighting?*—colonized his thoughts. But just for a half second, then Oya cleared her throat and called out his name.

"And Arés," Oya shouted from the cockpit and stepped out. "What's this?"

Sergeant Oya pinched the marble between a finger and thumb and aimed it at Paxton. Security still lingered, captains and lieutenants hovered in the wings, but they all either ignored or appeared oblivious to what it was.

"Something the old man gave me," Paxton said, reaching out for it.

"What?" Oya asked and closed the marble into her fist. She seemed to see something in his reaction.

"You got a fucking Spartan to pilot." Paxton held his palm out. "What's your issue with me, Oya? We're on the same team. Fighting the same war. What's your problem?"

Oya let it go. The marble hit his palm and his fingers closed in, a Venus flytrap eagerly gripping the ominous little ball. But Oya never answered his question. She simply coiled herself into the circle space and disappeared.

15

"What'd you see?"

But Bella didn't answer; she wasn't even listening. Her head was slung between her shoulders as if she were melting into herself. Her black, curly hair cascaded over her eyes. She looked smaller—deflated, drooping her shoulders and a deep hunch in her back. She was broken, her pieces sprawled out around her, fingers appearing unhooked from her hands and eyes detached from their sockets.

It was just them, her and Paxton. Five forty in the morning, crickets' trilled and a purple-blue tinge blistered across an awning-window skyline. Paxton hadn't slept since his last episode in the cockpit, and neither had she. They had found each other in the dark, roaming the corridors, barefoot and in tank tops.

Paxton's insomnia was in his paranoia, and that paranoia spoke with the old man's voice, the old man's drawl and off-tone enunciation. The old man whispered about the clues that Paxton might have left for Oya to find, footprints in the sand or data logs. The old man's voice was an alarm clock, ringing over and over again, and he couldn't turn it off.

But the alarm clock that rang in Bella's ear, Paxton assumed, was made of yesterday's defeat. Her chance to avenge brothers lost in the Ninety-Nine had come and gone. Her Androne had been picked apart, its limbs scattered in the wind, its signal snuffed out.

"I'm sorry," Paxton said, softer, and leaned in toward her to compensate. "You don't have to talk about it."

"I'm done," Bella said, even softer but leaning back, away from him. "I don't want to do this anymore."

"What?"

"War Machine Program, Androns, another SPQR."

"Another?"

"Brass said they'd issue me another Androne next week. No shame. No consequence. Just take another Androne and pick up where I left off."

"That's a good thing, though. Getting another chance at life."

"Rob and Tommy never got that chance," she said, likely speaking about her brothers. "I wasn't fighting for my life yesterday. I sat in the cockpit, and I knew I'd be okay. No desperation. No true threat. I mean I tried, I fought, but somewhere inside me I knew I could hold back, strategize; my life wasn't on the line."

"But Bells—" He tried, but she was a verbal freight train, her pent-up words moving at a hundred miles an hour. Bella didn't hear Paxton or didn't care what he had to say, and so she kept going.

"I had it," she said. "Right then, I had the opportunity there to hit back, but . . ."

Footsteps came from down the corridor . . . *no*, not steps but the snaillike drag of soles against tile. The base was waking up with all their morning fugue, and Bella seemed to realize that. Her expression awoke right then. She glanced back and dragged her chair closer to Paxton's, as if Bella knew that if she was going to say something, she had to say it now.

"I can't talk about it," she said in a quiet hurry. "It's classified, but I can tell you this. This much isn't a secret. I didn't fight the enemy yesterday. It was a traitor—a collaborator."

"Collaborator?" Paxton said, leaning in to her already-hunched posture. They were lip to ear now.

"That's what they called it, a collaborator. It's one of ours, *us*. Someone's helping them."

"Somebody flipped sides?"

"An Androne pilot, either from Nellis Base or one of the others on the West Coast. And they're fucking good. Whoever they are, their training was far, far beyond mine. Total *nother* level. I didn't even touch them. Their Androne picked mine apart."

"What Androne Series?" Paxton asked.

"I . . . didn't see."

"You started training on your Androne less than a month ago. There's no shame in losing to an elite."

"Not really," Bella said as she fixed her posture. "I trained before this. I've been training on and off for five years."

Five? The Androne Program was relatively new, so had she been involved in beta tests? Paxton nearly asked her but then remembered he was supposed to be sympathizing, cheering her up.

"You'll get your chance to hit back. Don't lose sleep over it."

"That's not it," she said as footsteps cracked the rec room threshold and shadows curled around the corner. "Yesterday I was fighting a god, Paxton. The reason I can't sleep, the real reason, is because after fighting someone that"—she searched for the word—"someone that indomitable . . . If they have an entire squadron of pilots on that level, I think we're going to lose this war."

And they went quiet. Conviction hardened her soft features, and all of that sureness from just one encounter, one clash with *a god*, as she called it. But he wouldn't believe it; no. This was Bella's combat failure talking. Her cockpit claustrophobia taking over. There were no gods out there in that desert. *None*, Paxton thought, because he had to believe he could win.

"Yo, Columbia!" A voice pounded in the distance and brought both Paxton and Bella's heads whipping backward.

Sergeant Woden swaggered inside with a thickly bearded lieutenant at his side. The lieutenant appeared younger than Paxton; he pinched a lit morning cigarette between his lips, and designer sunglasses stood high on his hairline, shielding its recession. He flaunted his uniform so obviously, tugging on his collar more than once, his bars advertising his rank, and yet the man stood in sandals, black against his tanned feet.

"Let me holler at you real quick," Sergeant Woden said to Bella.

"Your eyes," Paxton whispered, just out of Woden's earshot. Bella's eyes were dewy, and she swathed the tears with her sleeve.

"Hey, Woden." Paxton reached for a handshake, hoping to give Bella just that extra second to clean her face. "Heard you got a top pilot ranking?"

Which was true. Sergeant Woden was top ranked at the base, but Woden sidestepped Paxton's false gesture and whispered to the bearded lieutenant.

"That's Sergeant Arés. He's harmless." And it wasn't a compliment. The lieutenant smirked as he eyed Paxton. "This is Lieutenant Ogun," Woden said, now speaking to Bella. "Brass flew him in from Fort Hood. Second best Androne pilot in the United States."

"Oh, you got jokes now," Lieutenant Ogun said and smirked before turning to Bella. "Nice to meet you, Corporal Columbia." The officer reached out for Bella's hand. She lifted four limp fingers toward him. "Sergeant Woden is one of the top-ranked pilots on base. Together we're going to track this collaborator down."

"I gave a report," Bella said.

"We read it," Lieutenant Ogun said, and sat down in the space between Bella and Paxton. "But we have a few other questions on the civilians."

Civilians? Paxton thought, and he nearly spoke it out loud, but then he realized he wasn't supposed to know any of this. This was a private conversation shared between them and Bella.

"Don't worry," Woden said in Bella's direction. "Colonel's going to announce it all later today, so it's fine if he hears. Have all the pilots keep an eye out for the collaborator. You better head out, *Pax.*" Woden said the name with cynicism. "We got classy intel to talk."

For a half second, Paxton considered saying something back. He was the only ex-Marine among the pilots. And that meant boots on the ground, weapons and combat training. He considered it, and maybe considered for a second too long, because Woden seemed to notice.

"There a problem, Sarge?"

Yes, Paxton said with his unflinching expression.

"Jesus Christ," Lieutenant Ogun snapped. "You want a write-up, Private?"

"Sergeant," Paxton said.

"Yes, sir, no, sir, that's how you answer," Lieutenant Ogun said.

"I—" Paxton tried.

"Yes, sir! No, sir!" Ogun barked.

"Yes," Paxton said through gritted teeth. "Sir."

"I'll talk to you later, Pax," Bella said, implying that she'd be fine.

But it wasn't about her anymore; this was about manhood, and he felt his own shriveling, plum to prune, at the stem of his masculinity.

"Yeah," Paxton said. "Talk later."

But they wouldn't talk later. Later he would be back in his cockpit, exploring the monotony of his sandbox. Later he'd daydream at his controls about the hundred insults he could have hurled at Ogun and Woden. Later that same indignation would send him to Colonel Marson, searching for that next rung up the ladder toward making lieutenant. But it would all be later. For now, Paxton could only turn his back on Ogun's Santa Claus beard and the gap in Woden's grin.

He exited, dragging his feet, not giving them the satisfaction of a hasty retreat.

16

The admissions office was lined with fresh-faced recruits—shiny, brand new, that fresh-out-of-high-school smell. Many of them appeared younger than Paxton had remembered, barely adolescents from the looks of baby-fat faces and soprano-pitched conversations. The whole ensemble of young adults stood in a line that wrapped around the corner as, one by one, administrative assistants called their names into one office or another.

Paxton felt like an old man. He was illiterate to their small talk—this pop star, those lyrics, that line from that one movie, all of it was foreign to him. They hyphenated nonrelative words and bent nouns into verbs, like "I'm straight walleting this dude," or "Are you couching or weekending?" Their language was a sort of foreign futuristic, and Paxton strained his ears, a presbycusis tilt to his neck as he listened. He *was* the old man, witnessing this upcoming generation with new genders and jargon blossoming all around him.

But Paxton sat in the admissions office lobby, waiting for a meeting with his godfather. He hunched his back and curled his shoulders in, crawling into a shell made out of himself. He stared at his shoes and tugged the loops of perfectly tied laces. And still, with all the self-inflicted isolation, she spoke to him. A girl, probably just eighteen, an inept touch of makeup dotted across her face.

"Are you a pilot?" she asked, eyeing the insignia on his uniform.

Paxton nodded.

"They took us on a tour of things," she said as she gestured to something outside. "We saw the barracks, the medical whatever, and then they showed us the Androines. I'd only ever seen quadrupedals, but these Mongol Series. Shogun Series. It's intimidating. I like the Z Series. Its design is my favorite."

"Z," Paxton said as he nodded agreement. "Mobile. Flexible. Even at its weight."

"Yeah," she said as she wiped the drapes of hair from her eyes, wide and swelling with wonder. "Expertise." She breathed nervous laughter and kept batting the obvious blue of her eyes, in and out of curling lashes. "I really wanna learn how to pilot."

Paxton had never seen this before, the zeal of celebration—*celebrity*. Her smile shone on him. Her wide eyes paraded around every curve of his jaw and the edges of his cheekbones. What was this intoxication cascading from the endorphins in his head down the line of his spine? It was a soupy thing and hard to pick out its individual parts, some of it hubris, some of it the soft threads of adrenaline, but mostly it was power. He felt higher. He felt elevated by her praise, raised up as an idol, propelled by her worship. *Power.* Paxton felt it, like he could crush her as she crawled willingly into his palms.

"So which ones do you do?" she said, close enough that he could smell the flavor of bubble gum sponging her saliva. "I mean which Androne do you pilot?"

"I pilot a Series 1, the Spartan Series."

And it ended right there. The cadet reeled back. Her bubble gum seemed to sour in that exact moment. Her hands found their way to her lap, and her gaze tilted away.

"Oh," she said. "Nice." And she lowered her head toward the patterns in the tiles.

Series 1 stigma. Paxton himself had already hated the Spartan before he began using it, but now . . . "It's underrated," he thought and said simultaneously. "It's fast—if you know how to push it, it's fast."

But her thoughts were elsewhere and her eyes fixed on a sharp pair of high heels clicking on approach and stopping right in front of them.

"Sergeant Arés?" *Thank God*, or thank the fortysomething assistant with dried-up piercings in both nostrils and the end of a tattoo slipping out from under her sleeve.

"Yes," Paxton said as he stood and snatched at a handshake that wasn't even offered.

"Nice to meet you, Sergeant. And we're sorry, Colonel Marson has been swamped with this collaborator thing."

"No worries," he said. "Glad he could take the time out to see me."

"There's always time for family."

The reformed punk rocker led Paxton around corners, around bodies, and through the doorway of a conference room. It was spacious. Gusts of air-conditioning wiped against his forehead, and a ceiling fan cut the chill into even slices. Colonel Marson sat beneath it all with horn-rimmed glasses, eyeing the pile of papers on the conference table before him.

"Colonel—" Paxton started, but he never finished. He even started to lift his hand to salute but didn't quite get there either. There was an elephant in that room. In the corner behind the colonel was a gray face all too familiar to Paxton—Victoria, standing with a mug of coffee and papers in each hand.

"Sergeant Arés," Colonel Marson stood and lifted his arm in salute.

Paxton whipped his hand up to his forehead to catch up. "Thank you for taking the time out to see me, sir."

"That's all I have time for, molding the next generation." Marson pointed toward the coffee machine. "Coffee?"

"No, sir," Paxton said without even glancing in that direction. "Thank you."

"Sit down," Marson said, and gestured to the seat across from him as he himself returned to the soft cushions dressed in spongy leather. "Maria, get Paxton a brew of that mocha," he said to Punk Rock Maria.

"Just got the thing," Marson said of the coffee machine. "Nearly ten grand."

"You're kidding."

"No joke. I mean, a write-off, but still, right? How's the old man?" Marson slid the papers aside, taking a squinting interest in Paxton's features, as if they reminded him of someone.

"He's good. He had a checkup recently. Clean bill of health. And with as many cigarettes as he smokes . . ."

"Did always like his Marlboros. And the better half?"

"Good," Paxton said, and shoved two thumbs-up. "Third trimester."

"It's good. Good to have that. Reminds you of what we're fighting for."

What *were* they fighting for? Right now he was fighting for political position, clout, a career, pride even. But in the bigger picture of the war, Paxton had no idea, but he nodded all the same, rocking his skull up and down with a slow, contemplative rhythm.

"So what is this all about?" Marson asked as the coffee machine squealed behind him, its teeth chewing at a hundred coffee beans per second. "How can I help?"

"I'd like to take you up on your offer. You had mentioned the lieutenant program. I'm ready to take the first step."

"I had a feeling," Marson said as a smile lit his face.

Maria leaned in and placed Paxton's coffee on the table in front of him, a black mug with a white star, U.S. ARMY printed below it. Marson raised his own mug as if toasting, and Paxton followed, sipping and cringing at the hot burn.

"And like I said, Sergeant," Marson continued, almost winking his eye, "you'll rise up these ranks real quick."

Good, Paxton thought, and kept on thinking—thinking of how he'd have to keep these extra hours to himself. The ancillary studies and shadowing the colonel, Paxton would have to hide all of it, at least until he got his bars. And he'd have to get there before their other star pilot, Sergeant Woden. *Fuck that guy.*

"Victoria," Marson said, and he lifted his arm to wave her over. "Lieutenant, allow me to introduce you to Sergeant Paxton Arés, soon to be Lieutenant Arés. Long family history in the military. And a bright future here too."

His godfather had forgotten that Paxton had mentioned Victoria before, and she eyed Paxton as if for the first time. "Pilot?" As if she didn't know.

"War Machine Program," Paxton said, playing along.

Lieutenant Victoria let out a quiet gasp and nodded in reverence. "Nice to meet you, Sergeant Arés." She reached for a handshake.

"Likewise," Paxton said as their hands grappled and joggled back and forth.

Victoria handed Marson a folder but tilted it away from Paxton's line of sight.

"It's fine," Marson said, appearing to notice the strange tilt in Victoria's wrist. "We're all on the same team. And he'll have his clearance soon enough."

"Will he?" Victoria said as she laid the folder on the table.

On the folder's tab, Paxton noticed the word PEACEMAKER. He glanced, then glanced away, like a Peeping Tom caught in the open.

"Peacemaker op," Marson said, opening the folder with an exaggerated, almost seductive flip of the page, as if he wanted Paxton to look. "My most recent sleep problem."

"The collaborator thing?" Paxton asked.

"Ha!" Marson said without a smile. "See," he said to Victoria, "word spreads like wildfire in this desert." Then Marson twisted his eyes back to Paxton. "You heard?"

"Just that there might be a traitor or something . . ."

"Or something," Marson emphasized as he thumbed through the pages within the folder: maps, tracking routes, and diagrams with wings and rudders on strangely advanced aerial drones. "Twenty-seven Furies?" Marson turned to Victoria. "Is that enough?"

"Enough," Victoria said. "He's moving with civilians. E-class surveyors have infrared, echo-locale. It's enough."

"You know," Paxton started, fishing for answers. "I heard a friend of mine is heading the search for the collaborator. Sergeant Calum Woden?"

Victoria turned to Marson, as if looking for permission to answer. Marson didn't as much as flinch a response, and still she seemed to glean something from his poise, taking the colonel's silence as an answer.

"He and Lieutenant Ogun," Victoria said. "From Fort Hood."

"If Woden and Ogun find the collaborator—" Paxton started.

"When," Marson reassured him. "When they find them."

"When," Paxton agreed.

"They'll be the pride of the US military," Marson said. "And all the power that comes with."

And right then, two separate thoughts crashed at an intersection in Paxton's head: his vendetta against Woden and this whole collaborator crisis, they collided and created something new. What if Paxton found him, her, *it*, first? He could travel outside his sandbox. He wouldn't engage, but just finding a location could get him medals of service, valor, *honor*. And he just might become the type of father a kid could look up to.

"Good," Paxton said, the gears in his head spinning. "Let's find this collaborator."

17

The auditors, they called them, men and women in gray fatigues, roamed the hangar like wraiths. They carried tablets and stylus pens, scratching notes atop recently snapped photographs. They leaned into cockpit doors or stooped under ventilation, tiptoeing, bent over, but never standing straight, never immobile, as if each was competing with the other to appear busier.

They outnumbered the pilots two to one, with handfuls more stalking from the catwalk above. The night before, these same auditors had conducted interviews with half of the noncommissioned officers. Their watered-down interrogation techniques revealed nothing more than contraband vape stashes or siphoned-off electricity during brown-outs, and nothing on the collaborator's identity.

One of them hovered around Paxton's cockpit. Glasses thick as telescopes blurred the man's eyes, and still he leaned in and squinted at the ID number engraved just below the cockpit door, then leaned into the ajar doorway, checking the thick valves and wiring therein. He must have felt Paxton stop just behind him, because right on cue, this Galileo turned his Hubble-thick telescopes to him.

"A Spartan?" he asked, and pointed his stylus at the cockpit.

"Yes, sir," Paxton said. "The original."

"How does it operate?"

"Good," Paxton said, but then had to persuade himself and said it again. "It performs good enough."

"Really?" Galileo cracked a smile, and his brow twisted into a knot.

"That's to say, I haven't operated anything else. It's all I know."

Galileo gave a long, slow nod and made a few notes on his tablet. He circled around the oval cockpit—there wasn't much to see on that side, but then again Galileo seemed a little ways away from blind.

"You ever bring gadgets into your cockpit?" Galileo asked, coming around the other side of the cockpit.

"Gadgets?" Paxton said, his knees nearly buckling as his actual "gadget" seemed to suddenly weigh down his right pocket.

"You know," Galileo said, and held up his tablet. "Anything electronic."

"No," Paxton said, and shook his head, but it was his arm that did the real moving, migrating around his waist to his pants pocket and the marble therein. It happened so involuntarily in fact that Paxton himself didn't realize it until Galileo's telescope lenses aimed at that very hand and pocket.

"Nothing?" Galileo stepped closer. "Not even a wristwatch?"

The man's stare seemed exaggerated behind the carnival-mirror lenses, his wild eyes crossing and uncrossing like brown pennies rattling around in their sockets. Paxton couldn't decide whether Galileo was eyeing his pant leg or not. The angle that the glasses bent seemed to change the direction of his eyes.

"I don't even own a watch," Paxton said.

Galileo pointed at Paxton's pants as he fixed the glasses higher onto the bridge of his nose.

"What?" Paxton said. "What is it?"

"Oatmeal," Galileo said, and smiled.

The tiniest smear of dried oatmeal encrusted the lap of his pants. Paxton squinted at the minute gray smudge utterly camouflaged in gray pants and thought that it should be invisible to the naked eye.

"Thank you," Paxton said, sweeping his fingers along his pants.

Galileo nodded and stepped past Paxton but quickly spun on his heels for one more query. "By the way, what do you think about the woman who operates opposite your shift?"

"Sergeant Oya?" Paxton asked.

"Whatever," he said dismissively, a hint of distaste. "She came off a little . . ."

Paxton waited for it but quickly realized that there wasn't a word, just a feeling Galileo had about Sergeant Oya; they must have already met. Paxton wasn't close to her by any stretch of the imagination—in fact, of all the pilots, Oya might be the only one onto Paxton's trespasses. But this witch hunt had already aimed enough pitchforks and burning stakes at his fellow pilots. And Oya wasn't the collaborator; Paxton knew that with confidence.

"Sergeant Oya's an upstanding officer," Paxton said. "Good pilot too."

"You're sure? She seemed a little . . ." And again, gaps between Galileo's words. "A little headstrong."

"A little?" Paxton said sarcastically and smiled.

But Galileo didn't appear to understand sarcasm. "One of those . . . ," he said as he sketched a note on his tablet. "You're good to go. Thank you, Sergeant."

No, thank you.

Paxton led the Spartan Series out of the sandbox a second time, heading eastbound, moving with the direction of the wind. Thirsty blood-brown dirt flaked underneath the Spartan's heels, and a red mist orbited every step along the way. Dunes piled up into bunches, and the Spartan's shadow slithered over the uneven sand as it marched toward more dirt and more dunes, stretched out for near infinity. He turned around with four and a half hours left in his shift. It had taken him that long to get there and would take just as long to get back, or so he thought. The headwind slowed him down, and facing the glare of the setting sun squeezed Paxton's vision down to the finest squint. He arrived back at his sandbox a couple of minutes late. But fortunately for Paxton, Oya was a few minutes late herself with coffee-stained lips and sleep-strained eyes.

The following day, Paxton explored the north and quickly found a barrier of mountain ranges—craggy shark's teeth biting deep into a nicotine-yellow sky.

By the end of the week Paxton had spun the entire compass of direction—northwestern cold, southern steppes—and this country was dry for a thousand square miles. On the following Monday, he decided to return west, to sandstorm country. Clearer skies allowed him to trek forty-five miles farther than he'd had on his virgin voyage. By Wednesday, his growing aptitude for the Spartan's limitations allowed him to push double that—ninety miles west. Then, familiarity with the terrain, the shortcuts around ridges, and firmer dirt that allowed for deeper treading allowed Paxton to trek a total 108 miles out by Friday. And that was when it happened.

The landscape was an acne swath of swelled-up earth. The hilly ranges threatened to impede him, but they did exactly the opposite. A walking path had been carved into the hillside. The dirt was firm and elevating in squares, almost like stairs. The Spartan ascended in minutes. The setting sunlight exploded from the opposite end of the horizon, a dizzying brightness that lit the inside of the cockpit to a red-orange inferno. He was awed by the sunset. From that vantage point the landscape appeared flat, and sunburned dirt blushed in patches against the ground. And at the very edge of visibility, blown-out skyscrapers tiptoed to poke through filmy smog—civilization, or what was left of it.

A sudden gleam bent on something to his northwest, a luster that cut at the Spartan's eyepiece and blurred Paxton's vision. He shifted to the side, and it followed him. The swell of light shifted and again gleamed in the Spartan's lenses. Paxton zoomed in on it, magnifying the image.

He saw people, a crowd, thirty strong—children, adults, and the elderly, an extended family of men and women, and the scope of a rifle gleaming into the Spartan's eye.

18

The Spartan stood in the bull's-eye of the scope. Paxton had never seen that type of weapon before, but then again, he could only see down its muzzle. The barrel was long, just a few inches shorter than the old woman who held on to it. Civvies were known for auctioning scrap quadrupedal parts, and they'd probably get ten times that for an Androne.

Paxton knew he shouldn't engage, and still he unsheathed the Spartan's assault rifle and backpedaled from the edge of the hill. The Spartan crawled down to a prone position and attempted to remain still, but adrenaline beat through Paxton's chest, shaking his hands, melting his palms into puddles of perspiration. His trembling was relayed via satellite to the Androne's body. The Spartan shook in the dirt and wiped imaginary sweat from its dry brow, like a metal shadow of Paxton's nervous movements.

The cockpit's circular architecture had validated its design, rolling Paxton forward onto his elbows and knees but without the discomfort of the sand syringe stabbing into his skin. Paxton crawled in place while his half-ton shadow moved on the monitor a million miles away, inching toward the edge of the summit.

A sudden beeping pinged and ponged through the cockpit. Paxton twitched and the Spartan spasmed. The beeping echoed from the timer he had set at the beginning of his shift. He'd hit the halfway hour, and he needed to turn back.

"Breathe," Paxton whispered, as if speaking to the Spartan.

He didn't come out here to kill civilians. He had to remind himself of that. He took a deep breath, the oxygen like water cooling his burning heartbeat. He reminded himself that they breathed that same air, reminded himself that these civilians were the first living things he had seen amid all this desolation. War had that amnesic quality when it came to one's humanity, and he reminded himself of that too.

Paxton crawled ahead, the timer still screaming through the cockpit, drowning the sound of gravel snapping under the Spartan's elbows and knees. The Spartan's head hung low, and its chin grazed the ground as it approached the edge. He lifted the Spartan onto its knees, rifle tight against the shoulder, eyes zooming in, but its finger avoiding the trigger. And only then did Paxton finally breathe.

She wasn't there—none of them were. They had vanished into the extinct landscape so completely that Paxton had to second-guess whether they were real or just mirages on a sunburned CPU. *No.* Mirages didn't leave footprints. The Spartan zoomed in on thousands of them scattered across the ground.

For eighteen minutes the timer rang in his ear, and for eighteen minutes Paxton ignored it. He magnified the images below, following the patterns and path of the footprints, searching for a direction or design. But the prints circled, they intersected, footprints within footprints, yielding nothing but a shoe-size crater field.

Time was up, and Paxton twisted the pedals around and turned back. He raced down the incline, loose rocks and streams of dried, flowing soil making the descent more difficult than the climb up. Paxton hadn't left visual bread crumbs along the way and couldn't quite remember the path back. Still, he made good time and returned to the sandbox, arriving there a few minutes before the end of his shift. And even more fortunately, Oya was late, giving him the extra few minutes to sweep over the Spartan's footprints leading out of the sandbox. The wind would do the rest.

Oya arrived just as Paxton parked the Spartan in a position of perfect randomness. He felt that criminal cockiness of getting off scot-free, and it carried as he climbed out of the cockpit with a satisfied smirk on his expression.

"Sleep late, Oya?" Paxton asked, and smiled. Their banter had become regular now, but today Oya didn't even glance at him. She waited for him to climb out of the metal cave as she chewed her stick of gum and dug a pinky into her ear like she couldn't hear him. "Wrong side of the bed, Sarge?"

Oya turned her eyes to Paxton, and only her eyes. Her waist stood firm; her neck wouldn't pivot. "Keep my name out of your fucking mouth, Arés!" Oya said, nearly spitting the words at him. She barged into the narrow space between him and the cockpit door, clipping his shoulder, brushing his uniform, and Paxton sidestepped the rest of her. She climbed inside, snapping the cockpit door shut.

What was that? But Oya's bad day was tomorrow's problem; what was Paxton actually going to do about the civilians he saw out there? He felt an instinctive worry for them. Their fragile flesh and bone crashing against the titanium tide of the Androne Program. And if a Sergeant Woden or Lieutenant Ogun came across them, bloodhounds searching the desert, those civilians could end up as dead as the dust they crawled through.

19

Paxton toted handfuls of envelopes up to the Penthouse—personnel's nickname for the fourth floor of the administrative building. Many of the envelopes wore confidential seals, addressed to Colonel Marson or other men who only needed a one-name introduction. But as Paxton mounted each individual stair, his mind only sank deeper into the confines of yesterday's cockpit, that old woman and her pole-vault-long rifle, and their disappearing act at the end. Paxton daydreamed about it—even more than daydreamed, he embodied the memory, feeling the Spartan's springs recoiling in his heels, feeling the pistons popping in his knees. By the time he approached the ninth and final flight of stairs, Paxton *knew* he could bound over that entire batch of steps.

Thankfully, Colonel Marson's ex-punk-rocker assistant, Maria, stood at the top of the stairwell, hailing Paxton up and snapping him back to reality.

"Colonel's waiting, Paxton," she said as she snatched the mail out of his hands. "You daydreaming again?"

"No," Paxton said, catching his breath and catching up with Maria as she paced toward the glass palace that was the situation room. "Well, maybe," he said, rethinking his answer. "Not sure I'm getting enough sleep."

He wasn't. Paxton's non-cockpit hours were spent in the offices, shadowing Colonel Marson and couriering packages in and out of stairways. His days ended near midnight and mornings started at 4:00 a.m.

He might sneak a nap in the cockpit, but for all intents and purposes Paxton was a prisoner to the Penthouse.

The fourth floor was a glass mecca. Curved glass walls stretched down the corridors. Glass doors led into glass offices with ceiling-high windows. And skylights outshone the halogen light bulbs on the ceiling. The Penthouse was like a fishbowl, and Paxton floated upside down, almost sleepwalking his way to Marson's office.

His assignment this afternoon was to check Marson's next speech for typos, changing *atack* to *attack*, *air strike* to *airstrike*, *collaborater* to *collaborator*, and so on. Paxton brought the corrected memos into a conference room and was made to be social amid the arm-wrestling handshakes of analysts and investigators from the five major bases in the United States. He stood at the back of the room and listened to the war drum in Colonel Marson's voice beat, "This is the second *attack* now, an aggressive and brazen *airstrike* from the *collaborator* and his allies. We need to take measures."

"Can you believe he hit us again?" Maria whispered. She stood beside him at the back of the office. "Why's he so hard to catch?"

"He or she," Paxton said.

"Good point," Maria said, then flipped the subject. "Heard you're only like thirty-six office hours short of making lieutenant."

"Something like that." It sounded right, but Paxton had lost count. "You keeping track?"

"Hell, I'm counting down the hours I gotta spend with your ass."

"You'll miss me."

"Well," Maria said, and paused. She leaned in closer and her whisper grew quieter. "Whenever you get those bars, maybe you can tell me what in the fuck we're actually doing at this base."

Paxton smirked. "Who we're fighting?"

"More like who's fighting us."

"Sergeant Arés," Colonel Marson intruded into the quiet, his voice booming from the head of the room. "Lights."

Paxton flipped the switch and the room went black. A projector lit the barium screen with strange lists of numbers and coordinates, like a geometry class of shapes and graphs. Marson did his best to explain, but the inquisition that followed lasted twice as long as his speech. Questions about the collaborator's "demigod Androne," questions on the possibility of mods and augmentations, and the question that nearly every attendee was wondering: how the collaborator made an impossible shot to take down an Active Camouflage Aerial Drone, or ACAD.

"You following, Pax?" Maria asked.

"Nope," Paxton said.

But he was. Paxton hung on every menacing word and wondered if he should even be pursuing this collaborator and their demigod Androne.

The meeting ended even as questions kept rolling off the tongues of the overwrought attendees. Personnel washed out of the room, and Paxton waded through the stream of bodies, losing Maria somewhere therein.

He felt fatigued as he thought of it, the idea of stepping back into the cockpit without lunch or coffee. But he climbed in nonetheless, malnourished and dizzy from the morning proofread and late-night daydreams about Callie's chapped lips and the freckles on her back.

———

The sand turned somersaults, then pirouettes, an enlivened, frenzied soil that jostled the Spartan as it again escaped the sandbox confines.

Paxton ventured back to the scatter of footprints from the day before, but the desert chalkboard had been wiped clean in the winds. And still he walked the Spartan in circles around the region where the civvies had disappeared. The tedious merry-go-round of effort nearly put him to sleep, but right then the Spartan stumbled, its foot stuck heel deep in the sand.

Not sand but a thick wood panel covering a hole in the ground. He lifted the Spartan's leg out of the foot-size aperture and removed the splintered wood concealment. What little light remained in the day shone on a cavernous expanse with a pair of parallel metallic beams that ran on into an endless tunnel.

"Train tracks," he said.

His palms felt sweaty now in the gloves. His breath quickened too. These signs of civilization would lead to something—to Bella's *god*.

He switched to infrared, and though it clouded the details in the tunnel, those metal rails and intersecting crossties between them were as clear as day. Each plank of wood was like a stepping stone, a footprint unto itself. And he could follow the civvies right to their base of operations and right to the demigod—the collaborator.

20

Paxton had to turn back, of course. His shift was nearly half-up, and he estimated it would take just as long to get back to the sandbox. Sergeant Oya would be standing outside the cockpit doors at a punctual 8:55. No time to explore the tunnel nor follow the tracks to their eventuality. Paxton raced the Spartan back across the nameless desert, following his own footprints and arriving at the sandbox just minutes before nine.

Sergeant Oya stood waiting and didn't address Paxton as he stepped out, even as he nodded, even as he spoke.

"Hey, Sarge," Paxton said, and Oya somehow managed to climb into the cockpit and close the door before he finished his sentence.

But Paxton didn't put too much thought into it, as his attention span was withering. He had skipped meals and liquids, naps and dreams, and now tried to compensate for them all, hunched over lamb chops and bowls of oatmeal, three-quarters asleep. He stared in a daze at those gray, portly oats and didn't notice Bella taking a seat across from him until she tapped on his bowl.

"What's up?" she said.

Paxton hadn't seen her in a few days, but it somehow felt like more. She had her hair tied up in the back and her fatigues buttoned high. Her shoulders didn't curl in but were cocked back with an apparent confidence. She looked the part now. She had settled into the uniform and copper-stained shoes. And still Bella gave just enough of a smile that she seemed mostly herself.

"Hey," Paxton said after a second or two.

"Pax?" she said, squinting at him as if something about him seemed different too. "You look like shit."

"I am," he said, smirking now. "Feeling shitty."

"You smell the part too," Bella replied, a wicked smirk cracking the dimples in her cheeks. She was getting good at this. "You've been scarce, though. What've you been into?"

Paxton considered whether to tell her about the lieutenant program, the office hours, and the pending examination. "Nothing really."

"You sure?"

Or did she know? There weren't many secrets on this military campus, and she very well might have heard about Paxton's attempts to climb rungs and ranks.

"Nothing consequential."

"So what's the deal with you and Oya, then?"

He sat up now, the torpor washed away. "You heard about that?"

"Oya mentioned something to Woden. He mentioned it to me."

"Woden?"

"Yes." Bella shrugged. "He's all right." And she whispered it, like a shameful family relation. "I got to know him a little bit."

"All right?" Paxton couldn't believe what he was hearing. "So you two are cool all of a sudden?"

"Why not?"

He smiled, shook his head, and took a sip of the juice next to his oatmeal.

"You jealous, Pax?" Bella leaned in as she asked.

"Jealous?" But he was, wasn't he. Not a romantic jealousy, or even sentimental, but it felt off to him that his closest friend on base was warming up to his closest thing to an enemy.

"He's taught me a lot," Bella said. "I train with him now. Piloting."

"That's good," Paxton said, trying to shake off the notion of envy. "So what's Oya's beef with me?"

"He's going places," she continued.

"Who is?"

"Woden. He's looking to make officer."

"Good." And that was good. It would make it that much more satisfying when Paxton got there first. "Woden will get there soon. I'm sure. So what's with Oya—"

"And I'm not walleting," Bella said, cutting him off.

"Walleting?" Paxton asked, not sure if she had said *walleting* or *wallowing*; he didn't understand either.

"I'm not walleting Woden." Paxton stared at her, still not fully understanding the word. "I'm not using him. I'll work my own way up, but it doesn't hurt to have somebody looking out for you, right?"

"I guess."

"Anyway," Bella said, "Oya told him that you snitched her out to one of the inspectors the other day."

"Wait—what?" Paxton said, lagging a few steps behind the shift in topic. "I did what?"

"You told some inspector she looked suspicious? The inspector assigned to your cockpit. Oya got called in for questioning on it."

"Gali-*fucking*-leo," Paxton snapped.

"Galileo?" Now he was confusing her.

"The guy—the *fucking* guy; the one assigned to our cockpit. Glasses like telescopes. Like Galileo." Paxton rambled, his mouth moving forward as his mind rewound to the moments of that conversation.

He hadn't even halfway implied Oya. But Galileo and the other inspectors had a quota, a certain number of suspicious individuals that they had to tally. Galileo had used Oya and used Paxton's words against her.

"I didn't say shit about her," Paxton said.

"I know," Bella said. "I told him that—Woden."

"And no doubt Woden escalated shit when Oya told him about it."

"No," Bella said, though at that moment she herself seemed to consider it.

"No?"

"Maybe," she admitted. "Hey, I got a training session in a bit," she continued, and ambled away from the table. Bella had a skip in her step now. She seemed to be over the loss of her Androne a week earlier. "Catch you around, Pax."

Yes, around.

The lamb chops, oatmeal, and the rest of dinner didn't sit well in Paxton's stomach, or was it the conversation? Either way, he ran circles between his bunk and the bathroom. It'd be another sleepless night, then more office hours, more shadowing Colonel Marson on two hours of sleep.

But he did try. He closed his eyes and tossed around the bed, wrestling the blanket into a knot for an hour before giving in to insomnia. He called Callie, even though the brownout was ten minutes away and he knew she slept before nine. But Paxton had self-diagnosed what he was feeling and determined that his homesickness was far worse than his upset stomach.

Much to his surprise, Paxton heard from everyone in the house—the old man, Callie, even Hudson put in a bark or two. Callie had been to the hospital twice in the past three days and hadn't told him. *Complications*, the old man said. *It's nothing*, she said. But what was evident was the drift of the decimal place on the bills in his online medical account. Military insurance was a flimsy defense against an unborn child. He would have done better to suffer from facial scarring, PTSD, or erectile dysfunction. Gynecology and obstetrics were mostly ignored by the insurance.

"Poor thing." It was the last thing he remembered saying before drifting off.

He fell asleep against the banister of his bed and suddenly woke up at the colonel's desk in the Penthouse. The moments between his bunk and Marson's mahogany furnishings was a vague and dreamy fugue that barely registered in his remembrance. But Marson excused Paxton for napping, calling him one of the "good guys."

The colonel introduced Paxton to a foreign general and the secretary of state. He was moving up in the world and nearly moved up in rank, just a few hours short of lieutenant. But all the politics only sedated Paxton deeper into his stupor; he was too drowsy now, too fatigued, even for his bed to remedy. Yet strangely there was something about getting into that cockpit that felt dreamlike, like his mind was at rest in the Spartan's body. There was something about finding the refugees alive that was soothing. Even as he stalked them, he found watching them brought the tiniest sense of peace. His cockpit waited just an hour down the spin of that clock, and its swirling limbs of hours, minutes, and seconds couldn't move fast enough.

21

Sunlight waxed low on the horizon, shrouding the unnamed desert in that much more mystery. Paxton had pushed the Spartan hard against the desert, seventy miles per hour back to the tunnel beneath the sand. The space underneath the earth was the densest dark he had ever seen, a black hole, swallowing all light, all sound, and eventually even him.

The labyrinth of tunnels knotted into itself, a spaghetti-sprawl of passages that seemed to shape-shift around the Spartan each time it maneuvered around the next corner. The dark, artificial corridors seemed hellish in night-vision green. Every step inward he felt digested further into the guts of something sinister. Something was very wrong here.

The tunnels appeared lived in and ancient all at once. Years-old bonfire burns scarred the ground. Chipped cement archways patched with wooden bandages appeared ready for collapse. And graffitied cave paintings colored the walls in what appeared to be a Cyrillic text. He explored what he could for as long as he could, mapping the tunnels in a Picasso-style scrawling on the back of a lunch menu. Time was the problem, and he turned back. He always had to turn back.

It took a few more visits, a few more days of this for him to piece together the structure of things. And at the end of the tunnels—the end of a week—the Spartan ran into the first signs of life. Fresh graffiti had been sprayed along the walls and atop the ceilings. Nude feminine bodies and the faces of celebrated men, and farther in were images of Spartans, drawn to savage detail, the jet-tone of titanium bolts, the gleam around the alloys in the joints, and the single green eye. Mongol Series, Apaches, SPQRs—nearly the entire War Machine Program was drawn across the ceiling like a spray-painted Sistine Chapel.

Farther in, the Spartan felt the first hints of a breeze. Fat droplets of water drizzled down from cracks in the concrete ceiling. Fresh footprints cratered the muddy earth. He was close, and Paxton felt a cold sweat of nervousness, like that first date with Callie—fear cooked in excitement at the dinner table. There was that same rumbling in his gut now, hungry butterflies flapping up to his throat. He felt like he could smell them, in the empty pots and piles of shit, flies swooping kamikaze into open flames. He was so close, and all he wanted to see was whether life existed in this wilderness—to know that he wasn't alone in this universe.

Paxton slowed the Spartan down to a tiptoe, knees to the dirt and slinking forward with each step. Then something crackled in the dark, and the Spartan stopped altogether. Paxton lifted the Spartan's rifle as he inched it forward, hiding the pound of its footsteps in the occasional wheezing of wind. As it inched closer, the crackling more resembled a pattering—*no*, splashing. The sound of water.

The Spartan followed the trail of noise to a narrow service corridor, easily navigable for a five-foot-something engineer, but for the seven-foot Spartan it was a crawl space. The Spartan held its shoulders inward, angled itself to the side. The deeper it ventured, the tighter the corridor pinched in.

Soon the water splashed louder . . . closer. Light glinted around the corner. A voice emerged, a small voice, from an even smaller person. She looked four years old, *maybe*. Paxton was no good at guessing children's ages; to him the little rascals all looked alike from four to fourteen. A flashlight necklace swung on the collar of her shirt as the girl pranced barefoot through a sticky brown puddle and danced under a soft waterfall trickling in from the ceiling nearly a hundred feet above.

Her skin gleamed in a mix of water and light, a cocoa-brown sparkle amid all that night. Paxton considered, for the first time, the vast Saharan and Nubian deserts. He did the time zone mathematics in his head and it almost worked—add in a southern hemisphere, minus a few miles of sea level, and *maybe* . . . Were they in Africa?

Paxton lowered the Spartan's rifle. The Androne took a slow, stealthy step forward. Its tiny corridor was pitted in shadow, so it inched confidently toward the edge. The girl was alone aside from a backpack, nearly larger than the girl herself, and a lantern hanging next to it. The Spartan took another step forward—its last step, as a collection of gravel cracked under its heavy heel.

"Ma?" the girl asked as she twisted toward the sound.

The Spartan took a step back, and she must have seen the movement because she stepped toward it, out of the pool of contaminated water, and she kept coming, fearless of the pit of black ahead of her. The Spartan inched backward, its clumsy feet and the narrow corridor knotting into each other, and its back hit the wall. Now the girl ran playfully with the small flashlight bobbing between her chest and the bounce in her step. She climbed the small incline of the corridor and shined the light on the Spartan.

A good look at the scrawny girl revealed noodles of braided hair. Her shirt hung far below her knees, and she wore her hijab like a hoodie—it hung low on her forehead, so low that her eyes barely blinked out from underneath. The yolks of her eyes were drops of chocolate. Her smile was spaced out into tiny gaps.

"Daw," she said, and Paxton leaned in, trying to understand, but this wasn't English. The girl held the flashlight; it was large and she used two hands, as if offering it to him. "Daw?"

"Flashlight?" Paxton said, but without any audio output on the Spartan body, she wouldn't hear a word. "I can see, little girl. Go home."

"Daw!" She shouted it now, seemingly wanting him to take the flashlight. "En daw!"

Paxton eyed the muddy lagoon behind the girl and the path beyond. There had to be others, and whoever they were, they weren't far off, just minutes away, if that, and Paxton didn't want to shoot some South African civvy, or Sudanese, or Afghan, or wherever the fuck she was.

"Okay," Paxton said.

He moved the Spartan's hand to take the flashlight. He pinched it from her fingers as gently as he could, trying not to crush either her hand or the plastic flashlight handle. The girl smiled and spit an entire sentence of her dialect at the Spartan, drool dribbling out of her mouth with each word, yellow mucus hanging on the ring of her nostril.

"Okay," Paxton said, knowing she wouldn't hear. "Go back." The Spartan maneuvered around the bend in the wall and took a few more steps back, but the girl followed, wide eyed and wide mouthed, screaming happily at the top of her lungs. *Fuck.*

The Spartan stepped farther back, and the girl kept pace. She seemed ready to follow it all the way back to the sandbox. He had to do something. The Spartan stopped and leaned toward the girl, lifted a single finger, and nudged her, as gently as possible. The girl stumbled backward and tripped and crashed ass first against the dirt. She looked at him, eyes wide, full of awe and inquiry, then she exploded in laughter, holding tight to her stomach as if it tickled.

"Harum!"

The girl stopped laughing as she turned to the call of a name, her name in all likelihood, from a husky holler in the distance. There were other words too, but foreign, the same spiel of dislocated vowels and consonants that the girl had used.

The girl, *Harum*, raced toward an individual descending a stairway of crushed concrete and twisted steel, a jagged path that led out into the world beyond. As the stranger moved closer, Paxton saw a woman nearly twice his age. A backpack weighed on her shoulders, two massive rifles hung from her arms, but she didn't hunch or drag her feet. The woman was an old oak, her arms dense branches, her skin tan with wrinkles cracking like scales of bark.

The girl ran the length of the woman's shadow, stretching long from a sun that was setting beyond the rubble stairway. She wrapped herself around the old woman's trunk and sputtered with conversation.

The girl pointed into the shadows—pointing to a Spartan that wasn't there anymore. Paxton had retreated back but remained close enough to watch through infrared and zooming lenses.

The old woman didn't offer much attention to the girl's tantrum, giving the shadows less than a glance, then wrapping her wrinkled fingers around the girl's arm and tugging her toward the exit above. But Harum tugged back. She pointed and shrieked, but none of the words moved the old woman, except one.

"Daw!"

The flashlight sat about twenty feet or so in front of the Spartan's toes and shone in the old woman's direction. The woman glanced back at the wink of light, and she seemed to consider whether it was even worth going back for. But as Harum nearly choked on her own tears, the old woman dropped her backpack and rifles and approached. The only thing in her hand was the girl's arm.

Harum continued her large gestures, mimicking something big and heavy, and she mimicked it well. Paxton saw the obvious reference to the Spartan but grimaced as the subtle details of her pantomime began to convince the old woman too. Each exaggerated movement slowed the woman's steps to a crawl, then to a pause, and then she stopped altogether.

The woman tugged on the back of Harum's shirt and whispered something that sent the little girl running playfully back to her puddle. She exchanged the girl's arm for the larger of the two rifles, a long-barreled cannon with a fat muzzle—tank-buster rounds. Just the two of them now, separated by a long corridor, ink black in shadow.

The Spartan lifted its own rifle, but so slowly, so quietly, gripping the handle and pressing the butt against its shoulder. But Paxton didn't want a fight, because there wouldn't be one. The Spartan had infrared; it had laser sights, titanium armor, and bullets the size of the old woman's fists. But mostly he didn't want to fight because he had never killed anyone, besides maybe his mother, bleeding her out with his first breath. He couldn't do it, could he?

His trigger finger shook; his weapon wavered in his uncertainty.

But hers didn't. The old woman lifted her rifle steadily and aimed into the black. She aimed blindly yet with a level of control, firm grip yet loose enough to pivot, slowly swinging her weapon back and forth, back, then forth. The woman moved in a low military-style crouch, shoulders in, elbows tucked. She had training.

"Shhh," Paxton hushed the Spartan's finger as it wormed around the trigger, the whisper of metal clinking against metal. And the old woman stopped right there as if she heard something—*no*, it was a smell. Her nostrils flared. She sniffed. Paxton didn't know if the Androns had a particular smell to them, but it was the scent that seemed to turn her old expression in on itself. The old woman squinted hard, wrinkles cratered in around the hollow of her eyes. Regardless of the woman's prowess or the Spartan's weakness in comparison to other Androns, she was no match for a War Machine, and she had to know it. Paxton prayed that she did.

"Please don't," he pleaded, praying to her, his momentary goddess. "*Please.*"

The old woman glanced back at the girl waiting in the puddle, then returned her eyes to the thick dead of dark, appearing to consider whether to go deeper, meet the Spartan, or return for the girl. Paxton held his breath as she mulled—him or her?

She chose the girl. The old woman backed out of the narrow space. Her feet were heavy, splashing in the puddle. She picked up everything—rifles, backpacks, the lamp, and even the girl—and paced up the stairway of rubble. She didn't hunch or slow her pace; her posture was like an ancient oak tree, her arms narrow but branches fibrous, and the lean of the sunlight stretched her shadow back fifty feet or more.

Paxton panted, oxygen heavy in his lungs; he hadn't taken a single breath. He hadn't blinked either, and his eyes fluttered, a teary red. The Spartan's finger had vined around that trigger, and it took a full minute for him to unravel it. He would have killed her. He would have snapped that trigger back and watched her die. The same as Sergeant Woden or Lieutenant Ogun; he was no different, Paxton realized it now. The symbiosis of him and the machine was nearly complete. He would have fought for the Spartan's life and killed someone. And if Paxton continued venturing out into these wilds, he would eventually have to.

22

He would have followed them if he could, but time didn't allow it. Paxton boomeranged back to the sandbox and left the Spartan in a guiltless position in the sand. He skipped dinner, opting instead for the comforts of his pillow and the droopy mattress. But he overslept that evening, his dreams running longer than average. Paxton took an unconscious expedition beyond the black hole in the desert, beyond the tunnels and graffiti, beyond the narrow corridor and the little girl's puddle, and up that stairway of crushed concrete. And when he woke up, he climbed into the cockpit and did the same thing, traversing the desert and tunnels and up the rubble stairway, and there, in the light of a setting sun, civilization returned.

It was a city, or a blueprint for a city—that was what it looked like, a planned metropolis cut short by war. Unpaved streets ran in circles and street signs pointed to nowhere. Everest-size towers stretched taller than anything he'd ever seen in the skyscraper capital, New York City, but no windows, no doors or color, just structures climbing up to nowhere.

"Where the fuck are we?" Paxton said, but not to himself; he said *we*, he and the Spartan, recognizing the companion literally holding his hands for the first time.

The streets were abandoned—beyond the occasional ghosts of sand lifting off the dirt, nothing moved. Still, Paxton blanketed the Spartan in every shadow extending from buildings, walls, or mounds of debris piled like blockades in the road. After each deserted block, he thought up a new reason why the world was so empty—nuclear fallout, famine, biological outbreak. But by the fourth block, the answer came right into view.

Sonic thunder lashed down, contrails lacerated the sky, as a pair of Furies streaked violently overhead. Paxton trembled, and his Spartan shadow shuddered. The US military was in full force. Fort Bragg had approved the aid to Nellis Base with an additional four hundred aerial drones, while Fort Hood (Lieutenant Ogun's Texas-based bastion) afforded Colonel Marson ground-based War Machines, both Androne and quadrupedal.

The patrol was heavy. A second aerial smoke trail streaked to the north, and another sonic boom echoed toward the east. Marson had more than doubled his efforts in the search for the collaborator, and just as of today, Sergeant Woden and Lieutenant Ogun were reportedly closing in.

If this collaborator had butchered a top-twenty-rank pilot like Bella and her SPQR Series, Paxton and his baby Spartan didn't stand much of a chance. Every corner he rounded reminded him of that, the paranoia of running face-first into the demigod rogue War Machine. Yet in the back corner of his mind, Paxton wondered if his fear of the collaborator wasn't only because he knew he couldn't stand up to it, but also because he had an idea of who this pilot might be.

Lieutenant Victoria knew about the signal-jamming marble in Paxton's possession. She had it in her hand and gave it back to him. Her agenda wasn't clear, but she knew things. And if she wasn't the collaborator herself, Victoria likely knew who he or she was.

Night was settling in. Ghostly breezes swept up dust devils, and theatrical lighting leaned hard against skyscrapers, shadows toppling over into the streets. Paxton estimated he'd have another half hour before he needed to turn back. He had given up on the stopwatch; he had a feeling for it now, something in his gut that churned when the moment was right. He kept his eye in the sky, black swamps of cloud bubbling overhead, and if he zoomed deep enough through the layers of fatty, inked cumulus, he could see his satellite swinging in orbit overhead. That link, that *keyhole* between him and his Spartan, mesmerized Paxton, distracted him, and that was how he missed it. That was how it found him.

Two white suns exploded at the dark end of an alley. The Spartan immediately stripped its rifle from its sleeve, but it was clumsy, indecisive, unsure if this light was one of them or one of us. The Androne took precious seconds to adjust to the light and then he saw it—*us*; a quadrupedal with heavy iron legs, a bulldog rudder tail, and a tommy gun rib cage bulging at its sides. The quadrupedal galloped toward the Spartan, past the Spartan, swirled around the Spartan's body like a planet in orbit, and in an instant was right behind it. Paxton swung around on his steering and the Spartan pirouetted, trying to aim on spinning legs. But before he tugged on the trigger, Paxton realized the quadrupedal wasn't attacking; it was hiding. Hiding behind its Spartan ally. It had a tear on its left hind leg and cracks crawling across its optics lens. The quad was running, but from what?

"Collaborator," Paxton said, maybe to himself, maybe to his Spartan.

He heard approaching machinery and saw a dull light in the distance, sharpening in brightness as it came closer. The Spartan lunged backward, ramming through a window, and wall, of a nearby shack, leaving the quad to fend for itself.

The shack felt like another time zone. Full dark. No light. Strings of vine had twined into spaces on the ceiling. Weeds vomited up from cracks in the floor. Dust particles and mold spores sailed about the complicated air. The Spartan backpedaled to the darkest corner of the space, pressing its back against the wall—against a painting, a pregnant woman holding a flambeau in the dark.

A buggy skidded around the corner, topless and door-free, the three occupants inside hanging on to their seats as the half-naked vehicle circled around the back of the quadrupedal. First they hit it with high beams, catching the mechanical deer in its headlights; then a gunshot cracked the other hind leg. The quadrupedal floundered back as the buggy careened toward it. Its front bumper smashed into the quad and it piñataed across the road.

It wasn't the collaborator—just civvies, just scavengers, two passengers on the back, a young woman behind the wheel. The men hopped out, scrawny with long, graying beards melting off middle-aged chins. The woman, meatier than either of her male cohorts, sat behind the wheel with her neck craned up toward the sky, likely keeping an eye out for aerial drones.

The men moved fast, snatching up parts, any and everything, the legs, the tails, the ligaments in between. They shoved the scraps into backpacks but soon realized the real prize was still alive.

The head and the front legs of the quadrupedal crawled across the pavement toward the hole torn into the shack; it was crawling toward its Spartan ally.

The pilot of that quadrupedal was likely expecting the Spartan's assist. But Paxton wasn't performing any heroics this far outside his sandbox. Even on his home court he would have found it difficult to gun down a trio of civilians. Technically, it would be easy. The Spartan's stabilizers (they called it steady-cam) eliminated most of the shakiness from the pilot's hands. He could end all three lives in a second and a half, and they wouldn't know what hit them. But Paxton was just as terrified of gunning down civilians as these scavengers would be of seeing his Spartan. So he crouched and prayed it wouldn't come to that.

The two men hacked wildly at the neck of the quad, decapitating it with dull axes. The machine convulsed; its starry eyes faded. The top of the quad's spine split and the head rolled; bloodred sparks lit the dark. The men towed the carcass back to the buggy. *Hunter-gatherers*, Paxton thought, watching them tie their metal meat into a fishing net at the back of the buggy.

Paxton lowered the Spartan's rifle as the driver sped off, then he wondered—*Could the Spartan keep pace?* He didn't wonder long. He pushed the pedal to fifty miles per hour and the Spartan trampled the terrain, keeping up and still keeping its distance.

Overheard Penthouse conversation suggested the collaborator was in league with a certain sect of civvies. The odds that this bunch belonged to the collaborator was low enough. And still, Paxton wasn't sure if he wanted to take that low chance.

The few logos left on the buildings were as foreign to Paxton as Swahili or ancient Greek yet felt Eastern to him for some reason, neither Oriental nor Arabian but somewhere between, where the Far East and Middle East crossed. Africa seemed as farfetched now as Australia had been a week earlier. Where the fuck was he?

The city deteriorated the deeper in he followed. Building tops appeared to be bitten off with pointed, jagged summits. Other towers, cracked at their bases, leaned against sturdier skyscrapers like domino pieces. Belly-up steamboats drifted through flooded roads, salt water from an expanding ocean.

The War Machine patrol thinned, nearly all gone, except for a single close call with another Spartan. It was strange, looking in from the outside. Was his Spartan that frightening a thing, that massive an anatomy of metal? The civvies thought so, spotting *that* Spartan on the crest of the road and careening hard down the opposite street. But that Spartan either didn't see them or didn't care; scavengers like these were more pest than true threats.

The buggy skidded to a stop underneath a garage of piled-up concrete that sheltered pairs of other vehicles. They carried their spoils into an adjacent structure, what could be best described as a colosseum—Western architecture with columns and arches towering a hundred feet high.

To get a better look, Paxton would need altitude. An adjacent skyscraper, half bombed out, would do. Countless punctures had deflated it into slabs of slanted, twisted brick, barely standing, barely there. But it would do.

The building's interior was a graveyard of stray dogs and scavenger birds. The stairwell was torn out in places. The Spartan leaped over gaps in the ground where it could, and when it couldn't, when three full flights of stairs lay in a rubble pile in front of it, the Spartan spread its limbs against the walls of an elevator shaft and spider-crawled the last few floors.

The top floor was ripped off, and black skies hovered just a mile above. A man lay in the corner of the floor, his body pale and face smashed in. The blood on the floor had dried up around him, and one of those scavenger birds had started to peck at the soft gel of his eyes. The Spartan stepped over him and made its way to the edge, now some fifty-four floors up. It offered a vista of the entire city and a perfect peephole into the colosseum.

The colosseum—or *stadium*, now that he got a better look—was half filled with water. A nearby tributary had overflowed and drowned out the inside, making a fish tank of the old sports arena. Countless tiny boats meandered peacefully inside with lanterns lit like fireflies over the water. The stadium's stands, on the other hand, were dry, and elaborate tents towered tall in the renovated space. Computer keyboards and rusted car tires hung almost like decoration above the wide entrances. And light shone in those tents too—not lanterns, but torches, all built out of Androne or quadrupedal limbs.

Just a few minutes of bird's-eye observation revealed status and culture. The young danced for the elders, bowing and gesturing artfully. Those in the tents seemed to have brighter and cleaner clothing than those in the boats. A little more observation revealed the Old Oak—the woman from the day before—and the little girl, carrying a bowl of fruit between her and an elderly man dressed in worn-out robes. They had created a nice oasis for themselves amid all the devastation. A sprawl of grapevines ran along the ceiling. A garden of colored shrubs bore fruit, and various other plants thrived along the rim of the stadium walls. It seemed nice, until Paxton looked a little closer.

It was just a word, splayed wide across the side of the stadium wall, a simple word—how hadn't he seen it earlier, when the sunlight actually offered something? Now the shadows and infrared made the word appear ominous, eight foreboding letters half smeared in grime and rust, dirt and vegetation, but still legible. BASEBALL.

"Base . . . ball?" Paxton whispered to himself, like the English word was foreign and difficult to pronounce. "The fuck?"

And that opened his eyes to other words hidden in corrosion: PARKING, TICKETS, SEATING. Paxton strained his eyes into the stadium's flooded interior: the stands, the floating boats—this was a baseball stadium, the dugout and diamond flooded underneath the fishbowl lake.

Baseball, a sport already in the twilight of American popular culture. So where now? Cuba, Japan, Dominican Republic? He was quickly running out of nation-states to fit the puzzle piece of the cityscape.

"Where the fuck is this?"

Paxton thought he felt that biological alarm clock rattling inside of him—*time to go*, but no, that was his heart banging inside his chest. The anxiety of utter confusion. The time to leave had come and gone, but that didn't matter anymore. Paxton stretched the Spartan's eye farther, beyond the stadium to an all-too-familiar bridge. It changed everything. It made him pause for nearly twenty minutes, zooming in and out of every screw and beam. It was undeniably recognizable. What it looked like to him was a failed replica of the Golden Gate Bridge, half-collapsed and broken in its center.

"That's . . ." Paxton stopped short of saying *impossible*, but it was.

The impossible scale of the bridge, a one-to-one replica of the bridge he'd crossed just weeks earlier. The impossible detail on the San Francisco Giants baseball stadium. *Impossible*, he thought. What were these monuments and this made-up city? The questions tightened in Paxton's fist, the Spartan also clenching its metal hand as if mad at this world.

Laughter exploded from behind the Androne. The man Paxton had thought dead cackled, his laughter twisted as he gargled, choking on his own saliva. A hobo, in all likelihood, alcohol dried on his thorny beard and sunburned lips. He crouched in a corner with that haunting clattering of teeth and gums. And the laughter would follow Paxton, down the tower's stairwell, then echoing in through the tunnels, and all the way back to the sandbox, and even out through the cockpit doors to his bunk and bedsheets.

Could it be another simulation? *Maybe.* He had fought in those training sims just weeks earlier, but then how did they simulate the civvies? Could it be that advanced? The confusion made him sweat, liquid fear squeezing out of every pore. Why it frightened him, Paxton wasn't sure, but every nerve stood on edge, every heartbeat palpitating. Paxton didn't know what was real anymore, he knew nothing—*nothing*, except that dread beating into his chest.

23

The blanket twisted around him—leg locks, arm bars. Pillows smothered his breathing, pinching at his nostrils and lips. The bedsprings lashed at his back, and he squirmed around the mattress. There would be no sleep that night, not until he figured out what *the fuck* was going on. He had to see Lieutenant Victoria. No more beating around the bush—he had to know the truth of everything tonight.

It was just after midnight. The brownout was in effect; it snuffed out streetlights and any fluorescent shine inside the windows. Paxton couldn't see anything more than ten feet ahead and didn't recall the path to the lieutenant's trailer. He stumbled in the dark, lost, still feeling the thick cockpit pedals under his feet and the gloves on his palms and wrists. It'd take a couple of hours to shake off that cockpit posture.

But Paxton was willing to check every single trailer, sort through every lieutenant, captain, and major, until he found her. He'd make her talk this time. No more of the evasive, half-assed half answers—she'd tell him everything.

The brass's trailers didn't seem to have brownout regulations, and Paxton found a light shining in a familiar window, with familiar curtains and a familiar antenna on its roof. Had he found her in the dark, just like that? Paxton didn't hesitate or double-check. He pedaled up the stairs and barged in.

". . . gain a decade in ground—" a voice said, then stopped as Paxton stepped inside.

Eighteen eyes steered toward him all at once, eighteen pairs of arms and legs swiveled toward him. Generals, strategists, and the colonel himself watched Paxton with curious eyes. Victoria sat behind her desk, the sight of Paxton appearing to make her nauseous.

"Sergeant Arés?" Colonel Marson said as Paxton half considered stumbling back outside. "What are you doing here?"

"I needed to, uh . . ." His mind raced in that split-second stumble of the tongue. "Needed to ask the lieutenant about my office hours."

"This late?" Lieutenant Victoria chimed in, and leaned back, her swivel chair pivoting her left and right.

"The old man," Paxton said, not even sure how to finish the sentence. "He said, uh . . . the baby's not well." Paxton said the words and hated himself immediately, but suddenly all those hard stares thawed away, all except for hers.

"Jesus, boy," Colonel Marson said, his expression swelling red with compassion. "Is it serious?"

"It'll be okay, but I may need some extra time away from the office. For now at least."

"Take all the time you need," Victoria said, forcing a smile as she gestured for him to exit.

"No, wait," Marson said, gesturing for Paxton to come forward. "I want to show you something."

The other higher ranks watched Paxton's approach like rabid dogs, malnourished and ravenous and ready to bite. But Colonel Marson continued pulling at the air with a wave of his hand, smiling, inviting with the sheet of paper in his hand.

"What's your rank, son?" a big-bellied colonel asked Paxton while shooting a suspicious look at his godfather.

"Sergeant, sir," Victoria answered for him.

"Sergeant," the general said, disappointed, but not in Paxton; he aimed his derision at Marson. He tilted his disk-shaped body at an angle, eclipsing classified papers on the desk with the crest of his belly, hiding them from Paxton's view.

Marson's expression tightened, staring into the eyes of the general. There was something between these men, a history of politics and maneuvering that Paxton could only guess at. The two old men eyed each other like gunslingers in the desert.

"This young man's gonna have your job in twenty years, Wendell," Marson said, staring at Paxton as if trying to figure something out, calculating as his eyes narrowed to a squint. It took a second or two, but Marson eventually found a literally eye-opening epiphany. His eyes widened and as he spoke, he smiled. "You'll be getting your lieutenant bars tomorrow."

"Tomorrow?" Paxton said, surprised. "But—"

"I'll make it happen," Marson said, shooting a glance over to Wendell. "You put in your time. We'll get the old man and your lady to come out too, if she's well enough for travel."

"At tomorrow's commissioning ceremony?" Lieutenant Victoria said. "A little last minute."

"We'll make it happen," he said again. "Arés is ready."

Tomorrow? It was all too much, too fast for Paxton to take in. He had at least forty office hours left, plus exams, swear-ins, and the ceremony. Paxton might even have said no, but Marson immediately changed the subject.

"Few of us are young enough to have ever even piloted quadrupedals," Marson said. "The majority of us have never even stepped foot in a cockpit. We need the opinion of a pilot. And young Arés here would have been making lieutenant by what . . . ?" Marson paused and turned to Victoria.

He'd caught her off guard, but she recovered gracefully. "At his pace I'd say end of the month," Victoria said and turned to Paxton. "Right?"

"Give or take," Paxton said, and Victoria must have noticed something in his tone, an impatience maybe, like he had something more pressing to say. She watched him now; in fact, she couldn't take her eyes off him.

Marson showed Paxton a topographical map and aimed unclipped fingernails at red circles drawn onto it. "How fast would it take an Androne to cover that distance?"

"Hour, sir," Paxton said, and gauged their reactions—eyebrows rising, heads shaking—but he insisted. "Piloting a Spartan, I've done it in an hour."

"In your sandbox?"

"No." Paxton said it so quickly it sounded like he was correcting a mistake, and he was. He was incriminating himself. *Stay in your fucking sandbox*, he thought. "But I assume for that landscape, an hour at most."

"How?" Wendell asked. "In a Spartan of all things."

"Wind at my back?" Paxton asked, and they agreed. "I'd lean into the run, tighten the body to push off the wind. Just aerodynamics."

"And in something stronger than a Spartan?" Marson asked. "How fast then?"

"If they dropped their rifle, munitions, and armor, they could cover that ground in forty-five minutes."

"For sure?" Marson asked.

"For sure."

"We believe the collaborator's piloting a Kingsman Series as its weapon implies, but Sergeant Woden and the fellow from Fort Hood, what's his name . . . ?"

"Lieutenant Ogun," Paxton said.

"That's it," Marson agreed. "They're closing in."

"Good," Paxton lied, still wanting the collaborator for himself.

"I'll go ahead and set your new hours now, Sergeant," Victoria said, then turned to the colonel. "Colonel, perhaps we reconvene tomorrow?"

Colonel Marson nodded. He lifted his arm to a lazy salute. All the old men exhaled long, heavy sighs, like convicts awaiting escape. They stretched their tangled joints and fumbled for handshakes. They dwindled in small talk, one by one, thinning the space between Paxton and Victoria, until there were none. Colonel Marson was the last to step out into the middle of the night, leaving with another halfhearted salute aimed at Paxton.

"Good night, *Lieutenant* Arés." And he was gone. And they were alone.

Paxton turned hard toward her the second the door clicked shut. "*You're* the collaborator," he said, the words nearly vomiting out of him, his face screwed with rancor.

"*Shhh,*" Victoria hushed him and pulled the curtain shut behind her. "They have spies! Everywhere!"

"Jesus Christ, *you are*, aren't you," Paxton hissed. "And that's not even what I'm here for."

"What the hell *are* you here for Paxton?" Victoria got into his face. Insomnia sprawled red across the whites of her eyes.

"Where are we?" Paxton said.

"Where?"

"In the cockpit. Where are we? I've been out of my sandbox, as I'm sure you know."

"I don't."

"As I'm sure you expected."

She smiled. "Maybe."

"I've seen things. Skyscrapers. A first-world country. Baseball stadiums. A replica of the Golden Gate Bridge. Where is that? Where are we?"

The lieutenant turned her back on Paxton and flopped down in her seat as if she were suddenly ten pounds heavier. Victoria lifted a rum bottle from the bottom drawer of her desk, Mount Gay, a forty ounce. Yellow liquid belly-danced around the half-empty waist of the bottle. Victoria poured herself a shot-glassful, then aimed the bottle at Paxton.

"No," he said.

"Ballsy, what you did just now. Ballsy!" She drank to that. Her cheeks swelled as she sloshed it around on her tongue. "Ahhh!" Redness lifted into her cheeks. "You've gotten ambitious. All this first lieutenant talk, skipping a whole rung on the ladder, very ambitious. I used to be ambitious too. Like you. Took shrapnel in my left thumb. I can barely hear out of my right ear. All for this. To sit here."

"Answer the question," Paxton said. "Where are we? And what is the War Machine Program?"

Victoria's exhale, heavy and several seconds too long, was already half of that answer. The air leaving her body deflated her, shoulders, neck, all of it sagging in a sort of surrender. Her defenses—defensiveness, her worming her way around the questions, all of it was done.

"Right after the Ninety-Nine, I'm talking the week of, when I was a little younger than you are now, top brass thought it fitting to put one of their top recruits in a cell with a man who they found out was a Trojan horse, a traitor working with the other side. That top recruit was just supposed to watch him, feed him, but not supposed to listen to a thing he said, because he knew. He knew everything. And he told her everything. She tried not to listen, but what he told her was the answer to what everyone wants to know."

"Who we're fighting."

She nodded. "Right."

"Who?"

"If I tell you now, there's no going back, Paxton. Once you know, you know."

"Just tell me, already."

"It's not Colonel Sanders's secret recipe."

"I understand that."

"No, you don't!" Her voice exploded through the room. "You won't understand *until* you know. I didn't get this chance, and I wish . . . I wish I didn't know. I wish I could walk around here with the same jar-headed daze everyone else does. This is Pandora's box. There's no closing it back up. I want you to think about this. *Think!* Do you really want the burden of knowing?"

Paxton paused as Callie and the baby came to mind. Classified knowledge might endanger him from ever seeing them again. But then he thought of what he had seen: the bombed-out replica city, the hunter-gatherers, the fishbowl city in a baseball stadium, and the hobo's laughter still taunting him. It felt like hunger for the head, a growling of the mind. Paxton didn't want to know; he needed to.

"Tell me," he said. "I'm ready." And he could see the muscles in her face untwine and knots in her joints melt away. She was ready too.

"Okay," the lieutenant said, and took a final sip of the liquor still wet around the bottom of the glass. "*Okay!* Where to begin?" She paused. She recovered. "Your cockpit. When you pilot, a signal is sent from this base to a satellite and—"

"I know how it works," he interrupted.

"No," she snapped. "You don't. The signals are sent to the satellite but aren't bounced back down immediately. It hits the satellite and it stays there. Locked in place." She points up. "Every steer left, every steer right. Every footstep and full stop. Every movement you've piloted is still there, locked in that satellite. It hasn't been sent anywhere."

"How? I've seen it."

She grimaced then, either in frustration or angst. Her posture had crunched in on itself, and she hadn't seemed to notice. This was it. Like she said, there was no going back after this.

"The signals are set to be held in the satellite for years, decades. And after a couple hundred years or more, who knows, the signals are going to be shot back down into an Androne that hasn't even been built yet. The visual image you see isn't from today. That's why it takes so much power. That's why we're running on nine power plants, solar panels, generators, brownouts, and—"

"Wait—Wait . . ." Paxton interrupted with his hand in her face defensively, as if the lieutenant were aiming a weapon at his ears. "What the fuck are you saying?"

"Who we're fighting, Paxton—it's the future. We're at war with the future."

PART II

24

"First Lieutenant Paxton Victor Arés." He blared it over the speaker, blasting Paxton's name across the auditorium. Residual information like class, merit, and locality were drowned out by a detonation of applause.

Paxton lifted himself off the cold steel chair and strutted the aisle like a bride in his formal service wear. Colonel Marson stood at the podium, a godfather beaming with pride. He clipped a lieutenant's bars onto Paxton's uniform, then pulled him in for a strong embrace.

"You're one of us now," Marson whispered. "You're in."

In? Paxton had been "in on it" for the better part of the day, and for the past fifteen hours now her words had played in his head—a *war with the future.* This was the Enigma Campaign, this was World War Who, and as hard as it was to believe, he believed every word of it. The way Victoria had said it: the angst, the conviction, spooked by her very own words, afraid someone was listening; she had banished Paxton from her office without an explanation or another word. War with the future, that was all he knew. And even now, in the midst of celebration and advancement, Paxton's every synapse brooded on the true, terrifying nature of the conflict.

He'd been piecing it together, mental Jenga blocks, pulling from the bottom of his memory and fitting them on the top. Like the discussion on the nuclear reactors a couple of weeks ago—that made sense now. The power required to relay images from the future, however the fuck it was done, sounded about nine reactors worthy. The sandbox protocols, the unknown Androne locations, the secrecy and paranoia floating through the ranks . . . it all made sense.

What didn't make sense—that one Jenga block that tilted his thoughts toward total collapse—was why did he know when none of the other noncommissioned officers did? Why did Captain Laran give him the marble, why did Victoria take him on the tour—*Why, fucking, me?* He thought about it, and kept on thinking. Thinking that he was fast approaching the inner circle, too fast, on the threshold, pinned and striped, and that this revelation was only the beginning.

Thirty-six enlisted men and women had graduated to officer that afternoon, but none more meteoric than Paxton. The freshly minted first lieutenant had risen two levels in rank in a single ceremony, and Colonel Marson made sure he told any constituent willing to listen. The colonel flaunted Paxton like a newborn and didn't hide the nepotism. *The godson,* he would say as they zigzagged through navy and air force correspondents.

Family was in attendance. Callie, pregnant as ever, was wrapped in an emerald-green dress to match her eyes. The old man donned leather shoes and a belt, his satin tie, and his blue beret. But his muscle and height had trafficked to the bulges around his waist and neck, and the sleeves were like long noodles dangling over his wrists.

"Melting away in this thing," the old man said as he pulled at his collar like a noose on his damp neck. "How do you handle these functions on the regular?"

"A little sip of the old yellow burn," Marson said as he rocked a champagne glass of gold liqueur in his palm.

"Galliano," the old man said. "Never change."

"It's the fuel to my motor," he said, then toasted to the old man. They fell into a liqueur-fueled nostalgia about the old wars: the Gulf's Umm Qasr beaches, the Sri Lankan hookers, the Congolese moonshine. "Confidential," the colonel said, turning to Paxton. "All confidential."

He left them to their recollections and drifted through the network of mingling bodies, dodging handshakes and small talk to get back to her. Callie sat alone, resting her eyes, shoes half-off, kneading her knuckles into the dough of her hips. The old dress stretched around every inch of her swollen body; even her feet, naked from their high-heel girdles, had inflated, plump and purple from the heel to the toes.

"Did you eat?" she said without even a peek out of her closed eyes. "You look thinner."

"You too," Paxton said, and smiled as dimples fell into her cheeks.

"I have something for you," Callie said.

She scratched at the flimsy handles of a blue plastic bag underneath her seat. It read WHOLE FOODS and suffered a number of punctures toward the bottom. She pulled out edibles wrapped in foil and strapped in rubber bands. He could smell the deep-fried dough as she handed it to him. With these was a gift dressed in old Christmas wrapping paper, green and red with white snowflakes.

"What is it?" Paxton asked, reaching for the edges of the wrapping paper where he could fit his finger underneath.

"Don't open it now," she said. "Wait until I leave."

"Why?"

"If you don't like it . . ." Callie shrugged and lowered her gaze.

He nearly smiled. It would have been the first time today. Callie almost made him forget. She almost let him neglect that tomorrow he'd climb into an Androne cockpit and stare out into a wasteland future. *Almost*, but that thought stayed in his peripherals, warlords on front lines a hundred years north of now.

"Pax?" She caught him musing.

"Sorry," he said, remembering the gift in his hand. He held it up to his ear and shook it. "This lingerie?" he joked.

She smiled. "Maybe it is."

"You're not spending your uncle's money, are you?"

"A little bit," she said. "Just enough for this."

"Don't do that," he said.

Uncle Winal was six months into a two-year sentence but had given her a couple thousand dubious dollars for the baby before lockup.

"I don't need anything here," Paxton continued. "They give me all the necessary stuff."

"It's unnecessary. I saw it and I thought, *you*. You know?"

"You missed me," Paxton said, forcing a grin through the side of his cheek.

Callie blushed. She lowered her head and hung the entire bag of foil-wrapped foods on a single finger and dangled it out in front of him. Paxton leaned in with puckered lips, but she shook her head and recoiled away. *Always the prude*, his Callie.

"Why don't we save the awards for after," Colonel Marson said, scowling at the plastic bag and its foiled contents. He had sobered up enough to regain his American regality, that military posture, that soft southern drawl. He stood near attention with another old man he had yet to introduce. "This is Dr. Pallas."

The man was ancient—liver-spotted leopard skin, gray hair, gray-eyed cataracts, a frame whittled down to skin and bone. A man likely of South Asian descent based on the lapels on his dress jacket. Paxton had seen him somewhere before, but he couldn't quite put his finger on it.

"Nice to meet you," the ancient man said. "Paxton?"

"Yes, Sergeant—*no*, Lieutenant Paxton Arés."

"Pallas here," Marson started, "is the creator of the Androne Satellite Relay Systems. The true father of the War Machine Program."

"Arges," Pallas said as he shook his head, loose skin flapping under his neck. "Arges and his robotics team created the War Machines. Called it the War Machine Program." He took a breath. "My sciences are far, far afield from robotics."

"What types of science *do* you study?" Paxton asked.

"Quantum theory," he said. "Boring substance."

"Theory?" Paxton said, knowing it couldn't be further from. There were no more theories in this world anymore; every fictional science was possible. If he could see the future, then the rest, that should be easy.

It was then, under an arbitrary bend of the light and a crook in the ancient man's glare, that Paxton recalled where he had seen this face before—or a younger version of it. A training video. On the first day in the cockpits; the same Filipino flags in the background, the same erudite affections. It was him. A past him.

Pallas too appeared, in that moment, to glean something from Paxton's look. He leaned in to take a closer glare at Paxton's eyes, giving him a look of recognition. "How informed are you on the program?"

"Nothing classified," Marson said, and said it quickly. "But he'll get there."

"I hope I get to see the day," Pallas said, and seemed to think about it. His eyes drifted up to the embrace of high-arched ceilings—splintering, thinning mahogany curved like rib cages—before climbing back down to meet Paxton's gaze. "Paxton . . . I know you."

"Know . . . *me*?" Paxton said, confused both by the wording and the look in Pallas's eyes. "I don't understand," he said, then added, "sir."

"Your hackery of my systems, how else? You are consorting with the enemy."

Paxton pulled back half a step as the hundred-eyed monster of well-dressed patrons turned their gazes toward him. Pallas took an unsteady half step forward, not letting Paxton out of this cataract sight. *How did he know?* Paxton wondered so fervently that he nearly whispered it aloud, lips miming, tongue floundering. How did this wild-eyed old man know anything about what he was doing?

"Frederick Niet," Pallas said, his liver-spotted finger jittering as he pointed at Paxton. "Frederick! Still stowing away secrets."

A crowd had gathered, pointing, whispering, less like individuals but not quite a mob, not yet. Two men emerged from the pack of bodies, younger than Paxton and bigger, their physiques swelling underneath their uniforms. Their strides were long and veered directly toward him. It was a well-choreographed ambush to say the least. The crowd opened up, Pallas stepped aside. Callie and the old man watched from a distance.

He regretted it all in an instant: the curiosity, that marble, the sandbox trespass, and most of all the ego, that blowfish fucking ego. Jostling for rank and status was one thing, but the sanctimony of believing he might make a difference, that he might be the one to end a war. *Fuck!* The fucking ego.

Military prison ranked among his greatest fears. Like Uncle Winal, he'd be counting against time—counting for his time to run out. And what type of life would that be? And then there was the old man's legacy, and Callie, poor Callie. Even with the urge to turn to her one last time, he couldn't.

"I just watched them," Paxton pleaded to the brawny men, to Pallas, to anyone who would listen.

But they didn't. The men grabbed on either of Pallas's shoulders and gently tugged him back. "Give him some space," one of them said, then repeated, "give him some space."

"Sorry," Marson said. "He has episodes."

"Episodes?" Paxton said.

"Dementia. The onset of Alzheimer's."

Dementia—that sounded about right. He should have seen it in the old man's eyes, in the slur of his words, but Paxton's panicked, oxygen-starved brain couldn't piece it together. So he breathed now, finally, deeper than he ever had.

"Watched who?" Marson asked him.

"Sorry, what?" Paxton said, but he knew exactly what Marson was referring to. Paxton's little slip about his voyeurism into the future—about watching *them*.

"You said, 'I just watched them.' Watched who?"

"I, uh," he hiccuped his words. "I just watch . . . the Androne. There's much more going on in the cockpit. So I just watch my Androne."

But Marson had already lost interest halfway through the sentence. They led Pallas away as the ancient man prattled on about a "peacemaker" and someone named "Mr. Niet." Callie and the old man exited just as promptly, needing to catch the last bus back to California. Paxton sneaked a kiss out of Callie under the sunset-stretched shadows. Their lips lingered and Callie, eyes wide open, stared at him as if feeling a deeper breath of passion. Might have been his relief from that imagined military prison still breathing through him. Or maybe it was just her, pushing him playfully and skipping up the steps on the bus.

The world was still simple for her and for the old man. Breakfast, TV, remembering to feed Hudson—*simple*. There would be no more simple days for him.

25

Paxton received an invitation from a male model of a cadet to report to Victoria's office. He hustled along the quickest path to her trailer door, but she wasn't even there. Door locked, lights off. Paxton leaned against the door and texted Callie to sleep; then he sat on the steps and YouTubed his cell phone to death. Hours after arriving at her office door, Paxton, with an encyclopedia of questions, considered going back. But Victoria arrived on cue, the sight of her relieving him to such a degree that he'd forgotten how long he had waited. She kicked off her heels at the door and whistled relief as her toes danced like earthworms on the ends of her feet.

"Meeting ran late," Victoria said. "And sorry about yesterday. Kicking you out after just giving up the tip of the iceberg. Paranoia's a sickness."

"All good," Paxton said. He understood now the weight she carried; it was enough to fracture vertebrae, a crippling thing, and still he wanted more. He wanted to know everything.

"We're dead even now, First Lieutenant," Victoria said, flopping down on her swivel throne. "Congratulations."

"You've still got tenure," he said.

"And I hope you remember that." She smiled and sniffled. "But I'm sorry I missed the ceremony. Was the general there?"

"Didn't see him, but this doctor was there, a doctor, uh—"

"Pallas," she said and sniffled again, this time running her palm across the rim of her nostrils. "You met the great Dr. Pallas."

"He has Alzheimer's now, so . . ." Paxton shrugged. "Mistook me for a guy named Frederick Niet."

She turned to him in a sudden, twisted, spastic jerk, as if waking up to a loud noise. Her mouth hung ajar. Her eyes opened to a slithering squint.

"What?" Paxton asked.

"No." She shook her head. "Nothing . . ." But it *was* something. Had to be. The way her gaze lingered just below the edges of eye contact and wandered there, leading her into a slow stupor. "All the big names," Victoria said, eyes still dizzy in thought. "You'll be running this place in a few years."

"Speaking of the future . . ." Paxton let the words hang. "You never told me how it works."

"It works," she said. "Isn't that enough?"

"No," he said. "*How* does it work?"

Victoria sat up. She fixed her posture until they sat face-to-face. "You won't understand," she said. "I don't understand."

"That's okay. I don't understand Spanish music, but I still like to listen to it."

She nodded, then leaned back, dissolving into the cushion. "Spooky action at a distance." Victoria said it and shrugged all at once. "That's what the Cooks call it. Quantum entanglement."

"I don't understand."

"*Sí,*" she said. "But you like to listen, right?" Victoria sloshed the saliva around her mouth, as if moistening her tongue for a verbal slog. "Entanglement has been described as a yin and yang for subatomic particles. When two particles interact, they can become entangled—linked, whether separated by space or time. Cooks on either side of time have entangled the photopic sensors on the Androne's optics with the photopic output in your cockpit today."

"Photopic?"

"Photons are particles of light. Like a . . ." Victoria seemed to struggle to find the simplest word. "The smallest, tiniest fraction of light is called a photon. So crudely speaking, the light sensors on Androns in the future are entangled or connected with the image output in your cockpit. A bridge of light basically, between future and present."

"And we control the future Androns with our satellites?"

"The satellites will still be orbiting, two, three hundred years from now. When your Androne is manufactured, long after we're all dead, and its signal is switched on, all your movement will be sent down into its receiver."

"Switched on by who?"

"The military has its 'continuity allies' in the coming centuries."

"Entangled light particles to see, satellites to control. It's two separate sciences." He felt like he was understanding.

"Yes, but that's an oversimplification, of course. There's something about retrocausality—future influence on the past. Something about no definite fixed location. But the end result is information from the future can be observed in the present."

"It works," Paxton said with a shrug, as if giving up.

"It works," she agreed.

"So how do they attack us?" Paxton asked. "The Ninety-Nine? How'd they do that?"

"Same way, but reverse-engineered. They hacked into our Androns and quadrupeds, the aerial drones, aquatics. They hacked into the drones we have today, controlling them from cockpits in the future."

"Huh," he said, too engrossed in the revelation to form a word.

"It's call quantum hacking. And they're still doing it. The naval sinking in Nigeria. The rain of aerial debris over New Delhi last year; I'm sure you saw those. And just two weeks ago one of our submarines off the coast of Hawaii. That last one's classified."

That was how it all happened? How David died, Sergeant Vieira and Lieutenant Yan, and most of his squad on the day of the Ninety-Nine. That was how he stepped on that mine. How he ended up in a field hospital, transferred back to the US on medical release, all the way up to the day he met Callie. A chain of events in his life that all started with quantum hackers from the future.

"Fuck," Paxton said, and pointed in front of him, denoting the future. "How'd they do it? How'd they figure it all out? They're barely hunter-gatherers."

"They learn, slow, but they learn. Someone in the future, his name best translates as the Peacemaker, hacked our War Machines on the Ninety-Nine."

"Peacemaker," Paxton said, remembering Pallas's mention of the name. "Can we change it, the future?"

"No. You can't change the future. But we can create it, and that's what the War Machine Program is—creating and controlling the future from the past."

"So there's no changing that desert future?"

"No."

Paxton took a breath. It was too much. It was like a buffet of all he wanted to know, and she kept on feeding. Victoria eyed him now with her brow raised, ready to serve the next platter.

"You need a drink yet?" she asked.

"Almost there," he said, and smiled. "So why are we fighting?"

"That I can't tell you."

"Why not?"

"I just don't know." Victoria yawned, and Paxton knew the conversation was nearly over.

"Are you the collaborator?" he asked. "The truth."

"No. Someone in our ranks is railing against the system. They might not even be at our base. They could have trekked from the Texas base or even the East Coast."

"It's not you?"

"Not me."

He believed her. Officers of her tenure rarely saw the inside of the hangar, even less the inside of a cockpit.

"So how does it end?" he asked. "I mean, how do we end the war?"

"Think of time like ground to be covered in trench warfare, like front lines, and gaining ground on the enemy. Let's say we control the fourteen hundreds, give or take, they control the sixteen hundreds, and the real fight is for the middle, the fifteen hundreds. Who wins there wins it all."

"Why the fifteen hundreds?" Paxton knew it wasn't the fifteen hundreds she was actually talking about, but nonetheless, he'd use her analogy.

"In the sixteen hundreds, our satellites start falling. We can't fight anymore. That's why they're in control. If we can win in the fifteen hundreds, then we can get new satellites up in a future beyond the sixteen hundreds. And we win. We win the future. Our technology is far better than theirs, and resources in the future are scarce—rare earth metals, oil reserves, we have them all. But it's a difficult war to fight when you're trying not to wipe out your great-grandchildren."

"And what's your function in this whole thing?" he asked.

"My function?" she asked back.

"What is it you're trying to accomplish? What are you trying to do?"

"Just an observer, trying to find a side of the seesaw to stand on."

"You're not sure who's in the right."

"No one's ever in the right, but we can't . . ."

"Can't what?"

"We can't kill the future. We can't win this war." Lieutenant Victoria lifted forward in her seat, sitting eye to eye with Paxton. "You have to go, Lieutenant."

"Now?" He looked at her. The redness in her eyes had dissolved into the white. She seemed awake now. So, *why*? "Why now?"

"It's time for your shift."

26

For the past few days, Paxton had surveyed the future ruins of Union Square, the Financial District, and Mission Bay, attempting to reconstruct district lines in his head with the San Francisco Giants baseball stadium as his only point of reference. Each shift, Paxton raced four and a half hours to the ruins, then four and a half hours back to the sandbox, the equivalent of a round-trip drive from Los Angeles to the Bay Area just for a twenty-minute glance at the view.

It had become habit, this infatuation with society in a fishbowl. He had become familiar with them, the Fishies, and had started naming them. Like the Old Oak, or a man dressed in something like a business suit he dubbed Wall Street, or the leader, a narrow woman with a gold crown—he called her the Goldfish. Then there was Harum, of course, and the big-boned scavenger woman he named Bones.

That evening, lights bloomed blue and green in some sort of ceremony, shining above the stadium ring and reflected in the water. They had used broken-down quadrupedal parts to manufacture a caterpillar-looking creation. Women, and only women, held these painted pieces of metal over their heads and held hands, imitating the caterpillar's design. Their hips gyrated, they pirouetted and tiptoed, a mating dance between maiden and machine.

The lights, the instruments, the spectacle of it all was as far from American as Paxton could imagine. Their ethnicities weren't white or Black but an earthy gray that radiated in the twilight hours.

But the night seemed eager, making twenty minutes feel like five. Paxton took a final glance at smoky curtains smearing the tops of skyscrapers and pulled the Spartan into a retreat. He ran his hidden route through blown-out buildings and sewers to avoid quadrupedal and aerial surveillance. Through tunnels, across deserts, and back over the fence with minutes to spare, and still Oya was many more minutes early, waiting eagerly outside the door.

"Lieutenant," Oya said, raising a hand to her forehead in salute.

Paxton stared at her, surprised she'd even acknowledged him. The two hadn't spoken in a week, and tensions felt higher than ever.

"You were there?" he said. "At the ceremony?"

Oya nodded. "Saw the whole show."

"Show?" Paxton said.

"Dr. Pallas's Alzheimer's parade."

"Oh," he said. "That."

"*That,*" she repeated.

It should have ended there. He should have turned on his heels and escaped to the lunchroom, burying himself under a warm swamp of oatmeal. But he just had to continue it, didn't he. Just had to say one more thing, a gesture of friendship to warm that pinch of frostbite in her chest.

"I'm still just another pilot, though. No rank between me, you, them."

"Right," she said, and turning back toward Paxton, "By the way, who is *them*?"

"Them?"

"Yesterday, when Pallas had his little breakdown, you said, 'I just watched them.' Who?"

"I—" Paxton paused as he recalled his near confession. "I can't remember."

"I do," she said. "Who do you watch? Because sometimes I find things on its body, the Spartan—mud, a greenish, mosslike thing, even a feather one time, stuck to the back of its heel. Where does all that come from?"

Paxton shook his head without a real answer in mind as Oya stepped forward, nearly pressed up on him.

"You run off at the mouth so easy," she said. "Surprised you're so quiet now."

It took Paxton a second to figure out what she was talking about, but then he remembered Galileo and the cockpit inspection where he had actually defended Oya.

"I never said anything to that inspector about you."

"No?"

"They had already picked you to fill a quota of suspicious personnel. So no matter what I said they would've found a way to twist it against you."

Oya stared at him. Her wide brown eyes inquisitive, interrogating. And she kept looking, until it was uncomfortable, until Paxton couldn't bear the hefty strain of eye contact.

"Okay, Lieutenant," she said, then smiled as something in her head tickled her. She laughed with her lips but held her tongue.

"What?" Paxton said.

"No."

"What is it, Sergeant?"

"I've been at this for a while—longer than you. Trying to ascend that hill. But now I see how it's done, making rank, you just gotta be a snake."

There was venom in that bite. It bruised and swelled and carried on his demeanor all the way to the mess hall. The venom traveled down his back, and he hunched and his neck craned as he watched grease gleam on the floor.

What Oya had said was the intersection of lies and insecurities, and he understood that; it made sense. But still it made him feel shitty, like a dirtiness staining his insides, because Oya was right about one thing: she should be lieutenant, not him. No way should it be him.

He approached his accustomed table but found nearly every seat taken, and even the spaces in between those seats were packed with bodies leaning in with conversation. One seat appeared to shine under an incandescent spotlight, but a backpack sat on top of it. He nearly steered away, but then he recognized the military patches stitched into the pack.

"Paxton," Bella said and pointed to her backpack, beckoning him to sit next to her. Private Oro, Lieutenant Ogun, and Sergeant Woden sat in adjacent seats.

Woden smiled as Paxton approached. He leaned toward Bella's ear and half whispered, half chuckled something indistinct. Bella untied the knot in her lips and smiled but then shook her head, saying something back to him, her lips rounded into *no*s and *not*s.

Paxton pretended he didn't see their smiles or whispers. "What's going on, fellas?" he said, then turned to the only woman at the table. "Bells."

"Hey," Bella said, the only one with a verbal reply.

The others grunted and nodded their heads, more interested in their strings of pasta than Paxton's pleasantries. Solo managed eye contact, and even Lieutenant Ogun offered a lazy salute, but not Woden; he gave nothing. Woden stared with a smirk dug into the side of his cheek like it was a joke—like Paxton was a fucking joke. The venom started burning again.

"What's with the population?" Paxton asked, filling the void with words.

"We got a busload from Utah," Bella said, then turned to Woden. "And what, Seattle too?"

"About six hundred actives," Woden grunted, stabbing into a kale-spinach mix; the salad's olive oil shone gold in the incandescence, as did the yellowfin tuna blanketed in slices of avocado. "Give or take."

Paxton watched as the jocks grazed on their proteins, iron, uncarbed fibers, and the entire vitamin alphabet. And even then, Woden kept on smirking, his goofy tusks aimed at Paxton, a shred of flaxseed pinched between his grin. And still Paxton pretended not to notice. He wouldn't give Woden the pleasure of letting him know that he was getting into his head.

"You eyeing me, Sergeant?" Woden asked.

"Me?" Paxton asked, realizing that he was still staring at the flaxen crumb in between Sergeant Woden's teeth. "Eyeing you? No, man. You're not that pretty," he said with a playful smile.

"Prettier than that cave girl you're dating," Woden said, not playful at all.

"No, Calum," Bella interjected, evidently on first-name terms now.

But Woden cut through her soft dissent. "I've seen that photo in your bunk, Arés." He turned to Ogun. "The most basic of basic-looking bitches, dude."

Laughter gusted toward Paxton, scented in blooded meats and soured spices. Laughter that cracked like shrapnel against all the parts of Callie inside of him, the dimples in her smile, the blink of her beady little eyes, all the tiny facets that he had fallen for—and it hurt. Something bled inside of him. Cutting her was the same as cutting him, and they bled together.

"Dude," Woden continued, teeth shining yellow. "So there's this dog in the picture with her. It's like they're fucking related."

More laughter, and suddenly it was too hard to hide. Paxton felt it slipping, his expression tightening into a glower.

"Guys . . . ," Bella said, holding her hand up between him and them as if to separate.

"It's all good, Bells," Paxton said, smothering the wrath inside his chest. Moisture burned at the edge of his tear ducts, but he would dam that up too. "I'm good."

"No, you ain't either," Woden said, flicking flaxseed at Paxton's head. "I see it in your eyes. Reach into that pussy of yours and pull out your fucking balls, Sergeant. Say what you gotta say."

Paxton's even temper tilted, just enough for him to feel off balance, just enough for him to lean forward. And just enough for them to notice.

"There he is," Sergeant Woden said. "I know that look."

You don't know me, Paxton thought. Unlike the rest of these career pilots, Paxton was infantry. MCMAP trained. Combat hardened at Parris Island. He could pop every single one of them like the candy-filled piñatas that they were.

"You're not in your cockpit, Woden," Paxton said, staring him down. "You feel the hits out here."

Woden blinked. It was brief—the briefest—but Paxton discerned the visual backdown. "This fucking guy," Woden said, rolling his eyes and turning to Lieutenant Ogun. "We have orientation tomorrow at two, right?"

But Paxton wasn't satisfied. And he wouldn't be ignored. *No.* Not with Callie watching from inside his mind's eye, and not by the likes of Sergeant Woden. He snatched Woden's lunch tray and shoved the entire meal of kale, olive oil, and tuna onto the man's lap.

Sergeant Woden must have known Paxton was an infantry grunt in the Marine Corps, because right then, right there, Woden shriveled shrimplike into the basket of his seat.

"Fuck off, Arés," he said, and dropped his head toward the garden on his lap.

But Paxton was elevated. He stood on an altar of adrenaline and ego, flexors and biceps now reminiscing on all the training in their muscle memory. He picked up his fork and pelted it at Sergeant Woden's head.

"Man up, Woden," Paxton said.

"I'm calling rank, Sergeant Arés," Ogun said. "Sit your noncom-missioned ass down."

"First Lieutenant," Paxton said, pulling on the right side of his jacket to reveal the shining bars on his shoulder. "Fucking rent-a-pilot."

Onlookers had gathered together in bunches. They oohed and aahed. The mob was shifting in his favor, seeing things through his eyes, his point of view; they were his audience now.

"Paxton, stop," Bella said.

Too late, Bells. Paxton was already downhill and snowballing hard toward Woden. He was all wheels and gears, all mechanics, as steely eyed as his own Androne.

"How long have you two been looking for the collaborator and haven't found him, *huh?* Even in your cockpits, you're scared of a fight?"

"You want something?" Lieutenant Ogun lifted himself up from the seat, climbing to his lanky six-foot-two frame.

But Paxton had to wait. He had to make Ogun swing first.

"Fort Hood must have been glad to get rid of you when they did," Paxton said, watching Ogun's lips twitch and nostrils flare. "Now we're stuck with you."

And it was that easy. Lieutenant Ogun threw a haymaker and Paxton caught it. He tugged the lieutenant toward him, then used the momentum and body weight to flip Ogun over his shoulder. Something cracked when Ogun hit the ground, but that didn't stop Paxton from driving his knee down into Ogun's jaw and twisting his arm, locking him into an unsophisticated arm bar.

"Paxton!" Bella screamed his name now—there was power to it, power now in his own name.

"Arés," a few of them said. "Arés!" His name was infectious, spreading from table to table. They screamed for him. They worshipped him. "Arés! Arés! Arés!"

Woden grabbed Paxton by the neck from behind and dragged him back.

"You ain't no fucking lieutenant," Woden said as he dropped an elbow against the side of Paxton's head. "You ain't shit." Then another blow. "You ain't shit."

The blows kept coming, but Paxton couldn't pull himself free of Woden's grip. Woden was shorter than Paxton but stockier. There was meat in those arms, and Paxton couldn't climb out of his choke hold.

"Let him go," Bella said, pulling at Woden's arms.

"Cry mercy," Woden said, tightening his grip as Paxton started losing his breath. "Cry fucking mercy, motherfucker!"

He might have to. Not only was Paxton out of breath, but the canals of his lungs were gagged tight under Woden's fat forearm. He had a few breaths in him—*Two*, he thought, *maybe three?* And then he'd black out.

With his first breath, Paxton backpedaled, easily driving Woden backward. With his second breath, he lifted his shoulders and almost tossed Woden back, but suddenly Paxton blinked without blinking. Light flickered in his eyes, and Paxton knew he wouldn't get a third taste of air. So he dropped to his knees, leaned forward, and flung Sergeant Woden over his back.

Paxton stumbled forward and grabbed at Woden but missed completely, his eyes still flickering on and off. Woden lunged up with an uppercut, but Paxton sidestepped intuitively and countered with a haymaker of his own, cracking into Woden's nose and stubbing his knuckles in the process. Even with bruises, lungs half-empty, lights half-off, Paxton remained on his feet. Woden didn't.

"Break it up," someone said.

Four or five hands pulled Paxton away from Woden. A couple of the cadets carried Lieutenant Ogun to medical for a dislocated wrist. While Sergeant Woden hung around the scene of the crime, questioned by his superiors, Bella carted Paxton back to his bunk, guiding him hand in hand the entire way. Paxton was dizzy, and his limp revealed itself for the entire corridor of eyes to see. But she was a human crutch, and he felt shielded from their looks.

"It's okay," she said as Paxton flopped down on the hard mattress.

Bella tucked him in, blanket up over his neck, then folded it under his shoulders. And then she stared down at him. And then she kissed him, and kept kissing.

Her mouth pinched his upper lip. Their noses brushed. Breathing mingled. Moisture exchanged. It felt like minutes of contact and minutes more before she pulled back. And as she pulled away, their eyes locked, a conversation that neither knew how to start. Bella backpedaled from the bed, feet dragging reluctantly against the concrete floor, and then she was gone.

27

Paxton explained the altercation to his superiors, then wrote a formal apology and promise that it would never happen again. Colonel Marson gave the official "boys will be boys" pardon, and all was forgiven. But after the full day of formalities, Paxton could only think about the weight of Bella's lips on his. He still felt them there, weighing down his words. Why would she kiss him? Paxton's girlfriend situation was common knowledge, and he had just seen Callie a few days earlier, kissed her too. There was guilt in that thought. And the baby—Bella knew he had a baby. So why would she kiss him? Or the better question, why did he kiss back?

It wasn't until Paxton's shift in the cockpit later that day that her kiss or even the fight with Woden finally began to slip out of focus, dreamlike almost, as the Spartan opened its eye to an early future morning. By the time Paxton had trekked the desert, Bella's touch was, for the moment, absent from his thoughts.

The Spartan stood watch in its accustomed position high above the fishbowl. Celebration overflowed the stadium's rim. Fireworks popped green and blue, so deafening that lights seemed to echo and noise seemed to shine.

Boats raced around the interior of the flooded stadium, using long staffs to pick lanterns from spectators, competing in a water sport of some sort. Boats would race to the center of the lake with their lanterns in tow and hurl them into a furnace that would explode in either green or blue flames.

The Goldfish oversaw the games from the highest seat in the stadium, a throne painted jade with streaks of white. Harum saddled herself on a throne of her own, atop the Old Oak's steady shoulders. Paxton couldn't help but smile; he had watched them hunting rats and pigeons and eating scraps for so long that to see them celebrating gave him hope for the future. Celebrating what, he didn't know, but they were making it work, even in these ruins, even under a sun-choked, postapocalyptic sky—*we found our way.*

Fireworks exploded overhead, and the innards of the stadium flashed in all the shades of autumn foliage. A thunderous applause came immediately after. Somebody had won something. But the noises reminded him of that biological alarm clock going off in his head. Paxton settled back into his controls and descended the stairway as always, but tonight he didn't need infrared vision to see the steps. Fireworks lit his way and the stairway caught those shrapnels of light, one step blue, the next step green, the next step purple. Disco balls of color bouncing down the stairs.

He took his time, appreciating the rainbow brick stairway. But halfway down, the colors changed; now only an orange-reddish flare brightened the sky above, the popping somehow blasting even louder than before. *Strange*, and yet he continued down.

The Spartan rounded the last flight of the stairwell and exited the ruins of the skyscraper. The ancient metropolis porcupined on the skyline, puncturing a black and bruised sky. It seemed impossible, all those centuries between now and then, consumed by a war between the now and them.

The Spartan lifted its head to a brightness above, and Paxton saw something even more impossible. Blood snowed down from the sky, scarlet red and glowing, drifting down to the Spartan's open palm. It caught one—not blood, but a fiery ember dying in color and curling to a black flake of ash.

Something was burning, and it didn't take him long to discover what. The Spartan rounded the corner of the skyscraper and found an entire wall of the stadium had cratered open. Boulders of brick had torn off, and the dam had broken. Waterfalls gushed out, tossing boats and bodies out into the rubble.

Paxton considered climbing back up to get a look back inside, but there wasn't time. He raced the Spartan directly toward the ancient stadium. The closer he came, the more those pops from within sounded like gunfire. The entrance had caved in on itself, and flames consumed anything that would burn. No way in and no way out, thousands of screaming people inside. The Old Oak, the little girl—he imagined them boiling in the heat.

"Climb it," Paxton said, hoping that the Spartan could lift its titanium obesity up the wall.

It couldn't. Barely five feet up, the Spartan stumbled, and ten feet higher it flat-out crashed down and kept falling, its body too heavy and the bricks too loose to find stable footing.

The Spartan rounded the backside of the stadium. Paxton noticed another adjacent structure, something like a clock tower but too battered and broken to tell. The stairwell inside was sturdy, likely renovated by the natives over the years. Paxton didn't hear a single crack as the Spartan laid its heavy feet on the stone steps, but then again, any noise would have been muffled by the choir of gunfire and explosions pouring out from the stadium.

Gunfire? Why had it taken him so long to consider that? Whose gunfire? Who had destroyed the stadium—who was capable? Was his own military gunning down hapless civvies and scavengers? And what the fuck was he going to do if they were? Heavy questions slowed the Spartan's footsteps, like an extra hug of gravity around its heels.

The gunfire cracked louder, the reds and yellows flashed brighter against the stairway walls. The Spartan stopped before that final step, immobilized by Paxton's indecision. But an opening blown into the wall in front of the Spartan revealed the enemy.

The vantage from the top of the structure exposed the massacre within. Corpses lay atop corpses with limbs twisted underneath them. Other cadavers floated in nearby pools, lit by the yellow-orange glow of flames. Any survivors were already half-dead, crawling up the stands with holes in their backs or dousing the pain of their scorched bodies as they choked in the water.

It was massacre, ruin, and fire, and it mangled Paxton's insides, twisting his stomach, his chest, his every thought turned sideways and nearly upside down, and his Spartan nearly toppled over with him. It stumbled as the recall hit him, memories in full color and sound from that mine in Sri Lanka—from Ninety-Nine. It was like that same flash, that same fire that danced in front of him now. Memories that squeezed at every inch of him, but more immediately at his leg, and the metal in his knees. It fucking burned, and Paxton felt their pain with seething, stabbing phantom pains.

Gunfire erupted from the far corner of the stadium. The Spartan zoomed in to discover adolescents clinging on to their infant siblings, absentee parents presumably dead. They raced out from a hollow in the stands, a hiding spot, and were swiftly gunned down with vicious accuracy. It was a War Machine, a Kingsman Series, seven feet plus of blood-painted titanium, emptying entire clips of ammunition on the civilians. It fired incendiary grenades out onto the boats that were still afloat, setting the water ablaze. The gunfire was sniper elite—not one bullet from its 135-round magazine was wasted. This Androne was a harbinger of death, a masochist, a cannibal of the soul, and quite possibly *the collaborator*.

"What the fuck?" Paxton said to himself, the cruelty so hard to watch and even harder to believe. *"Why?"*

But this was the collaborator, not a god but a devil. And from what he'd overheard in the Penthouse, it was a Kingsman Series, based on the weapons it used. If this Kingsman Series, a Series 8, *was* the collaborator, and Paxton was as sure as anything that it was, it would eviscerate his Spartan, a Series 1. It would tear the Spartan apart, limb by limb, and suck on its metal bones. But they might escape. Harum, the Old Oak, even the Goldfish, at least a few of them could get out. At least he could buy them some time. And the longer Paxton thought on it, the more he realized he didn't have much of a choice. He had to face the collaborator.

28

The Spartan lunged off the top of the clock tower and crashed through a hollowed-out window on the side of the stadium. The Androne's weight cratered into the floor, ceramics snapped, concrete gave way, and the Spartan tumbled down to a lower level.

Rock rained for a moment, then the space went quiet, quiet enough for Paxton to hear the direction of distant gunfire. The wood floors had rotted out, and each step was a minefield of loose planks and hardwood potholes. Deeper inside, full-on chasms tore through the ground, and the Spartan hopscotched over the breaks in the floor.

Graffiti decorated the walls in that space, chalklike depictions of Androngs carrying men and women toward a light. Or maybe it was art, all those carvings on the ceiling, bees toting torches, or the pagan decor with buck antlers and goat horns welded onto quadrupedal and hexapod bodies.

The room led to a corridor, which led to a stairway, which climbed to the top floor of the stadium. The top floor was a long, circular corridor that ran the circumference of the arena. Ancient luxury-box spaces, once marble and glossed in garnish finishes, had abraded down to the basic grays of cinder blocks.

Gunfire ebbed from underneath the exits leading out to the stands. But the exits were blocked with brick piles and steel beams that seemed deliberate, trapping the civvies inside.

The Spartan was far stronger than a few piled-up bricks and the twisted steel bones of rusted metal. It rammed shoulder first into the door, and the hinges spattered and the locks snapped, and the Androne stumbled out into a colosseum of smog and blood.

In the distance, civilians avalanched down the stands as fires chased behind them. Blood lubricated the steps as they slipped and rolled and trampled, and were trampled. The lake at the center of it all flickered yellow and orange flames. The boats burned, and white ash floated up like an opposite to snow.

Gunfire rang out and echoed and seemed to come from everywhere at once. The screaming and the crackle of burning wood and the singeing of hot metals made it harder to pinpoint the collaborator's position.

Footsteps trampled the ground behind the Spartan. Paxton whipped around and found the double barrels on a sawed-off shotgun staring him in the face. Light flashed but did little more than momentarily blind Paxton. The buckshot bounced like rubber off the titanium armor. The Spartan snatched the gun, crushed it between its fingers, but she held on—*Bones*, the "big-boned" young woman. She shrieked, her eyes wide and wild as if she were expecting the Spartan to end her life. But the Spartan tossed her aside, a simple flick of Paxton's wrist, hurling her ten feet across the stands.

Flickers of gunfire flashed from the other side of the stadium. A quick zoom of the Spartan's lenses revealed the Kingsman Series ramming the bayonet on its rifle through the back of an elderly man.

"Fuck," Paxton exclaimed, in momentary shell shock from the savagery.

Instead of running the circumference of the stadium, the Spartan raced directly toward the lake of fire. It sprang hard from the railing and landed on a burning boat. It ran the length of the boat and leaped onto another, then another, a titanium stone skipping across the water, surging through nebulas of black smoke.

The Spartan landed on the boat closest to the opposite side, twenty feet away and seven feet below the edge of the stadium. Andrones couldn't swim, and Paxton had never made a jump that far.

Paxton stepped on the pedals, charging toward the edge of the boat. The Spartan slammed its feet deep into the wood planks, splinters stripping from the wood as it exploded upward. The cockpit shook as the Spartan soared. It hit the wall and barely hooked its fingers onto the railings at the bottom of the stands.

The Spartan lifted itself onto the platform just in time to witness the old man he had nicknamed Wall Street lying limbless underneath the Kingsman's boot, dark red plasma squirting from the four corners of his corpse.

"The fuck is wrong with you?" Paxton exclaimed.

Paxton felt it in his chest, an agony, a heartbreak that bent at his sternum, cracking at his rib cage, and his heart felt liquid, like it could pour out of him. He had never seen such cruelty, *never*. The sadism of that kill was beyond him, beyond words, and Paxton understood right there, right then, that he wasn't trying to buy time anymore; he was trying to put this motherfucker into the dirt.

A feminine voice cracked into the quiet, charging out from the smoke and acrid smolder—the Old Oak, her face lit by her own gunfire. She shot wildly, hitting the Kingsman's back and doing little more than garnering its attention. The Kingsman swung back and aimed its rifle at the Old Oak just as Paxton lifted the Spartan onto the stands and took aim.

The Spartan landed a headshot that sent the Kingsman into a stumble. But Paxton didn't stop firing. He kept his finger tight against the trigger. He kept his gunfire concentrated on the Kingsman's abdomen, where the satellite receiver was positioned.

But even under the hail of high-caliber rounds, the Kingsman managed to aim its rifle at the Spartan. But the Kingsman didn't fire. It stood like a deer in headlights, not returning a single bullet, as if the gunpowder had drained out of them.

But why? The collaborator certainly wasn't scared. It had taken out bigger, badder Androne than a Series 1. It somehow seemed surprised to see the Spartan, and Paxton would take full advantage.

The Spartan lunged forward and swung its rifle against the Kingsman's optical lens, hoping to blind the larger Androne. Then it swung its rifle against the Kingsman's left shoulder, knowing those joints were the most vulnerable. The Kingsman didn't counter, seemingly still under the spell of surprise. Paxton swung again, same shoulder, same joint. The Kingsman stumbled back, fumbling its rifle and nearly dropping the weapon before managing to get a hold of the thing and finally fighting back.

In such close quarters, the Kingsman could only swing its rifle. Paxton dodged the slow body shot, then dipped under an even slower head strike. The Kingsman's left arm wasn't moving at full capacity. Paxton had done some damage with all those bullets and shoulder hits. There were tears in the Kingsman's anatomy, metal scraping against metal. But the pilot wouldn't switch hands even as cauterized strings of metal snapped on the Kingsman's left shoulder—the collaborator was left-handed.

The Spartan angled itself to the Kingsman's right side, and at a foot away, the Spartan was untouchable. Paxton needled the Spartan's fingers into the Kingsman's wounds and yanked down. Sparks flew and the Kingsman stumbled back toward the edge of the fishbowl. *And Andrones can't swim.*

Paxton pressed his Androne forward, charging the Kingsman shoulder first, hoping to drive it toward the edge. But with a single thrust, the Kingsman lifted the Spartan off its feet and brought it back down so hard that it nearly shattered the wood planks beneath.

The Spartan dropped its rifle at the Kingsman's feet as it tumbled, dizzied and dazed, to the bottom of the stands. The Kingsman stepped on the Spartan's rifle and aimed its own weapon, but didn't fire. It waited, or seemed to, for seconds and moments on end. It stood and aimed, not pulling its trigger.

What is he waiting for? And more importantly, how could Paxton take advantage? He'd have only this one moment of distraction. The Spartan's rifle lay on the rotting wood just ten feet ahead of him. The Androne bounded forward and raced toward the weapon, the wood bending and rattling under each step as the collaborator finally pulled the trigger. The Spartan angled its body like a hammer, ramming itself into the wood. The ground snapped and the Spartan fell beneath the floorboards.

Paxton switched on infrared and saw through the floor. The Kingsman's orange-yellow heat shone on the visor, as did the green-gray outline of the Spartan's assault rifle.

The Spartan leaped up and ripped the skeletal wood away. Both the rifle and the Kingsman came crashing down. The Spartan regained its weapon and unloaded an entire magazine on his enemy's shoulder, shredding through layers of dense metal and circuitry. As the magazine went dry, the Kingsman's arm twitched uncontrollably. The rifle shook in its hand. Yet the collaborator didn't seem ready to attack, as if it didn't have the desire to fight or was ready to throw in the towel.

But that lasted only a second as the Kingsman lifted the rifle and its bayonet blade and aimed at the Spartan. Paxton too took aim and pulled the trigger but had forgotten that the magazine was empty. *Shit!* The Kingsman's bullet cracked the air, sonic-booming across the space and shattering the rifle in the Spartan's hands.

Was it aiming for the gun?

Unarmed, the Spartan pulled the pins from the smoke grenades on its side. A green mist blossomed through the space underneath the stands. Paxton knew it would take the collaborator at least a second to switch to infrared and another second for their eyes to adjust, and one last second for them to react. And three seconds later, the Spartan ran within striking distance of its enemy. Paxton hit the Kingsman Series in its shoulder, snatched the rifle from its devastated arm, and rammed the bayonet through its chest.

"Holy shit," Paxton said. "Holy fucking shit."

The Kingsman stumbled backward as yellow fluid spewed from its chest and dripped to its feet like urine. Paxton pulled the blade out, ready to stab again, but the Kingsman retreated to a ladder at the back of the space. Its arms flailed at the rungs, and it more so fell upward than climbed. Paxton followed the collaborator up the ladder to the stands.

A few civvies had returned to the stands for the injured and the dead. They stared in awe at what they saw: Androne versus Androne. A Spartan Series stalking a crippled Kingsman, the drip of yellow fluid trailing behind it. The Old Oak stood at the head of the crowd, holding her waist, blood dripping down her leg. Harum held on to the other leg and pointed at the Spartan as if she recognized the machine.

He had to end this now. Paxton aimed, and the Spartan pulled the trigger. The bullet hit the Kingsman's wound and it exploded into flames. It crawled forward as it burned, aiming a flare gun at the black sky and shooting a streak of red light into the clouds. Then the Kingsman tumbled into a pile of titanium flames as, somewhere out there, the collaborator exited his cockpit.

The collaborator had allies, though, and they were coming. The Spartan pointed the civvies toward the exits, but they stared instead at the skies. Furies swooped by overhead, and seemingly at the Kingsman's bequest. *But why?* Those were Nellis Base aerials, four of them, circling overhead like mechanical vultures.

As the civilians retreated to the exits of the stadium, Paxton did the math of it all. It took him a minute or two to put it all together, but in the end the beginnings of an idea had started to form. The Kingsman's hesitation to fight. It shooting at the Spartan's rifle instead of the Spartan itself. The Kingsman's signaling the military. It wasn't the collaborator, was it?

"Oh God," he said, and thought, and said it again. "Oh my God."

Paxton knew it the second it crossed his mind. If they had the technology to connect to the future, then each individual cockpit could, in theory, be locked in at a different point in that future, some in April, some in May, some in June—and what if his cockpit was locked into March? He could be positioned days or weeks behind the others, which led Paxton to the next and far more terrifying possibility.

This Kingsman Series wasn't the collaborator. He was.

29

He wouldn't make it back in time, not with the few hours left in his shift, and definitely not with the quartet of Furies whistling over the stadium's airspace. He took the Spartan underground and crawled about in the dirt before making a mad dash for the blown-out buildings nearby. It stooped beneath a rubble-made skylight and watched the reinforcements congregate in the sky. Gunships, Furies, and aerial drones he didn't have names for blazed across the sky like semi-suns. Reinforcements gathered on the ground: Z Series and Apaches and packs of quadrupedals hounded the civvies like wolves. He was stuck, beneath all the rocks and hard places as the minutes trickled down on his screen, as Oya knocked against the cockpit door, as he realized this was it; this was how it ends.

The burn of perspiration scorched under Paxton's armpits. Sweat slimed on his palms. His heart throbbed hard against his chest—*no*, that was Oya again, knocking impatiently at the door. He'd have to tell the truth, admit, confess, plead ignorance. If he did it now, he might serve only ten to twenty years. With time off for good behavior and lip service from the old man, Paxton might just get out in time to see his son graduate from high school.

He reached for the door and lifted the heavy handle. The gauges clicked, internal locks dislodged, and the hinges hummed open. The hangar's acrid musk wafted in, and he felt choked by it. He felt like he couldn't breathe.

"What the fuck, Arés?" Sergeant Oya said. "You don't get paid overtime."

"Right," he murmured, barely there, barely paying attention.

"Corporal Columbia's looking for you," she said, referencing Bella by her surname.

"Where?"

"She was just . . ." Oya glanced back at the hangar crowds, searching for Bella. Then she brought impatient eyes back to Paxton, as if waiting for him to say or do something. "You planning on spending the night, Arés?"

Paxton's gaze sliced past Oya and fixed on the armed officers in the distance, holding coffee cups and Coke cans like microphones to their conversation. The men's casual vigilance flickered toward Paxton. Static buzzed from a nearby walkie-talkie. The click of high heels Dopplered by. Every crackle and conversation, every glance in his direction wasn't like the butterflies in his stomach but more like caterpillars crawling around the walls of his gut.

Then Paxton snapped. His arm flung toward Sergeant Oya, and he snatched her, dragged her into the cockpit, and she landed on top of him as Paxton pulled the door shut.

"What the fuck are you doing?"

He didn't know. Paxton had no idea why Oya's flexing biceps was bundled in his sweaty fingers, why the door, though still ajar, was held in place by his other hand, keeping it quiet, keeping it dark. *Why?* What was he going to tell her? What could he tell her? What was the solution to this equation he had etched out so haphazardly in front of him? *What?*

"What's wrong with you?" she snapped.

"We're in the future," he said and winced.

"What?"

"We're in the future, Oya." Paxton gestured to the cockpit screen, which was only at half optical output. Without the visor over their eyes, neither could clearly see what was on-screen. "This is the future." He gestured harder toward the screen. "That's where we're monitoring, *when* we're monitoring."

"Are you on something?"

"Think," he whispered, glancing at the door, still ajar. Footsteps roamed around outside. "Think about it." He said it quieter now.

"Why's there so much secrecy? Why do you think there's no country on Earth that has an appropriate time zone to match the sunsets and sunrises? Why are we using so much damn power? Come on, you've been here longer. You had to have noticed something."

Oya glanced at the blurred screen and the visor hanging around Paxton's neck like a techno pendant from a wiry necklace. That was good, though—at least she was listening.

"The cockpits shoot signals up to the sats," Paxton said, pointing up to an imagined satellite above them. "The signal is going to be held there for years, maybe a hundred, I don't know; then it's shot back down a hundred years later into Androncs that aren't even built yet."

There was a struggle on her face. Her expression screwed up in a sort of disgust, as if Paxton's voice had a scent of soured fish. At the same time, one of her eyebrows peaked, and her eyes bounced back and forth between him and self-reflection.

"You know it, don't you," Paxton said, feeling the resistance in her biceps slip. "You've been here longer. You've seen more. Heard more."

"You're the collaborator," Oya said, her lips and jaw awed open.

"I . . ." He considered it. *Maybe?* "I don't know."

Sergeant Oya reached for the door. Paxton grabbed her arm and pulled her back.

"Please," he pleaded "Just listen."

"No," she yelped, and swung her elbow against his jaw. She grabbed the door handle. "Let me out, Arés."

"I will, but just let me say one last thing, and it's the truth." Oya paused. Her muscles unwound beneath the grip of his hand. "No matter what happens, there's something sinister going on. We *are* in the future. We *are* at war with the future. And I don't know how the brass is going to react when they know that you know too."

"That a threat?"

Was it? The words had come out reflexively, knee-jerk-like, defense mechanisms that ran like undercurrents beneath his conscious mind. He remembered the story then, the one Victoria had told him about the man who had incriminated her just by telling her the truth. *It was a threat*; his conscious mind was just catching up to his subconscious, like sound chasing its bullet.

"If I tell them, it incriminates you," he said.

"A threat," she said, smirking.

"I'm not the threat, Oya. I just don't know what they're going to do. If you tell—"

"*When,*" she interrupted. "When I tell them."

"Fine. When you tell them," he said, nodding.

She paused then, as if reconsidering everything. "How do you know we're in the future? I mean, how do you know for sure?"

"Pax?" Bella's voice came from the outside, and he could see her eyes peeking in through the crack in the cockpit door. "What are you . . ."

He didn't understand Bella's expression at first, the embarrassment burning red underneath her cheeks, the strings of wrinkles as her eyes narrowed to a squint. But as she stepped away, he realized what she must have seen. Sergeant Oya sitting in his lap, the two of them face-to-face in his cockpit, a nod away from a kiss.

"Bella," Paxton shouted, but she was gone.

"Get out," Oya said.

"Oya—" he tried, but she interrupted.

"I don't want anyone seeing us together. Get out."

"What are you going to do?"

"Get. Out!"

Oya's gaze rolled away from Paxton in a way that he had seen before—elementary school teachers giving him a pass or how the old man ignored his childhood misgivings. Oya would eventually tell. Two children and a husband back home guaranteed that. But he felt like her confusion would buy him some time, a few minutes at least, and he left the marble in a crease behind the cockpit seat to buy a few more. And Paxton had to get to Lieutenant Victoria before that time ran out.

30

Paxton carried that burden of uncertainty quietly down the corridor and out into the night. He had hoped to resolve things with Bella, their kiss and misunderstanding, but he hadn't seen her that week, and maybe that was for the best.

He dialed Callie's number on the way out. No response. He imagined her taking a nap on the couch downstairs.

"Just checking in," Paxton said after the voice mail requested a message at the tone. "And make sure you're taking your meds on time," he finished, remembering that she often forgot.

He paced along the sandy paths leading to Lieutenant Victoria's trailer, hoping for closure. The sunset left cold winds drifting between the corridors of mobile homes. But Paxton was greeted by lightless windows in Victoria's trailer and a hollow echo as he knocked on the fiberglass door. He waited for hours, until just after midnight, before retreating to the quiet of his bunk and bed.

Fraught silence howled through the night. Forced air pushed against the sheets; the bedsprings were ocean waves and twisted Paxton's body around the coiling tide. Sleep and consciousness blurred to a lucid gray that rushed the morning to a premature dawn.

Paxton was on his feet before anyone else. His muscle memory navigated him through the unlit room. He had slept in his fatigues and didn't need to change, just a splash of water across his face and he was out into the hangar, watching his cockpit from afar. Forty-five minutes until Oya finished her shift, and he glanced at his watch every five minutes. No alarms. No crowds around the cockpit doors. Just business as usual.

Sergeant Oya crumbled out of the cockpit in pieces, a lazy leg, then an arm, a torso, her head peeking out halfway, the rest of her dragging behind. She approached Paxton, but her eyes shot straight past him, like he was a ghost, and she could step right through him. It wasn't until Paxton waved that Oya seemed to notice he was there.

"What happened?" he said.

Oya stepped past Paxton, not even glancing at him. "I said I don't want to be seen with you."

"No one's here but janitors," he said, trying to keep pace. "What happened?"

"They're cameras." Oya gave a soft gesture with her head, identifying the many security cameras on the ceiling. "And when they find out what you're doing, they'll look at those cameras and see that we spoke."

"Are you going to say anything?"

"What am I gonna say? I support aerial drones shooting down the civilians out there?"

"The Furies are shooting them?"

"Those that are left, yes."

Paxton turned back to the cockpit.

"They're waiting for you," Oya said. "I took the Spartan to this old factory or something. And they followed me. A little girl and uh . . ."

"An old woman?" Paxton said, nearly saying *the Old Oak*.

"Right, scrappy old chick and a few others. I don't understand what they're saying. What's that, Arabic or something?" Paxton didn't know, but before he could tell her that Oya cut herself off. "You know what, I don't want to know."

"If you're going to say anything, you should say it now. They might listen if you said it now."

"Could say the same for you," Oya said. "It just happened, just now, last night. If you keep going, you'll become this great collaborator they're all talking about."

"Why aren't you going to say anything?" Paxton asked.

"Who said I wasn't?"

"So what are you going to do?"

"I don't know," she said. "I don't understand. Why are we at war with the future?"

Paxton didn't have the answer, and she must have seen that. Sergeant Oya hung a sharp left and paced toward a crowd of other second-shift pilots, Maria the only nonpilot among them. Maria waved at Paxton. He didn't wave back. Paxton felt the cockpit calling. He imagined the voices screaming from within. He turned back to a cockpit he never thought he'd pilot again, and in an instant he was a million miles and minutes away.

———

The Spartan opened its eye and found itself in a Rubik's Cube of broken architecture. Ceiling fixtures jutted out from the wall, and hollowed-out windows were half buried in dirt. The building had collapsed and was still collapsing, as rubble peppered down in a fine powder and the walls hiccuped and moaned in exhaustion.

Survivors surrounded the Spartan like a cornfield of gray bodies stacked boundlessly still. They were like a black-and-white snapshot from some third-world war, a hundred black pitted eyes staring out from under their ashen faces. Puppy eyed like Hudson soliciting scraps at the dinner table. But their cloned postures, tight in the shoulders, with a slight buckle in the knees, was like nothing he had ever seen.

Oya had parked the Spartan under this broken garage to hide from aerial surveillance, not to lead refugees to shelter. What were they expecting?

Movement rippled from the back and drifted to the surface of the crowd. The Old Oak limped out from the mass with gauze mummifying her waist. The Goldfish followed close behind, still wearing her gold crown atop a frizz of hair. They stopped ahead of the Spartan, still a few arm's lengths away, and discussed something with all the body language and passion they could muster. Then they turned that same passion toward the Spartan.

"*Dekek lukeen endakk?*" the Goldfish said, or seemed to ask, in a language like nothing Paxton had ever heard. It was a croaking dialect filled with clapping *k* articulations, far from any Romance language or the Germanic relatives of English.

"*Nawa shwa jong wenna?*" the Goldfish said or asked. The rising, falling intonations were hard to grasp, but Paxton seemed sure that this was a different language than the first, or a different dialect. The rhythm of the language fluttered like a butterfly on her tongue. "*Jong way na?*"

"*Ubu,*" the Old Oak said to the Goldfish, shaking her head.

The duo discussed some more, strategizing it seemed, but never coming to a conclusion.

"*Juel Spanna?*" Another voice, in another language, from someone in the crowd.

The Goldfish hushed him harshly, then turned to the Spartan and asked what sounded like the same thing. "*Juel Spanna?*"

"Oh!" Paxton said, finally figuring them out.

The Goldfish was spinning the wheel of language, trying to find one that he could understand. But even if they were speaking something as familiar as French, Paxton could only say the *hellos* and *goodbyes*.

"Sorry," Paxton said, aware they wouldn't hear. "I don't understand."

Then, almost as if they did hear him, the Old Oak and the Goldfish shuffled off toward a crowd filled with questions, essentially giving up.

Harum followed the Old Oak and knotted her little limbs around the woman, peeking out from behind her legs. Her half smile simpered at the Spartan; the other half of her face was lost behind the old woman's bloodstained pants. Harum held a quadrupedal sensor in her hands. She fiddled with it aimlessly, unplugging and reattaching wires with unimaginable speed and accuracy, like a four-year-old savant. Harum played with the billion-dollar hardware like a toy as she eyed an even bigger toy—the Spartan.

Harum tiptoed up, trying to reach the Old Oak's ear, and shouted in that same foreign language. Whatever she said, it hit the old woman like a truck. The Old Oak twisted, unbalanced, to face the Spartan, her lips ajar but nothing coming out, her thinking outpacing her voice.

"Angles," the Old Oak said, her accent almost French. "You recognize Angles script?"

Paxton spasmed with excitement, and his Spartan shadow perked up with the same charge of fervor. The Old Oak stumbled back, her arm dropping fast to her waist and the revolver holstered to her belt. They all stumbled back, except Harum. She stepped forward.

"You speak the Angles?" she asked in that same French-like twang. "Can you speak Angles?"

Paxton gestured a thumbs-up, though he didn't know what Angles was and wasn't even sure what a thumbs-up gesture meant to them. But the Old Oak stepped toward the Spartan nonetheless and stared up two full feet into its eye.

"Stride forward," she said, and gestured. "Stride forward, please."

The Spartan took two small steps forward. The Old Oak took two wider steps back, nodding, half smiling, but not yet convinced.

"Bound," she said, this time without a gesture. "Bound upward."

Paxton complied, lifting the Spartan off the ground with a soft tiptoe on his pedals. The Spartan's head cracked the ceiling. Cement chipped and flaked down around it.

"Proffer me your weapon."

The Kingsman Series bayonet-rifle had to be at least two hundred pounds, probably heavier. She couldn't carry it. And still Paxton reached his metaled gloves toward his back, the Spartan in turn lifting the rifle off the holster on its own back, then offered the rifle to her.

The crowd gathered. Questions came from all of them and all at once, all except the Goldfish. She closed her eyes and pressed her palm against the Spartan's abdomen, almost exactly where its satellite receiver rested. Meanwhile the Old Oak fielded questions from the crowd and tried to interpret them to the Spartan.

"Do you bear messages from the Mother?" she asked, but Paxton didn't know how to answer. "Will the Mother of I appease?" she asked again, translating the Goldfish's questions, and still Paxton didn't understand the question. "Mother of I, what message do you provide?"

This continued. Mind-numbing minutes turned into coma-inducing hours. Puzzling questions about a "mother" and a "Church of I." Questions about bees that carried "the light." But no questions about the War Machine Program, aerial drones, or the landrones. No questions about satellites or signals or quantum entanglement, just religion, spiritual translators, and a fear of bees.

Paxton studied their confusion. He investigated the puzzle of questions and put together a picture of their history, made up of folklore and superstition. More puzzle pieces lay at the Spartan's feet, pairs of men kneeling and clasping their hands and speaking in tongues as they worshipped the Spartan. Did they think the machine was a god?

These people were blind, sleepwalking through a world far larger than they were conscious of. *How could they know nothing?* he thought, then he thought, *How could they know?* Stark naked in the dark medieval future: illiterate, lost, they were children, without a school for them to learn.

"How do you come to speak a dead language?" the Old Oak asked. "Why is it that you speak Angles?"

"English?" Paxton asked the air.

The Spartan shrugged its shoulders, hoping that was a gesture she could understand. And she did. She dropped her gaze to the Spartan's feet, and her eyes squirmed in thought.

"Will you lead us to the interpreter?" She whispered her own question now, deftly quiet, so the Spartan and only the Spartan would hear. Then she glanced back to the Goldfish, who stood in conversation with the religiously fervent. "Is that why they attacked?" the Old Oak asked and again glanced back at the Goldfish, who now noticed their secret conversation.

"I don't understand," Paxton said, but how could he express that over the gap of hundreds of years?

He pointed to his head—the Spartan pointed to its head, and shrugged, and lifted its arms.

"Did you know what we took from the church?" she asked.

"You stole something?"

Paxton lurched forward in his seat. The military had to have known about the civilians in the stadium, and for a while now. Surveillance drones, satellite imaging . . . and the civilians weren't exactly hiding either, with their bright boat lights against the water and firework celebrations. So the attack *was* provoked by something.

"What?" Paxton asked. "What did you steal?" *But how do I gesture that?*

A fist banged on the cockpit door from outside. At first he thought it might be Sergeant Oya, but Paxton had spent only a few hours in the cockpit. A few hours, just enough time for Oya to alert the literal heavy hand of the military guard. Paxton nearly smiled as he peeled the visor off his head and opened the door. He almost felt comforted now. This would be the end of it, the hiding, the lying. He almost felt his lungs fill with relief—*almost*, until he saw Sergeant Oya with a coffee cup wrapped between her fingers. Mocha-black waves crashed around the navel of the cup, sprinkling out as she leaned in and shoved her face into the barely opened cockpit door.

"Look," she said. "I've been thinking. What you did in saving them was good. I'll admit that now; it was the right thing to do."

Her throat jerked, like old Buick engines cutting out prematurely. There was more to that sentence, and if she wouldn't say it, he would.

"But . . . ," Paxton said, his voice hanging on the word as he tried to reel the rest of it out of her.

"But," she started. "If we take the Spartan back to the sandbox now, before anything else happens, then we'll be okay. No one knows. No one finds out."

Paxton noticed a redness in the corner of Oya's left eye. She hadn't gotten much sleep. That led his gaze to the braids on the left side of her head, and right there was the myopic blur of a person in the distance behind her, their body half-hidden behind a post, but Paxton felt sure that person's gaze was fixed on them.

"Paxton?" Oya said as she followed the direction of his eyes, ready to turn around to see what he was looking at.

"Don't turn around," he said.

"Who's there?"

"I can't see," Paxton said. "I can't see who."

"They're watching us?"

"Seems like it, yeah."

"Get back in," she whispered. "We'll talk later."

He nodded and grabbed the door, but before closing it Paxton returned his gaze to the human blur in the distance. They had disappeared, lost to the stream of bodies and faces flowing in and out of the hangar.

31

Paxton and Lieutenant Victoria planned to meet at a specific time; the place, though, was a bit less particular. They would meet on the west end of the solar array that night, and separately, as to avoid being seen together. Paxton arrived first, minutes before the brownout, with a baseball cap casting a dull moonlight shadow on his face and an ancient kale-green sweater billowing in the breeze.

It was a fifteen-minute walk and a thirty-minute wait, and Paxton kept his arms wrapped tight against his chest the entire time. He watched his exhales glimmer ghostly against the air and filled those hollow moments with imaginations of his son. He imagined eyes like his and lips like Callie's, or maybe a nose like his and eyes like hers. He even considered the old man's salt-and-pepper stubble on that imagined baby face. He dissolved into his subconscious so completely that the black of night was just background for daydreams to paint upon. Paxton watched an infant's drunken baby steps tiptoe across the cosmos.

"What's funny?" Victoria said, stepping in from the shadows and surveying the spaces behind him.

Paxton had been smiling without realizing it, but those dimples and the swell in his cheeks flattened as Victoria emerged. He remembered where his mind had been before all that. He remembered his paranoia. His muscles tightened from his fists up to his shoulders, and he remembered the cold.

"The hat makes you look conspicuous," Victoria said, settling in under the solar panel beside him. "What's this all about?"

"I'm pretty sure that I'm the collaborator," he said.

Lieutenant Victoria didn't respond. She leaned against the trunk of a solar panel, eyes stained a sleepy shade of red. She observed Paxton as if searching for something else, some other piece of information, as if she already knew that part—*as if she knew this entire time.*

"You knew," he said.

"No," the lieutenant answered, rubbing her eyes and yawning into her palm. "But I suspected."

"How? How could you know?"

"Because you killed me, Paxton." She paused, letting the word settle into his head. "You shot down my Fury. Nearly a year ago, I piloted an aerial drone over an old stadium and watched a Spartan Series kill one of its own. Sound familiar? I didn't report that I saw a Spartan or the serial code for this base. Kept it all to myself."

"That was you?" he said, doing the math in his head. "So the cockpits aren't all set to the same time in the future?"

"Wouldn't make sense, if territory is time, to have every soldier standing on the same day. You're all locked into a two-year span of each other. Your friend, Corporal Columbia, she's already fought and lost against you. Or your wingman."

"Wing-woman," he corrected, still not sure if Oya was in or not. "How'd you know that it was me in the Spartan's driver's seat?"

"Did my due diligence. Knew it would be someone in this recruiting class based on the time period of the battle. So I kept an eye on all the new Spartan pilots, about nine in all. But there's something about you, your walk, your posture, that felt familiar. But I didn't know for sure."

"Now you know."

"Sergeant Woden's Apache Series is looking for you and your wing-woman as we speak. And unlike the fight with me or Corporal Bella Columbia, it hasn't been decided yet. So I suggest you keep an ear open to what their strategies might be. My guess is you and Woden are locked into a similar time pattern. Days or hours apart."

"What've you heard?"

"Nobody tells me anything," she said, then seemed to remember something right then. "Oh, but Lieutenant Ogun was discharged this afternoon. You hear about that?"

"Discharged?"

"Guess you didn't."

Paxton shook his head.

"And Woden got a write-up. One more strike and he's all the way gone."

"Over the fight?" Paxton said in genuine surprise. "It's because of our fight?"

"I guess you didn't even feel a slap on the wrist," she said with her first smile. "Your godfather favors you. There are advantages to that."

"I'm not spying for you."

"And I'm not going to push you." Victoria stepped toward him. "I'm being transferred, Paxton."

"What?"

"They're sending me to Fairchild." Victoria paused and seemed to clock Paxton's confusion. "Fairchild Air Force Base in Washington."

His heart dropped. It fell to the gut and boiled in its acids. And soon he felt like he was falling too, plummeting into himself. He was trapped in the brown skin, trapped in frizzy hair with Hispanic roots. Paxton felt ensnared in himself, his accent and eye color, his gender and his name, and he felt the strongest desire to be anyone else, just not Paxton Arés. He had to get out of himself. His lizard brain calling for him to shed his skin and crawl the fuck out.

"I'm sorry," she said, taking some hint from his muted reaction. "I'll be on staff for another couple weeks, but . . . I made captain."

"Congrats." Sarcasm.

"We lost Captain Laran a few weeks back, and the other couple of insiders on base are losing enthusiasm."

"There's more than just me?" Paxton said. "Who else?"

"They don't know who you are, and I'm giving them the same confidentiality. If you're ever found out, they'd be safe, and vice versa."

"You said the other couple of insiders? So, what, like two people? I thought this was some sort of revolution."

"This was never a revolution, just whistleblowers running out of breath."

"So what do I do?" he said, sounding smaller, like a little boy losing a friend.

"What do you mean?" Victoria asked, digging fingers into the pockets of her khakis.

"What do I do when I get back into the pilot's seat?"

"The right thing."

Victoria tugged an empty cigarette package out from her pocket and tossed it into the dirt. The wind carried the yellow plastic and paper off into the dark, following behind Victoria's footsteps as she faded into the black.

32

The air in the hangar was stale that morning. The light beamed down at an angle, and the cockpits resembled a hundred silver Easter eggs gleaming under nuclear incubation. The wires and valves underneath were like metaled veins sprawling out from the eggs and brought to mind the old "chicken or the egg" adage. The future or the now, which came first, the future or these eggs?

Paxton sniffed the stagnant air, filled with pit fuels, blowtorch fumes, and singed metals. It was a convoluted scent that wafted to the back of his nasal passages and made them water. Ten weeks and he still hadn't adapted.

He had decided not to arrive early so as to avoid suspicion, and somehow he still ended up arriving prematurely and waiting outside the cockpit for over twenty minutes. This time Oya was late, nearly thirty minutes so. She climbed out red eyed, with a carpal tunnel grip bending her knuckles.

"They're moving," she said. "They split. Most of the survivors are staying in the ruins. The old woman is leading a small band out."

"Why'd they split?" Paxton asked, a shade quieter than her.

"Don't know. *Oh!*" she shouted, remembering something. "The old woman speaks English."

"I know," he whispered. "Let's keep our voices down."

"She said she wants us to shepherd her—her words—to some Church of Intelligence."

"And what did you do?"

Oya breathed heavy in the same way a doctor might before he gave a terminal diagnosis.

"Sergeant?" Paxton said. This type of loitering outside the cockpit was exactly what he was trying to avoid.

"I followed her."

Oya did a quick scan of their neighborhood and their neighbors, stepping by midconversation with half glances, all of them with fractions of interest in the duo standing like speed bumps in the middle of morning traffic.

"Don't make eye contact," Paxton said. "Just play it normal."

"Normal," she scoffed. "There was half a ton's worth of supplies that they need to carry. Food. Water. Medical stuff."

"And you're carrying it?"

"Yes."

"So this is how it starts," he said out loud, his insides out now, as he considered that there was still time to go back to the sandbox, change the narrative of history, even though they said that was impossible. *This is how it all starts.*

"What starts?" Oya said, her voice rising again. "You're putting this on me?"

"No. No," he repeated, holding his hands up in surrender. "No, this is on me."

"And don't fucking forget it."

Oya seemed to feel the scowl on her expression. She seemed to hear her own volume as curious gazes darted in her direction. In a single inhale, Oya gathered together every grimace and expletive into the flare of her nostrils and, in the next moment, exhaled.

"So what were you saying?" she asked.

"Some of these cockpits are a few days ahead of when we are, maybe weeks. Sergeant Woden said last week that he was tracking the collaborator through the desert—tracking us."

"We're not all locked into the same time?"

"No," he said with a stern shake of the head. "We're all sort of spaced out over a two-year period."

"Bella."

Paxton nodded.

"Oh God," Oya said. "She already ran into one of us, already—"

Paxton held his finger to his lips. Her epiphany raised her voice just enough to leak out of their personal space. "Yes," he said with a nod. "It already happened to her. Will happen to us. Which direction are they heading?"

"Southeast toward the mountains."

"Okay, so we carry them to where they want to go and then get back to the sandbox. It could work."

"Another thing, they seem to think that the Spartan is AI, that it's controlling itself. They think all the Androne Series are artificial intelligence, that machines have become sentient. They have no idea what this really is."

Paxton grabbed the cockpit door and lifted himself inside. "I know. It's fucked up. It's all fucked up."

"And Paxton," she said, leaning into the cockpit as he pulled himself inside. "They stole something. I think that's why the military attacked."

"Stole what?"

She shrugged, ignoring the question. "By the way, there's some weight on your back, supplies, so make sure to adjust your posture."

"Will do."

She shut the door for him, all ladylike, and the cockpit went dark. Alone at last, he and his future, and Paxton decided it was time to figure out which side of time he was on.

33

A half ton's worth of supplies weighed on the Spartan's back, and it stumbled right out of the gate. They had tied the cargo with braided bamboo fibers, but too loosely, and the cargo, mostly water from the sound of it, sloshed back and forth, twisting the Spartan's path into a drunken sashay.

The Old Oak led a party of nineteen, which quickly slipped to eighteen as one fell into hypovolemic shock. They all carried injuries to some degree, hauling burns, broken bones, and fractures across a searing desert. Their feet sunk in the dunes and emerged heavier as sand trickled out from between their toes. They drowned in their own perspiration, stumbling, hallucinating, stripping off shirts and hijab-like headgear, until they started to fall, and the Old Oak, like a mother Moses, finally stopped.

They set up tents that wobbled in the wind and a fire that fizzled before sunset. They would probably die out here, but the sooner they did, the sooner he could get back to the sandbox. That was wrong, but he wasn't sure that *they* were in the right, this old woman and her nonconformist entourage. Penthouse intel had pointed to someone associated with this group drawing first blood in World War Who.

The Fishies kept their distance from the Spartan, all except for a balding man, kneeling at the Androne's feet. A man of fifty maybe, his sun-beaten skin peeling, his naked scalp soured and spotted in pinks. The man clasped his hands and bowed his head and prayed, or chanted, for an hour straight, a rhythmic and yet monotone hymn. Paxton took off his headphones and just watched the man, maybe a monk, whittle his vocal cords down to screeching threads.

And then there was Harum. A fugitive of adult conversation, the little girl had sneaked off from the failing bonfire and hid in the Spartan's shadow. Harum began timid small talk but quickly found her boldness and hugged the Spartan's leg and later tried to climb it. She even managed to get halfway up the Spartan's waist before the monk scolded and dragged her back to camp. The little girl was the cutest Paxton had ever seen, present or future, and she made him smile consistently.

Paxton's fingers and toes uncoiled from the controls as sunset squeezed light out of the cockpit and wind lullabied him into a daze. But the wind picked up, and he watched the Fishies settle into their swaying tents. Even the monk departed, but not before leaving an offering of bread at the Spartan's feet before heading in for the night.

The Old Oak crawled out from her tent almost on cue. She surveyed the encampment, then strayed toward the Spartan with a blanket hugging her shoulders and dangling cape-like on her back. She sat in front of the monk's offering, a fat loaf of bread frosted in sand and held in place by a rock.

"He believes you to be a god," the Old Oak said, lifting the bread from underneath the rock. "Most of the others do too, and those that don't, well, they believe you were sent by God, an angel, a metal messenger of heaven."

Paxton smiled and she smiled with him. She shook most of the sand off the bread and started to chew the Spartan's offering. Grains of sand snapped under each bite.

"You have any messages for us?" she asked with a mouthful of wheat muffling her voice.

Paxton shook his head and the Old Oak took a bite, seemingly satisfied with his answer. A thought occurred to Paxton then—why communicate through these simple gestures? Why not write?

The Spartan injected its finger into the sand and dragged it down to form an *I*, then looped an *a* and dubbed an *m*.

"I cannot read the script," she said before he could get to the next letter.

"Okay," he said, and considered.

He pointed to her, and the Old Oak looked up at him. "What do *you* . . ." Then he pointed to the Spartan's head. "Think . . ." Finally he pointed to the Spartan's chest. "*I* am?"

"My head on you?" she said, mimicking, pointing to her own head, then to the Spartan's chest. "Oh, what do I believe you are?"

Paxton and the Spartan nodded.

"I believe you are malfunctioned. Just a glitch in the AI overlords' system. And as long as you allow us to use you, I will use you."

"AI overlord," Paxton said. "You really don't have any idea."

They didn't. This world appeared dried completely of every ounce of knowledge that had come before. Like cavemen without the cave, and still completely in the dark. Little children flaunting fairy tales like philosophy.

"We need to turn hard south once we hit the mountains," she said, and gestured to mountain ranges stabbing into a Milky Way ceiling. "Give them another hour, yeah?"

Paxton figured the question was rhetorical, and still he lifted the Spartan's right hand and poked two fingers out of its fist.

"Two hours?" she said and chuckled. "Okay. Two hours."

It was quiet then for a while. Her mind likely wandering—wondering about what she believed was a sentient machine. Paxton wished he could explain to her, tell her about the satellites, show her the cockpit. He wished he could ask her what had happened in the hundreds of years between them.

Harum wandered out of her tent, rubbing the reds of her eyes. The Old Oak held out her hands in embrace, but Harum returned to the Spartan's legs, tangling her tiny body around its heels, jabbing her fingers and toes into the bolts and grooves, and climbing up its waist. The Spartan stared down at the girl hiking up its seven-foot frame. She stared up at it, grinning wide from cheek to cheek, excitement in her marble eyes.

"Her name is *Harum*," the Old Oak said, but he already knew that, or did he? There was something different in the way she pronounced it just now. "Her mother and I *mostly* agreed on the name. Something to define a warrior and an inflictor of pain—*Harm*."

"You named her Harm?" Paxton said, and smiled. "Her mother agreed to that?"

"She will be a warrior someday. Live up to her name."

"And what's your name?" Paxton said, mostly to himself, but he hoped she might say.

"You know . . . ," she started, but paused, as if considering whether to finish. She must have felt it strange talking to what in her mind was a walking calculator. "They call me Mute," she said, then gestured to the crowd of sleeping bodies. "*Them.* They've been calling me Mute since I was a child. My family spoke Angles, a language that nobody else knew, and . . ." Another pause, this one was longer and heavier. Her toes curled into the sand, and she wrapped her arms around her chest. "Ma spoke it, but Grandmama taught me the spelling and reading of things. I've forgotten most all of it now. My family didn't believe in AI gods, so we weren't protected when they came. AI, like you, killed Gran when I was seven. Killed my momma when I was . . ." Her voice cracked, she bit her lip, and for the first time the Old Oak bent, hunching over the sands of time and staring into them. "It took me a long while to speak their language, and in the meantime I *was* mute. The name sort of stuck—even though I speak Javan well enough now, even with my accent."

He watched her, naked in the moment, arms wrapped tight around herself, trying to hide all that she had just revealed. Sergeant Oya knocked from the outside. Paxton's shift was over, and it had felt so fast. He couldn't leave, not now, not when there was something else to say. It bore down on top of her. She wouldn't cry, not her. She was an Old Oak. Instead she blushed like the maples in October.

"For forty years, I haven't spoken a word of Angles, because machines killed my family, and now the only person in the world I can speak my mother tongue to is an AI." The Old Oak chuckled and shook her head. "A fucking War Machine."

34

It was their third day into the desert when Paxton spotted Bella's Shogun Series. It stood amid a maze of fat rocks and smooth boulders that led to the foot of a hill. The Shogun marched dutifully around the stone plot, stopping still only moments at a time. Paxton imagined Bella taking off her gloves to rub her eyes or pick her nose; then a moment later the Shogun would continue the march across its path, the very path the civilians needed to take.

They were all armed to varying degrees; even Harm carried advanced electronic components that Paxton himself couldn't name, connecting the wiring like Lego bricks. But not the monk. His palms were pressed into the sand and his head bowed as he prayed at the foot of his Spartan god, arming himself only in faith.

The Old Oak believed in weaponry. She carried the heaviest artillery of them all, what looked like a sniper rifle, with a barrel the size of an eight ball. "Now we find out which side you're truly on," she whispered, crouched at the bottom of a foothill with the rest of them.

The foothill's peak offered a clear view of Bella's Shogun. But Paxton already knew he would win this fight. What he didn't know was how it played out, whether the Spartan took serious damage, the number of civilians injured or killed—all of it was classified. Bella hadn't given away much besides the fact that she hadn't seen which series of Androne attacked her.

The Shogun was superior to the Spartan—they all were, though Paxton had noticed an advantage in the Spartan's quickness, not foot speed but like Ali's "phantom fist" that broke Sonny Liston's jaw, the Spartan seemed faster in close-quarter combat. Less armor weighing down the limbs, he figured.

The Goldfish drew shapes into the sand and positioned stones at different points in those shapes. Bones complained about the Spartan, at the Spartan. She used her wide body to block the Spartan's view of their strategies. Bones didn't seem to trust him, and Paxton thought it prudent. He wouldn't trust him either. The Old Oak, though, had a look about her, as if she knew what Paxton knew—this would be his fight, not theirs.

Three Fishies crawled barefoot up the hill: Bones, a grizzled man who might have been the Goldfish's lover, and another, a boy with twiggy arms and a head topped in ginger hair. They pinched the dirt with their tiptoes to get a firmer grip, their hands preoccupied with fancy rifles and scopes. The Goldfish crouched with a handful of others at the base of the hill. Only the monk, Harm, and the Old Oak stood with the ostracized Spartan. Harm sat nestled between the pillars of the Spartan's feet as Old Oak squinted curiously at the pair, as if something was out of place about a child so cozy with a War Machine.

"They suggested that I keep an eye on you," she said as she reached for Harm, still between the Spartan's legs. "None of them quite trust you, myself included, no one except for her." The Old Oak pulled Harm in a kicking protest from the Spartan's legs, then nodded to the monk. "She thinks you are a toy, and him, he believes you are a god."

The monk kneeled in front of the Androne, praying for deliverance as Bones, the Goldfish, and her grizzled friend mounted the hill and craned over the top. They aimed their scopes and rifles and paused. The panic was almost immediate. Bones turned to crawl down the hill first, followed by the Grizzly and then the Ginger, the slowest of the three. Their shouting was loud—*too loud*, and erratic. Paxton couldn't distinguish much from their gestures and less from the panicked conversation. The Spartan turned to the old woman and gestured to where its ears would be.

"It's gone," she said. "The other AI is gone." *Bella knows they're here.* Paxton thought it, and the Old Oak said it. "It's watching us," she said. "It knows we're here."

Androne sensors can detect movement even behind cover. It's just that in the day-to-day monotony, one might not focus on that minutia, but Bella, she was sharp as fuck.

Training exercises came to mind then. Instructors trained pilots to first go high and signal for aerial support. The Spartan lifted its gaze, searching for an aerial support signal—nothing. Was Bella going to try to fight them herself?

The Old Oak and Bones followed the Spartan's line of sight, looking through scopes and binoculars at the high horizons around them with too many hills and plateaus to count.

Their sudden silence squeezed details out from the crannies in the landscape—the whistles of wind, the screeches of insects, and then those mystery noises that could be anything and were everything in their minds.

The Goldfish gestured for the Grizzly to move back up that hill. He did, and Bones followed. The Goldfish circled around the base of the hill with another duo of brutish men. Every eye and gun and binocular lens was aimed up, searching for Bella's metal war god.

But it found them first.

The Grizzly was lifted off the ground like a rag doll, a spatter of dark red exploding out from his chest. The Ginger dropped nearly immediately after, his rib cage cracked open like a hundred wine bottles gushing with liquid.

"The fuck, Bella?" Paxton shouted.

The Spartan wrapped itself around Harm's tiny body, and right then the third bullet cracked against the Spartan's back, intended for her.

"What the *fuck*? Bells! They're civvies!"

The Old Oak raced off in what seemed like retreat to the others, but Paxton knew the heavy weapon in her hand was meant for something else.

But what *the fuck* was Bella's problem? These were civvies, he thought, as another headless body flopped to the dirt, and that one might have been the Goldfish.

Paxton spun a 180, clutched his rifle, and aimed up at a glint of bent light atop the plateau. He zoomed in hard—*too hard*. The Shogun Series disappeared into a blur of stone and sand and sky.

"Motherfucker!"

Paxton pulled the trigger anyway, a warning shot that might bring the Shogun off its trigger to take cover. It didn't work. The next bullet cracked against the Spartan's skull and just as suddenly the screen blacked out.

"Goddamn it!" Paxton shouted, panic beating out of his chest. "I win this one! What the fuck?"

Could time be changed? Was this an alternative reality being formed in real time? Or were there inaccuracies in Bella's report? She had officially declared not seeing what series of Androne attacked her, but with that accurate a shot she had to have seen the Spartan Series clearly in her scope. The titanium plating, its unmistakable cyclops eye—Bella had seen it all. And how the fuck was she this good already? This was Bella six weeks ago, when she had just barely started training in her cockpit.

His gloves suddenly went cold. The pedals sagged flaccid underneath his feet. The audio feed fizzed sharp with static. Paxton stripped the visor off his head to find the entire cockpit drenched in an inky midnight black, and for the first time he could hear his own heartbeat battering against his chest, that beat, beat, beat, instead of the thrum of the electrical current coursing through the cockpit's veins. He felt his own gloveless fingers folded up into a fist, his unclipped toenails scratching at the inside of his shoe. Paxton was now aware of himself in the cold, black space.

The screen exploded with light, scorching his pupils. The Spartan was on its back staring into the afternoon sun. Paxton donned the visor and gloves and lifted the Spartan to a crawl across the bloody sand. The Spartan reached blindly for the rifle, then zoomed carefully up the plateau. But as the lenses and light focused, he realized that the gleam of the Shogun's rifle was aimed directly at the Spartan's eye.

Gunfire cracked across the corridor of hills, and Paxton's entire body spasmed as if it had hit him. The Shogun's body snapped back and it dropped its rifle. The Androne's two-ton frame rolled down the incline of the hill, reaching and grabbing for some grip in the loose dirt.

Paxton knew it was the Old Oak that had hit the Shogun and didn't offer even a glance toward her. He raced the Spartan as fast as its feet would carry it, rifle in tow, toward Bella's Androne. Paxton was like a lancer atop a mechanical steed. As the Shogun hit the last length of the incline, the Spartan lunged up and rammed the bayonet into its chest.

The Shogun looked up at the Spartan, lens to lens. Out on the other side of the Shogun's eyes was Bella, pre-kiss, pre-breakup, staring out at the Spartan, likely confused. Paxton twisted the bayonet in the Shogun's chest, and the light in its eyes went out.

Their numbers were cut in half. Nine dead. The Old Oak and Harm and three others were untouched. The monk had caught shrapnel in his leg, and Bones had sustained a few bruises from falling in the dirt. The Goldfish's wounds were emotional, standing over the Grizzly's body. His name was Jiyo, Paxton learned, as the Goldfish hollered the name out into the night.

"Jiyo." Her breathing juggled in her throat. "Jiyo!"

Paxton's shift wouldn't end for another few hours, but he was done right then. He snatched off the visor and muted the audio feed. He folded into himself, arms around his chest and fingers under his arm-pits. Between the cockpit shifts and the office hours, Paxton had little left in him.

And Bella. She had lied to him—to them. Bella had said that the Androne was like some sort of war god, but it was the Old Oak that laid the real blow against her Shogun. Somehow, Bella hadn't seen that it was a Spartan, even though they stood lens to lens at the end, or had she lied about that? Either way it was lucky for him, because that would have narrowed the search for the collaborator to Spartan pilots only, barely thirty or so at Nellis Base.

"Fuck," he moaned in the dark.

The dulled sunlight darkened the details inside. Only the greens and reds of the knobs and switches shone in the black. He noticed the Old Oak miming in front of the Spartan, gesturing and shouting without audio. But Paxton didn't rush to slip on the gloves or return the audio feed. He slowly dressed himself in his Spartan armor, like slipping into the sleeves and shoes of one's own funeral dress, then switched the audio feed back on.

"Are you there?" she asked.

The Spartan nodded and offered two thumbs-up.

"Lost you for a while." The Old Oak squinted into the Spartan's lens and tiptoed and craned her neck up, and he felt that she saw him. "What goes on in there?"

If you only knew.

"They'll need time. We're just a day and a half away now from the interpreter's palace," she said, and flapped her arm out toward the hills. "A day for us, half for them."

"Good," Paxton said. "Just one more day."

35

Sleep was luxury. It was the Cartier bracelets, the twin-deck private yachts; it was the aged chardonnays and mink coats. Sleep was as much a dream to Paxton now as any of those things, and base personnel kept it guarded behind store-brand cappuccinos and espressos and foam-cup graffiti-leaving caffeine rings on their desktops. Sleep was luxury and never offered freely; it had to be stolen.

And Paxton stole it as he dozed off under the shade of bathroom stalls or took full-on naps as lights dimmed in the meeting room and projectors lit a laminated screen. Paxton stole away minutes at a time. Dreams were like short stories, he and Callie wrapped in green mink coats watching yachts sail in that future fishbowl. Paxton lay facedown against the coffee-ring pillows on his cubicle desk, and not even the buzz of his own ringtone could lift his head from his desktop.

"Hey, Paxton," Maria said, jabbing his shoulders with turquoise fingernails. "You're ringing."

"Ringing?" he said as he sniffled back to life. "What's ringing?"

"Your cell phone."

Paxton groped at his pockets, but the cell phone was on the desk where he had hidden it under the pension files for some nameless retiree.

"Here," Maria said, fishing it out for him.

It was the old man, his name highlighted as GRANDAD on-screen. Paxton ignored the call, then found a text message underneath, a message from VIC, Lieutenant Victoria's moniker: need to chat about things, getting kinda hairy.

Paxton's head throbbed. His eyes burned. He squinted into the screen and texted back, or attempted to. His fingers were like fins, fumbling over the touch screen display.

"When's the last time you slept?" Maria asked.

"Just now."

"Nap in your cockpit," she said. "That's what all the pilots do."

Paxton nodded, but Maria didn't know why he didn't have the luxury of daily cockpit monotony. He managed to type two words onto the screen without typos or autocorrect putting words into his mouth—will do—and he sent it off.

But as Paxton lifted his head from the cell phone screen, he discovered the ant nest of personnel crawling into the tight spaces between cubicles, desks, and each other. Nearly fifty additional noncommissioned staffers bumbled between the office aisles.

"What's this?" Paxton asked.

"Extra staffers."

"Why?"

"Not sure," Maria said and shrugged. "Think it has to do with catching the collaborator."

A shot of ice stiffened Paxton's spine. He sat up, proper posture tightening from his lower back, his eyelids peeling back just wide enough for a smile to press into Maria's cheek.

"That woke you up," she said, her smile widening even further.

"Not . . . No." He muddled the words and dropped out of eye contact. "I'm just surprised."

"Don't worry, I know you ride a Spartan."

"Spartan? What does that have to do with anything?"

"The meeting?" Maria said, and she must have seen the question lingering in his eyes, because she kept going. "You were sleeping there too?" It was barely a question, barely a rise in her inflection.

Paxton *had* slept through the entire thing, that dim room, the lullaby hum of a projector. It might as well had been general anesthesia pumping through the projector's cables like an IV.

"The collaborator is a Kingsman Series," she said.

"They're sure of it now?" Paxton said. "How do they know for sure?" But he knew now—when they discovered the corpse of Bella's Shogun Series and examined the bayonet wound on its chest, they would have assumed a Kingsman.

"I don't know how they know anything," Maria said.

Paxton's cell phone rang again. The old man, *again*, and Paxton switched it to silent.

"Heads up," Maria whispered and gestured to someone on approach.

"Lieutenant Arés," Colonel Marson said just as Paxton turned in his direction.

"Colonel," Paxton said as he popped to his feet, hand to his forehead in salute. "Sir?"

"At ease, Lieutenant. At ease." Marson put his hand on Paxton's shoulder. "Things are crazy around here right now, and trust me when I say they're about to get crazier real soon."

"What's going on exactly?" Paxton asked, genuinely curious. "All the new staffers, the helter-skelter."

"Well, that's actually what I came to speak to you about. I've got some good news."

"Good?" Paxton said.

"Very good news," the colonel said as his smile widened. "Come with me."

It never was "good news," but Paxton followed the colonel nonetheless, through secure access doors and down an oblong corridor with its vaulted ceiling lit by dots of fluorescent bloom. The "Black Box," as he called it, stood at the end of the corridor, a room with the highest security clearance on base. Two human pillars stood on either side of the door in matching navy-blue uniforms, steely-faced human decor, staring ahead without a glance at either Paxton or Marson.

The Black Box didn't live up to its name. The windowless room was white and well lit, with a birchwood conference table at the center and comfortable cushioned seats positioned around it.

A quartet of officers populated the room. Lieutenant Victoria stood behind her seat, eyeing Paxton's hand resting on the cell phone in his pocket. She had texted him minutes earlier. *Was it about this?* There were two others, whom Paxton didn't recognize, and then Sergeant Woden, sitting on the opposite side of the table. He stood to salute.

"Colonel," Sergeant Woden said and saluted, then turned to Paxton. "Lieutenant." And it sounded sincere. The bruises on Woden's nose had nearly dissolved away.

"Nice to see you again, Paxton," Lieutenant Victoria said. "Welcome to the box."

"Thank you," Paxton said, responding to both of them.

"Arés." The colonel's voice was accompanied by a burst of light and the hum of the projector above. "Take a look at this map."

The labyrinthine swirl of geographic lines dizzied Paxton. It was like geometry and French stir-fried onto watermarked paper. Yet everyone else appeared to follow, pointing and nodding, so he nodded too, as if in agreement with his own bewilderment.

"These ranges here," the colonel said as he passed his hand over the map, his gnarled fingernails seeming to scratch away acres of mountain ranges. "This is the collaborator's trail."

Fuck. Paxton mouthed the words. This was about him—about the Spartan. They were closing in. *Fuck me!*

"Didn't think we'd get him?" Woden said, appearing to notice the bounce in his lips.

"The fight's behind you now," the colonel said. He pointed at the duo, the aim of his finger bouncing off Paxton but lingering on Sergeant Woden. "Focus on the now. Focus on capturing him."

The mountain range in question was split into three main peaks, all with red marker wrapped around them. The word *triangle* had been written underneath in the same red ink.

"Triangle?" Paxton said, knowing now was the time to focus.

He rubbed the floaters skimming across his eyes and squinted deep into the greens and the grays, the dotted lines denoting separations in elevation, and the coordinates, 36 by 117. He didn't blink—every detail was suctioned into the swirl of his eyes. This was his future, his *literal* future; these were the decisions he would make, and Paxton had to remember how to counter himself, or at least how to counter his instinct with the knowledge of things to come.

"The triangle, as Sergeant Woden has been referring to it, is a set of three mountains and the end of this mountain range."

"Like," Sergeant Woden said, then paused, as if unsure whether he should finish. "I thought of a triangle because it's . . ." Again, a pause. "It's like our Bermuda Triangle to capture the collaborator."

So very creative, Woden. You should've been a poet.

"The collaborator and his allies have gathered at the foothills of this triangle, and unbeknownst to them, Sergeant Woden tracked them there a few days ago. In which time we have been analyzing this data to prep for a final assault."

"That *is* good news," Paxton said, trying to figure out when this would be. It hadn't happened in his cockpit yet, obviously. So he still had time to counter; he just had to find this triangle mountain range. "So where exactly—"

"The good news that I was referring to wasn't that exactly," the colonel said, cutting Paxton off.

"Oh," Lieutenant Victoria said, her posture rearing up like a horse on high-heeled hooves. "You haven't told him yet?"

"Not yet," Marson said.

Told me what? Their "good news" sounded like some movie twist to keep an audience guessing. And, Paxton guessed, it could be anything from "you've been promoted again" to "we know you're the collaborator." But the buzz returned right there, right then, echoing through the empty spaces in Paxton's pocket. It felt heavier than ever, like it could tear through the bottom of his pocket. This was the third time now, and the old man wasn't that persistent. Something was wrong.

"Callie." He said it as he thought it, the words just bubbling up to his lips like a kettle at boiling point.

"Cell phone?" the colonel said, nearly scolding, nearly, but still with a nepotistic softness.

"Sorry," Paxton said, lifting the phone out of his pocket. "I have to," he said. "Family emergency."

"Go," Marson said. "We'll talk tomorrow."

"Thank you, sir." He offered a flaccid-wrist salute and paced toward the exit, answering the phone midstep but not bringing the receiver to his ear until he stepped through the Black Box doors.

36

The doctors called it false labor contractions, the results of which could lead to stillbirth or cervical hemorrhaging and death, all-too-familiar territory for Paxton. He had murdered his mother at birth in a similar way. Like father, like son.

Paxton thought he might avoid thinking of her by submerging his head in the cafeteria cacophony, submerging his nostrils into coppery peppers, charred meats, and floral muffins or the eye dazzle of colorful boots, sandals, and sneakers maneuvering the bodily gridlock; the sensory overload should mute the thought of her. But the breakfast chatter wasn't loud enough, the buoyancy of breakfast not pungent enough. She was a resilient sensation.

He squinted into the white hole of an empty foam cup and saw Callie's eyes in two black beads of leftover coffee. She stared back at him, quarantined to the corner of his cup, white hospital gown swathed around her. He saw her everywhere, lying alone in a hospital bed awaiting another round of testing. It was in these moments that he loved her the most and felt all the guilt that came with it.

Paxton refilled the cup with coffee, then tried the hangar. It was louder there, and the closer he approached the cockpit, the louder it became, muzzling thoughts of her, thoughts of his own mother—his own matricide. His shift was hours away, and still Paxton orbited the egg-shaped globe as if it were another world that he could escape to. For hours, he dragged his soles in circles around it until the caffeine fueling him dried out and he crashed against it.

Sergeant Oya had the same undead look about her as she slithered out of the metal shell, the same shrimplike posture, the same eyes, red dyed with irises floating aimlessly across the white, the same scent, the same weathered lips, like dizygotic siblings of their mechanical egg.

"I shot down another Fury," Oya said. The words came sighing out of her.

"They're on our asses," he said. "We need to turn back to the sandbox."

Oya glanced over Paxton's shoulder then and stepped closer. "I know what it is."

"What *what* is?"

"What they stole," she said, then lowered her voice. "What brought the War Machine hell hammer down on their stadium."

Now Paxton glanced over her shoulder and stepped closer yet. "And?"

"A map," she said.

"A map of what?"

"Don't know, but it's digital, and they don't have the means of displaying it. The technology is too old and therefore too advanced. That's why they need an interpreter."

"So we turn back now. They're good. They don't need us."

"We lost another one," she said, seeming to not even register what he had just said.

"Who?"

"Boy," Oya said, then gestured to the vining plaits running like velvet rope along her scalp. "The one with the mohawk. The desert took him."

Oya lowered her head then as moisture swelled in her eyes. She fought the tears, she fought hard, but her sensitivity brimmed over, attracting the attention of only the nosiest of pilots and maintenance men. And he couldn't console her. Not now. Not with all his emotion tethered into Callie and the non-recollections of a dead mother. Or could he? Could he redirect the current of his sympathies toward Oya?

"It's okay," he said, and stepped around her, blocking her eyes from curious pilots and crew. "You need sleep."

"They're dying, Pax." *Pax* now—had they grown that amicable? "We need to get them out of the desert."

And here, Paxton nearly thought of insisting that they leave the Fishies. Tell Oya that Woden and his new scout were closing in on them in his "Bermuda Triangle." But he wouldn't say it now. Maybe tomorrow, maybe the day after.

"Get some sleep," he suggested as he crawled into the cockpit; then he demanded it. "Sleep!"

37

The desert whipped muscular gusts of sand at their limbs and necks and made them rag dolls in its tantrum. It mauled their ankles, then knees, then swallowed them wholly, snakelike as sand inched up to their waists. Its tentacles choked their orifices, gagging them and gouging their lines of sight. And they stumbled and fell and crawled to unmarked graves under a blotted-out sun.

The Goldfish had become an anchor of grief as she dragged behind them. She sank in the loose sand, she tripped and stumbled, drunk with despair, and eventually she dissolved away. They lost her to the sand, but not for a lack of searching. The Old Oak had said a day and a half, but it was going on three days and there was still no sign of anything but sand.

The few survivors lined themselves up behind the Spartan's body, a millipede of footsteps stumbling behind the robotic physique. Bones, the monk, and the Old Oak among them, and Harm nestled in the Spartan's arms under two layers of blankets. The Fishies offered her up without protest, their technophobia giving way to desperation, all of them except the monk.

Even now with the winds lashing at their backs, the monk disapproved. *Sacrilege*, Paxton imagined him saying as he prayed his incantations at Harm, hissing the words with a lisp and nearly sneezing out the nasal language. The Old Oak had told Paxton the old monk seemed jealous, that somehow he felt it unfair that she, unordained, could commune with the Spartan, and he, wholly devout, could not.

The monk reached up for Harm right then, but Paxton pulled away. She was so tiny, so infinitely fragile in the Spartan's titanium arms. He held her as gently as the controls would allow and rocked her—she liked that. She would smile and close her eyes as she nestled herself deeper in the blanket.

Glints on the horizon shone like night-lights against the overcast sky. The glints swelled into a gleam, and as they pushed farther the gleam split into nine points of light, like chandeliers on a sunless sky.

It resembled a mosque or some kind of religious structure—gold domes, harpooning spires, in reverence to an AI god. A vast wall snaked around smaller structures inside and obscured most of the buildings therein. Nine pillars shot out of the corners of the wall with boisterous light swinging lighthouse-style inside.

The pace picked up as the sound of civilization spilled over the walls, words both foreign and distant, and yet he knew their meaning—hope. The sand there suddenly spun like yellow fog trying to hold them back and only thinning moments before they reached the trail. Paved in stray rocks like lazy cobble, the path tightened and led to a steep climb of steps crested by a heavy gate that towered just over ten feet. Baseball-size gold emblems jutted out from the outer edges of the gate with what appeared like Arabic calligraphy etched into their round, smooth surfaces.

"If they assail us," the Old Oak said as she veered into the Spartan's path, "you take her and flee." She touched Harm's head, stirring the little girl's eyes to open. "You flee."

The Spartan nodded confidently as it watched Harm unfolding from sleep, though Paxton prayed that it wouldn't come to that. They had come so far and lost so much. And here they were, standing on the dais of their final destination. But it wasn't about them, not completely, and he knew it. He knew that this bubbling anticipation popping like pyrotechnics in his brain was about getting back home—back to the sandbox and back to Callie.

The Old Oak made her way toward the door without even a hint of fatigue, bags on her back, bags on her shoulder, bouncing as she skipped up the last few steps. She lifted a long pipe and swathed it in a lime-shaded cloth. She lit the end of it, and a green flame bloomed bright in the overcast evening.

Harm peeked out from her blanket as flames hissed louder than the desert itself, firecracker-like snaps, out-voluming the wind. The Old Oak lifted the flame over the gate and swung it back and forth, again and again, until drips of green flame trickled down, until the fire soured to a pickle green, until it went black.

"This is it," the Old Oak said.

"This is what?" Paxton asked as he lowered Harm to the ground. He shrugged and the Spartan followed, as he hoped to convey his confusion.

"Your church," she said as she grabbed Harm by the hand. "Sometimes I wonder about you. It's like you're not part of the AI construct. Like you're from another world or something."

"You're the one praying to drones," he said.

"She will teach you the history of things," she said. "The interpreter will teach us everything."

Paxton felt curiosity's tickle in his cerebrum. *Interpreter.* Any individual with know-how enough to translate advanced technology—older technology—likely had answers to even more questions. Who was the Peacemaker, and why did he attack?

Voices came from the other side of the gate. Their shouts were like whispers at that distance. The Old Oak shouted for Bones; she was slouched in a stupor on the stairs. Bones eyed the Old Oak but didn't move except for an abnormal tremble in her feet. Her thick thighs appeared to shake at the mere thought of standing.

"It's my accent," the Old Oak said as she rested her hand against the Spartan's frame, where a rib cage might wrap around a body. She slouched there and heaved a breath. It was so casual that she didn't even seem to know she was doing it, until she did, and flinched away. "It's better for her to speak," she continued. "My accent might confuse them."

It happens like that, camaraderie, friendship, *love*. It happens in the invisible moments that get forgotten in the nooks of perception, things that are difficult to see, like an arthritis for the eye. But standing there in the Spartan's shoes, Paxton took a second to unthread the blur of the moment. Its significance shone from the screen, a woman and the machine standing beside her.

Bones eventually heaved herself up the remaining stairs. Her legs were squid-like, tentacles that seemed to tangle into the stairs' knots and bends. She pressed both hands against the wall and shouted something foreign. A man's voice returned from the other side and Bones spoke again; then he responded, then her, and back and forth, volleying their wrangle for ten full minutes, more even. By the end, Bones's voice was a fingernail scratch. She slouched against the wall, defeated, and gestured to the Spartan.

"They will not open," the Old Oak said. "Time to show our hand . . . time to show them you."

The Old Oak shouted something different over the wall, and she shouted it louder, an arrogance in her tone, without a care of her off-putting accent. The doors opened immediately, not on hinges but like barn doors, the two sides rolling away from each other as shadows from inside spilled out. Ten of them, and all carrying guns. They marched out in a single line, brushing past Bones, knocking her on her ass. They stepped over Harm, past the monk and Old Oak, and then dropped their weapons and dropped to their knees. They pressed their foreheads against the stone and dirt, and they prayed in a loud panic, and the puffs of their breath blew sand away from their lips.

"Mater," they said as their hands trembled against the dirt, their fingernails scratching gravel and concrete. "Mater," they repeated. "Mater," they huffed as grains of sand fell out from under their lips, saliva dribbling. "Mater," they screamed in a hysteria, as mad as any rabid pack of dogs howling at a moon.

The Spartan was the moon; the Spartan was their god.

The Old Oak helped Bones to her feet as the monk joined the men in worship. Harm ignored them all, plugging in and unplugging circuits on a small motherboard the Old Oak had given her, lighting up green and yellow nodes as if it were a coloring book. The girl seemed more like an Einstein than the "harmful" princess-warrior the Old Oak wanted her to be.

"Mater?" Paxton said, and cocked his head at the men kneeled in front of him.

And the Old Oak must have noticed something in the Spartan's posture. She stood between them and the Spartan and watched the Spartan's neck cock to the side like a confused pup.

"It's your name," she said. "The one I chose for you. They just can't pronounce it properly. Mother. Your name is Mother."

38

The cockpit was like his cocoon. He would go in one end and come out on the other side of that screen a god. A strange metamorphosis. Radio waves spun through the circuits like silk, and suddenly he was omnipresent, wearing an armor of titanium and a helmet of steel alloys. His golden fleece, the whole armor of God, and they worshipped him.

Fanatics packed the roads, globules of arms and eyes reaching out to the Spartan. They were drowning in each other, just to get a glimpse of *mater*. Circuit-chip pendants hung on many necks, yellow cables braided into their hair. Scrawny arms hoisted paintings of Andro021 donning halo crowns or aerial drones with feathered wings or honeybees spraying a gold nectar across the sky.

Children ran alongside the Spartan holding X symbols; the Old Oak pointed out that this X represented the intersection of man and machine. This was just one sect of the Javan religion, and they were half-right—Andro021 were, after all, men inside of machines.

Zealous middle-aged men hoisted banners overhead. The symbols printed on these banners seemed familiar and foreign all at once. Paxton squinted at the symbols, the dots and parentheses, the forward slashes and colons, and he stared long enough to think that the symbols somehow resembled computer code. *But why?*

The township within the walls was monstrously larger than Paxton had imagined. Some structures rose nearly ten stories high. It was a world made of machinery. Recycled brass shells instead of brick, a patchwork of colorful alloys instead of walls, and on the rare occasion a vintage twentieth-century car door that opened as a window. In the other windows, circuit wiring, reds and yellows, hung together like a sort of curtain. And a single jet engine crested the tallest of their buildings, its turbine spinning like a low-tech windmill.

They filled their world with such empty technologies, and Paxton slowed his Spartan gait as he marveled at it all. A complex spiderweb of clotheslines twined the upper floors of every domicile, made up of ancient cables. Loose coats and vests writhed there uncomfortably in the wind.

A woman led them through the crowds, wearing what looked like a wool cloak with a hijab that covered only her hair, and even then the features of her face were lost to a mask of tattoos; the moss-green ink appeared everywhere light found her skin. She was a walking tapestry, swirling shapes and Arabic-like calligraphy dancing across her hands and face and even the heels of her feet, slipping, as she stepped, from underneath the cover of her cloak.

The monk stalked close behind the woman—too close, as he stomped on her heels and sandals. They shared similarly patterned vestments, a gender-neutral robe that dragged on the sand and lifted in the breeze. It might have been a similar religious sect or maybe just fashion sense, but he preached to the poor woman ad nauseam.

Bones lagged, basically sleepwalking on the path behind them. At one point she was nearly swept up in the hounding crowds as she half hibernated beneath the Spartan's long evening shadow. But Harm called out to her from atop the Spartan's shoulder. The little girl kicked her feet, gleeful as she peered back to her laggard cohort.

The robed woman untangled herself from the monk's one-way conversation and returned to the Old Oak. Now the woman monologued without a space for the Old Oak to respond, as if seeking a type of verbal revenge. But as the woman spoke, the Old Oak's eyes continually rolled toward the Spartan. The conversation likely focused on the Androne. Was this woman the interpreter?

"She said your coming was prophesied," the Old Oak said. "They call you . . ." She searched for words. "Package Embryos? Or something that sounds like this."

"Package Embryos?" Paxton said, and smiled, thinking that with monikers like Harm and Package Embryos, naming his son something like Eddie wasn't that bad after all.

"Haven't been here since I was a little girl," the Old Oak said, staring up at the buildings behind her. "It's changed." She glanced ahead. "It's stayed the same." She squinted then, eyes sinking through craters of wrinkles, her vision aimed at buildings and faces that must have appeared foreign and familiar all at once.

He wanted to ask how her mother had died. They shared that heartbreak. It was that type of pain that never fully sank to the bottom of memory but buoyed in the quiet of self-reflection. The Spartan was her mirror, her image cast against its shiny titanium body, and she didn't seem to have the heart to look at herself.

They came to a clearing at exactly sunset, that exact moment when light stone-skips off the horizon and flickers into mush. But it made the night-lights seem brighter. Lanterns lit rainbows in the windows and doorways behind them.

Another heavy climb of stairs came next, seventy-two steps high, and he counted, ticking off another number in his head as he heard the crunch of gravel under the Spartan's feet. Bones nearly collapsed halfway up, but the Spartan caught her on the way down. She pulled away as if the Spartan had violated her. She cursed, or at least it sounded like that, as she flailed her arms and regained her step.

A verdant meadow sprawled for nearly a mile, unpopulated besides the few hundred sentries roaming the grass. Beyond that was the church. It towered over everything, hundreds of feet high, with an *x* above two massive yellow doors. It was made to resemble gold, but the Spartan's scanners revealed an alloy of copper and brass.

The woman stopped them there. She had said little to nothing the entire hike up the stairs and seemed to try to make up for that lost time. Her lips moved fast, careening past punctuation, without a single breath between her words. The monk leaned into her monologue, his posture literally tilting toward her with his mouth agape. The Old Oak listened with a different sort of scrutiny. The glower of suspicion ran around the ring of her eyes as she glanced at the Spartan every few seconds or so, as if ready to translate, but then got caught up in another string of words.

"The priestess will take you in," the Old Oak said, gesturing to the woman—*the priestess*. "Only you get to see the interpreter. So . . ." The Old Oak dangled the word in front of him, waiting for a response. "We'll wait for you here?" It sounded almost like a question.

"I can't speak their language," he said as the Spartan pointed to the side of its head where would-be ears might hang.

"You won't understand, right?" she said and quickly turned her attention and language back toward this woman, this Priestess.

The Priestess eyed the Spartan. She pressed her palm against its thick titanium abdomen and whispered something to it in Javan. Neither Paxton nor the Spartan responded, and she returned a quick spiel to the Old Oak. They bickered for a moment as if they were haggling down the price at a garage sale. Even Bones chimed in for moments at a time while slouched on the grass. But it seemed to be the monk who veered the direction of the argument. His voice was calm and persuasive, and the Priestess seemed to agree.

"Do you speak the language of palms?" the Old Oak asked.

"Language of palms?" Paxton and the Spartan shook their heads.

"Then they'll let me in with you."

"Good," Paxton said, and the Spartan nodded.

The Old Oak kneeled in front of Harm and took something from the girl's backpack. It was a smartphone-size device with a touch screen interface and exposed hardware at its back. This was the map they needed translated. She pocketed the device as she whispered to Harm. The girl protested when it was obvious that she wasn't going with them.

"Mater," the girl hollered, running to the Spartan instead of the Old Oak, and latched herself, arms and legs alike, around the Androne's leg. "Mater."

Her eyes, her beautiful little eyes, stared up at the Spartan with a fear that Paxton hadn't seen before. He wished then that he could hold her, not in the Spartan's metal flesh but in his arms. He imagined rocking her back and forth to snoring sleep. But then the monk peeled her away from the Spartan's body, and they disappeared down the stairs.

The Priestess, the Old Oak, and the Androne entered the church's massive main hall. A stained-glass ceiling yawned open above, a sky unto itself, hundreds of feet high, dizzying at the mere glance of it. Light bounced off the stained-glass fixtures, and the space was a crayon swirl of shine and shade. Invisible bourgeoisie huddled in the pews, their silhouettes shifting back and forth.

He thought of Callie then. Her parents wanted the baby christened in a traditional Chinook pseudo-Christian church; something like this—something like a soupy mix of centuries-old theologies built into bricks and mortar. This renovated cathedral had lost its meaning and found new ones, kind of like him and Callie, he thought.

An altar stood at the anterior of the room, but the Priestess gestured to a passage behind it and a stairway coiling upward. She stopped there, at the foot of the stairs, and said something to the Old Oak. The Old Oak responded, then glanced back at the Spartan, but not to translate, just to watch. And the conversation continued, nods and shaking heads, large gestures and curious expressions. For over a minute they spoke, and the Old Oak glanced back more than twice to meet the Spartan in its eye. When they finally stopped, she seemed different. She stared at the Spartan with a narrower cut in her eyes, as if the Spartan stood farther away than it was and she had to squint to see it.

Was that it? Paxton asked himself. Had the Priestess said something to the Old Oak about the Androne that twisted her eye contact away from the Spartan's and pushed her a few cautious steps farther away.

"The interpreter is up this way," the Old Oak said without even a glance of eye contact. "The path leads to the valley of the trident."

Paxton eyed the carvings of tridents etched into the ribbed ceiling, the arches, the curves, and the bends of the room. There was an oblique sexuality to the sprawling interior, and while the outsides were erected in phallic spires, the interiors bowed and bent to the feminine.

A brick stairway spiraled upward. Long curtains of shadow stuck to the curved gray brick. Jade lanterns hung on the walls and swayed as a draft drained down from above. On the third spin around, Paxton began to notice a few hanging wires; by the fifth spin, he was surrounded by fat circuit cables, red power lines, black transition cords with exposed filament. So much of the stuff hung that by the eighth rung, they covered the walls entirely. The wires knotted into each other and hung over the steps as they rounded the final twist of stairs.

Right then, two things happened simultaneously. A knocking boomed from the cockpit door—*Oya already?* And second, a large shadow loomed against the wall at the top of the stairway. Her shadow, the interpreter's, and with her came answers. Another round of knocking, and Paxton considered shutting down and climbing out, *but no*, he had to see her. Even as the knocking persisted, Paxton kept moving forward, asking himself the questions.

"What is the importance of this map?" he said as he squinted into the monitor, into the image of a large body standing in the distance. "Does this have anything to do with the Peacemaker?"

"Pax?" a voice came muffled from the other side of the door along with the *beat, beat, beat* knocking.

But then he saw her. "Jesus. *Christ?*" Paxton said as he stared beady eyed at her. "Interpreter?"

Her, sitting on a dais of dirt and piled-up rock, weeds, and vine. The entire spaghetti spoil of wiring led to her—a Macedonian, a Series 0, a prototype.

The fabled interpreter was a fucking Androne.

39

The Macedonian was dead. It was a fossil of Androne architecture, an artifact, high-tech vestiges at its joints and fractures on its glass eye. Buried under shadow, weeds, layers of rust, the Androne was like a memory of the past, faded and fading into the amnesiac future.

Nature nibbled away at the metals, moss biting at chrome heels, needlegrass acupuncture through corrosion on the right foot. Vines had coiled into rusted-out hollows where bolts had once aligned leg to knee. And more vines wrapped around the waist, tightened like corsets. Cobwebs between the chin and chest seemed to be the only thing holding the head to its shoulders. Nature nibbled like green maggots—like caterpillars, eating away at the fruits of their past.

But the Priestess wasn't satisfied to let it rest. She extracted metal organs, transplanted inputs and outputs, Frankensteining the machine. Soon, those hundred cables and cords snapped with current, and the ancient Androne spasmed back to a half life. But then there was knocking on the cockpit door right beside him, the clatter of stiff knuckles against metal invading the sounds of the future.

"Shit."

He shut it all down, the visor winked out, the screen went black, and the suction on the gloves exhaled off Paxton's sweaty palms. He cringed as he lifted the door open, adjusting to the thousand incandescent suns' novas above.

"We made it," he said, still wincing at the light, but then it wasn't Oya, *was it?* That sugary aroma wafting in, the shine on the boots, the narrow figure silhouetted in the light.

"Paxton?" she said, *Bella* said. Cherry eyeliner twinkled as she blinked, her lips gleaming as she spoke. "You made it where?"

Paxton's gaze snagged onto the balls of Bella's eyes like there were hooks there. He couldn't blink away. He barely recognized her, dressed to the nines, and she looked like a ten under the drawn-out cheekbones and color breathed on her pale face. Bella was beautiful in a way that he hadn't noticed before, and not unnaturally so. It was as if the cosmetic sketch lifted her own natural features up to their surfaces, eyes swirling to blink, and lips buoyant as she spoke.

"Paxton?" Bella said again, and smiled as he stared lost into her eyes. "Made it where?"

"I'm, uh, I'm right where I'm supposed to be," he said, glancing at the clock in the cockpit. There were still forty-five minutes until Sergeant Oya's shift. "What are you doing here?"

"Playing hooky. Didn't wanna train on the Androne today."

"Americana Series?"

"Right. So I figured I'd catch you for lunch. But . . . you haven't taken a lunch, or bathroom break, in the past hour."

Now that he thought about it, Paxton did feel a bulge in his bladder and a growing echo in his empty stomach, which had become all too familiar in the past weeks. He had been neglecting himself. The waist of his pants felt looser, shirt sleeves sagged on his shoulders, a few months short of muscle atrophy, and all just to be a voyeur into the future.

"How long have you been waiting?" Paxton asked.

"Around two hours, but I mean, I've been bouncing back and forth."

"Oh," he said, not sure what to say about what sounded like stalking. "So what's up?"

"I just wanted to talk . . ." She paused. "I wanted to apologize."

"No." Paxton waved it off. "Don't."

"No, I do," she insisted. "I should. You're with somebody. You have a kid on the way. I shouldn't have . . ."

Kissed? No, she shouldn't have. He shouldn't have let her either. But for a moment there, Bella had accomplished something. Paxton's attention turned away from the warmth of the cockpit, away from Old Oak and the Macedonian, and that peephole to the future. For a moment, Bella had made Paxton present. But it wasn't the mascara or counters or the five-o'clock eyeshadow's heart beating behind the blink of her eyes. It was Callie; Bella had reminded him of her. He imagined her on Bella's face, eyes narrower, skin tone a few shades darker. He could see Callie on Bella's features, and he thought of the hospital bed in the North Novato and the pregnant bump weighing on Callie's hips.

"Listen, *Callie*, I—" Paxton cringed as he said it and so did she. "Sorry, *Bella*." He held her name and paused. "Bella, stuff happens. It's in the past."

She smiled. "You wanna maybe lunch it out?"

No, not now, not with the future loitering in orbit twenty-two thousand miles above. Not with answers under his fingernails and at his fingertips. But he smiled to balance the negativity on his tongue, the *no, sorry* souring on his taste buds, but she kept speaking, pushing past the half smile, half frown seesawing on Paxton's lips.

"You haven't eaten, have you?" she said. "We could head to the mess hall. You have to try their oatmeal cookies."

"Sure," he said, giving in. *But fuck*, his mind and his lips at odds. "Yes," he continued, hating himself as he said it. "Let's go."

"Cool," Bella said.

"Sergeant Columbia," a cadet shouted as he raced up to her. "General Mattis needs to speak to you immediately."

"Shit," she hissed, then turned a smirk to Paxton. "Red-handed."

"It's an active emergency, Sergeant," the cadet insisted. "We should . . ." And he gestured the last words of the sentence as he pointed to a crew of men in the distance.

Bella's expression went dark. "'Kay," she said as the cadet led her toward a crowd in the distance, which included Woden and other high-level pilots. "I'm in real trouble now," she said. "Rain check?"

"Rain check," Paxton said.

Paxton climbed back into the cockpit, dragging the door in behind him, as a cell phone signal slipped between the gap in the ajar door. The phone rang as if it knew the space was closing. A quick, terse shrill slithered into the cockpit just before Paxton closed the door and closed out all signals to the space.

"Paxton?" the old man yelled through the receiver. "You can talk?"

"I can talk," Paxton whispered.

"Called you, ten times almost."

"I was in the cockpit. No signal. How's Callie?"

"There's . . ." The old man's voice bounced up and down, not going anywhere. "There's, uh, there's complications."

"What complications?"

"What'd he say?" the old man asked himself. "Preterm labor or something or the other."

"False labor contractions," Callie said, her voice adrift in the background current.

"She there?" Paxton said, and didn't wait for the answer. "Give her the phone." He said it but didn't mean it. Paxton didn't want to talk to her. Not that he didn't want to, but he didn't know what to say, and yet he said it again anyway. "Let me talk to her."

"Hello?" Callie said, a soft, warbling cadence and heavy breathing. *Had she been crying?*

"Callie," he said. "You okay? What's going on?"

"Nothing. Waiting. I have an IV," she said.

"They gave you something?" he asked.

"Something," she replied, seemingly implying that she didn't know what, but he could tell from the drawl in her tone that it was likely some sort of sedative. "Waiting for the doctor to come back in."

"Okay, good. That's good." *Isn't it?* "How do you feel?"

"I'm scared," she said—the drugs said. Callie would never have admitted it otherwise. "I don't know what's happening."

"You're gonna be okay." Easy for him to say, so he said it again. "You'll be fine."

"I'm scared." The drugs again.

"What did the doctor say?"

He couldn't hear her breathing. Her voice disappeared into an abyss of white noise, and he halfway thought the phone had cut out.

"Callie?" he said.

"Yes." She sniffled.

"What did they say?"

"I may have to lose the baby," she said, and took in a deep breath. "I may have to make that choice, the baby or me."

Now he went quiet. But he couldn't go quiet, *no*, he had to be the strong one. He had to fill the dead spaces with something.

"No," he said, but that *was* what he had wanted, right? A way out, from the baby, from her.

"I am," she continued her drug-induced slur. "If I lose the baby, you'll break up with me."

"I don't know what you mean."

"You don't like me."

"That's . . . not true."

"After I lose this baby, I lose you too."

"Are you wearing the bracelet?" he asked. "The jade one?"

"Yes," she said.

"I bought it because that first day we met, you lost your green watch. Larry and I had sat down to eat a few tables down, and you came back to your table and asked the waitress, did she see a green watch."

"You remember that?"

Paxton nodded even though she wouldn't see. He scratched at his head, fingernails shoveling into the dirt of his mind. He dug deeper into himself than he ever had, searching for her; searching for the part of his mind that Callie lived in. But she was everywhere, in every thought and every decision. She was everything, and how had he not noticed it before?

"You there," she asked. "Paxton?"

"I can't say how *you* think about love, Cal," he said delicately. "I don't know how you define it, or interpret it. But for me love is a . . ." He searched for the right words. "Love is this cocktail of feelings: a little bit of affection, fondness, a little bit of lust, maybe even a bit of pity. The intoxication is hard to parse out, but I am intoxicated by you. I love you, Callie," Paxton said for the first time. For the first time, she heard it. "I love you."

Paxton heard nothing from the other end of the receiver, but waited, replaying the words in his head. Did he get it right? It was messy and maybe sounded insincere, but it was true.

Suddenly, and for seemingly no good reason, the volume in the hangar outside went up. Footsteps came pounding in. Voices elevated to a fevered pitch. His curiosity piqued, but he recoiled. He reached for the cockpit door and pulled it down, leaving just enough space for a cell phone signal to slip in.

"You remembered?" she asked. "The watch?"

"I remember you said it was green, probably set to match your green Ninja Turtles T-shirt, or those green flip-flops you had on. No, the flip-flops weren't green, but they had so much grass on them that they looked green. You were like this salad of a girl that day, yes, I remember."

She laughed.

"Love you too, Pax," she said.

Paxton smiled. "I love you, Callie Arés."

Quiet again, after that nearly indirect proposal. It seemed that Callie had believed his improvised rant about love, and what was far more surprising, Paxton seemed to believe it too.

"What you smiling like that 'bout?" the old man said in the background of the call, and Paxton imagined Callie smiling, cheeks curved, lips covering any chance of teeth. "What's he saying to you?"

Callie gave the phone back to the old man, but Paxton hung up. The hangar was a riot of noise now, louder than he had ever heard. Something was happening, something big, but still Paxton pulled the cockpit door shut. Still he tapped into the digital interface and dressed himself in the Androne's armor. He had to see this interpreter. He had to find out what the war was all about.

40

The Macedonian's eye, composed of a thousand microscopic hexagons, a replica of a fly's compound vision, blinked light. The rusted metal head jerked forward, shoulders spasmed, seesawing into balance. Rust rained from between the joints, and its fingers twitched like a dance across invisible piano keys. The Macedonian dragged its left foot backward across the sand, lining up with the right. Then the ancient Androne thrust itself forward, knees bounding, legs lifting, but couldn't quite climb to its rusted feet.

The Priestess kneeled in front of the Macedonian, her knees melted into dirt, her head bowed toward the soil, and yet there was no reverence in her movement. Long, exaggerated exhales belched from her nostrils as she wormed fingers into soil like scratching an itch in the earth. She cursed, or at least it sounded like it—vulgarity was that same genre of sound in any language. She scowled at the metal monster in front of her, a look that implied a resentment deeper than the dirt she dug into.

The Priestess dug a cable out of the soil, caked in clumps of black dirt, its rubbery silicone skin cracked and peeling away, revealing the copper soul within. She bent the wire slightly, like squeezing a narrow sponge for all its juice, but the Macedonian continued its spastic dance, its body language implying *not enough power*. The Priestess bent the wire more, a 45-degree angle, then 90 degrees; then she folded the wire into her fist and squeezed it until the Macedonian orgasmed into a flailing of limbs, then eyes lit, bloomed bright—*alive*.

The Macedonian hunched over with its hands on its lap, its compound eyes aimed down toward its feet. It stared at its hands as if seeing them for the first time, squeezing them into fists, then opening their wide, rusted palms. It looked up at the room, glanced past the Old Oak, then past the Priestess even faster. Finally its compound vision settled on the Spartan, and it paused as if dying its battery-dead death again. But Paxton knew this lull in movement was from the pilot. Their jaw dropping, eyes narrowing, as it stared into an Androne mirror.

The Macedonian's gestures were almost immediate. It splayed its fingers, showed its palm, then made a fist. It lifted and dropped its hands in circular motions. It brought its thumb to its chin and nodded. The Priestess nodded and spoke to the Old Oak, and she turned to the Spartan and translated the third leg in this relay of words.

"You shouldn't be here," the Old Oak said. "That is what she said—*she*." The Old Oak's thumb pointed to the Macedonian. "She said you shouldn't be here, because they'll find you."

Sign language, Paxton realized, as the Macedonian began another round of clumsy motions. He saw it now as it bent its knuckles, carpal spins, palms out, then fists in against its chest, and the Priestess seemed fluent in every mimed gesture.

"And she said . . . ," the Old Oak continued, translating the second round of hand signals. "She's further ahead of you?" the Old Oak asked the Spartan, and didn't seem to understand the words she was translating. "She said she's further ahead, but . . . I don't understand. Do you?"

He understood. That pilot was months, years, maybe decades ahead of Paxton. But what he didn't understand was how the pilot would know what time Paxton and his Spartan were from.

"There are general things you should know," the Old Oak translated. "Firstly, these people's dialects are a spoken form of computer language—some of the C languages, PHP, and a number of computer languages yet to be created. And Java, a lot of it is Java code."

"Javan," Paxton said, and nodded.

"The grammatical influences of Allah and Laozi dialects," the Old Oak said, seeming to struggle with the translation of it, and Paxton wondered if her strange interpretations, Allah and Laozi, were due to the Middle East and Asia no longer existing as they were. She continued, "Most of what you're hearing is verbalized computer language, in reverence of the all-powerful AI."

"I don't care," Paxton said. "Why are we fighting them?"

"The religion has its roots in the present Middle Eastern religion of Baháʼí, and the church is designed in the Baháʼí tradition. And they've probably given you a feminine name?"

"Mother," Paxton said and nodded.

"That's because in their religion, the Andro99s are all female," the Old Oak continued. "And that is because the antennae that receive the satellite signals are located in the base of the belly." The Old Oak stepped closer and pressed her palm against the Spartan's stomach as the Priestess continued to speak. "The antennae are where a womb would be and . . ." The Old Oak paused and turned back to the Priestess in disbelief. "They believe the Andro99s are receiving a signal from an AI god, not a bunch of grunts in a worn-down . . . hangar?"

The Old Oak seemed confused; every word of her translation was a revelation to her. Paxton imagined the trauma of having one's beliefs churned upside down and having to reerect them right side up to translate, to make sense of the nonsense she was hearing. But she wouldn't get any time to adjust as the Macedonian held out its rusted hands, she handed the device to the Priestess, and the Priestess placed the device into the Macedonian's palm.

"Who the fuck are you?" Paxton asked in vain. "Who?"

The Macedonian gestured to the device and began another gestured spiel to the Priestess.

"It's a map," the Old Oak translated with an eyebrow raised and an ear cocked toward her own words as if revealing secrets to herself. "It's a device with encrypted intelligence on a map to a place beyond the mountains and desert. A place that controls the satellites."

The Macedonian's body seizured, its eyes winking in and out of consciousness, dead for a second then back again, like the flicker of a light bulb. In seconds the Macedonian came back refreshed and began signing.

"I've forgotten what I was saying before," the Old Oak translated. "My equipment malfunctions, and it has been over . . . eight months? Eight months since we began?"

The Old Oak shook her head in complete bewilderment, but Paxton understood. The pilot was using shoddy equipment and was likely not even at any base. The pilot had lost connection with them for nearly a year before getting the equipment working again. What was seconds for them had been eight months for the pilot.

"It's a map," the Old Oak said. "The device is a map. And she keeps calling you Packaged Embryos, but I don't know how to translate that."

"Packaged Embryos?" Paxton repeated it to himself.

"Are you an embryo? Or . . ." The Old Oak played with the pronunciation on her tongue. "Packet Eros."

"What?" Paxton huffed, just as confused as her. "Packet Er . . ."

And right there he understood. The Old Oak couldn't translate it because it was a name.

"Is it Eros?" she continued, needlessly, licking her dry lips, letting the words roll on her tongue, getting a taste for the name. "Packet Son Eros?"

Not quite, he thought. "It's pronounced Paxton Arés."

"Packet Son Errands?" she tried one last time. "She wants you to know that the map leads to the source."

Paxton heard the words *map* and *source*, but he wasn't listening anymore. Every word skipped across the skin of his subconscious. Who was this pilot? Who was this person tossing his name so recklessly across the centuries?

"How do you know my name?" he asked but wouldn't get the answer. The Macedonian went dead again. Its compound eye faded dark.

"I don't understand what I'm interpreting for you," the Old Oak said, her eyes wet with fright, red with angst. "Do you understand?"

He did, but he wouldn't respond to her. She seemed too unbalanced in that moment, like even a whisper could tip her over.

The Macedonian spasmed back and forth, fighting for its life. Its eyes lit up, then dimmed, then shone again. It did eventually stabilize, and the Macedonian immediately attempted to sign, but its hands shook so violently that the Priestess took longer to interpret, and the Old Oak took longer yet to interpret to the Spartan.

"The Macedonian is dying," the Old Oak translated. "For the past four years, I have been trying to get back in touch with you, but my man-made cockpit is failing." The Old Oak's expression twisted into a knot. "I believe this will be my last connection to . . . ?"

The Old Oak paused and turned back to the Priestess with her face contorted in confusion. Whatever that last word was, it didn't seem to make any sense to her. She asked the Priestess other questions, maybe other translations of the word, but the Priestess nodded, confirming whatever the word was.

The word rolled around the coils of the Old Oak's outer ear, through the strings of the eardrum, to the back of her throat, and by the time it hit her tongue, it had bittered and her expression spun into a wrinkled web of confusion. And still, she translated.

"I believe this will be my last connection to . . . *the future?*"

The Macedonian moved its arms out and in, pressed an index finger against the side of its head, and scratched a circle around its chest. The Priestess nodded and turned to the Old Oak's back. She spoke, but the Old Oak didn't turn to the Priestess. She wouldn't translate, not until she understood.

"You're a man?" the Old Oak asked and poked the Spartan's abdomen, its womb. "In there?"

"Yes," he said, and the Spartan nodded.

"You're in the past?" the Old Oak said as the Priestess raised her voice, so she raised hers. "You're in our past?"

"Yeah." And the Spartan nodded, even as it aimed its eye at the Macedonian's hands and the Priestess's mouth, translating invaluable information.

"There is no all-seeing, all-knowing AI god?"

"No!" And the Spartan shook its head. "Now translate, what is he saying—*she*—the Androne, what is she saying?"

"You're just a person?" She said it with a tone of betrayal, with heartbreak, like a hiccup in her heart.

"What are they saying?" Paxton shouted. "Translate, please."

"Tell me," the Old Oak shouted as the Priestess tapped her shoulder, something important on her lips. "That means that it was men that killed her," the Old Oak said. "My mother was killed by men like you."

Drums began beating outside, and only the Spartan seemed to notice, its enhanced audio feed picking up some ceremony miles out in the distance. The drums were the only distraction from the betrayal on the Old Oak's expression. She pouted, a child failed by her mother, and her eyes dampened, but she'd never cry. She was an old oak.

Then she sucked it all in—the shock, the betrayal, the look of angst; all of it swirled down into her lungs and lingered there. Then she exhaled, and it was gone.

"The map leads to the source of the AI's satellite control," she said. "And it's also the place that could bring them all down."

"Jesus Christ," Paxton exclaimed. That was why a thousand civilians in the fishbowl stadium died, why the Fishies and his Spartan were hunted through the desert. "No fucking wonder." *This map could end the war.*

The Priestess watched the pantomimic flow of the Macedonian's limbs. The wind whistled in the stairway. The drumming in the distance pounded louder, like a soundtrack to the moment reaching its climax. But then the Old Oak didn't translate, she replied, and the Priestess responded back, and back and forth, both women speaking among themselves with the muted Andrones at their backs. Not until they stopped, not until there was a quiet agreement between the two, did the Old Oak twist her back and turn to the Spartan.

"I said yes," she said. "I said yes for you."

"Well, what the hell was the question?" Paxton asked, not expecting an answer, but this time he got one.

"She asked if I wanted the map transcribed. Knowing that they'll hunt us to the ends of the earth, do we still want the map?" Right then the Priestess handed the device back to her. "And I said yes." The Old Oak pointed to a mountain range in the distance. "It's at a location beyond the trident."

Paxton lifted the Spartan's eye toward the landscape ahead. The moonlight outside the window accentuated the view beyond the balcony—the trident, *the fucking trident*. A trio of snowy peaks, the tallest of the three flanked by two jagged mountains: a trident, or as Sergeant Woden would describe them, *"the Bermuda Triangle."*

The drumming pounded louder as it closed in. Not drums but the sound of cruise missiles cracking into the tiny metropolis outside. He could see what he was hearing now, flames flashing in the distance. They were here, Sergeant Woden and his new copilot. Now Paxton heard aerial warbirds singing overhead.

This was their endgame. This was the end.

"Harm!" the Old Oak screamed, spinning back into the stairway they'd ascended minutes earlier.

The Macedonian died, its pilot still a mystery positioned sometime in the future. But no one out there in the hangar was ahead in time or behind anymore. They were fighting in as close to parallel time as ever, and for the first time, Paxton didn't know what would happen.

41

Furies shrieked overhead. Black, muscular carbon-fiber bodies screamed into the sonic barrier. Four wings ran parallel on either side, and long black rudders, like shark fins beneath them, cut through the bottom of the clouds. These were the monsters that the Cooks had stirred up in their kitchens. Recipes that had stewed for centuries on end. Recipes for grandchild engineers to package—for great-grandchildren to seal away and wait for this, the farthest future, to arrive. For these monsters to kill their greatest and grandest of children.

Another trio of Furies streaked over the church. Every window shattered, every eardrum burst. Gray brick towers popped like fiery kernels in that microwave, noises shaking like earthquakes of the air, like gusts, like tornadoes, just as much felt as they were heard. Soon building tops enflamed, towering candles flaring orange in the black of night.

The Old Oak sprinted past the Spartan and into the falling city. The Spartan kept pace, trying not to run any people over with its half jog, half stroll. *Its*, Paxton thought now, *it* or *her*? How could an Androne be a her? *Andro* the male hormone, *drone* the male bee—fertilizers of the queen, and still, his Androne was a her now. And somehow it felt right. Just like Larry engendered the Oldsmobiles back at his shop. *She's a dame, ain't she?* he'd say. And *she* was. His Spartan was a dame—*his* Spartan now. She was beautiful.

She. He let the thought of it marinate on the mind. *She* moved ahead of the Old Oak as claps of gunfire ricocheted from around the corner. *She* leaned into a space between two buildings and switched to infrared. And what she saw squeezed a knot into Paxton's chest.

"Fucking . . ." His voice echoed through the cockpit. "They brought a donkey."

The donkey, a mammoth-size quadrupedal built far heavier than any of the now-extinct tanks. Built with the same impenetrability of a bank vault, donkeys were made with foot-thick steel alloys, a reverberating shell that ricocheted bullets like a force field of vibrations. And then there were the guns, a Gatling on its head, Gatlings on its tail, grenade launchers on its sides, and its namesake, a thermonuclear weapon that echoed like a donkey's caw when fired. A team of at least six pilots handled this quadrupedal, on the guns, motors, and controls, and this one was in the future, so who knew what other bells and whistles they'd incorporated by then.

The Spartan gestured for the Old Oak to stop; she didn't. She ran through a minefield of burning debris. But the Spartan didn't follow. There were so many fleeing civilians, squealing like swine in slaughter, that she would likely be lost in the chaos. The donkey wouldn't notice her, but it would most certainly notice the Spartan.

"Be safe," Paxton said quietly, backing into the alley. "You all be safe."

It almost seemed like she heard him, or heard the absence of the Spartan. Those heavy footsteps were no longer shadowing behind her. The Old Oak turned to *her*, staring into the Spartan's lone eye. And without taking another step, the Old Oak dissolved into the swarm of bodies and then was gone.

"Find her," Paxton said, and meant it with every muscle. From the grip in his fingers to the grit in his face, he meant it. "You have to find Harm."

For a split second, Paxton considered how to get back, how to delve into his footpath databanks and retrace the steps back to the sandbox. For a split second more, he considered where to discard the bayonet-rifle that didn't match the Spartan's titanium apparel. In that last split of the second, Paxton eyed a path out of the falling city, between twists of brick and iron trails. All he got was a second, because in that next second it hit him—hit her—a semiautomatic round, cracking against the Spartan's metal chest plate, knocking the rifle from her hand, and laying her to the dirt.

Apaches, two of them, opened fire with massive Geronimo rifles in the distance.

"Fuck!"

The Apache Series had a triceratops eyeline, three equilateral red dots on its tungsten-framed face. Iodine-inked skin was painted on a thinner, sharper body, edges at its shoulders, edges at its hips, angular at every single joint. The Apaches reached for the side of their heads, where the headset would be for their pilots. They were calling for someone—*something*.

Apaches were trackers above all else. And knowing the significance of what that map in the Old Oak's hand was, Marson would go all out. Even beyond his fleet of Furies, beyond the donkey and this pair of Series 6 Apaches, there had to be something else—*someone else*, and they were coming for the Spartan.

One Apache surged forward and unloaded everything in its magazine. The Spartan scrambled to her feet, somehow avoiding every single bullet. She lunged toward her bayonet-rifle, snatched it, hugged it against her chest, and spun around the corner of the alley, still avoiding every bullet, every crack of shrapnel at nearly point-blank range. Paxton almost thought himself lucky until he saw the light and heard the donkey's caw—*heeeeeeeee-hah!*

Brilliance lit the cockpit like daylight. Blinded, Paxton didn't see the Spartan hit the concrete wall at her back, nor did he hear it. A razored ringing cut into his ear, and he ripped the headset off. But Paxton's clumsy reeling in his seat saved the Spartan. As he fell back, she fell back, and the blast flashed just above the Spartan's head. It shattered brick, mortar, and metal like dandelion spores.

The Spartan lifted itself into an immediate sprint. It snatched a "flasher" from its belt, what the Cooks called a flash-bang grenade. The

Spartan lifted its right hand as it raced ahead, and the donkey's multiple night-vision optics followed and zoomed in.

"Keep looking," Paxton screamed as his finger flicked in the gloves, and the Spartan flicked the pin from the flasher. "Look!"

Light exploded into the donkey's night-vision lenses and likely blinded the pilots on the other side of time. The donkey stuttered backward, and Paxton pedaled harder than he ever had, not thinking, not contemplating that he was careening toward a donkey, the second most powerful weapon in the War Machine arsenal.

The Spartan lunged seven feet up, gripped her titanium fingers into the donkey's head, then scratched-clawed her way onto its back. Polygon solar panels covered the donkey's spine and gleamed from the surrounding flames. The Spartan didn't waste a second, dropping to her knees, digging her fingers on the panels, and she heaved. Bolts in her wrists crackled, hinges in her shoulders rattled.

"Come on," Paxton hissed through the grit of his teeth, squeezing his gloves tighter than ever before. "Come. On."

Furies circled above the Spartan, four of them, then five, six, swooping in low and firing indiscriminately. The donkey's back lit up in sparks of shrapnel that dotted the Spartan's armor. And yet she kept heaving, fingertips grating against the panel's inner surface, peeling back just enough to get beneath the wires within. Just enough to shove her arm elbow-deep into the cables and let go of her entire arsenal of grenades: two incendiaries, two frags, and that second flasher.

An Apache lunged off an adjacent rooftop to the donkey's back, racing forward without a skip in its step and barreling through the hailstorm of aerial drone artillery. The Spartan's arm seemed stuck underneath the panel. She yanked and wriggled her arm as the Apache roller-coastered forward, but they were pretending—*performing*, Paxton the director, her the thespian, struggling to get unstuck from underneath the panel as the Apache trampled closer, *closer*, and just close enough for the Spartan to lunge forward and swing the edge of its bayonet against the Apache's momentum. The blade pinched right through the chest. Guts of wiring and fluid hung and dribbled out, and the Apache collapsed onto that same open panel.

The Spartan leaped off the behemoth just as the grenades flashed and clanged and tore at the donkey's insides. The quadrupedal monster spasmed and hunkered, and its bowels spewed fiery orange and black mushrooms. The flames consumed the donkey, the eviscerated Apache, and a pair of Furies that had swooped a few feet too low.

"One fucking stone," Paxton said, leaving the first half of the idiom in his imagination.

The Spartan had leaped off the donkey's back with mere seconds to spare, and Paxton felt the thud on the dirt in his pedals. Smoke clouds swelled all around her and still the Furies followed, thermal images likely guiding them through the smoke, infrared through the building tops. They had stopped shooting and he knew why—*ammo-less*, he thought. *Flaccid mechanical fowl.* Every turn she took, every alley the Spartan ducked into, they stalked, not there to attack but to monitor. They were leading something toward his Spartan.

"Good," he said, still high off his heroic kills. "Bring the mother-fucker on."

42

Hours had passed, long hours, hours of drizzling gunfire, hours of Furies droning overhead and flames fizzling into ember, and hours past the end of Paxton's shift. For some reason the punctual Sergeant Oya hadn't arrived.

Still, any thought of the present played softly in his head. Like this drizzle of gunfire, it was the background noise in his mind. He was in the future, and whatever or whoever was keeping Oya was ancient history now, hundreds of years bygone.

Sunlight cracked a curved eggshell horizon, and its yolk seeped yellow against the sky. Smoke billowed from obliterated structures and wound serpentine through the cracks in the broken city. The Spartan had stopped running. The mechanical vultures couldn't be outpaced. Their aerial horsepower spun merry-go-rounds above the wounded Spartan. The axle on her left knee had been punctured. It whistled with each seesawing step.

Paxton tried not to eye the cadavers beneath the Spartan's feet. He kept the perspective high on that hard-boiled horizon. He had learned early on that no matter what the movies tell you, you never look them in the eyes. Their faces, their features, and especially their eyes had a way of dissolving into the subconscious and reemerging in his dreams, blinking on his grandfather's or girlfriend's face, and after waking, Paxton was never quite able to place where he remembered those eyes—until he could. Until those eyes multiplied and they were all he could see, on every face, in every dream, staring at him in every flavor of ethnicity—Congolese, Iraqi, Sri Lankan. Paxton had enough dead eyes peeking out from his past and didn't need any more staring out from the future.

A girl's voice hissed in the distance, less than a scream, but sharp enough that her vocals carried across the rubble, over the crackling of fire, and above the Spartan's own heavy footsteps. The Spartan followed, stepping across cinders of brick and bone, and found the girl underneath the floorboards.

She was as close to dead as he had ever seen anyone. Her face was burned to a ghoulish black. Wisps of hair dangled on her scalp. Her ears were warped out of shape, and her lips had melted into her black gums. The girl wheezed like the whistle of a kettle through the gaps in her baby teeth.

Her eyes were cringed shut, but Paxton needed to see them. He needed to make sure it wasn't her—*not Harm*, he prayed. The Spartan stepped closer, her heavy feet cracking into the rubble, and he woke the girl up. Her hazel eyes popped open. She gasped her last choking breath as if the Spartan had scared the life out of her, and she died, eyes wide and staring back at Paxton. But at least it wasn't her. It wasn't Harm.

Another noise whistled from what sounded like a million miles away. He held the Spartan still and listened, believing at first that it might be civilians trapped underneath the rubble, and it almost sounded like it—voices right beneath the Spartan's feet. The Spartan twisted her ear toward the dirt, but the root of noise never sprouted.

"Wait," Paxton said as the epiphany hit. "That's outside?"

Paxton turned to the cockpit door and peeled the earpiece from his sweat-moist skin. Shouting pounded from the other side of the door. He leaned in, cocking his ear to an ever-shifting epicenter of noise, hollers to the left of him, bellows to the right.

What the fuck is going on out there?

He took his eyes off the screen for a second, lifted his feet off the pedals for a few seconds more, and pressed his ear against the door. It was *then* that his Spartan stood comatose in the postapocalypse.

And they saw their moment—those shadows moving in the Spartan's peripherals.

Paxton glanced at the screen but didn't notice them, two shadows flanking from either side, squeezing in on the Spartan. So he didn't see the flasher tossed in front of the Spartan, and its flash didn't blind him but instead woke him. Paxton's feet stomped back into the pedals, and his fists snatched at the gloves. He brought his eyes squinting into the residual light.

"Jesus," he shouted, and squinted into the blurred bodies in the distance. "Christ!"

The second Apache charged toward the Spartan from the left flank, gunfire exploding from its unsteady trample, hitting everything but the Spartan's body. The Spartan remained still, firing with godlike accuracy, clap after clap after clap hitting the Apache, and it stumbled. Clap after clap knocked the Apache off balance, clap after clap after *clap*, and the Apache's knees hit the dirt right ahead of the dead girl. Paxton swung the bayonet. And the Apache lost its head.

A second shadow emerged from the Spartan's right flank. Paxton swiveled hard on the steering and whipped around, ready to shoot, but his finger never reached the trigger.

"Americana," he said, and stood doe-eyed like a reindeer in the Americana's headlights.

The Americana stared back, feminine, a full-figured chromium body—*fucking chromium*, the strongest metal on Earth. Long, thick legs with a hundred pistons between the heels and hips, an entire stampede of horsepower. And then the spider-eyed OO, nine black lenses at every corner of the face, like the blackest of widows on two feet. The most powerful Androne in the War Machine Program was also female—mother of all monsters.

Knocking echoed from the cockpit door, but he couldn't take an eye off the controls at this point. Handing it off to Oya would only guarantee destruction. It would be like a NASCAR driver handing off the wheel in the middle of the most dangerous turn. He'd have to see this through himself, one way or the other.

Paxton knew he couldn't outrun an Americana Series but tried anyway. The Spartan skidded on the rubble as she took off on unbalanced footing, stumbled down the mound and into an alley. The Spartan treaded as fast as she could, and still the Americana nearly beat her to the alley, coming in fast on her right. It cracked the ground as it ran, each footstep like a meteor pounding craters into cobblestone concrete.

The alley was tight. It squeezed in on the Spartan, tapering like a concrete noose, tighter after every step forward. The Americana trampled in like a locomotive chugging a few feet behind. But there was the light at the end of this alley. It shone from a round window cut into the brick wall, a window just large enough for the Spartan to squeeze into, and just small enough to shackle around the Americana's waist.

But the Americana lunged forward just as Paxton thought it up, as if he were thinking out loud, as if the Americana had heard his thoughts. Its fingertips clawed at the Spartan's shoulder; sparks flickered. The Spartan stumbled but didn't fall. *It's now or never*, Paxton thought and this time said out loud, "Now or fucking never."

The Spartan lunged toward the window, ten feet out and eight feet above. She straightened her titanium body like an Olympic diver but diving up, diving out, hitting the stained-glass window and just barely grating through.

"Yod!" Paxton screamed, some word between *yes* and *god*, rejoicing with a pump of his fist, grunting excitement, and the Spartan shadowed him, punching into the dry interior space.

The room was cut in slices of light, shaft upon shaft upon shaft of sunshine intersecting like an expressway of light. High ceilings emphasized the scant vacancy of the space, thick with dust particles and ash. The Spartan stood, stumbled, and stood again; the split in her knee kept her off balance.

A strident *bang* rattled and echoed from behind him. Paxton pulled the gloves in to his chest, and the Spartan in turn ripped the rifle from the holster on her chest. She aimed at the jagged window frame behind her, but there was nothing there—from infrared to thermal imaging, there was nothing on the other side of that wall. And still the pounding came again, and then it hit him: the noise was coming from the outside of the cockpit door, Sergeant Oya's impatient fists hammering against metal. But she'd have to wait.

"Where are you?" he said, staring through infrared imaging at a blank space where the Americana should be. "Where the fuck—"

He didn't finish. Knocking pounded on the cockpit door—and harder. It had to be at least two of them now, because there was knocking on either side of the cockpit, one at the door and one on the opposite side. Sergeant Oya wasn't alone, if it was her at all, and Paxton could still hear that hollering from the hangar beyond. Something was going on out there, and he had a feeling he'd have to deal with far worse once he finished with the Americana—or it finished with him.

A drumbeat of footsteps echoed through the space. The Americana splashed through the wall like it was a champagne glass and grabbed the Spartan by its rifle. The Spartan let go and tumbled backward and turned too fast, its knees giving out underneath, and it fell. The Americana raced forward, though the rotting floor gave way under its heavy chromium feet, giving the Spartan a second to grab her rifle and get a few seconds' head start.

"Fucking chromium," Paxton said, and then he said again, "Fucking chromium!" but it was different then. It was an epiphany.

The Spartan scrambled forward and made a ladder out of a crack in the wall. She climbed through a hole in the ceiling and kept going up. Every stairway, every wall, every floor that she could climb she did, leaping from structure to taller structure, and the Americana tracked and trampled behind her. In less than a minute, the pistons had taken the Spartan a hundred feet up and nine stories high. And now she jogged toward the adjacent building—jogging just slow enough to let the Americana catch up—and it did.

The Americana closed in so fast and leaped up from the adjacent building with such a bound it seemed it might land on the Spartan herself, but instead it was just close enough to grab the Spartan's foot. She hit the ground but wriggled and wormed her leg out from the Americana's grip. The Spartan clawed, fingers and toes, back to her feet and careened forward. The Americana followed a foot or two behind.

The Spartan reached the edge of the building and leaped down to an adjacent structure, the Americana on its tail. The Spartan hit the roof and kept running. The Americana hit right after, *but chromium is a heavy metal*. The Americana pierced the ceiling and the monster fell. Floor after floor gave way under its deca-ton body. Floor after floor, like it was falling through glass.

And the Americana Series had fallen.

"Motherfucker!" Paxton snarled, his heart beating hard at the inside of his chest.

Furies scratched smoky lacerations across the sky. High-pitched squeals suddenly whistled all around the Spartan. And as she glanced up, the sky fell.

Endless Furies came kamikaziing down onto the Spartan. Fires blossomed like mushrooms, metal spatter like confetti. The Spartan ran through the rain of flames, through the desperation of aerial pilots without a bullet to spare; they never hit, but proximate fires burned away her skin. The noise was so much that Paxton couldn't distinguish the pounding from the door and the pounding around the Spartan.

As she neared the city walls, Paxton found a hollow on the side of what had once been a building. The Spartan crawled in, palms and knees crushing the pebbles underneath. She huddled into its darkest corner, then aimed her rifle at the hole she'd just crawled through.

The Spartan was bleeding. The scratches on her veneer and even the breakage in her knee were nothing, but the fluid dripping out of the side of her abdomen was a problem. Paxton held his hand against his belly and halfway felt the life seeping out of her. But the knocking kept coming.

"Hang on," he said to the pounding on the door outside, or to the Spartan? *To himself?* He wasn't sure where his subconscious aimed at that moment but kept saying it. "Hang on. Hang on."

As he opened the cockpit door, the noise startled him. A hundred bellowing voices sucked into the airlock as he lifted it ajar. He couldn't tell whether it was an atmosphere of happiness, anger, or fear. He lifted the door slower, eased his head underneath. Sergeant Oya was the first face he saw, smiling the way one might after receiving a Christmas gift they didn't like. Behind her stood Colonel Marson, smiling like he *had* gotten the gift he wanted. And there were others, technicians, men in fatigues, men in suits, men in uniform, all of them staring at Paxton.

"They got 'em," Oya said, widening that Christmas smile. "We got 'em, Pax."

As Paxton's lips broke to speak, another round of shouting echoed around the corner. Applause exploded from the corridor—the cheer was moving, like dominos of voices, rolling out of the hangar and out through the barracks.

"Got 'em?" Paxton eventually said. "Got who?"

"We got him, Arés," Marson said. "We got the collaborator."

43

A fly buzzed. It passed over the mess of contracts, résumés, and NDAs on the colonel's desk. It lit on the mahogany finish and danced its native dance. Then it buzzed into a mad orbit around the lamp and it clinked. It clinked and clinked against the incandescent bulb. It would swing around the empty office again, visiting curtains, picture frames, and the pockets of Paxton's ear, but it kept coming back to that light and clinking.

Paxton couldn't help but notice these tiny six-legged details. He had been sitting idle for an hour in the un-air-conditioned stew. Sweat pockets weighed on his armpits and the back of his shirt. They got the collaborator, but what did that mean? They wanted to talk to Paxton, but they couldn't do it in the hangar. They had particulars that couldn't be overheard, intel that couldn't be made public.

They knew something. What they knew, how much they knew, he couldn't say, but they knew enough to incarcerate him in this work-space sauna. They should know it all by now, from the marble to the Americana—they should know, and yet it felt like they didn't. It felt like there was a piece missing from their puzzle that only he could fill. Would he?

Could he give up Victoria in some sort of plea deal? Or even Oya? And what about the future—the map and the Old Oak's position in the desert, the monk, Bones. Could every name he'd offer up cut years from his sentence? Paxton didn't think he could; he was panicky, desperate, but not a snitch, never a snitch. But then what about Callie in her hospital bed alone? She'd become just another single mother in the Oakland slums, overlooked and preyed upon, and because of his recklessness.

As he debated with himself, seven others debated in the corridor outside the office, old men wrapped tight in tailor-made uniforms. The office door dangled ajar; words leaked inside, but never the full stream of conversation. Paxton picked out a word here and there and eventually came up with a best guess at the dialogue. It seemed the colonel was on Paxton's side. It seemed he was making a plea to the officers present. It seemed as if the colonel was trying to save him.

Right then the colonel turned the corner and stepped inside, closing the door behind him. "You're probably tired, Lieutenant," Colonel Marson said as Paxton took his wandering eyes off the fly. "Bouncing between the cockpit and lieutenant duties, I mean."

Paxton's response felt stuck, a lump in his throat. The colonel's bearing seemed too casual for someone seated across from a traitor.

"Not really, sir. Thrive on adversity, right?" he said, repeating the military mantra.

"Right answer," Marson said, and pointed at Paxton. "Lieutenant, what I am about to tell you is classified. What I'm about to tell you is going to change the way you see this war."

They don't know. Paxton sighed as if he'd held his breath for the entire time he'd been sitting in the office. He thawed from a block of clenched muscle into the cushions on the seat. They didn't know. *Yet*, he thought. *They didn't know yet.* All the secrecy, the show of force in the hangar, it was because they were about to tell Paxton what he already knew. This was a war against the future.

"Change the way I see the war?" Paxton asked, shrugging and cocking his head, giving his best performance.

"There are NDAs to be signed and multiple levels of approval to be had, but I want to hear it from you, Lieutenant. I want to hear you say it."

"Hear what, Colonel?"

"Are you a career?"

A career, a.k.a. the military life sentence. Paxton knew what he had to say. It had become clear to him over the past couple of months that he had the colonel's full favor. If Marson was his godfather, then the nepotism was devout. The colonel wanted to pass it all down—the knowledge, the power, the holy spirit. And part of Paxton wanted it, his father's part in all likelihood.

"This is my life, Colonel. More than my career. It's in my blood."

Colonel Marson breathed his own sigh of relief. His hands rested over the contracts and pen and he leaned in. "You're going to hear things," Marson said. "Things you may not understand. But bear with me and believe me, it's the truth."

"Yes, sir."

"Well, there's no other way to put it, Lieutenant. We are engaged in a military campaign against the future, and I understand that may sound like some analogous declaration, but I assure you that is as literal a statement as has ever been made. The Androne you pilot are not in our present time but occupy the decades and centuries ahead of us. This is a future war—a war with the future."

The colonel scoured through Paxton's eyes, searching, hunting for the squints and gasps of awe or disbelief. But Paxton had forgotten to portray surprise, his body still unwinding, the euphoria of remaining in the clear flowing like a narcotic through his posture. Then he remembered—he wasn't supposed to know about the war or the future or where the two intersected.

"You're not serious?" Paxton said. "That's impossible." And he reeled back in his seat. He shook his head. He squinted back at the colonel's scouring eyes. It was overlong and overacted, and yet his thespian shortcomings managed to suffice.

Marson explained the satellites, the signal delay, the actual manufacturing of Androne still many decades out. He described the science of the Androne's carbon-sealed airlock, how they remained in a zero-kelvin stasis for another hundred years. He described everything Paxton knew and more. And at the end of an hour-long explanation and minutes more of reexplanation, Paxton could finally ask his godfather a genuine question.

"Why?" he asked. "Why are we fighting?"

"The Peacemaker," the colonel said, taking off his glasses like they burdened his eyes. "The Peacemaker is a man who will be born at some point in the future that this base patrols. He leads the first attacks against us. He discovers how to hack our satellites. He reverse-engineers the system controlling the War Machines that we manufacture now, in the present, from cockpits in the future. He's responsible for the Ninety-Nine. And not just War Machines—missiles, submarines, he even got his hands on an Israeli nuclear silo. The Peacemaker, as his name's been translated, will be responsible for hundreds of millions of deaths. The Peacemaker is the most deadly single individual in human history."

"Was he provoked?" Paxton asked.

"When we first entangled those photons, we opened our eyes in the future and saw our civilization decimated. So we occupied the future and allied with local militias who share our ideals. We provided medicines, supplies, technologies that had been long forgotten. We have to guide the future. We have to show them the way. There are those who rebel, who don't believe in the old ways, like the Peacemaker. He fights against our occupation of time."

"Who is he?"

"A man," Marson said, dismissively. "We have little information on him beyond his name."

"How do we stop him?"

The colonel smiled, and wrinkles wrapped around his eyes. Marson slid an envelope toward Paxton. CONFIDENTIAL. The black imprint was pressed into the manila skin of the folder. Inside, Marson revealed a time line that spanned from the present to the deep future, half shaded yellow, the other in green.

"In this war, we're not quite as interested in gaining ground as much as we are in gaining time. You see we have control of the rest of this century and the century to come." The colonel pointed to the present, marked in yellow, and dragged his finger forward on the time line. "We control most of the subsequent century." Then his finger stopped at a point on the time line where the yellow and green merged. He prodded the chartreuse-colored area and pressed against it as if it would change the color. "Then the sky falls. Gravity begins to run its course, and the satellites begin dropping. We lose control." His finger then ran across the green into the deep future. "They control this future because our few satellites are barely functioning." Then the colonel's finger returned to the mix of green and yellow and tapped on it. "But it's here, where their front lines and ours meet. Front lines or front times? This is the critical battle, as we prepare to launch new satellites for a new wave of War Machines to be unleashed into the deep future. If we launch successfully, we win the war."

"I understand," Paxton said. "Where are we on this time line?"

"Here," he said, tapping a point of yellow just before it mixed into the green. "A few years before the Peacemaker enters the scene."

Clink. That fly again, that bulb again, interrupting the colonel as he fanned it away. Paxton had always wondered what flies were searching for. What was going on in their tiny brains that spun them headfirst into light or into picnic bonfires or the neon of bug zappers? What was it about light that made them seem mad with envy?

"I mentioned yesterday there might be good news," the colonel said, glancing at the minute hand on his Swiss Army timepiece. "Two days ago we located the collaborator's position, and in that time we've strategized, brought in key personnel and international specialists, and in a few hours will run a strike against the collaborator and his or her allies with extreme prejudice. We have them cornered, Lieutenant, and I want you to be part of the assault that brings the collaborator down."

A burning fizzled at the inside of Paxton's chest, and he suddenly realized that he was holding his breath. A burn of CO_2 in his lungs, the sprinkling of ice down his backbone. He was, and he would be, a part of the massive assault team that tore apart the city just hours ago and from now. It dizzied him, confounded his thoughts, and still Paxton managed to find the words.

"My God," he said, not performing this time; this time he meant it. "Oh my God!"

"Right?" the colonel replied with excitement and a matching smile. "We need to get you prepped ASAP—briefing starts in an hour. Welcome to the other side of the looking glass, Lieutenant Arés. Your name." The colonel gestured to a pen and the dotted line on his NDAs. "Sign here."

And Paxton did.

44

They led Paxton to the restricted end of the hangar but didn't say much, an escort of jarheads, with heavy arms weighed down in tattoos—strong, silent, vacant-minded men trained to be like machines. Paxton eyed these outdated mounds of meat like relics, like fossils of war. And somewhere in his malnourished mind Paxton felt like he was his Spartan. He felt like he could swing his titanium arm across their backs and snap them in two. But reality was a twinge in his knee that brought him stumbling forward. Reality was a body so malnourished, so dizzied in insomnia, that he couldn't recover. Reality hit him before he hit the ground.

"Just a stumble," he said, picking himself up and dusting himself off, but they hadn't even noticed he fell.

A few card swipes and key turns guided Paxton through glass doors, where his security escort couldn't follow. He stepped into a twilight-lit arena with sixty-six cockpits positioned like stadium seating on three levels. Thirty-three cockpits sat in a circle on the highest deck, twenty-two cockpits were positioned a few feet below that, and on the final ring, eleven cockpits sat at the bottom.

This was the Rooster's Nest. While the cockpits outside were each connected to a different date in the future, some of them years apart, this network of cockpits were all synced to the same point in space and time. The arena he hadn't even known existed was used for coordinated assaults, like the one on the fishbowl, and today Paxton would be a part of an assault on the collaborator—an assault on himself.

Many of the pilots sat with their cockpit doors ajar to a sliver, watching Paxton's unguided footsteps swerving back and forth. He noticed one familiar face in Sergeant Woden, who offered a wry smile and affirmative nod as if they were old battle buddies who shared memories. The others were from out of state, Washington or Georgia. They had German accents or spoke in Indonesian dialects. They were the best among the best shipped in from every corner of the globe, and Paxton walked among them.

He felt outclassed here, in awe of the space, studying the shapes and colors, learning midstep with no time to digest. They led him past the first ring of thirty-three cockpits, reserved for the aerial pilots. Twenty-two Androne cockpits occupied the second ring, and the third ring, eleven cockpits strong, was likely for the donkey and other quadrupedals.

Paxton was directed to his cockpit and the Apache Series therein. It felt strange inside. New smells, new designs, a different grip to the controls, and heavier pedals beneath him. A voice under the influence of an accent, British, maybe Australian, began by discussing the topography, the temperature, and the sandstorm now brushing over the terrain.

The briefing also went into the details of the collaborator's skill set, everything from marksmanship to close-quarters combat. They made his Spartan out to be the voice of God, and him Mozart at the controls, to be tackled with no less than two Andrones and accompanying aerial support. He smiled and it widened as they detailed what he and Oya had been able to accomplish. There was, for the first time, a sense of pride in his acts, hearing his story put into words with the speaker's noble accent.

Paxton hung on every word for as long as he could, like hanging from a cliff over his own subconscious, but the gravity of thirty-some-odd hours with no rest other than a lazy blink pulled on his eyelids.

Sleep forced itself onto him, and he drifted farther back into the seat, farther back into the dark. He slept, but briefly—so briefly, with the social media post of a dream, and all he saw was Callie. Then there was noise, circuits and satellites sinking into place, and Paxton woke up to a stranger reality, staring out of the triple-eyed Apache Series a thousand miles and a hundred million minutes away.

The desert spun like a top, sand gyrating on sand. It was like an avalanche caught in a loop, like a blizzard dyed gold and eclipsing the world ahead. And still the tall tent in the distance appeared to shine through the sandstorm, white and ruffling in the wind. It almost seemed to flicker as it inflated and deflated under random whips of wind. Everything else was invisible in the sand; even the Apache Series' own feet were shrouded as it lumbered forward, toward the white heartbeat of the tent.

Paxton's Apache followed behind a long line of War Machines. Ranks and rows of quadrupedals, Z Series and Apaches, and a pair of horse-size hexapods. He had never seen so many, moving in unison toward the tent.

Just a few steps into the mustard whirlwind and the corpse of a Shogun Series came to light—Bella's Shogun, a few days dead with a congregation of men hovering around the laceration on its chest.

A noodle-net of wires ran from the lifeless Androne to 1990s-style CPUs with fat monitors and big-buttoned keyboards. They were faceless, these men. Breathing apparatuses muzzled their lips and nostrils, steel goggles swallowed their eyes, and hoods flapped wild in the wind, struggling to get off their heads.

Paxton assumed these men to be the allies the military had in the future, traitors of their own time. One of them even turned his techno-eyes toward Paxton's Apache as if he knew Paxton was a wolf in sheep's clothing.

———

The tent did little to keep the sand out. It stood about fifteen feet high, and the tarps on its side sagged in as the gales came to a crescendo. At the center of the tent a familiar voice hummed, almost singing or maybe just repeating the same Javan phrase over and over again, like a chorus to her discourse—*her*, distinctly feminine vocals and without a break in her verbosity. The Apache leaned forward. Its gaze bent toward a figure, a shine gleaming behind her. The silhouette hinted at her identity but wouldn't give it away so easily.

The Apache stepped farther out of line and rank and lurched even farther forward. It found a peephole of space between the shoulder of a Z Series and armpit of a Shogun. She was gold, blonde hair sprinkled with streaks of yellow sand, and the yellowy sheen of prenoon sunlight. It *was* her—the Goldfish.

She spoke to a pair of ancient men, old enough, it seemed, to remember some hearsay of the now. They were human strands, not standing but bent, arched, lurched in primordial postures, the early half of Darwin's evolution-of-man mural. They took her words and translated to a Z Series, not in English, but an older form of Javan. And someone on Paxton's side of time was listening.

Paxton had a thought then as the Goldfish prodded a digital map in front of her. She was colluding with the enemy, that was obvious, but the gentle bend in her wrist, the sleepy roll in her eyes, there was calmness to it, a familiarity. The Goldfish didn't seem forced but a willing participant. *And for how long?* Had she been leading the War Machines toward them the entire time? As these questions spun in Paxton's head, the Goldfish turned to his Apache and paused and leaned in and squinted. There was recognition in her look. She crooked her head and narrowed her eyes further—*recognition*. Be it the Apache's posture or a glimmer in its triceratops eyes, somehow the Goldfish appeared to recognize him.

She climbed to the tips of her toes, to the top of her lungs, kicking, screaming, stomping, and aiming it all at the Apache. Paxton couldn't understand but watched as she danced her ire across the sandy canopy, kicking up mini dust devils under each stomp of her feet, but it wasn't stomping, *was it?* She pretending to limp? Was that it? Was that the crux of this improvised caricature? The limp itself was exaggerated, but the design of it was the same, the divvying of leg against lurch, concealing a stumble in swagger, all paralleling Paxton's movement.

Was there a noticeable tilt to his gait as a pilot? *Maybe.* And if she could see it, who else would notice? The prongs of anxiety scratched against the insides of Paxton's chest; even his breathing paused as her zombielike stagger lurched closer. Then the youngest of those ancient men held her back with a torpid gesture of outstretched hands.

The British accent whispered into their earpieces. "Sorry, mates, she's dying her hair red these next few days," he said. "You know which hairs I'm talking about."

A more official report suggested that the presence of so many Androne had made her nervous, and thus the War Machines were ordered out to a sandy tarmac under the shade of an aircraft, half helo, half jet, like they had cut holes into the wings and shoved in helicopter propellers. The propellers spun to a blur within the wings themselves, allowing for vertical takeoff, and yet avoiding drag when the aircraft hit Mach 6.

They loaded the Androne on the aircraft like cattle. Paxton followed behind a reluctant Shogun Series, stepping on its heels as if the pilot were hesitant to step into the dark. It was an assembly line, leading them through the bay door, then into the cargo hold, then harnessing them into shoulder locks. The engines rattled as the bay doors closed in and the light went out.

Paxton saw his cell phone light up in the black. For all their security, he could still receive text messages in this cockpit, when he never could with his Spartan. His phone lit up again—old texts piled up from Callie, newer ones from Victoria. He sifted through them in order, starting from Callie's first text.

You said you would call, she had written. Then, Dr. Flaxen said surgery. And her last text: I don't want to.

His cell signal was half-full, or half-empty, but that was enough, and he had to try. Callie had a fear of hospitals. Her mother had wasted away in Saint Mary's during her sophomore year of high school, a fact that she hadn't given freely. Paxton had gathered this from a friend of a friend of an acquaintance. He dialed, and her numbers lit the dark, but as the ringtone hummed from the receiver, the electronics in the cockpit buzzed—that eerie fizz of static when signals collided.

That same British voice came scolding on the speaker. "Whose electronics?"

"Hello?" Callie said, just as Paxton hung up.

"Stay off all coms," the Brit said. "All coms."

Paxton winced and waited and thankfully didn't hear anymore from the Churchill-styled baritone chiding. Then the image of Callie's reaction marinated in his mind: her pressing the phone tighter to her ear, whispering *hello* once more, listening to dial tone, then pouting or maybe even crying?

"Sorry," he said. "Sorry, Callie."

Victoria's messages were still lighting up the dark. They know, the first one read, and Paxton jerked forward. The messages had been sent over an hour ago.

Paxton scrolled down to the next message. They're coming for you.

His heart paddled hard and fast, upstream, climbing into his throat. He choked on it. Paxton couldn't breathe. He shook and barely had the steadiness of hand to hold his cell phone. But still he managed to scroll deeper into Victoria's messages.

The next message, sent just thirty minutes earlier, read: They're going to bring you into the inner circle.

But he knew that already, and Paxton breathed easier, knowing that what she meant by *they're coming for you* was his initiation into the inner circle of knowledge. As he started scrolling deeper into her messages, the British cadence started spouting on about a "prep for landing" and orders to "begin recon."

Light burned into the cockpit from the monitor as the bay doors opened and the Androns marched out into a sunset, twenty-two strong, onto mist-wrapped mountaintops with brown weeds sucking on gray dirt. Paxton kept one hand on the controls and the other on his cell phone, reading or trying to, as he marched his Apache out with one limp arm.

There is a space in the inner circle that you're taking. Paxton leaned in as he read her last two words. My space.

How was he taking her place? Paxton questioned himself as he read the text again.

"Where are my aerials?" the British voice shouted into their headsets. "Shoguns, run me up a perimeter. Fort Boxer! Fort Boxer! Apaches magnify on sector 3645."

Paxton magnified the image on-screen but wasn't quite aiming right. He still eyed the messages on his cell phone.

Dont trrust anyone, a fifth message read.

I cant held u anymore, the next text read.

Scrolling down farther, the next text read: The coming in, ill dell eat alk text, u do to.

A last message lit the screen, this one live, not even a half second old, and already it was completely incomprehensible. Fist fore he further.

"What?" Paxton said and he texted back just that. WHAT????

Paxton read through the messages again. Her disorderly penmanship grew as he descended down. *Fist fore he further.* He wondered if *further* might be *future*, or *father*. But he would never know. Victoria never responded, and his cell phone faded to black.

"We got a lock," the British voice said. "Apache confirm?"

Paxton turned back to the screen and magnified onto sector 3645. Right then it was no longer a screen but a mirror. Paxton saw himself, captured in the belly of a Spartan, as he led the Old Oak and Harm and the others toward the city of the future.

"Fixed in on collab," the British voice said. "Repeat. Kingsman in fix. Kingsman in fix. Confirmed sighting of the collaborator. But . . ." He paused. "It's not a Kingsman Series. It's a Spartan?"

45

Radio chatter ping-ponged through Paxton's earpiece. "It was a Spartan," they said, and still had trouble believing it. Furies maintained aerial distance many miles overhead and squinted their lenses in onto the Spartan, the "bald accomplice," the "fat lady," the "girl," and the "old bitch." The Old Oak had a habit of glancing over her shoulders, occasionally staring out at the military's position on the triangular mountain range, and though her gaze could never span that hundred-mile trek, she almost appeared to be staring right at them.

He watched the Spartan—watched himself, and cringed at every step. A déjà vu–induced coma washed over him, an out-of-body stillness, as the Spartan roamed the city's lanky buildings and anorexic roads with a Jesus-like entourage in tow.

He felt like a father watching his Spartan make those same old mistakes, the same mistakes he had. He wanted to tell them to stop. He wanted to shout out, "Turn the fuck around, stupid." But he could only watch as the Spartan and the Old Oak approached the church or cathedral or whatever it was. The British voice called it Locus Delta A66.

Paxton held out hope that somehow it might play out differently. Or maybe he had remembered it wrong and they never went inside. But as the Spartan and the Old Oak followed the Priestess toward Locus Delta A66, he knew time was a constant that he couldn't change. It would play out exactly how it had played out, with his Spartan bleeding to death in the ruins of the city.

"We have a cover of visual," a voice said in an accent that Paxton couldn't place; English wasn't her first language. "Switching to the infrared."

"Aerials," the British voice shouted. "I want his allies lit up. That fat bitch, midlife monk, anybody else who spoke or interacted with the target, light them up. Light them the fuck up!"

It happened so fast after, too fast, and Paxton lost track of what was happening. The Apaches raced back into the helo-jet aircraft and then swooped down over the city. Its propellers flapped mad; monsoons of rock and dust lifted off the earth. It lowered the Andrones on steel lines that linked to holes on their backs and dropped them into the middle of a civilian population.

Paxton's dizzy Apache hit the dirt with a thud. The city was already in flames. The sun was gone, and Furies lit the streets with umbrella missiles.

"Arés," Woden's voice came over his headset. "You're in company."

"Copy that," Paxton said, understanding that he would follow Woden's lead. "Two man?"

"Yes, sir," he said with a seeming genuine respect. "Two-man company. I'm on point. We wanna track east of Locus Delta."

"Solid copy."

Paxton followed Woden's Apache toward a decapitated steeple. Its mounds of burning brick and timber planks clogged the road, and they detoured into an alley barely wide enough for them to squeeze through.

A dozen civilians raced out from the shadows therein, children mostly, fleeing toward a familiar-looking building at the other end. Paxton didn't react to the civilians but saw Woden's Apache turn back to him.

"Civvies," Woden shouted. "Hold fire."

Obviously, Paxton thought, but only replied with a "Copy that."

He had to at least appear vigilant, even as the surreal nature of reliving the same day in a different body hit his brain like a stub to the toe. As they passed the building and the children peeking out from its windows, a bludgeoning of déjà vu hit. He knew that pair of eyes staring out from behind the glass, that little one, she was about to die.

"No!" Paxton shouted or tried to.

A roar of fire belched upward, phoenix-like, and wrapped its orange wings around the building in embrace, puffing the bricks away like a dandelion dust. The Apache fell backward, consumed by boiling black smoke. The temperature gauge burst and burned out a circuit or two. These were flesh wounds for an Androne body, but that girl was now melting into the metal, still alive.

"God," he said. But he was the god that she worshipped, and he'd let her die.

The speed of sound hit milliseconds after the speed of thought as a Fury tore through the sonic barrier overhead. It launched two more air-to-surface missiles into tightly packed civilian crowds. A bloodred flash and fire evaporated the bodies into smoke and ash.

Paxton wondered what the civilians might have been thinking right now. Angry gods, screaming down fire from heaven. Androne angels walking among them, armed with swords made of fire, and carrying messages of wrath from the AI god.

He couldn't know for sure; he didn't even know what the military was thinking. Aerial missiles lit the night like fireworks. Death was indiscriminate. It was like they didn't care about lives in the future.

"Matchbox, this is Overwatch, copy?"

"We copy, Overwatch," Woden said. "Over."

"We've got eyes on your tag. Spartan is on a southeast heading."

"Solid copy, Overwatch," Sergeant Woden said as his Apache crouched and raised a pair of fingers, gesturing ahead. "Oscar Mike."

The sergeant's Apache moved in a slow trot around the burning building. Paxton's Apache followed, slower and less spritely. His fingers trembled. Butterflies flapped and drowned in the washing machine of coffee spinning around his gut. He was footsteps from facing himself. *The fucking odds*, he thought. What were the fucking odds?

"You wanna take point, Lieutenant?" Sergeant Woden asked, and Paxton suddenly remembered he held rank.

"I'll, uh . . . ," Paxton said, trying to decide. He held on to that last syllable for as long as his breath would allow, calculating whether he'd be better set to lead or hang behind.

"Lieutenant?" Sergeant Woden said, not impatiently, but getting there.

"Uh . . . ," he started on that same syllable, finally flipping the coin of indecision. "You hold," Paxton said, and gestured toward a corner.

Before they could take another step, a shadow eclipsed them, a Spartan's shadow—his Spartan, racing forward in a panic.

"Light him up!" Sergeant Woden shouted.

Her, Paxton thought, *Andrones are hers.*

Sergeant Woden's Apache raised its Geronimo rifle and choked down on the trigger. But Paxton raced his Apache into his line of fire, making it into a tungsten steel barrier between Woden's Apache and the Spartan.

"Friendly fire," Sergeant Woden hollered as his gunfire went quiet. "You're in my line of sight."

But Paxton remained directly in the sergeant's aim. He watched his Spartan, frozen in time. Those moments felt like minutes, felt like hours, as Paxton's Apache and the Spartan stood like opposites in the old westerns, hands at their waists as sand swept by. But instead of tumbleweeds, lit embers and ash wafted across the dark.

"Come on," Paxton huffed under his breath, begging that old image of himself to fall back.

He didn't—she didn't. The Spartan idled away for what felt like minutes of a moment. Paxton would have to scare himself off. He lifted the Geronimo, aiming at the Spartan's flanks, and emptied an entire magazine, hitting nothing but thin air.

The Spartan reeled back but kept posture, arms upright and chest in frame. Even off balance and backpedaling, she lifted her rifle and aimed dead-center-mass at Paxton's Apache. He watched in shock at the

Spartan's posture under such duress, barely recognized himself. Paxton had remembered himself stumbling back and shooting wildly into the night, but now, on the receiving end of the rifle, he felt every bullet hit as the Spartan shot off five volleys of gunfire, each cracking against the Apache's chest plate and arm. Deft form. Flawless aim. Mozart.

Paxton's Apache collapsed, not dead but damaged, his controls and satellite feed fluctuating back and forth. By the time the Apache struggled back to its feet, the Spartan was gone, the smoke and nighttime dark closing like a curtain around her.

"You good, Lieutenant?" Sergeant Woden asked as his Apache raced up from behind.

"I'm good."

But he wasn't—beeping and eerie rings howled through the Apache's cockpit. Its chest had been punctured, three metallic lacerations torn into the tissue under the right shoulder.

"Asshole's accurate," Sergeant Woden said, noticing the Apache's chest plate and the torn wiring under its armpit.

Paxton felt a restrictive stiffness in his right arm controls. The Spartan's gunfire had torn away some of the copper wiring that acted as the Androne's tendons.

"Can you move?" Woden asked. "Can we pursue?"

"No, he's too talented," Paxton said with as much modesty as he could endeavor, though the truth was, Paxton was just buying the Spartan as many minutes as he could—buying himself time, and that was a mindfuck unto itself. "We need to take a second to strategize."

"'Kay," Sergeant Woden said with a stain of impatience. "What's the stratty?"

Paxton didn't have one. He tried to remember what had happened after he'd shot back at the Apache ambush hours before. That was when he heard it, a noise so piercing that Paxton nearly tore the earpieces out of his ear, and a flash of light that clamped his eyes hard shut. It was the donkey.

"Let's move," Sergeant Woden said as his Apache spun hard on its heel and trampled forward.

Paxton followed, stumbling behind with one arm swinging, nearly limp, and fluid running from its chest. *Center mass*, he thought again. The Spartan's aim and poise, her soon-to-be defeat of the donkey minutes later. And the evasion of an Americana Series. They wouldn't catch him; time couldn't change. But Harm, and even the Old Oak—where were they?

Paxton's Apache slowed from a run to a slow trot to a labored walk, and then it stopped altogether. Sergeant Woden's Apache raced off into the black of smoke and night as Paxton turned his attention to the radio chatter, switching to a different frequency.

"No visual on AR. Please advise."

Then switching.

"We've got the southern entrance locked down. Civvies are in herd."

Then switching.

"Eeyore is down, HQ—I repeat, Spartan is loose, our Eeyore is down!"

Then he found it: "Solid copy, Overwatch, we've got eyes on her. Dispatching drones to the old bitch."

He hated that they called her that: *old bitch*. The Old Oak felt as much a daughter to him as she did a mother. *Fuck*, he thought. Only curse words ran through his head now, because he couldn't help her, not with all of them watching. So he would have to watch too, whether it was murder or torture; he would have to watch the Old Oak die.

46

The road was ash. The city's skin flaked away. Its cinders snowed down and lost their glint as they touched the ground. Paxton's Apache trampled across vapored earth, moving top speed; it was faster than the Spartan, a lot faster, seventy miles per hour plus, and it got to that speed twice as fast as her. And even with all that speed, Paxton had trouble keeping up with the jumping markers on the map and locations shouted over the radio.

"Tracking lost on accomplices," one said.

"Granny's on the move in sector E-I-zero," another said, repeating nursery rhymes.

"Aussie bot in pursuit, got her at sector E-I-aught," the British voice said, who it seemed was actually an Australian.

Sector E-I-zero was at the far end of the town, nearly three miles out. How the Old Oak had made it that far in just over fifteen minutes confounded Paxton. His best time on the mile was six minutes, and that was before his knee injury, when he was actually in shape.

Gunfire popped in the same direction that the comms had suggested for the Old Oak's position. The Apache twisted on its heels and moved toward it as structures on either side of him burned into nothing. He switched infrared under those blankets of smoke and came out on the other side to an impossible sight—she had won.

The Old Oak stood over a Shogun's fiery corpse. An ooze of battery fluid dripped from its orifices. Wires snapped and wriggled like glowing maggots eating away at the wound. The Shogun lay in its coffin of fire, and still she fired off one last shot into its chest.

Harm hollered out from a shadow; the monk, Bones, and the Priestess all crouched in the dark behind her. Paxton's Apache nearly stepped forward; then he realized she wouldn't recognize him. He'd end up like the Shogun Series underneath her feet. But she saw him in that moment of movement and quickly aimed her rifle but didn't shoot. Instead the Old Oak lifted her rifle and aimed up, way up.

"Time on target?" a voice spoke into Paxton's earpiece.

"Uno Mico," the Aussie replied.

Paxton lifted the Apache's head to the squadron of aerials streaking down toward the Old Oak kamikaze-style, a half dozen of them at least. But with all their eyes fixed on the Old Oak, would anyone notice him? His little Apache, his little gun; he might just get away with it. Paxton lifted the Geronimo rifle, aiming at a pair of plunging aerials. He rattled off an entire magazine of ammo. The pair of them popped in flashes and flame just as the mag went dry.

Four other aerials dove through the smoke. The closest of these suddenly combusted into flames barely a hundred feet up, so close and loud that the gunfire that had destroyed it was drowned out. Another duo of aerials zoomed through that smoke, descending nearly sixty feet closer to the ground but then detonating into balls of fire forty feet up, knocking the Old Oak on her ass. Where was it coming from? The mystery gunfire continued clapping, but that last aerial cratered into the ground, and the Old Oak disappeared into its smoke.

"No," Paxton shouted as he charged his Apache out from the shadows and into the fiery light of the night.

The Old Oak's anatomy sprawled across the blackened earth. Her arms and legs seemed to spill out from her torso, rubbery and deflated like tires torn from their wheels. Her cotton-thick blouse crackled in flames, and the ends of her hair were singed.

The Apache approached, dragging its feet. Heavy, dilatory steps scratched the ash-black path. Harm screamed for the Old Oak. He saw the girl in night-vision green, springing out from her hiding place, but Bones dragged her back into a corner. But not because of the Apache; she hadn't seen it yet. Another figure emerged slow from the shadows, tall and steely, massive footsteps cracking into burning wood, snuffing out fires. The world grew darker as it drew nearer, a Shogun Series. Its massive, dark frame was hazy in the smoky night.

"Shit," he said, knowing that now he couldn't do anything in the Apache's body.

"I got a hit A-P at sec E-I-zero," the pilot said, a woman, American accent, a New England cadence. Her Shogun Series turned to Paxton's Apache, eyeing the wound on its chest. "You try a patch?"

Paxton shook his head, subconsciously hiding his voice, not even aware of why.

They stood over the Old Oak and peered down at her from the balconies of their seven-foot frames. She seemed smaller than she had from the Spartan's eye. Whether it was the Apache's height or its lenses or the Old Oak's deflated state, she seemed smaller now. His little, old girl, dead in front of him, and there was nothing he could do.

Paxton felt his rifle slipping from his fingers. An arthritic angst cutting away at the tautness between the knuckles; his wrist, his very grip just slipping away. But he caught himself. He caught himself and he held on as tight as he could, because if he didn't he would fall apart limb by limb. There was nothing holding him together anymore. Grief dissolved him so fast—so fucking fast.

"Not breathing, right?" the Kingsman pilot asked but didn't wait for the answer. "Granny is KOS. Calling in a retrieval, over?"

They responded in accents, military lingo, and all peppered in static. The Apache was dying. The screen flickered; the audio feed rang sharp with the static, like a kettle pot at its boiling point. An aerial whizzed overhead, maybe two; he didn't look up. He lowered his head in uncontrollable reverence. It was finished. Whatever the fuck *it* was, it was finished now.

"You need a patch, Lieutenant," she said and pointed at the fluid leaking from the Apache's chest. "Keep away from the fire."

The leak on the Apache's chest plate dripped into a liquid lithium puddle on the sand. And even that image of slowly crystalizing cathodes flickered in the Apache's trilogy of eyes. The visual feed blinked in and out, not dying, but falling into a battery-deficient coma.

"Calling in support," she said. "We need a mend at Echo India zero. Repeat, calling a mend capacity quad at sector E-I-zero for . . ."

She stopped short. She saw something. Her Shogun turned toward it, lifting the I-stinggar rifle, but *it* shot first. That gunfire again, gunfire with that same ring that had brought down the aerials.

"Spartan," he said and she said, simultaneously dubbing one another.

"Spartan," the pilot hollered.

Her Shogun stumbled but recovered quickly and took aim as the Spartan and Sergeant Oya—her stance and posture, her weaving sprint maneuvers, bobble-stepping side to side to avoid the Shogun's aim.

And the Shogun returned fire—the I-stinggar used slower semiautomatic rounds, but a single shot would put down a tank. Each shell cracked like a cannon round, and even the Old Oak's flaccid body shook. The Spartan emerged from the shadows, running and gunning, semiauto rounds aimed at both the Shogun and Apache, but the Spartan's ammunition ping-ponged off the Shogun's heavy armor. The Shogun didn't stumble, not even a flinch, just poise and concentrated aim, following the Spartan's swerving footsteps, finding the pattern, until it was ready, aiming, and gunfire.

That gunshot hit. The metal cracked like fractured ice on the Spartan's right shoulder, and she stumbled off to the side but found her footing. The Shogun's subsequent shot hit the dirt, presumably where the Spartan would have fallen, and left a crater the size of a volleyball. The next shot cracked the butt of the Spartan's rifle and the weapon fell to the dirt, but the Spartan didn't stop—she kept on moving, unarmed and nearing point-blank range.

The Old Oak started an infant-like crawl out from under the spray of shrapnel, abandoning her shoes and rifle and a pair of grenades lying like Easter eggs in the dirt. He thought of it then, an idea, that stretched the moment to an infinity. There are moments where the body reacts without the mind, when indecision forces fate to take over. Paxton was like a rag doll then, and fate his puppeteer.

There was no thought; it sort of happened, like a reflex, a knee jerk in his subconscious. He bent down, and the Apache bent down and lifted a grenade in either hand, flicked the pins, and pressed the grenades against the leak on its chest. He approached the Shogun from behind, the silent timer on the grenades ticking, ticking; then Paxton's screen went white.

47

"Requesting sitrep, all comms, Overwatch out," the squad leader announced, giving the command to exit their cockpits.

But Paxton had sunk deeper into his seat. There was a tightness pulling at his chest and in nearly the same spot that the Apache had held the grenades against its breast. There was something about playing both sides of this war that was tearing Paxton in half—in thirds. How many pieces of him lay scattered across these cockpits? The trust from his godfather, the code of the pilots, and his care for the Old Oak or Harm, and then his love for Callie and the boy growing inside of her.

It all beat at his brain like his head had a heartbeat, right at the edge, right at the frontal fucking lobe, cratering into his skull, fracturing every thought into pieces: past, present, future, and all at once. *What fucking side are you on?*

Paxton kicked open the cockpit door, swallowing mouthfuls of tasteless oxygen. The other pilots snailed toward the barracks in a tight huddle, a sticky sweat lathered between them. Paxton followed, trolleying behind a zombie line of disheartened pilots. He felt them watching. He felt them following. He knew that they knew—they had to. But there was no one in his bunk and no one following. And still he waited. He sat on his bed in full uniform; he didn't even untie the tight noose of his shoelaces or loosen his belt. Paxton sat prepared to be taken to the off-site disciplinary post, never to be heard from again.

But an hour passed, then two, and Paxton finally felt himself breathe. He unpeeled his socks like banana skins, his belt like orange rind. He lay back and smothered his face into the pillow. He melted into saliva, evaporated into the snoring of oral exhalation. The languor was heavy and dragged him under in seconds. He slept and was too tired to dream.

It wouldn't last long. A vibrating against his chest lifted his eyes open. He woke up to the shake of his cell phone underneath him. Lieutenant Victoria's text messages were coming in, one after the other, flashing across the screen.

We have to meet, she texted.

Meet where, he replied, arching his back, listening to the cartilage pop.

Lunchroom. Yellow table in the back row.

Yellow table?

NOW, Victoria replied.

Paxton shoved his feet into his shoes without the notion of socks and dragged his heels back down the corridor to the mess hall. He had barely slept two hours. It was just after four. The population was scarce, sixtysomething strong and the perfect time for him to take advantage of a flimsy lunch line. Victoria would have to wait.

He filed into the entrails of the line: a dozen pilots debating earlier failures, a duo of men in suits, analysts on their cell phones, a janitor tiptoeing around the broad-shouldered Marine in front of her, and another pilot, Bella, turning back almost on cue, noticing him as he noticed her.

"Hey," she said stepping out of line and weaving her way back to him. "You look like your bed beat you up."

"Yeah," he said, taking his time now, picking up a foam cup of green tea and taking a sip as he surveyed the oatmeal muffins and blueberry bagels under heat lamps. "KOed for a couple hours."

"Well, with the cockpits out for the next thirty-six hours, you can sleep late."

"Thirty-six?" he said.

"You didn't hear? After today's . . . happenings, Washington's stepping in."

"Oh, wow," Paxton said, searching for Victoria now, finally waking the fuck up and remembering the shit that he was in.

"You looking for someone?"

"No," he said, and shook his head. "This new responsibility's got me all twisted. Regular cockpit hours, plus office time, and today they decided to put me on the strike team."

"I heard. Congrats."

Congrats? "We got fucked up," Paxton said, and shrugged.

"The collaborator." Bella gasped as if in awe. "Wiped an entire army by himself."

"Him?"

"Or her."

They swiped their meal cards and carried their lunch trays down the aisles of the tables. Paxton hoped to lose Bella when they ran into Victoria but wasn't sure if Vic had even arrived yet. They moved toward tables in the back, adjacent both the latrines and the garbage bins.

"We'll get the collaborator," Paxton said, searching table after table for the one with a yellow tint. "Eventually, we will."

"Confidence," Bella said, but shook her head. "It's out of control now, though. First that siege earlier and then letting the Spartan slip between our fingers this morning."

"What siege?" he asked as he finally eyed the only yellow table in the cafeteria and swerved toward it.

"You're out of the loop," she said, still following. He had to get rid of her.

"Seems so," he said, and stopped at the unpopulated yellow table.

"There was a siege at Lieutenant Victoria's trailer."

Bella put her tray down on the table first. The way Paxton slowed down and his eyes locked onto the table, all his body language must have suggested that this was the final destination. But he didn't place his tray down and he didn't stop. He only paused—a stutter step.

"Victoria?" Paxton said.

"The MPs took her," Bella continued. "And she didn't go quietly, that's for sure."

Fuck! Not Victoria. He couldn't ask about her well-being either. He couldn't show the splinters pinching at eyes as he considered her fate. He just could only stutter-step again, and so hard this time that he worried he might trip. If Victoria was dead or in detention, then who the fuck was sending him texts?

"Her phone," he mouthed, and maybe even murmured, but it was too quiet for even himself to hear. "They have her phone . . ."

"Fucking crazy, right?" she said, eyeing his surprise. "Somebody that high up?"

He didn't respond. The only conversation to be had now was with himself. He had found his footing and he kept on walking, not even glancing back at the table. It was invisible to him, even as Bella had taken her seat, sipping on grape juice and picking at fries on her plate.

"You're not eating?" she said, leaning onto the table, as if not sure whether to get back up.

"Latrine," he said abruptly. "Gotta hit the latrine."

And he walked off. He moved toward the blur of an exit sign in his peripherals while his gaze strayed to the random bodies around him. Eye contact was a minefield, and Paxton kept his head down, eyes on the white diamond tiles and the monotony of military footwear.

He glanced up just in time to catch a duo of burly men moving in tandem from separate corners of the room and converging on Paxton. Earpieces clogged their ears, listening to commands, moving like puppets on radio strings. And as they closed in on either side of Paxton, he didn't try to fight. He gave in. He felt relief. At least now he could finally sleep.

But the men brushed by Paxton, jostling him in their wake.

He knew he shouldn't glance back. He knew it, and still he did. He spun around, a little in the neck, a little in the waist, a little in the corner of his eye.

The men approached the table. They approached Bella. They grabbed at her armpits, lifting her to her feet, and dragged her out from under the table. She wormed her flimsy arms against their brawn and asked something, but they didn't answer. She looked out into the crowd, his patsy being hauled across the cafeteria floor, her feet like skates on ice. Her eyes darted left, then right, searching for someone—*for him?* And it was right then that Paxton turned away.

48

Paxton shuffled down the corridor but he couldn't breathe, his heart muscles flexing, his lungs panting to keep up. Even his limbs felt stringy, and his torso was just a thread. He was like a rope caught in a tug-of-war between his heart and lungs. The corridor narrowed in his eyes as if the walls themselves were squinting at him. He was having a panic attack, but he didn't realize that until the end, until his knees buckled and he fell over.

Fortunately Paxton had made it back to his bunk, to his bed. It was all collapsing in now, the lies, the alliance, his own body. Victoria gone, now Bella, sitting in a trap set for him. Her unwitting sacrifice would last long. They would eventually find the root to the tree they were chipping away at. This was the end, and he wasn't ready. He called Callie but got nothing. The old man's phone was similarly silent. He could leave a message, but that might only incriminate her.

He knew what he would say, though, mouthing those very words to himself, telling an imagined Callie that she was the most beautiful thing he had ever seen; clichéd, sure, but Paxton was never very smart. He knew that; she did too. She was dreamlike to him right then, every imperfection perfect. He felt starved of her: Callie's smell, Callie's touch. The thought of curling up next to her was sustenance for his soul.

Fuck it, he should tell her, even if it was just a text message, but Paxton was asleep and he hadn't even remembered drifting. All these thoughts were in his subconscious. His mind had thirsted for sleep and now it guzzled at every hour, every minute of it. He was washed away in fevered dreams that hauled him off to a military hole forever. Even in his subconscious, Paxton knew Marson would grind him under his boots. He would never see Callie again. He wasn't ready for that.

"Paxton?" He heard the voice but didn't wake up. So someone shook at his shoulder and said it again. "Paxton, wake up."

Sergeant Oya waited for the blur to slip out of his eyes before she said anything. She sat at the edge of his bed with her arms folded formally over her lap.

"Oya?" Paxton said. "What time is it?"

"We're safe," she said, moving to the floor with her back against the frame of his bed. "For now. We're safe."

Paxton wasn't sure when she had stepped into his room, but he was still half submerged in the cotton of his pillow, watching floaters drift across the red of his eyes like single-celled sheep.

"Safe? They just set up a fucking sting for me, Oya. They might have killed Vic. We couldn't be further from safe."

"*They,*" she emphasized. "They're safe. I got them out of the city."

"Where are they now?"

"About sixty miles southeast of the city," she said. "Oldie analyzed the map and—"

"Oldie?"

"The old woman," Oya said. "There's Baldie and Wonder Woman, the Kid, and Oldie." Oya smiled now and seemed to wait for Paxton to return the same. He didn't. "Anyway, she analyzed the map. Oldie's headed to the location."

Why? Why did she keep tempting fate? They had barely gotten out of the Bermuda Triangle and now she wanted to go to the epicenter of it all. Bring down the satellites. End the war. *For what?*

"No," he said. "We're done. They're on their own."

"We have to."

"Have to?" he said, maybe a notch too loud.

"Quiet," Oya said, eyeing the door. "Look, we're close."

"They . . ." He pointed through the walls and ceiling to the Penthouse half a mile away. "They know it's a Spartan now."

"One week," Oya said. "Six days' journey. Couple hundred miles."

"Why?" he asked, leaning toward her, his voice barely escaping his lips. "Why are we doing this?"

"For our future."

He had never put it into words, the *why* to what he was doing. For the future? *No.* And yet it made the conflict on the inside of his chest feel noble.

"For the future," he said, not so much to her but for himself. "I don't know . . ."

"Shhh," Oya hushed him, hearing the patter of footsteps a moment before he did.

"What?" But just as he said it, he knew what. He heard what, stepping into the doorway.

"Lieutenant Arés." Sergeant Woden stood in the doorway at full attention, heels parallel and arms folded behind his back. "They're calling for us in the Penthouse."

"For what?" he asked.

Woden answered with a shrug.

Paxton didn't budge. So Woden appeared to think up something right there on the spot. "Something to do with our run-in with the collaborator."

Fuck.

They took a shortcut through a service hall that custodians and maintenance workers traversed. Woden bragged about his connections with the "common civvies" on base; *a man of the fucking people,* Paxton mused. That passage led to a stairway that led to an elevator that led to the Penthouse.

Security was lax. Maria pointed them toward Colonel Marson's office; the door was atypically wide open. Marson sat at the desk with his head down, eyeing a stack of papers. And he must have heard their footsteps dragging against the floor, because Marson didn't so much as glance up from the documents; he just waved them in with a curl of his hand.

"Sir," Paxton said, and noticed that Marson wasn't looking at the documents but staring at a fly, its wing strangely amputated.

"Have you ever thought of it?" Marson said as he gestured for them to sit down. "A wingless fly? A *fly*, defined right there in its very name, and the irony that in taking its wings, it is no longer a fly. Doesn't walk like a fly, squawk like a fly—is it a fly?"

Paxton shrugged, very aware that the colonel was implying something, but not sure what.

"So what about humanity? If you take the man out of human, what *do* you have? *Hu? Who* do you have? We are defined by our names. We are our fathers' sons."

Paxton and Woden both nodded and waited for more, but it never came. Instead Marson sipped on a ribbed glass of what looked and smelled like gin.

"You piloted a Spartan?" Marson asked, the distilled spirit warm on his breath.

Paxton's heart dropped, but he knew immediately that he couldn't show it.

"Yes, sir," Sergeant Woden said, taking the words out of Paxton's lips. "I piloted a Spartan before switching to an Apache."

"Serial number?" the colonel asked.

"SP 105," Sergeant Woden replied.

"Lieutenant?" Marson asked of Paxton.

"SP 450," Paxton said.

"Formality," the colonel said. "Just formalities. There are over thirty Spartan pilots at this base and hundreds of Spartans nationwide. I'm sure we'll find the collaborator elsewhere."

It went quiet again, and this time the silence stretched on for the full length of a minute. Paxton's and Woden's eyes met and agreed to leave. Woden went first, backpedaling, as he searched the colonel's demeanor. Paxton followed, turning to the door, and they almost made it too. But the colonel turned to them one last time.

"One last thing," he said. "Corporal Bella Columbia—a friend of yours?"

"Yes, sir," Sergeant Woden responded, cutting Paxton off before he could answer in kind.

"We tagged her earlier today. May be nothing. I just thought I'd let you know. You're dismissed, gentlemen."

They took the long way back, either forgetting the shortcut that led them there or feeling the need for the walk. As they rounded the bend to their bunks, Paxton's and Woden's paths should have diverged, but Woden followed Paxton down his corridor. He seemed to have something deeper on his mind. It dragged at his heels and choked him, a heavy pant on his breath.

"We need to talk," Sergeant Woden said.

"About . . . ?"

"I can't say for sure, but I think something's happening. It's more complicated than it looks."

"What are you talking about?" Paxton said, searching the confusion on the sergeant's expression. "What are you saying?"

"It's not him . . ."

"Who?" Paxton said, now leaning in and shaking his head in confusion. "Sergeant?"

"But I can't say for sure," Woden said.

"I don't get what you're saying."

Sergeant Woden nodded as if indicating that he knew that Paxton didn't understand. He stared at Paxton, wanting to say something—it burned in Woden's eyes, bubbled on his lips, but he backed away. "We'll talk, Paxton," he said, stepping backward into shadows. "We'll talk."

49

They released Bella after days of interrogation. Innocent on all charges was the official call, but Paxton knew that Bella must have given them something. Her release ran parallel with new intel on the collaborator. Rumors ebbed and flowed through the Penthouse cubicles. Every individual was simultaneously suspect and accuser. McCarthyism, Maoism, and now Marson inherited the rest. Maria and half the office had been polygraphed. Oya was questioned, Woden disappeared for a day, everyone was a suspect—everyone but him. His godfather made sure of it, filial affiliations at their most obvious.

By the next day, most of the pilots were back to regular sleep patterns. Only Paxton remained caught in future jet lag. He kept cockpit hours, owllike, waking up at noon and missing the most important phone call of his life. Callie was in labor.

He flipped open his laptop and watched a low-definition image from the old man's cell phone. There was a lag, choppy signals on the crowded Wi-Fi, and thus Paxton was seeing into the past, however infinitesimal. The fluorescent hospital lights, the blur of bodies on the shaky camera—all of it had already passed, haunting, ghostly almost, like staring into a memory, like communing with the past.

The old man brought the arthritic sway of the camera into the delivery room, showing images of nurses in scrubs, Callie's bearded uncle holding a flowery bouquet, and Larry, waving a pair of middle fingers toward the lens. Beyond the throng of smiling faces was Callie as she cradled the fleshy, wrinkled newborn in her arms.

"A girl," Paxton said to himself.

A girl so small, so microscopic, she was a hummingbird swathed in green and rose-patterned linen. Her eyes, brown, earthy puddles, melted on her face, tears streaming down her cheeks. Her eyes, like his eyes, stared out from that screen as if it were a mirror, and soon Paxton's eyes melted into a stream of tears.

Callie held her up to the camera, assisting the old man's wavering aim, and for a moment she saw him. His daughter stopped scream-ing and she looked at Paxton. For him it was love, first glance—first glimpse, the hypnotic swirl of her baby blinks and her brown eyes. She was a pageantry of him and Callie; she gleamed in their shiniest parts. He couldn't love her without loving those parts of Callie. And he did. He loved her too, the mother of his child.

Word had spread through the barracks. A few bodies gathered behind Paxton and orbited the screen. Privates Qamaits and Solo kneeled at his sides, and Sergeant Oya watched from a distance by the doorway. Even Bella arrived and stood behind Paxton with her hands on the back of his chair; he could feel her fingers scratching at his back. Every eye was locked on the screen, every eye fixed on his hummingbird.

"Hi," Paxton said, waving at her through the laptop.

"Your eyes," Sergeant Oya said.

"And your hair," Solo said, pointing to Paxton's scalp. "Air's getting kinda thin up there."

"You still want Eddie?" Paxton asked, leaning toward the screen, making sure Callie heard him over the noise. "Eddie, the king?"

"Ellie," she said, then lowered her lips to her daughter's head. "Ellie, the queen."

Ellie cried and it sounded like a melody, soprano-esque wails inter-mediated by a chorus of coos. The nurse politely ordered them out and locked the door behind them, but the old man hovered around the glass window, and they watched Callie's rockaby together.

"Sometimes," the old man said, lifting a Pepsi can to his lips for a sip, "I didn't think I'd ever see you—see great-grandkids, y'know. You're in the fight, guts and gunfire they used to say, your face is in the dirt, swallowing soil, mud in lungs, you start to think: I won't see my kids grow up. Won't ever see grandkids." He chuckled then. "But look at me now." And he took another sip. "Look at me now."

Ellie the Queen quickly fell asleep on her mother's milky chest, and Callie fell asleep on similarly milk-white sheets and pillows. The crowd began to scatter, on-screen and off. Callie's family exited to the waiting area, and the old man said his goodbyes. Solo and Private Qamaits returned to their bunks. Oya loitered in the doorway, tapping her cell phone, likely wanting to discuss the pending reopening of the hangar with him, but Bella occupied the space beside him.

Sergeant Woden appeared in the doorway, a smirk on his face, a wink in his eye, likely ready to offer some passing congratulations, but then his eyes lit on Bella and her eyes on him, and immediately the sergeant spasmed in hesitation. His shoulders lurch backward. His leg jerked to a sudden stop, and he retreated from the door.

"What's the deal with you and him?" Paxton asked.

"We had something. It's over," Bella said, then turned her eye toward Sergeant Oya still loitering outside. "What's the deal with you and Oya?"

"Oya?" he asked with a half smile on his face. "She's my copilot."

"But the way she looks at you, though. You'd think she's jealous."

Paxton glanced over at his copilot lingering in the doorway, an impatient knot in her frown. He understood Sergeant Oya's leering, and it had nothing to do with romance. Her eyes were filled with the dirty business of mutiny.

"Lieutenant Arés," Oya said and waved him over. "Can I . . ."

Paxton nodded. He turned to Bella and asked her, "Gimme a second?"

Bella smiled and cocked her eyebrow suggestively. "Sure."

As Paxton made his way to the door, Oya winced and tilted her head, suggesting that he move even nearer.

"Closer," Oya whispered, her voice barely audible.

"What?" Paxton mouthed, stepping within a kisser's range.

"One week," Oya said a bit too loud, and she leaned forward, seemingly ready to kneel. "We lead them out in a few more days."

"No," he said emphatically. "I have a daughter now, a little girl that I'm responsible for. There's too much heat now, Washington's stepping in. Even Woden's been acting strange, saying he needs to talk. We can't."

"Regardless," she said as her eyes roamed the hall, looking at everything besides him. "I have first shift tomorrow and I'm going with them. And if you turn around in your shift, I'll go back, again and again if I have to. I'm not leaving them. Not now."

"I have a family now. *We* have families."

"You got me pregnant with this, Paxton," she said. "And I'm seeing it through to the end."

Fuck, he thought, knowing that no matter what he said, she would do it.

"See you tomorrow," he said.

"Tomorrow," she said, then disappeared into the distance.

50

It had begun again, a packed hangar with sweaty bodies entering and exiting the techno-patterned eggs they called cockpits. The conveyor belt of pilot in, pilot out had returned to form. Paxton was back behind the Spartan's controls and Oya was still his copilot, or maybe, it seemed now, he was hers.

He was happy to see Harm again, joyous even, but Oya had promised it would be only a few more days of accompanying the Fishies across the desert. It wasn't. By the sixth day, the desert appeared like a yellow-dyed ocean that ran beyond the ends of the earth, never-ending dust and ash.

On the ninth day, one section of the desert had unfolded into a gargantuan crater that descended a hundred feet at its deepest. It had been a lake, and its memory lingered on in the broken fishing ships and the yachts that buoyed in the sway of shifting sand. The Spartan found an intact rowboat and used it to drag his fatigued entourage through the sand. The Old Oak, the monk, Harm, Bones, and the Priestess slept in a rib cage of a rowboat. The Spartan moved slow over and down the wavelike dunes and toward a destination that didn't seem to exist.

The evening sky was overcast. Portly, white cumulus filled every hole on the horizon, and the day aged prematurely. Noon seemed evening-lit as the sky teased rain. But any miracle of water would be wasted on the yellow, dried ground. The smooth sand was now replaced by pebbles and coarser dirt that rattled the boat and shot splinters out of the hundred-year-old plywood.

"We should stop," a hoarse voice came from the boat behind the Spartan, but Paxton didn't recognize it at first, even in the obviousness of the English language. The Old Oak's voice sounded like it had been squeezed through glass shards in her throat.

The Spartan stood still and Paxton took a genuine breath. He turned to a crowd of bodies huddled in the back of the boat, all of them either asleep or in a free fall toward their subconscious. Only the Priestess and the Old Oak remained alert.

"The terrain is becoming rockier," the Old Oak said. "Let them rest."

The Spartan didn't let go of the rope but loosened her grip around it, letting it hang in her palm and flap in the wind. The Old Oak stared out of an ever-narrowing squint at her metal companion. Her gaze aimed at the belly and satellite receiver therein.

"You're just a driver," she said, and smiled. "Just flesh and blood, piloting her from hundreds of years ago."

The Spartan nodded.

"And you're long gone," she said. "Long dead."

Paxton flinched and the Spartan tensed up. Just the thought of it, having been dead nine lifetimes over, beyond bones, beyond ash and dust. And then to think that this old woman was hundreds of years younger than his infant daughter. It took him moments to fathom the absurdity, but Paxton came to terms with his mortality and nodded the Spartan's head.

"A man or a woman," she said and paused. "You?"

Paxton considered how to say both, him male, Oya female. He hesitated, and the Old Oak rephrased her question.

"Are you a woman?"

"Yes," Paxton said and nodded. "Oya is, but . . ."

It didn't matter—for the Old Oak at least, it seemed like a passing curiosity. She turned to Harm and brushed sand from the girl's hair. Harm barely flinched, drained completely by the heat.

"I heard stories as a girl. My grandmother spoke of her grandfather. A time of change. The old languages were dying. Angles was already a minority dialect. Factions rose up after the great diminishing.

Liberty Bloc, Bahá'í sects, the Futurists, any of them would have been preferred over a fledgling cult called the Machinists, living in these deserts, worshipping dead satellites in old city ruins. But they were too small, too unassuming, until the machine gods they prophesied rose from the ground with ancient technology. The Machinists changed the world, changed its language. We were wiped out . . ." She turned to the Spartan. "You died, buried yourselves in these machines, and now reincarnated yourselves to haunt our future."

Paxton turned to Harm, lying on the Old Oak's lap, asleep with a circuit board on her belly, rising and falling with her breathing. He felt a strange urge to poke her bubbly cheeks, but not now, not while she was sleeping, and not with the Spartan's cold, metallic finger. Paxton knew he would miss her the most, because he couldn't imagine her gone.

"She's smart," the Old Oak said, following the direction of the Spartan's eye. "You likely believed that I was the one who figured out how to use this map." The Old Oak shook her head and smiled. "It was Harm. Her name is a variation of the name her mother made for her—Harm: destroyer of worlds. But she's a thinker, a creator. She isn't meant for this world."

He poked her then. The Spartan's metal finger pressed against her cheek as gently as humanly possible. She didn't wake.

Sunlight had found a hole in the smog. Brightness trickled down and bounced off something, something that could bend its light. The Old Oak saw it first, stepping out of the sand-washed boat without saying a word. The Spartan followed her footsteps, then followed her eyes toward a glint twenty miles out.

"You see it?" she asked.

He did. He leaned into the binocular vision and saw a thousand ruined pieces of metal like the ruins of an ancient city.

"We are here?" she asked, as if he would answer.

"I think so," he said, as if she would hear.

Nine days in the desert and the end was just over the horizon. But Paxton wouldn't get to see any of it. Sergeant Oya was already outside and the baton had to be passed. He whispered last goodbyes to the Old Oak, and Harm, and even his biggest fanboy, the old monk. He was holding her now, cuddling Harm, yawning and heavy eyed, in his weathered hands. Somehow this little posse had become family, and they would need that after the Spartan was gone.

Yet there was a heaviness in his chest that made his breathing hot and melted sniffles into his nostrils. He could love them as much as he pitied them, and as he stepped out into the hangar Paxton pitied the future more than anything.

"Where are we at?" Oya asked, not noticing the sniffles.

"Location's due west about twenty miles," he said. "And we're turning back to our sandbox the minute they get there."

"I will."

"You're sure?" he said, unable to leave it at just that. Oya cared more now than he ever had. Even though he cared, passionately, desperately for those eventual children, Oya cared just that bit more. "Turn back. Without them to slow us down, we're back in the sandbox in a couple days."

"I understand," she said as she closed the cockpit door. "Once I get them there, we turn back."

She pulled the door in fast, as if she was tired of hearing him talk. They'd become an old couple, nagging and tired of the sight of one another, but still allied. He smiled at that, and the twinkle held on his face. There was hope now. They might still make it out of this disorder. Between their two shifts, they could make it back to the sandbox.

———

He slept well that night. No dreams, just the sound of his own breathing. He woke up early, bright eyed, and found Bella by the doorway.

"Morning," she said, stepping outside, as if she had been watching him sleep.

"Bells?" he said, rubbing the sleep out of his eyes.

"Bella," she said, moving into the hallway. "Just Bella."

And she was gone. *Strange*, but he didn't think much of it. Whatever feelings Bella had for him were irrelevant now. Paxton knew where he wanted to be, back with Callie and baby Ellie, Hudson and the old man in the background. He framed the picture in his mind, all of them together. He was almost home.

The morning was quiet, the corridors empty. Even in the hangar, only human shadows drifted against the walls like ghosts with no bodies. Paxton was only a minute late but had missed most of the traffic of switching shifts. Only a minute late and Oya was still inside, still in function, the light on her cockpit's display still green. Paxton knocked, waited, then knocked harder, but nothing changed. The light remained green and the door remained closed. And Paxton's mind found room enough to wander—*What is happening in there, hundreds of years away?*

One minute became two, and it was nearly three minutes before the first distraction came swaggering into view. Sergeant Woden sashayed by, and Paxton quickly remembered that Woden had wanted to say something the other day.

"Hey," Paxton shouted, and waved, but didn't catch a flinch of the sergeant's attention. Paxton stepped forward, raised his hand—raised his voice. "Hey, Sarge!"

Sergeant Woden stutter-stepped and twisted back. He watched Paxton for a second before eventually offering him a nod but didn't take a single step toward him. The impasse of distance between the two lingered awkwardly before Paxton finally abandoned his post beside the cockpit and paced toward the sergeant.

"Haven't seen you around the last couple days," Paxton said.

Sergeant Woden nodded again, partly distracted as he waved to someone behind Paxton and held up one finger as if to say, *Wait a minute.*

"So, uh . . . ," Paxton started, hoping Sergeant Woden would remember what he wanted to say those few days ago.

"Isn't it your shift?" Woden said, seemingly not remembering.

"Yes," Paxton said, and gestured to his cockpit a few rows back. "Oya's still in there."

"They're not keen on that shit," he said. "Staying in over your time. But, hey, I'm heading out at the end of the week, so if I don't see you . . . thanks for the broken nose."

"Heading out?" Paxton said. "Where you headed?"

"Transfer," he said, and gestured toward the ceiling. "Up north."

"What's that?" Paxton said, trying to remember the drone bases the US had up north. "Fairchild?"

"Fort Wainwright," Sergeant Woden said without a spot of eye contact.

"Wainwright?" Paxton asked, familiar with the name but not the location. "Where's . . ."

"Fairbanks," he said. "Alaska."

Paxton cocked his head as if looking for more—reasons, logic, or even sarcasm—but it never came. "That's not air force," Paxton said, still in the duality of asking and stating at once.

"Boots on ground," he said. "Fieldwork."

"Not piloting?"

"No," Sergeant Woden said. "Not anymore."

"Anymore? You're a career."

"Well," Woden said, and shrugged. "New chapter."

"Why?"

"Got my theories, but . . ." Then he paused as if reconsidering those theories and shook his head. "Honestly, I don't know anymore."

Sergeant Woden started to drag his feet away as if those last words were his soft and informal goodbye. But Paxton followed, not even realizing that he was trying to get ahead of Woden to see the look in the sergeant's eyes, a look the sergeant seemed to be trying to hide.

"What was it you wanted to say to me the other day?" Paxton finally asked.

"Right," Sergeant Woden said, as if he had forgotten. "That. You know what, forget I even said anything."

"No, what was it?"

"Probably nothing, dude."

"Woden," Paxton insisted, even resting a hand on the sergeant's shoulder. "What was it?"

"It was probably paranoia, y'know, the whole collaborator thing. But the questions she asks, like, I didn't even notice them at first: time line this, piloting that. Sneaky questions. Where do you pilot? What do you pilot? You know?"

"Questions?" Paxton asked, not understanding a word.

"Once she found out, I mean."

"Who?" Paxton said. "Found out what?"

"Bella," Sergeant Woden whispered as if she were listening. "Once she found out I piloted an Androne, she started acting funny—flirty."

"You hit on her," Paxton insisted, as if he knew.

"No. She came on to me."

"Why?"

"It was like she was looking for something, and when she didn't find it, she moved on. I just wanted to tell you to be careful with her."

Paxton patted his pockets on a hunch. His cell phone was gone. He stepped backward in his mind and traced the steps to his path with Bella. She *had* asked questions about the Spartan but so few that it had just been like white noise. And Bella was in Paxton's room that morning; did she take his cell phone and all the incriminating texts from Lieutenant Victoria? He spun on his heels, twisting around and crashing into Sergeant Oya.

"Hey, Oya," Paxton said. "Need a favor. Need you to hold the cockpit for a few minutes more. Ten, fifteen."

"Pax!" Sergeant Oya nearly shouted his name but then noticed Sergeant Woden. "I need to talk to you for a sec."

She dragged him aside, but Sergeant Woden didn't stray. Their expressions seemingly gave them away. Woden lingered. He watched them in the shadow of the cockpit with its door hanging ajar.

"We found it," she said.

"I told you that yesterday," Paxton said, straying away with each word. "I have to go."

"You don't understand," she said. "Something's happening."

"Bigger fish, Oya," Paxton insisted. "I can't be here right now."

"I don't think it gets bigger than this," Sergeant Oya said, panic pulsing on her expression. "Trust me!"

Paxton caught her look, but so did Sergeant Woden. Tears had dried into the corners of Oya's eyes, and a soggy redness lingered in the whites of her eyes. She had seen something, and whatever it was waited for Paxton on the other end of that cockpit. But he had to see Bella first.

"Whatever it is, you're going to have to handle it, Oya. I'm sorry."

Sergeant Woden picked up on that, leaning in, taking a single step closer. "Handle?" Woden said to Oya as Paxton abandoned her for the hangar exit. And now she would have to deal with him too.

The corridors had thickened with bodies, and Paxton tiptoed and slinked sideways to slip in between them. He hooked a right around the second corridor, taking the long way around, but being that the back corridor was usually empty, he could move faster. He walked as quickly as he could without running, coming up on his bunk door and barging inside.

Bella sat on the edge of his bed. She noticed him and smiled; it seemed sincere, and so he smiled back.

"Hey, Lieutenant," she said.

"Hey," he said.

"You're back early."

"Forgot something."

Paxton stepped deeper into the room, keeping his distance from Bella, like she was some wild animal that couldn't be predicted. As he stepped closer to the locker, he noticed that same sock hanging out like a dog's panting tongue, just like he had left it in the morning. Paxton pulled the locker door open and reached for his cell phone under the half-folded underwear. He dug deeper and deeper yet, but it wasn't there.

"It's here," Bella said, holding up Paxton's phone.

"Why do . . ." But he knew why, and as that realization hit him, she grinned. "Bella?"

"Bellum," she said, looking out from under twisted snakes of hair over her eyes, Medusa turning his heart to stone, and pebbles pumped through his veins.

"What?" he said, stepping toward her—toward his cell phone. She staggered back from the bed.

"My name and names in general are important in my culture—family names, given names."

"Give me the phone, Bells," he said as she backpedaled to the door.

"In my culture, family names are from our fathers. Given names from our mothers. But my fuckup of a mother was in and out of rehab. So Dad named me. And everybody gets it wrong. It's not Bella, for beauty, but Bellum. Bellum! My name is War."

Bella stood at the edge of the room, having retreated all the way to the door, her posture serpentine, hunched and bent at the knees. She seemed changed now, and completely so, all the wildness of an animal, a wolf naked of her sheep's clothing.

"What are you going to do?" Paxton asked.

"If you think there's a chance you're not spending the rest of your life in a military prison, then you're all the way wrong. You will. They don't know yet, but they will."

"We're fighting our future," he said. "Future generations."

"I know who we're fighting. I know we're in the future. I've always known. And I agree fully. Completely. Absolutely."

"So why am I not in handcuffs right now?" he asked. "Why aren't they here?"

"Poor thing," she said. "I'm giving you time to get back to your cockpit. You beat me last time, and I want another chance. So go. Save as many as you can." Bella paused as if waiting for something, as if waiting for him to retreat. "Now, Paxton! Get to your fucking Spartan. And we'll fight. Same space. Same time. Go and try to save your future."

51

Sergeant Oya sat in the cockpit door with her head hung and her legs dangling outside. She almost appeared to be oozing out like a yolk from a fractured shell. Oya was alone, but still her lips mouthed out silent conversation, madness seeming to have taken hold. She didn't see Paxton approaching until the very last footstep, even with his breath heavy and feet lumbering loud against the ground.

"Oya," he said, resting a hand on the cockpit and leaning forward for support. "I need to get in."

She looked at Paxton with her own tiredness on her expression. "Woden knows," she said. "He figured it out."

"Yes," Paxton said, figuring as much. "What'd he say?"

"He didn't. It was in his look. The questions he asked. The way he reacted. He knows, though I don't think he cared for some reason."

"Bella knows too," he said. "She knows and she cares."

"So that's what you had to handle just now." Oya nodded contemplatively. "What's the plan?"

"You had nothing to do with it," he said. "I started this. I got you into it. If you tell them before Bella, like you're snitching on me, they'll let you off with something lighter. You can even say I threatened you. I'll back up the story."

Sergeant Oya considered it. She bit her lips and looked down at the scuffed ends of her boots. Oya stayed that way for half a minute, and by the end he knew she would say yes. Before she started nodding, before she let that hunch of compliance take hold of her posture, Paxton knew.

"You'll back up my story?" she asked. "If I told them that?"

"I will," he said, his tone softer as she abandoned their sinking ship, but then again Oya had kids, but then again and again, so did he. "I'll say . . ." What would he say? "I'll say I coerced you."

She nodded, moisture closing the vacuum of her eyes. "Thank you," she said, her voice weak and wavering, so she said it again. "Thank you, Paxton."

And now he was utterly alone, a solitary gear turning against a global war machine. And he felt that isolation. It undulated out from his chest and moved wavelike through his joints and his limbs, and all of a sudden he felt like this liquid; he felt like he was dripping—leaking out of himself, like a nausea of the arms and legs, scalp and toes, and he could vomit himself into oblivion.

"You okay?" Oya asked.

"Not sure," he said as he leaned against the cockpit, the only thing keeping him afloat. "But I've gotta get inside."

The cockpit was the only thing that could contain Paxton in this liquid form, like a yolk to an Androne egg. He needed to hold her hands; they trembled without her. He needed her feet beneath his limp—his liquid legs. Gods could walk on water.

He turned to the cockpit but noticed Maria racing toward them, out of breath, out of her mind it seemed. Her irises were like beady dots in the whites of her eyes as she tried to say something that wouldn't quite come out.

"I . . . ," she gasped, ". . . rigged it!" Another whirling breath. "To the panels."

"Rigged what?" Oya asked.

"They're coming for you," Maria said. "Right now."

"You know," Paxton said, discovering in that moment that Maria had been on Victoria's side longer than him, and still he asked her. "You and Victoria . . ."

"Since day one," Maria said with a nod. "You're going back into the cockpit?" she asked, but continued before Paxton could respond. "I rigged the SPL to link with your cockpit. Security won't be able to shut off power unless they tear the cockpit door off its hinges."

"Which they will," he said, his eyes selling his angst wholesale, out there for everyone to see.

"They will," Oya agreed, observing Paxton through the narrow of her eyes.

"There's another option," Maria said with a sudden crack in her voice, as though something had abruptly rear-ended her train of thought. "Because . . ." And Maria paused then. "I lo . . . ," she said, stuttering. "Lost t . . ." And whatever that thought was had her now. Maria had shut down, standing comatose and unable to fall.

"Maria?" Paxton said, looking over her shoulder for any security personnel. "What's the other option?"

"I lost her. Victoria. Lost her . . . for nothing." A misery poured out of her, not in tears—her blinking beat the water back—but her tone gave it away. Her cadence rolling like waves: In. Out. In. "We gained nothing. Better sometimes to run, hide, fight another day."

She didn't answer the question, this other option.

"The other option?" Oya asked this time.

"There's a depot on base. South side. About a minute from the bunks. Jess, our driver, she'll get you out on the kits transpo. But you have to leave now."

Run. He told himself not with words but the pricks of neural snaps, electrical synapses firing—fireworks lighting up the gray of his brain. Run or fight? This was his final chance to decide. Run and he might watch Callie from a distance, see his daughter grow up from afar. Call from time to time with just three words of affection before they traced his call. There was some freedom in that. But if Paxton climbed into that cockpit to fight, they would lock him at the bottom of some hole, some Guantanamo-inspired abyss. No sunlight, no news or knowledge of the world. He would be locked in, not unlike a ghost in its shell, a sandbox, six feet by six, with no future beyond it.

"How do I . . . ?" Paxton said it sheepishly. "Transpo—is your driver there?"

"She stays on call," Maria said. "But we have to go."

The exit widened as they marched forward, the traffic quieter at this time of day. The doors opened up as if embracing them. But it was there at that moment that Paxton saw a light within the cockpit gleam, like a lighthouse, he thought, across that ocean of time. Harm, the Old Oak, even that jealous little monk. The children of all their children. He would be sacrificing everything to go back to them—go forward to them; his life for theirs. This would be his sacrifice.

"No," he said and swerved hard back toward the cockpit. "She'll slaughter them if I'm not there."

"She?" Oya said.

"Bellum," he said as he pointed toward the exit. "Get out of here. If they see us together now—"

"Doesn't matter anymore," Maria said. "Taking down those satellites will end the war. While you're in there, we'll hold them off as long as we can."

Paxton turned to Sergeant Oya as she turned to him.

"She's not in this anymore—" Paxton started, but Oya interrupted.

"Fuck!" Oya said to herself, and then her eyes suddenly lit up like she knew something. "Sector nine." She said it to herself, then him. "Sector nine."

"Sector nine?" Paxton asked.

As Sergeant Oya opened her mouth to respond, a sudden explosion of alarms screamed over her. The vibration echoed through every corner of the base and echoed through him, still that liquid, still leaking into an ever-deepening puddle on the floor. It was all falling apart, and him too, falling apart in pieces.

"The ENB," Sergeant Oya screamed over the alarms as she raced into the distance. "Sector nine has the ENB!"

A tremor hit the hangar floor, not quite an earthquake, but the ground shook just enough for him to notice.

"Get in," Maria said, and ushered Paxton toward the cockpit door. "They'll try to shut off the power to your cockpit first and fail. That'll buy you a few minutes."

"What did she mean?" he asked. "Oya, she said sector nine? ENB?"

"Go!" she said, shoving him into the cockpit and closing the door. "End the *wa*—"

The door shut. The alarms shrank to low murmurs and the tremors lulled, a soft pulse at his toes. He switched the cockpit controls on, lights and hums and vibrations. He liquefied into spaces inside, filling the gloves, filling the pedals and overflowing even. And he took her shape, made in a goddess's image. He once again embodied the Spartan.

52

Sunlight fractured on the horizon, divvied up into splashes of yellows and twisted red-orange hues. The light molded shadows in a bizarre forest of corroded metals—a metal jungle with stalks of cast iron that stretched on for miles, bending the light far into the horizon.

Paxton saw Harm first, doodling on the ground, her finger a brush, the sand her canvas. But she wasn't drawing, was she? Numbers and symbols were etched into the sand, a miniature Einstein in her wasteland classroom. The Priestess stood behind Harm, her shadow consuming half of the light on the girl's face. The monk slumped nearly lifelessly against one rusted metal stalk, and Bones rubbed the blisters on her heel, then the ones between her toes.

They were all there except the Old Oak. Paxton whipped his controls into a scan around the surrounding area and found nothing but dead metal and dirt.

"Where is she?"

The Spartan ran a radial scan that spanned nearly half a mile, and still no signs of life. The metal jungle stretched for miles longer than her scanners reached. It was endless, seemingly, and Paxton decided to move toward the center of it all—toward a tower that loomed more than sixty feet high and a shadow that at that moment in the day was practically infinite. The Spartan moved at a quick trot, slow enough to maneuver the metal thicket, fast enough to beat the internal clock ticking away in Paxton's head. He knew gunships and aerials were en route. They had likely already hacked around the marble's fail-safes, now that they knew which cockpit to search, and they would trace him to that very spot.

The Old Oak stood at the foot of the looming tower, staring up at the blown-open windows and ceiling. She noticed the Spartan but didn't glance back; in fact, she stepped forward and tiptoed and stretched her neck, distancing herself miles in her posture. But the Spartan rounded the old woman's invisible barrier and stared down at her, and still she ignored, eyes squinting so thin that they appeared closed.

"How do we take them down?" she asked.

She wasn't staring at the tower, he realized, but beyond it, beyond the silver-gray clouded sky and into an imagination of those ancient orbiting ruins in the exosphere beyond. The Spartan followed the Old Oak's gaze upward, and even with its enhanced vision saw nothing but the choking of clouds.

"How do we do it?" she asked again.

"I don't know," Paxton said, knowing she wouldn't hear.

"There's this admiration," she said, looking at the tower. "And I can't explain it. You created so much. You tower over us and we . . ." She paused in thought. "It's almost as if I want to bring those satellites down just to make you proud. But how?" The Old Oak gestured to inscriptions faded nearly completely on the wall. "I'm illiterate to it all."

The Spartan stepped forward and leaned toward the encryption on the wall. There was grime there and Paxton pursed his lips, ready to blow it away, and at the last moment remembered he couldn't. So he squinted. He squeeze his gaze between the grime and saw numbers, ones and nines and decimal points, and a name—

"Nellis," Paxton read the name off the sign posting. "We're at . . ."

His eyes climbed up the numerical ladder, reading the base coordinates and titles. First Floor: Nellis Base Public Office (11999.0910). Second Floor: Intelligence Security Access (22996.0920). And he kept reading, third floor, fourth floor, fifth and now sixth, an as-yet unbuilt renovation to the structure.

"Nellis?" he asked himself. "The Penthouse?"

He peered out at the low-hanging cumulus, heavy gray and sagging under its own weight. Those scraps of corroding iron were the solar panels just outside his hangar. It was all there, history, future, and present all knotting into itself into a paradox in his brain.

"What the fuck?"

"Dupré," the Old Oak said. "It's my surname. My grandmother's name was Jules Dupré. Maybe you know her great-great-grandfather." She smiled, likely knowing the odds of that were next to none and a century too early. "They said she had a boy's name."

Harm raced up to the Spartan, clutching its knees and hanging between the Androne's legs like they were an open doorway. Bones limped her way under the Spartan's shadow, wiping her slippery brow underneath its shade. The monk bowed at the Spartan's feet. And the Priestess kept her distance, keeping her eyes on the skies above.

The Old Oak appeared to glean something more in their looks. She stepped past the Spartan and spoke in the Javan language, and they replied in kind, loud with mad physical motions and heads directed upward.

"What's going on?" he asked himself, trying to follow the dance of their gestures.

Then, as if she could hear him, Harm pointed upward, tiptoeing, elevating herself and her finger to something above—a drop-ship.

A stadium-size behemoth, blimp-type architecture, with all the engine power of a 747 fleet. Paxton had never seen it in any schematics. This was a new monster inching silently along the sky.

Harpies, hundreds of them, orbited the aircraft that could house a hundred more Andrones. This was overkill. This was Marson not making the mistake of underestimating the Spartan twice.

"Take Harm and run," the Old Oak said.

"I can't," Paxton said, and shook his head. And the Spartan shook her head. "They're tracking *me*." The Spartan pointed to herself. "Wherever I run they'll follow."

The sound barrier cracked open and thundered down as the drop-ship's shadow consumed the day, bite by blackening bite. The aerials hummed whizzing circles around the ship—vultures in a mad orbit ready to scavenge anything it left behind.

"It's a shield," the Old Oak said. "Their larger aeroplanes are not sturdy under fire. I've seen them fall before. The smaller ones are protecting it."

The drop-ship descended, its shadow seeming to scratch across the earth as sand and gravel lifted up. Its engines, still a mile high, gusting tornadoes against the landscape.

"Fuck," he whispered as the drop-ship swallowed up the sun. "What the fuck do I do?"

The Priestess scrambled her way in front of the Spartan, shouting and gesturing, impatience in her tone. The Old Oak responded louder, shouting her down, then turning to the Spartan.

"I told her you don't understand," the Old Oak said. "But she wants to know the strategy. Is there a strategy?"

No. But he couldn't say that. Paxton couldn't say anything. Tongue-tied and choking on his own voice, only his sputtered breathing filled the cockpit.

The Old Oak seemed to understand the posture—the recoiling of the Spartan's mechanical corporeal. She turned to Bones, pointing upward, shouting commands.

Bones raced toward the Spartan so quickly that Paxton worried she might knock it over. She stripped something out of the car-trunk-size backpack on the Spartan's shoulders and pulled down an arsenal of metal and missiles.

They assembled it together, Bones, the Priestess, and the Old Oak, putting together the puzzle pieces with an octopus-like synchrony. Six arms twisting and screwing packs of metal together and all in unison. A mortar was being born right there beneath the three toiling women, with a large missile resting on its tip.

"We need you to distract them," the Old Oak shouted with her fingers in between the sharp edges of the mortar's inner workings. "Make them aim at you."

Sacrifice? He could do that. Simple enough. The Spartan nodded to the Old Oak, and she nodded back but with a softness he had never seen before. Her wrinkles deepened into dales. Her eyes watered into lakes. This was goodbye, and she said it with a look, with that same bark-like skin that had before seemed immovable.

"Good luck, Ms. Dupré," he said.

"Thank you," she replied, eerily.

The Spartan raced forward, stripped her rifle, and took aim at the metal engine screaming above. She didn't hesitate. Bullets popped and the rifle recoiled, popping and recoiling into a steady rhythm, and still all that noise was silenced by the deafening thrum of the drop-ship. Paxton wasn't sure they had even noticed the Spartan. She must have appeared like a firefly, like a flicking of a cigarette lighter.

But they had noticed. They noticed, and they responded with a hundred aerials diving down and spitting out a hundred more missiles toward the Spartan . . . guided cruise missiles, heat seekers, everything in their arsenal.

The Spartan crouched under a pair of solar panels, but it didn't matter. The missiles tore through them—tore through her. Light flared on-screen, blinding white, as static exploded into the headset. Then the screen went black. Then the audio fizzed out. It was done, *finally*, it was done.

53

Paxton felt his heartbeat and remembered he was alive. He blinked. He exhaled. He ungloved his sweaty palms and wiped them on his pants before rubbing the stars out of his eyes.

"They'll be all right," he said aloud, loud enough to drown out that voice telling him: *No, they're fucked.*

Then another noise, a rattling, beating against the cockpit's exterior. He hadn't heard it with the headset on, but now the clangs and shouts of disorder seeped through. He heard Maria, screaming, fighting—fighting for him, for them. Fighting for nothing.

Security personnel were trying to tear the door open, but they wouldn't have to. Paxton reached for the cockpit door and pulled on its handle, but just before it clicked he heard a crackle, static hissing into his ear. Light flickered from the screen.

Paxton twisted back to the controls, wrestling arms and legs back into the Spartan armor. He lifted the Spartan up from the dirt and sheets of metal shards. She had lost fingers on her left hand and a thumb on her right. The audio feed bubbled in his ear as if submerged in water.

A dust cloud swarmed around the Spartan. A switch to infrared revealed a buzz of aerials still whipping around a few hundred feet above. The Spartan turned her binocular vision toward the crowd of women (and the man) in the distance. Harm rested in Bones's embrace as the Old Oak fixed her missile into the improvised mortar. Paxton knew it wouldn't work—fifteenth-century technology against the future—but what else could he do but watch as it shuttled off into the gridlocked skies.

The missile whistled upward, a red flame ablaze behind it. In seconds it climbed fifty feet high, then sixty, seventy, but by the eightieth foot it had begun to shake like a spindly man struggling to do his last pull-up. And by ninety it stopped.

But then something happened that Paxton hadn't expected. The missile split, and a hundred smaller shards of explosive material rocketed upward, each of them the size of fireworks and all with flames of their own ablaze and soaring toward the mechanical whale. And they hit, spears against its sides, and it bled fire and smoke. The missiles appeared to be like bunker busters, penetrating the ballonet fabrics and thin metal framework. And the monster fell.

The drop-ship immediately dipped its head and plummeted, like it was deflating into flames. Fiery bubbles popped open new orifices on the ship. Human-size parts splintered from its body as quadrupedals, aerials, and Andrones fell to the earth. Shoguns, Apaches, Mongols all free-falling at suicidal speed and exploded into the soil, limbs split off like shrapnel. Z Series shattered like glass to the left of her. SPQRs and Kingsman cratered into the fire-lit sand.

The Spartan raced through the falling canopy. Flames drizzled down from storm clouds of swirling smoke. Gunfire cracked in the distant corners of the smog. The Spartan careened toward the Old Oak, and Harm, and the others. He found them in infrared, orange bodies racing toward the tower behind them. The Spartan took chase and in seconds was running alongside them, reaching to take Harm from the Old Oak's embrace. The Old Oak shouted something, but Paxton couldn't hear over the noises suddenly echoing in the present day. A hammering of tools reverberated through his cockpit, metal clanging against metal. They were breaking in.

"Take her inside," the Old Oak shouted again, one hand embracing her own rib, the other holding the shoulder of the girl's shirt. "Take Harm inside!"

Tears ran down Harm's eyes. Not fear but sadness, like she knew the eventual consequence of all the noise around her. Gunfire continued to escalate, louder—closer. More guns. More fire. And it seemed that not all of the Androns had broken as they fell. A handful of Apaches with their light frames and sturdy joints had landed mostly intact. Aerials swooped down, and the Spartan widened its frame to shield Harm and the Old Oak from the pelt of bullets raining from above.

The Spartan shot back and hit an aerial with her first tug of the trigger. It burst into an orange meteor and flamed down to the dirt. The Spartan shifted aim and fired and clipped the wing of a second aerial. It spun into a swing dance downward, trailing smoke, and blew into a bonfire on the ground. *Two for two.* The third aerial she shot down exploded and consumed another aerial on its left side. *Four for three?* The Spartan couldn't miss. The enemy appeared nearly magnetic to the edge of her hollow-point.

The Old Oak returned gunfire of her own but caught a chestful of shrapnel as nine-millimeter rounds chipped into the Spartan's armor. And still she kept shooting. Her arms unsteady. Her aim careless. But she got hers; an aerial dressed in jet black ate half her magazine and exploded, and descended, and died in a fiery grave.

Somehow the old monk had managed to keep pace, even pulling ahead as the Old Oak slowed down. Her attention was aimed at something in the distance, a weighty distraction that hooked to the balls of her eyes. The Spartan followed her grievous look.

A body lay beneath a cloud of ash and smoke, slumped over, face-down, ass up, limbs bundled underneath her. Either the Priestess or Bones, the lifeless cluster of limbs in that smoke and at that distance revealed little distinction.

"Get inside," Paxton shouted as he lifted the Spartan's arm and pointed to the ancient Penthouse's interior. "Move!"

The Old Oak slithered inside a large crack in the wall, and the Spartan lifted Harm into her arms. The little girl screamed and reached out for her, but the Androne wouldn't follow. The monk lauded the

Spartan before crawling his way into the space, dipping his forehead against the Androne's wound. And finally the Priestess limped toward the Spartan, meaning the body slumped dead in that wasteland was Bones, *may she rest in peace*. The Priestess didn't so much as glance at the Spartan as she bent her body into the angles of the breach in the wall. And suddenly the Spartan was alone. And suddenly again, she wasn't.

An Apache was the first to emerge from the smoke, firing wildly, nervously, seemingly fearful of facing off against the legend—the collaborator and his war goddess. The Spartan fired back—headshot, between the eyes, all three of them, and as it stumbled the Spartan surged forward and ran her bayonet through its neck.

A second Apache and a Kingsman caught the Spartan with gunfire, bringing her to her knees. But she recovered fast, rolling, dodging, lifting her rifle and hitting the Kingsman in the chest. It stumbled. She sprang forward, leaping over the Apache and lancing the bayonet through the Kingsman's chest, then swinging the blade backward to guillotine the Apache.

More came. A Zulu Series took bullets to the chest and fell and crawled toward the Spartan, and she waited and stomped its face into the dirt. More Apaches, a Shogun, a Mongol, and all of them fell. Their problem was that they approached one at a time or two at most, and in one-on-one combat there was no contest. Paxton outclassed every one of them.

His cockpit rattled under hydraulic cutters chewing into the door like the Jaws of Life. He heard the hinges tearing back. He knew he had only minutes before the door tore off, but he would buy them every second that he could.

Then a hiss of static buzzed into his earpiece, just as the frame of an Americana stepped through the smoke. "Arés," a feminine voice said in the earpiece—*Bella's voice*. "Surrender your Spartan now."

54

The Americana rammed the Spartan, hitting at sixty-six miles per hour and flinging its metal anatomy into a recoiling pirouette. The Spartan's body hit the ground and bounced stonelike, grated to a slow stop, leaving drag marks along the ground. And she didn't stand up immediately. The Spartan shuddered. Her titanium arms seemed spongy beneath her, and her legs were liquid.

The Americana's shadow loomed over her, blocking out what little light endured on the cusp of the day.

"Come on, Arés." Bella was in his head now, literally, figuratively. The powers that be had obviously hacked his headset. "You still there?" Her Americana stepped closer. "You hear me?" The Americana stepped closer yet.

She stepped too close. The Spartan lunged forward, fist first, and the Americana parried, catching her arm, dragging her forward, and tossed her into the wind. The Spartan hit the dirt. She stood even slower this time.

Paxton knew he couldn't beat the Americana, but he could delay her. Oya had said she had a plan. She had said something about getting to sector 9, something about an ENB.

"The collaborator," Bella said, contempt hissing in her accent. "You wanted this."

"No," he said, lifting the Spartan to her feet. "Not like this."

"Not like what?" she asked.

The Spartan rolled, snatched up her rifle, and swung the bayonet. The Americana caught the blunt end of the blade and stumbled backward. The Spartan took a shot at point-blank range and hit the Americana's chest. It stumbled to its knees. The Spartan brought the bayonet down toward the Americana's neck, but a gunshot hit her shoulder and the Spartan fell back to the dirt.

"Almost, Arés," she said with a soft chuckle. "Almost."

In the distance an SPQR Series held the smoking gun—a Rhino X2061 rifle. Behind the SPQR, a collection of Apaches huddled in the background, a few Shogun Series and Zulu Series among the ranks, and a single Mongol Series stood at the head of the pack. An entire squadron of War Machines, gunned up, as they would say, and all ready for war.

Paxton's control on the Spartan's right arm felt wonky. He moved it forward but it twitched. He lifted it upward and it twisted left. Only half of her remaining fingers had any reaction at all. She was broken. She was finished.

"You know we're killing off the future," he said.

"They're killing themselves," she said. "Misused everything we gave them. Civil wars in nations we created, genocide against their own people. They're killing themselves. We're making it right."

"Right for who?"

"For all of us."

"Us?" Paxton shouted. "We're dead, Bella. We're long dead."

"We're fighting for what's right."

"We're killing them," he said. "And you don't even know why."

"Do you, Lieutenant?" she asked.

"Yes," Paxton said, finally with confidence. "We are at war with the future because they won't take ideologies, *Bella*. They don't want our capitalist dreams or Marxist programs. They don't want our Buddhas or Allahs or Holy Ghosts. We're at war with the future because they won't take our name."

"Cute," Bella said, aiming her rifle at the broken Spartan. "See you on the other side."

Thwack. A gunshot tore through the metal casing, and the shrapnel spattered across the Spartan's face, and for a moment Paxton thought the round had hit his Spartan, but as the Americana stumbled back, he saw the dent in the Americana's chest. And he knew immediately what had happened—who had happened.

"The Old Oak."

She had shot from the fifth floor of the tower and was already cocking and reloading for the next. The Americana noticed her too and in that instant swiveled toward her. The flash from a second gunshot glinted in the distance, but this time the Americana parried, adjusted, and aimed, and as it yanked the trigger, the Spartan sprang forward with her one good arm and jabbed at the Americana Series. It misfired and still tore a hole into the building's facade. And she fell. The Old Oak fell five stories.

"No!"

The Americana dropped its elbow and noosed the Spartan's shoulder, tying her into an armlock. The Spartan twisted her already half-severed arm back but couldn't get free, not under the raw power of an Americana, and still Paxton heaved forward, hearing the titanium tendons in the Spartan's arm snapping away. He pulled harder against the controls as the Americana tugged back, tearing the inner lining of tungsten steel in the Spartan's shoulder joint. Paxton screamed as if he felt his own cartilage crumbling under that pressure, as if pulling against the very cords of past and present, and then it snapped, and the Spartan ripped her own body away from her arm.

Sparks flashed both on-screen and inside the cockpit—the saws and drills had penetrated the cockpit door. He flinched away as the needle-hot flashes pinpricked his exposed skin—his arm and his neck.

The Americana exploited the Spartan's momentary glance at three-hundred-year-old sparks. It hit the Spartan in the chest, lifting her off the ground, then in one fluid motion switched to a rifle and lit her up midair, midfall, and kept shooting. The Spartan rolled onto her own rifle as her vision flickered black and white on the cockpit screen. It grabbed the rifle, a single bullet in its magazine, and javelined the entire gun toward the Americana's womb, hitting it center mass. The Spartan lunged forward, driving the bayonet in deeper.

"See you on the other side, Bells," he said as he pulled the trigger.

The bullet shot into the already cauterized wound of metal, and the Americana's womb detonated. Bella's voice warbled in that last moment and then disappeared.

The Spartan's body was dotted with holes. Her single arm twitched at her side. Her shoulders sagged on her frame. Her knees pulled down on her legs. And yet she turned toward a hundred Andro07nes ready to fight as many as she could for as long as she could.

"Who the fuck's next?"

None of them budged, likely waiting for a command from dumbfounded strategists, mystified that the Spartan had butchered their Americana.

Paxton squinted through the cracks in the Spartan's plexiglass eye and searched for the Old Oak. He found her nearly immediately, climbing out of the rubble at the base of the building. She hobbled on her one intact leg; the other was twisted into a red knot of flesh and rags. She was nearly naked. A wisp of cloth hung around her neck, another draped like a half curtain around one leg. She dragged herself toward the Spartan, hopelessly slow, so Paxton turned the Spartan toward her, backpedaling to the Old Oak while keeping an eye on the Andro07nes ahead.

The Old Oak sat as the Spartan stepped in front of her. Her breathing was deep and slow and seemed hard to pull in and push out.

"Get to Harm," she said, and tried to point to the Penthouse ruins, but her broken arm couldn't make it that high. "I was wrong. Harm isn't a warrior. She shouldn't be. I don't want her to be like me. That's not what her mother wanted. I . . ." The Old Oak's voice struggled to escape her lips, her lungs collapsing under the pressure of inflicted wounds. "I wanted her to . . . I called her Harm, but that's not her name . . ." The Old Oak's voice drained down her throat, and that might have been it, but she quickly blinked back to life and seemed to have forgotten what she was saying. And somehow Paxton knew, right there and then, her next few words would be the last utterance of the English language. "Harmony," she said. "Her name is Harmony."

The Old Oak died just after sunset that day to an audience of a hundred pilots, all of them long dead and somehow still killing. None of them wept for her, not even Paxton, force-fed so much emotion he had no time to digest. But he could pity, and he did—he pitied the life she had lived and the future they had created for her. But not pity, *no*. She didn't deserve pity. The Old Oak deserved love, and he did, he loved her.

55

The saw-toothed monster minced the metal door like a blender. Steel peeled away like fruit and spattered through the cockpit. The shrapnel scratched at Paxton's arms, metal fingernails cutting at his skin, hot enough to singe the hairs on his arm. The audio feed in from the future had drowned under the heavy clatter. They were almost inside the cockpit now. One way or the other, this was almost over.

Sergeant Oya wasn't going to save them. What did she mean by sector 9? She had run in that direction, but how could that help him here, now—in the future . . .

She hid something?

Paxton remembered now. The basement level of sector 9 was being filled with concrete—if she hid something now, there was a strong chance that it would still be there in the future. *Maybe?* It was all he had. Paxton twisted the pedals at his ankles but caught a shoulder full of hot metal shrapnel spitting in from the door.

"Goddamn it!" he cursed as loud as he could, and still couldn't hear himself over the boisterous machine.

The Spartan veered to the right—veered toward the building ahead. The Old Oak wasn't an afterthought behind her, she wasn't forgotten, but Harm was the future—*Harmony*, and he had to protect her.

The Spartan's feet pummeled gravel and dirt and left craters in her wake. And yet she was moving at only half her normal pace. With her right arm just a stub, without her balance and her momentum, she sprinted with a topsy-turvy inclination.

Footsteps came from behind. A Zulu and Mongol Series approached at nearly twice the Spartan's foot speed. The Spartan grabbed a grenade in the midswing of her left arm and dropped it behind her in a single motion. It exploded in the Zulu's face, and it tripped and dropped and rolled in the dirt. Far from damaged, but shaken and stirred and now too far behind to catch up.

But the Mongol did catch up. It lifted its rifle to aim—a Rhino rifle that could tear the Spartan's head clean off. The Spartan stopped on a dime, twisted back, and sprinted toward the Mongol. The Mongol's trigger snapped and the bullet grazed the side of the Spartan's neck, but it missed, and it wouldn't get another shot.

The Spartan's first strike hit the Mongol's right eye. The bulky machine stumbled back and countered with slow, lumbering movement. The Spartan dipped and swung an elbow toward the eye again. The Mongol swung again, even slower, and the Spartan dropped a haymaker into the eye. It cracked but didn't break, and that would have to be good enough.

She stabbed her heels into the dirt and pushed off again and lunged through a hole in the blown-out wall. Paxton knew the way and would run the course. He would go through the corridors, along the hall, and down the stairway. But there was no corridor. No hallway. No stairway. The building was rubble and shadow and dust. And so dark that the sparks inside his cockpit made it impossible to see.

A Shogun Series fired a single shot from outside, hitting the Spartan's leg, accurate as fuck. The Spartan's knee joint split but didn't break. She hobbled now, with bullets still whizzing by.

"Fuck," Paxton shouted, and they could hear him now as the monster saw shut off.

"Lieutenant Paxton V. Arés," they shouted from outside. "Surrender yourself or we will have no choice but to enter by force."

Aren't you already doing that? Paxton considered as he squinted into the dark screen. The saw had dug deep enough and wide enough for hands to reach through. And they did. Fingers wormed into the hole and pulled against the metal, opening it wider. Time was up.

The Shogun caught Paxton distracted. It tackled the Spartan, brought them both to the ground. The decaying concrete beneath them fractured. Cracks snaked across the floor as the Shogun pummeled the Spartan's body, denting and bending the metal rib cage.

The Spartan heaved her body upward, against the weight of the Shogun's. The Shogun shoved back down, and the Spartan's back cracked the ground underneath her; the floor was caving in.

"One more," Paxton whispered through gritted teeth, feeling the Shogun's punches and hoping that one more body slam would break the floor underneath them. "Just one more."

The Spartan planted her one hand on the ground and lifted up, titanium muscle stretching, steel bolts rattling, bending under the weight of a mad Shogun's fists. The Shogun grabbed the Spartan's chest and shoved her back to the ground. And it broke. The floor caved in.

As the Andrones fell, the Spartan grabbed the Shogun and twisted in the air, a tango and tangling of alloy anatomies. They hit the ground, the Shogun first, the Spartan on top, and with that gravity, that inertia, that megaton momentum, the Spartan's fist struck down harder than it ever had. The Spartan punched through the Shogun's chest. Her wrist broke as the Shogun went limp.

"Mater!" a voice echoed, and Paxton recognized it immediately.

"Harm!" Paxton shouted before even seeing her. Then, as she emerged barefoot and tiptoeing on the gravel-sharpened floor, Paxton corrected himself. "Harmony."

The Spartan lifted Harmony into her arm and staggered forward, limping each step of the way. A hundred more metaled feet rattled overhead, shaking the entire structure and stretching the unstable concrete.

The monk was propped up against a wall, bullet holes in belly and jaw, and still he bowed as the Spartan hobbled past him. The Priestess stood a few feet ahead, herding them toward a corridor that ran deep into the structure, but the Spartan turned her head in the opposite direction, toward a faded arrow that directed her to sector 7.

"Seven?" Paxton said, doing the math of it in his head. "Seven, that means . . ."

That meant he was close. As the Spartan veered toward a tiny space, clogged with rock and rubble, her foot was pulled from underneath her—from underneath him.

A trio of gloved arms reached into the jagged break in the cockpit door. They snatched at Paxton's heels and dragged. Paxton pulled back—kicked back, knocking their arms against the jagged maw.

"No," he shouted, slipping his foot back into the pedal. "Not yet."

And as if they were listening, the men slid their arms out of the cockpit. As if they knew he just needed a few more minutes to get Harm to sector 9 and whatever Oya had waiting there.

Paxton flinched back to the controls just as an Apache and SPQR Series dropped into the hole that the Spartan had dug. Harmony had watched confused as the Spartan kicked at invisible arms reaching in from the past. But the Spartan quickly picked herself up and turned to sector 9.

"What is it?" Paxton asked, voicing his subconscious to Sergeant Oya. "What am I looking for?"

The Spartan limped into the doorless rubble of sector 9. Harmony ran alongside her. She stubbed her toe on something metal and hollered out. The Priestess followed close behind, watching as the swarm of Andrones fell down the rabbit hole in the ceiling.

The Spartan switched to infrared, searching underneath the ground for heat signatures, and she saw it immediately. It lay at the center of the room, a burning orange-yellow of a thing. The Spartan kicked away at brick and rubble, and before she even got it out, Paxton knew what it was.

"EMP," he said, recalling Sergeant Oya's indistinct words. "An electromagnetic pulse switch!"

Sergeant Oya had worked her way up to pilot through the tech/maintenance track. It made sense that she would know where to get them, where to hide one, *here*, under the layers of century-old concrete. There was still a chance, however small, that they could win.

The Spartan dropped to her knees and hammered her broken fist against the concrete. It barely cracked. She recoiled, cocked back, and hammered again, but the stubborn flooring didn't give an inch. This was going to take time, Paxton knew it, time that he didn't have. Mechanical hooves rumbled to the left of her. And to the right of him, a clamp widened the tear in the cockpit door.

"Jeez-US!" Paxton hissed out of his grinding teeth, striking at the ground on-screen in front of him. "Come, the fuck, on."

The Spartan peeled off another slab of concrete, revealing the beginnings of a bronzed rust of metal. Infrareds revealed the EMP's full body buried under four feet of concrete. But this was all she needed, just the lever at the top. The Spartan grabbed at the handle and pulled, but an SPQR Series emerged from behind her and ran its bayonet through the Spartan's wrist, cutting off her hand. The Spartan fell back, exposed wiring squirming like earthworms at her wrist.

Paxton screamed as if he could feel it, pulling his own hands from the gloves.

The Priestess lunged for the handle, ready to lift it herself, but gunfire tore through her shoulder like a water balloon, gushing red. A pair of Apaches rushed into the space, all of them unloading their weapons on her. And none of them hit. The monk threw his body in front of the Priestess. His chest dotted in red but he didn't fall. He stood. Bloodied and beaten, arms shredded away by inch-long bullets, jaw torn to reveal gum and teeth, and still the monk wouldn't drop, not even to his knees.

The Priestess grabbed the lever and lifted with every ounce of energy left in her bloodied, dangling arm. And the EMP exploded, sending its invisible charge of electromagnetic energy miles in every direction.

And that was it.

Paxton's controls went dead. Every Androne went dead. And the last things he heard were Harmony's yelp and the *click* of machine death. There was a moment of light, a brilliant nova of electrical current running haywire through the centuries. Then the screen cut to black.

56

They snatched Paxton by his jacket, by his belt, by the laces on his shoes, anything they could grip their knuckles around or their fingernails into, and dragged him toward the tear in the cockpit door. And he let them. He folded his body in, shaping himself into the size of that jagged tear, loosening his fingers from the gloves and his soles from the pedals.

Paxton felt some muddy sense of closure. The future might be safe; *maybe*, he thought. But then he thought about how far the electromagnetic pulse carried and whether any Andrones would have survived. And he thought about Harmony and her little hands and her little feet. If the Priestess didn't survive her gunshot wound, who would take care of her?

He may not have done the right thing, but he did do the only thing that he knew how to. He acted with empathy. Not looking down anymore from the hubris of pity. Paxton did what he did for love. For the love of little Harmony and the Old Oak, and even the monk and Bones. He loved them like he loved Callie, and he loved his little girl. *I have a future*, he told himself. *She is my future.*

And Paxton dreamed of the future with his eyes cringed shut. The light outside was prickly, cutting at angles. The tug on his shoelaces threatened to peel the shoes off Paxton's sockless feet. The jagged aperture seemed to aim the barbed metal at his skin. But whatever happened from here on out, he had done what he could. *It's over*, he thought, but then it wasn't.

The cockpit screen burst into a scalding white. A pyrotechnic light show detonated across his optic nerves. He was seeing stars, seeing quasars and supernovae. But soon the light either dulled or his eyes had adjusted to it. He fretted with his visor, struggling to fix it back on, even as the soldiers kept pulling, but now Paxton dropped his shoulder and let his arm snake through the sleeve of his jacket—the old man's jacket, actually. He slipped his feet out of his right and left shoes, and suddenly he was barefoot and bareback and squeezing himself against the left corner of the cockpit just for a few more seconds—a moment's more glimpse.

On the screen in front of him, Paxton saw a room, a window painted in grease and grime, and a cord, running from the Spartan's satellite receiver to a makeshift satellite dish sitting on the pane of the window. The cord was lubricated in greenish goo that dripped into a puddle on the floor.

Voices echoed, none of them familiar, tennising a Javan conversation back and forth over the Spartan's head. Their shadows stretched along the floor, then bent and sprawled up the wall.

Paxton climbed back into the pedals and made fists into the gloves, and immediately the Spartan moved, making fists in both hands. *Both hands?* He had just lost a hand and an entire arm. Paxton stared at his palms, one white and made of an alloy of rhodium and iron, the other rusted red, appearing to be a retooled version of the original hand. But as he moved the pedals, the Spartan remained still. She couldn't even swivel her neck. The Spartan could only stare straight ahead as if paralyzed from the neck down.

In the fringes of the Spartan's peripheral vision, Paxton noticed someone he had never seen before, a scrawny young woman with narrow, sinewy arms. Her braided hair swung on her scalp as she approached, then kneeled. She leaned toward the Spartan and smiled a familiar smile on her unfamiliar face.

"Harmony," Paxton gasped, now calculating her age in his head. Tears filled the corners of his eyes as he squinted at her. "Oh God, Harmony."

She was twelve—thirteen? *Maybe?* Those same brown button eyes, that same kinky auburn hair. But her smile had thinned. Her baby-fat fingers had dried to sandpaper grinds, and her cheeks had melted into their cheekbones. And there was a scar on her neck that hadn't been there before. An entire decade of growth in an instant. His little Einstein had put the Spartan back together.

He fell apart then. It felt like invisible syringes stabbing at his eyes, an invisible rope on his throat, and he choked and cried. She had grown so much, so fast, and he felt strangely amputated of her, like a lost connection. He reached out and the Spartan reached with him, grasping at the space between Harmony and him, hundreds of years in time.

She said something to the Spartan in Javan. She spoke slowly and enunciated as if it might adapt some of the foreignness of her words, but Paxton understood none of it.

Two middle-aged women stepped into the Spartan's view, lugging a 180-pound bayonet-rifle. They dropped it in front of the Spartan, gasping as they did, one of the women wringing her wrists in pain. The other woman was the Priestess, grayer, thinner, and because she was thinner it made her look taller. She towered over the Spartan with her same skeptical squint.

The Spartan raised her hand and splayed her fingers in front of Harmony. Harmony understood and pressed her hand against the metal palm. They reconnected, metal and humankind, as her smile swirled around Harmony's face.

"How?" he thought and whispered all at once.

How many years had it taken for her to piece the broken puzzle together? Harmony had waited and worked on the Spartan for what had to have been a decade. The poor thing, scavenging parts, reconnecting satellite links—she was a little genius. Harmony hadn't become a warrior, not yet at least. She was a creator, living up to the Old Oak's hopes, living up to her name.

"Harmony," he said, then paused, then thought. "Living up to her . . . *name.*"

Paxton squinted at the girl's hard features propped up on her yellowed smile. He wondered how Harmony might be translated into

Javan. And how would the Javan then be reinterpreted back into English by military linguists?

"Peacemaker?"

Maybe. Harmony understood the satellite technology. She understood how to hack the Andrones. She had done it already, here and now, at barely thirteen years old. And according to Marson's intel, the time period was right. A new young leader would emerge in the next few years, one who would hack present-day Andrones and be responsible for the Ninety-Nine, responsible for hundreds of thousands of deaths.

Paxton tried to shake it out of his head, but at the same time new suspicions trickled in. The timing of it all, *right?* And Harmony's name, her fucking name meant peace. And then there was Harmony's unique skill set, robotics, likely an understanding of hacking, hacking into the past and controlling present-day Andrones from the future. Everything pointed to her, *everything*, including the Spartan's rifle lying on the floor and pointed directly at her.

Could he shoot her? Could he end all this on a hunch? *No.* He could never, not even the thought of it, but she could—the Spartan.

Harmony turned back to the Priestess and spoke. The woman replied with a tepid groan and turned that same unenthusiastic gaze to the Spartan. The Priestess had never been fond of Andrones, and maybe she was the one who turned Harmony as she raised her, and would continue to raise the future Peacemaker. Or maybe someone else in her life right now would flip the switch and turn her against the past.

More gloved hands reached into the cockpit. They snatched at Paxton's belt and pants, tugging him toward the light. Paxton kicked back, but the squid-like swirl of arms snatching at his legs were too many. He had this last moment to steer Harmony in the right direction.

The Spartan aimed her finger at her own chest, at her heart, at the humanity within her—*Paxton*. He made a fist against his chest, and the Spartan shadowed him. Harmony lunged forward and threw her arms around the Spartan's titanium back and rested her head on the Spartan's shoulder.

"Daw," she said in her language. "Na daw."

Light, he remembered, that word meant light. And he remembered everything, all at once. Her first smile underneath that desert. The day she first wrapped herself around the Spartan's legs. She was so tiny, even now, that he couldn't embrace her.

Security tugged at Paxton's legs in such a way that he couldn't kick, knotting their arms around his ankles and dragging him out. He could only wriggle against their arms as he looked at Harmony, at the Priestess, and the other woman with a shirt hanging off her bony shoulders. Then he looked at the rifle. It lay right there, right next to him. A slender chrome body and extended magazine, an elegant carbon-steel bayonet, a violent beauty right at the Spartan's fingertips. He knew what had to be done.

There are moments where the body reacts without the mind, when indecision forces fate to take over. Paxton was like a rag doll then, and fate his puppeteer. There was no thought; it sort of happened, like a reflex, a knee jerk in his subconscious. The Spartan's arm dropped to the rifle, lifted it, and felt the weight of the ammunition within and heard bullets rattling inside. Harmony only flinched, a jerk in her neck and a flutter of her eyes. And then she just watched as the Spartan brought the rifle down to aim, and still her only movement was a twitch in her eyebrow as she seemed to ponder what her machine mother was doing.

There was no hesitation. Paxton's finger dragged the trigger back, point blank, and her chest tore open, a thick ruby-black blood volcanoing from her rib cage. Her body buckled and her limbs spasmed as a last shock hit her nerves and *she, the Spartan*, fell into a puddle of combustible fluid at her feet.

Techno suicide. That was the only path out. Paxton knew the powers that be would use the Spartan to murder Harmony. Then use the Androne to kill them all. Whatever base that was and whatever year the Spartan was in, it would be re-piloted and they'd murder every last one of them. Paxton loved Harmony like his own daughter, a daughter that he now knew he'd never see.

Harmony had stammered back to the window in that split-second flash of gunfire. Her image flickered on his screen, everything flickered, walls, bodies, it all blurred together in smudges of static and light. As the Spartan's body spasmed, Harmony's audio jerked in and out audibly. It was a scream, a mad shriek of horror—anguish, and he felt that. Tears lit his eyes too. Then that last image of Harmony froze on-screen, tears in her little eyes, Androne blood speckled on her face, and she appeared changed. Maybe it was interference in the image as it flickered on-screen, the interference making her skin seem darker, thicker, like bark. She *was* changed. Now. Then. Forever. And before Paxton could take a second look at her, they shoved a hose into the cockpit and pumped pepper spray inside.

Paxton let go of the controls, and they dragged him out headfirst. His skin and the hair on his arms grated against the shredded metal, and he bled. But they didn't care. They tugged even harder. His bare back cut against the pointed steel, his belt buckle caught on the metal as they pulled, and it tore his pants off. Paxton hit the ground, bloodied and blind and naked. Tears dripped out through his eyes and nostrils. He was dead to the future now. He was bone and ash in that deep and present future. He had truly killed himself in that Spartan's body, dead, but *she* would live. And that was love, transcending the self, transcending time; his love transcended it all.

Paxton squinted into the incandescent flare as the boom of hollers beat at his eardrums. Their voices were so simultaneous that it sounded like nothing, all those incestuous syllables like blunt trauma to his brain. They dragged him naked, deaf, blind, dripping in blood, away from his cockpit and into the present. The future was lost to him. It was there, *then*, that Paxton thought he heard the old man's voice intermixed in all that hollering, quoting the old Shakespeare verse, *Nothing against Time's scythe can make defense. Save breed, to brave him when he takes thee hence.*

EPILOGUE

Inmate 092745. That was all they told her, just the name. All the rest was locked in binders that she didn't have clearance for. But she knew the story. *Shit*, who didn't? A man eight years into nine consecutive life sentences. *Nine*, and by that math the man's fossils would be released into a future he was responsible for.

The prisoner was held in solitary. The last stop down on a warbling elevator shaft. Then security checks, metal detectors, and hundreds of cells in a Guantanamo-inspired abyss. But his cell within a cell hid many lengths away from any others. A steel door blocked the corridor leading to his single cell inside. This prisoner—*her prisoner*—he was different.

She stood outside the first steel door in a $1,000 dress suit, pressed, professional, indicating scholarship and rank. But the armed guard, bearded and tattooed in American miseducation, looked past the suit— looked through it, eyeing every edge of her curvature.

"Door," she said, and pointed as if it wasn't the only door in any direction.

He unlocked it with a keycard and a nine-digit password, eyes still on her. She thought the guard might accompany her, but no; he scowled at the dark corridor beyond the door and she ventured in alone.

The passageway was long and empty. She noticed the light first, or the lack of it. The farther she ventured toward his cell, the weaker the fluorescence flitted above her. The icy air too, it gripped her exposed arms, it rolled up her sleeves and sprayed down her back. And darker yet as she approached the cell. Snotty yellow mold curdled on the ceiling and wall, and she tasted the stink of it, like something dying, something rotting away.

As she stepped closer to the cell, the woman noticed a single wrinkle in her uniform and ironed it out with the back of her hand. Appearances were everything for her, a West Point grad with Naval Academy ambitions. Everyone was top of their class, politically savvy, and every inch of advantage was necessary.

He would be her advantage. This broken, nameless man slumped at the edge of his bed. Their most coveted prisoner, the one who never spoke to anyone but himself. There were documents thirty pages long with recorded conversations between him and his dreams. Was he mumbling those same names now? *Callie, Victoria, the Ol' Polk* . . . Mumbles they had recorded in his cell with twelve hidden microphones and cameras staring in at his every move.

He had been interrogated for seven years, according to the intel she had surveilled. The inmate hadn't spoken to a single guard or interrogator in all that time, at least nothing substantial. And the military in turn had given the prisoner very little in the way of conversation or any information he truly wanted, like that on his wife and daughter. Thinking of that almost made her pity him as he lay crumpled up in the corner of his bed, blanket hanging off his chapped, bony legs, underwear torn ragged, and a single sock on his left foot.

"Lieutenant Paxton Arés," she said, hoping that showing him the respect of his military rank might give her some reaction. "It's an honor to meet you."

She wasn't expecting a response, but she got one. Nothing verbal, just a shift in movement, a shuffle in his bed to turn toward her. And she had to keep speaking. She didn't want him to lose interest.

"I'm with the NSA. A separate branch of the US government than you've been dealing with for the past eight years. I have a few questions."

The man shook his head, and she didn't know whether that meant he didn't understand or it meant he wasn't going to tell her anything. His expression was a Picasso, broken into lips, and eyes, and brow, all with their own emotions.

"Who's Polk?" she asked. "Ol' Polk. Who is he?"

The man hesitated this time. Lips broke open to speak but pulled back, a retreating tide of conversation. But now she knew she had him. Now the game of seduction was done—she would reveal everything now.

"Have you heard of the Santana Clause?" She'd barely said the words before he turned away. She was losing him. "The Santana Clause is a code we use to describe a specific article in federal law—a Christmas gift. And once I describe it to you, the military"—she pointed to the camera above her—"who I do not answer to, will end this conversation."

The man twisted back toward her now, his eye opening just a bit wider, letting her in.

"The Santana Clause states that title 18, chapter 115 of the US Code on sedition and treason can be nullified if federal security deems it necessary. A fancy way of saying that there is a way out of this prison for you. In days. Weeks, maybe."

The man sat up and nearly stood, but something held him back. *Doubt?* His blanket fell off him. He was thinner than the picture she had seen, the one of him with the dog and the girl.

"You get to see her. The little girl. Your little girl."

The man started shaking. Fingers flicking, lips too, and eyes aflutter, and all of it out of sync. There was a landslide of his anatomy cracking from the inside, individual parts falling away. His resistance diminishing, the man finally looked her in her eyes.

"I want you to see her," she continued, knowing that one more push would send him over the edge, break this camel's back. One more push. "Because I made her a promise that I'd get you out."

"You spoke to her?" the man finally said, and surprised himself, as if he wasn't sure whether he could still speak.

"Yes. And Callie, and even your grandfather. He's in . . . there's still time to see them all. You'd be in protective custody, of course, under house arrest, and the strictest of surveillance, but you would be with them again."

"What do you want?" the man said, his tone still dubious.

She smiled now, realizing how little he knew about anything that had happened in the past eight years—the attacks, the weather, the disarray. And there was so much more to say.

"You're a god, Paxton." She chuckled at this. "You will be. A literal religion will live in your name. I just thought you should know that, but that's not why I'm here. The powers that be need to know that you will cooperate. Sergeant Oya took a deal. She has thirty-six months left, possibly shorter."

"You want me to help you kill the future."

"No," she said with a curt shake of her head. "We just need to make sure that you won't help them destroy us."

The man leaned back with that Picasso look again, confusion, scrutiny, and genuine curiosity bending his micro-expressions in countless different ways.

"Won't help them destroy us? What does that mean?" the man asked.

"That means someone is coming for you, Paxton. And we don't know what they'll do when they get to you."

"I . . . Is this another thing?" The man made a spinning gesture with his finger and placed it against his head. "Are you guys fucking with me again?"

"No," she said. "What I'm here to find out is if the extract was part of a plan. Something you'd set up beforehand."

"What are you talking about?" the man said, shaking his head, almost rattling it in confusion.

"I'm asking, why are they coming, Paxton?"

"They?" he said, leaning in now. She had him in the palm of her hands. "Who are *they*?"

"Harmony?" she said.

"Har . . ." The name got caught in his throat. He was choking on it. He knew her, didn't he.

"You know the name," she said, and it wasn't a question. She was sure of it.

"Harmony," Paxton said, as if making sure he had heard it right.

"The Peacemaker. She is coming for you."

"She's . . ." He paused again—again as if making sure he got this right. "Harmony is *coming* for me?"

"Well . . ." The woman thought about this for a moment. His words weren't quite accurate. "No, not coming," she said. "She's already here."

ACKNOWLEDGMENTS

To my mother, Rosaline Maxine, who amid a conservative time and culture and household gave me freedom enough to draw outside the lines, to think outside that box. Invention requires more room, and she gave me the space to stretch the muscles of imagination.

To my father, Wayne Anderson, whose strictness inadvertently birthed inner worlds in my head. He taught me responsibility. Hard work. The ability to push through adversity.

To the Georgia State English professor whose name I can't remember and whose class I can't recall. But it was him who imparted on me the greatest advice of my life: "You gotta go with your heart," he said in a conversation about writing. And he changed the trajectory of my life. I switched majors, from the sciences to theater and creative writing. Instructor, inspiration, starting me on my literary path—all that, and he'll never know.

To my sister, Delicia: strong, brave, intelligent, single. To Dorian, my brother: smart, dedicated, responsible. To another Dorian, my literary agent, who believed in this novel when no one else did, who saw the diamond within the rough drafts. To my editors, top to bottom—Adrienne, Clarence, Lauren, Jon, James, Ashley, everyone for every commitment—and 47 North for trusting in the written word and our beloved science fiction. To lifelong friends who supported me when I struggled: Paulo, Scott, Matty Free, Sands aka Grim, Carnell, 王思懿.

And I dedicate this to you, reader, whoever you are. Thank you for your investment in these words, this world.

About the Author

Dwain Worrell is a filmmaker, traveler, and novelist. A Caribbean native who resettled in the US in the nineties, Dwain currently resides in Los Angeles where he works as a film and television writer and producer. His writing credits include Marvel's *Iron Fist*, CBS's *Fire Country*, Amazon Studios' *The Wall*, and the Disney+ series *National Treasure*, among others. For more information visit www.dwainworrell.com.